IN VIOLENT WAVES

PRONOUNCIATION GUIDE

Aine — AWN-yuh

Alfor — AL-for

Auris — OR-iss

Aradia — ah-RAY-dee-uh

Baelywn — BAY-lin

Cyrus — SY-russ

Daisy — DAY-zee

Drystan — DRISS-tan

Ennosidas — EN-oh-sigh-dass

Fionn — FYUN

Lyra — LYE-ruh

Maelys — MAY-liss

Mab — MAB

Marina — mah-REE-nuh

Oberon — OH-ber-on

Ophelia — oh-FEEL-ee-uh

Ridge — RIJ

Seraphina — seh-rah-FEE-nuh

Tiandra — tee-ANN-druh

Titania — tie-TAY-nee-uh

Wilder — WILD-er

For the first daughters, the loud ones, the "too much" ones—don't ever lose your voice.

HIGH LANDS
WILDS
THREE SISTERS SWAMP
Pinna
VALEWOOD FOREST
EMERALD CO
FRESIA VILLAGE
TERRA BADENVARIA
MANNEREDS
BRITON

ISLE OF ELVETHAMIAN
DANES
ATLANTIS

In Violent Waves is a fantasy romance set in a mythical realm. However, it does include elements of war, battle, blood, violence, injuries, death, graphic language, attempted rape, and sexual activities that are explicitly detailed on the page. Readers who are sensitive to these elements, please take note.

PROLOGUE

"And the mermaids, they come once a year
They climb the struts of Brighton Pier
They come to drink, they come to dance
To sacrifice a human heart
And the world is so much wilder than you think ..."
-Mermaids, Florence & the Machine

I

TIDAL TITHE

L yra drummed her long nails against the driftwood chair, staring out at the sea of merfolk in the throne room, waiting for her father to begin the Tidal Tithe ceremony. Other than drinking the vial to gain legs, the speech was pretty pointless, with a few nonsense rules and reminders about the dangers of the surface world.

She switched to tugging on the charm at the end of her silver necklace. The tiny shell was made of a single sapphire and shimmered as she pulled it back and forth between the diamond-encrusted clam shells that cupped her breasts.

Tonight was the night Lyra had looked forward to her entire miserable existence. It was a sip of true freedom. Her only opportunity before her wedding tomorrow.

Her dark red hair was pinned up painfully in coils against her scalp, yet she left the bottom half unbound. Having loose hair was a burden, a tangled mass of indecency in the water, but that seemed no worse than the headache that was those gods-forsaken pins. And it was the message it sent that was the most important to her, anyway. It caused more than a few stares, but that was the curse of being not only a mermaid, but the king's daughter.

"Drystan is most displeased that you have accepted none of his attempts to plan the wedding together."

It had taken years to train her body not to react, not to flinch at the savagery in her father's voice.

Lyra met his gaze with something other than loathing. That attempt at small talk was most unusual for him.

"Wedding planning really isn't my thing, and given I actually had a choice this time—I declined."

King Auris sat upon his silver throne, composed of glimmering stalagmites that had been sharpened over a millennium. His long white hair and beard were the same shade as the tumultuous waves during storm season. A crown of narwhal horns rested upon his brow, and the turquoise shade of his eyes was the exact shade of the sea in which he was born centuries ago, before humans polluted the oceans. They bore into her. He snorted, and a few crabs that had crawled up the stairs of the dais scuttled away.

"Your sisters all enjoyed planning their weddings. And marrying a handsome prince is usually most princesses' 'thing'."

She ground her teeth, and the sharp points clacked together.

Her father's path to ruling the seven seas was wrought with cruelty and manipulation. He had bartered each of Lyra's six sisters into strategic marriages. But Lyra was his favorite, and he had arranged her marriage to the most volatile of territories beneath his control—Ithicais.

King Auris had planned this marriage since her infancy. From the moment he looked upon the fire-hued hair of his last child and gleaned the power that danced within her veins.

It was ironic that such a powerful king had sired only daughters. But that was the intended consequence. Only a powerful ruler would have spawned male offspring to carry his mantle.

Fate cursed a weak ruler, dooming him to father only daughters who would become pawns in the game of power.

And such a game was already afoot.

Drystan was a handsome prince. But his depravity corrupted any semblance of attractiveness. He was attractive by their societal standards. A strong chin, brawny muscles, and golden hair were common for that territory. Yet it was the wickedness within him that seeped into the deadness of his eyes.

It was a small boon that she would get to kill him. This one order that would secure the territory, thus tightening her father's control, and it would get her out from under his thumb. It wasn't true independence—but it was close.

But that was a conversation that would require a much emptier throne room.

Her face slipped back into its usual mask of boredom as she tried to stifle the undercurrent of *something* that was now thrumming through her veins. It was an emotion she couldn't quite place. It was not fear. She had tasted her fair share of fear. That was sour. And it was not excitement either. That was sharp.

No, this was a joining of the two.

"You are to return immediately after the tithe. Your wedding is tomorrow, and you must not be late." King Auris stared at Lyra for any hint of disobedience. Apparently, he wasn't finished speaking to her after all. "And steer clear of the elves, Lyra. I mean it."

She snorted this time, unable to grasp the warning in his tone. "There hasn't been an elf sighting in our hunting grounds for centuries."

His knuckles turned white as he gripped the golden trident. It had once belonged to Ennosidas, the god of the sea. The muscles of his shapely forearm and bicep rippled with the movement. The trident was merely a prop now. Mermen didn't have magic—not anymore. But it was still a fearsome sight to behold.

"Our scouts have heard whispers that the elves have been spotted. The war between their courts has spilled across borders."

Lyra didn't even try to hide her rolling eyes.

The scouts were unreliable at best. Males that gave up their fins to live out their lives as spies on land. No one in their right mind would do that, and she couldn't find it in her to trust their word. But that information was surprising to her.

King Auris didn't care about the elves or their wars. He had only ever cared about controlling her.

The small bit of fight she had left in her rose to the surface. "And what exactly are you afraid of me doing?"

King Auris slid his eyes across his daughter's face before returning them to the crowd of merfolk.

"An elf harnessing your magic could turn the tide of their war. If you were to be caught, you would be enslaved and used in ways beyond your worst nightmares." His words were bitter, utterly uncaring of his youngest daughter. But they were not a lie.

Lyra had been wrong in her earlier assumption. This wasn't about controlling her; it was about controlling her magic. If he could cut it out of her and use it himself—he would. And had tried long ago.

Her nostrils flared as she remembered the pain.

"The sea witch was wrong," Lyra replied with quiet menace.

The memories from that day, the horror and the sea witch's dark, swampy cave in Ithicais still gnawed on her mind from time to time.

Trials and prophecies.

Blood and death.

Her power would bring nothing but pain and destruction. And it had already brought death.

But even as she said the words, she felt that the lie was obvious.

Her magic had come, and she was terrified of it.

She could feel it even now, a thread of pure gold around her heart, waiting to be plucked. She recoiled from it.

It had happened only once.

An accident.

She was so young she hardly remembered how it had happened or what she had said, but that male had died. And it was of her doing.

Her father turned back to the gentry, and Lyra looked around. She tried to look past the creatures and at the room itself. The mosaic tile floor depicted waves, coral reefs, and Ennosidas. A merman of infinite power, with hair as black as night and eyes of emerald green, he gripped the golden trident in one hand while the other was outstretched at his side.

As a child, she had lain on the floor, pretending to hold the trident herself while dreaming of the sky.

The memory elicited a tightness in her ribs as she looked up to the towering pillars of stunning white granite that held up the open-domed roof that caught and guided the murky light around the room.

Lyra wondered briefly what the day had looked like above the water. She had still never seen the sky—not the sun, nor the moon, nor stars.

It was the one rule she hadn't broken.

The water in the hall was warm, kindling something inside her—a flicker she imagined was fire. She'd read about fire. Read about everything related to life above the sea, how to survive it, and the vileness of men.

Well, men—and the elves.

Far more nefarious than the humans were the elves.

Murderous creatures who defiled, pillaged, and conquered. They had been at war between themselves for centuries, and she was grateful. Utterly grateful that they hadn't ever turned their sights on conquering her home.

The thought of them sent a shiver gliding down her spine. Tales of cruelty that surpassed even her father. At least under his rule, their kingdom had seen peace. But if the scouts were right—tonight became even more treacherous.

She pulled her eyes away from the faint light and turned to the gazes that raked across her skin. The high-ranking men and their families were always positioned closer to the dais, while the lower-ranking members were pushed to the back. It was easy to pinpoint who was high-ranking. They had the most children.

A family of four hovered at the foot of the dais. A father and three daughters. The oldest daughter stood dutifully at her father's side. Chin lowered, eyes averted, silent. The middle daughter still held a quizzical eye as her gaze darted around. But when her attention clashed with Lyra's, she lowered her eyes at once.

The youngest daughter, however, was studying Lyra with a curious expression. Her hair was pinned up so tightly that it pulled at the delicate skin around her eyes. She was so small, no more than eight, but had already mastered the correct chin level to appear superior to her older sisters. Her eyes narrowed in on Lyra's unbound hair, and she tilted her head.

Lyra ran her fingers through her hair and met the girl's stare head-on. The child's eyes widened at the indecency. Lyra smiled with all her teeth. The girl looked up to her father, who was locked in conversation, and then back to Lyra as she ripped the lower half of her hair from the tight updo.

It was satisfying to see that small act of rebellion and to know she had caused it.

To stop herself from laughing and brushing against that thread of power, Lyra studied her nails and then exhaled. She hated engagements like this and wanted to flee this place. Her tail swished and shimmered from pale lavender to light green.

She loved her tail, loved how powerful and graceful she could streak through the water and to the sanctuary of the reef.

The slamming of King Auris's trident brought her out of her daydreams. He struck it two more times, and the sound brought forth immediate silence from the crowd.

"Tidal Tithe is upon us!" His voice boomed throughout the room. It rattled the crystal champagne glasses spread across tables, the glasses bewitched to keep the champagne inside, and the tower of vials set up for the rite. "To honor the ancestors before us and the mighty Ennosidas, our blessed thirteen maidens head to the surface this evening. I know they will do each of us proud." He threw Lyra a sneer masked as an adoring smile. She stifled a snort. Her selection as a maiden was guaranteed as the daughter of the king, but the others had entered a lottery. Though it wasn't truly a lottery. They had all bought their way in, just as Lyra had won through nepotism. "As always, each maiden must sacrifice a heart by first light. Fail, and you will be cursed to walk the land forever. Choose any mortal you wish—man, woman, or child. But not royalty."

A hush fell over the crowd before the murmurings began.

His eyes scanned the hall, falling onto the two mermaids who scuttled in late, Seraphina and Marina, the closest things Lyra had to friends. They were night and day. Seraphina was the epitome of the day. Fair hair, fair skin, pale eyes. Marina was the night. Black hair, umber skin, and dark eyes.

"Under no circumstances," the king continued, "may you engage with any elf you see on land. And if they realize what you are—Ennosidas have mercy on your soul."

With that foreboding warning and a final strike of his trident, the speech ended.

Lyra rose from her small driftwood chair, trying her best to float out of his line of sight without him realizing she was gone.

"Do not deviate from the two marked paths," he said, not once taking his eyes off the crowd in front of him. The maidens swam single file to the golden table set up with amber vials. One small vial and your tail splits in two, and legs emerge. Lyra had heard it was excruciating, but no one had ever refused to take part.

She halted, squeezing her lips together over her razor-sharp teeth. "Of course."

"Of course, *what?*"

"Of course, Father," she drew out each syllable as she raised her chin.

The only bit of defiance she could muster.

He came closer, grasping her chin between his thumb and forefinger so he could lower it. Lyra locked her muscles in place to keep herself from trembling. His eyes beseeched hers, and it was an effort to weather that gaze.

"My favorite daughter, things will be better soon," he whispered.

It had been a long-standing promise. That those "things" would be better.

At first, the promise had meant more independence or more books, but now it rang hollow. Nothing would change. He would continue ordering, demanding her obedience like he did to all the others in his realm.

A throat clearing nearby halted the tension bubbling between them.

Drystan waited beside the throne, bowing low in supplication. His emerald-green tail flicked with impatience.

"King Auris," Drystan crooned with forced respect. "Might I have a moment with my intended before she goes topside?"

His leering smile set Lyra's teeth on edge. His coiffed golden hair didn't ripple at all in the current, and the dimple in his chin would be the perfect place for her to pierce through his skull with her favorite dagger.

"Of course," the king replied, gesturing with a smirk. "She's all yours."

All yours.

As if she were property to be bought and owned. Lyra's shoulders rose imperceptibly at the arrogance of it all. She was not property, a bartered womb for the taking.

No—she was the ocean.

Unattainable, unruly, and vast.

Drystan didn't wait before seizing her arm and dragging her behind a pillar.

"Ouch," she mumbled as he tightened his grip.

He pinched the freshly healed skin on the inside of her arm. The damage he had caused. If she hadn't been ordered to murder him on their wedding night, she would have attempted it then.

"You are not to make a fool of me tonight."

His chest, broad and gleaming, pressed into her. His cologne —heavy with musk and sea jelly—sickened her.

"Why must everyone say the same thing to me?"

"Because you're not known to behave." Drystan reached for her chin like her father had done.

Lyra snapped her teeth in close proximity to his fingers. Barely missing biting them off his hand.

"Point proven," he chuckled.

"I've had enough of this conversation."

She spun, heading towards the dwindling line of maidens plucking the remaining vials, but Drystan grabbed a fistful of her hair and pulled her body against his. The feel of his scales against hers had her jaws snapping shut to staunch the bile that surged up the back of her throat.

Drystan leaned in close. "I will skin you alive, scale by glittering scale, if you even think about staying topside. You will return to me and be my wife."

Lyra tugged against his hold. The sting of her hair being ripped from her scalp was nothing compared to swallowing down her words and letting him treat her with such disrespect.

Drystan let go.

"Are you an imbecile? I don't belong on the surface." Lyra's chest heaved, and her eyes pierced him with the promise of retribution.

His gaze slid from the strands of hair still tucked in his fist to her face. "You belong to me, and you will come to love me—as much, or perhaps even more, than I love you."

"You're not capable of loving anyone but yourself."

He smiled, tracing a fingertip from her temple to her lips. "I know that if I can't have you—no one can. Is that not love?"

She swatted his hand away, and he gripped it, squeezing her fingers. Lyra felt her knuckles crack before he kissed each finger tenderly.

"You deserve to be loved just as violently as is your nature, Lyra. Let your monster out so that I may worship her."

Her breath hitched, and the gold thread around her heart flared.

Long ago, Lyra had yearned for love. A folly that had since turned to silt on the seabed floor. Now, all she knew was rage. She was so very close to showing Drystan who she was and ripping his heart from his chest.

"There you are!" Marina called. "It's time. Let's go!"

She thrust a vial of amber liquid into Lyra's hand before tugging her along, not once sparing a look in Drystan's direction.

Marina's jet black hair, like a pile of nets upon her head, bobbed as she led them briskly towards the exit and after the maidens who had already begun heading for the trails.

"You're going to get yourself dragged back to the castle again if you keep running your mouth," she murmured.

Lyra threw a glance over her shoulder to see Drystan staring after her. He winked, and she bit her tongue to keep from cursing him. She couldn't wait to end his life.

2
TOPSIDE

ioluminescent lights glowed along the lane and lit their
path into the darkness beyond the kingdom. She couldn't
help herself. Lyra stole yet another glance behind her. The
spires of the castle shimmered a muted gold. It was beautiful in
the way the architects deemed it should be.

All that glittering gold; it veils the rotting within.

Marina hummed as they continued. Her black scales shimmered in the glow of the luminescence.

Seraphina was a few paces ahead of them, conversing with
the other mermaids, her shock of white hair shifting into shades
of pink or green depending on which light she passed.

Lyra's ears pricked at snippets of their conversations. Some
were nervous about what they would find on land. Others were
so delighted about the promise of the tithe that it bordered on
pain.

But almost too quietly to be heard were the murmurs about
those who had not returned from past tithes. There was always

one who did not have the stomach to complete the ritual and became cursed. However, one out of thirteen was forgettable. A fear not worthy of being acknowledged. They were never spoken of, the maidens who had failed, not even by their own families.

But a twinge of excitement stabbed between Lyra's ribs.

The taste of a human heart was second to none. Something about the life force in their blood that sates the cruel loneliness that dwells within each mermaid. And the gratification of supplying more magic to their realm, specifically to the fertility magic that had dwindled.

Magic in general had diminished. There were tales of mighty mermen that could sink ships with a wave of their hand centuries ago. Now, only mermaids retained any semblance of magic, but it was dull in comparison to what it had been. Ranging from foretelling better fishing grounds, bewitching small items, or the gift of song.

Marina slowed, sidling up beside Lyra. "The tide will run crimson this night."

"I suppose it will." Lyra flashed a semblance of a smile to Marina.

She was unusual for a mermaid. Probably because her father was doting. Marina couldn't do anything wrong, even if she tried, which is probably why she enjoyed Lyra's antics so much. Marina had nothing to fear.

"Do you think the humans who butchered your mother are still alive?"

Her question brought Lyra up short.

A flash of a kind smile sprang to her mind, and nausea took hold. She never knew her mother.

The foolish woman had begged and pleaded with King Auris to spare their daughter from his plans. He had her bound and dragged to shore. Mermaids weren't allowed to disobey their husbands.

Her mother's fate was unknown. But if Lyra knew anything about the humans from the books she had read, then it was not hard to imagine her tail as a trophy on a wall somewhere.

Lyra choked on a snarl at the thought. "Doubt it."

Marina glanced sidelong at her. "At least no one speaks of her. That would be distressing."

Seraphina interrupted, "Coral's older sister said that we should go to Briton instead of Danes. They're a bit larger, and their diet makes the heart less appetizing."

"Fine. That's fine," Lyra replied, placing Seraphina between her and Marina.

Seraphina's family had fallen out of favor, and thus her father had more to concern himself with than his daughter's whereabouts. It was obvious he rarely thought of her at all, which was apparent in Seraphina's desire for attention at all times. But Lyra didn't mind, especially when it took the attention off her.

And Lyra didn't know if she could stomach any more questions about her parentage from Marina.

She always seemed to ask pointed questions, the questions that got her thinking. Itching with curiosity and the desire to change things that were out of her control.

Desire strangles you slowly in a world designed to play you.

Lyra raged against the idea that all she had to offer the world was her womb. She was smart, exceedingly so, and once had dreams. Dreams of making her own way, her own decisions. And those decisions had nothing to do with how many children she should bear. But the practicality of achieving those dreams had snuffed them out.

It simply wasn't possible without using her magic—magic that would only make the suffering worse—and so she killed the very idea of them.

Even now, the ceremony for mermaids and how they

increased the magic of the kingdom was guided and controlled by a male.

A lone guard led the procession from Atlantis to the fork between the two landings the maidens could choose from: Briton or Dane. From there, they were on their own.

The guard's orange tail was a beacon guiding them through the depths. The light from the surface was gone. Only the bioluminescence and their keen eyes allowed them to see.

At the fork, Lyra hesitated.

Her father's voice echoed through her mind: stick to the two paths. But that just wouldn't do.

How could she follow directions from a male who only wanted to control her for his gain?

The guard continued, leading the larger group of mermaids down the Briton path. There were two discernible paths. One to the left, to Briton, and the other to the right, to Dane.

But straight ahead, through the darkened kelp forest, were the faint lines of another path. Something about that choice seemed like the first in a long line of decisions that would lead Lyra to her destiny.

Whether she was ready for it or not, it was coming.

"Which path are we taking?" Marina asked, though she knew the answer already.

Lyra swam forward and turned a devilish grin back at them. Marina followed Lyra everywhere, and Seraphina, though not as close, was never far behind.

"Let's see where this takes us."

Their swim through the kelp forest was a quick one.

Tall, turbid green spires rose high above their heads, undulating in the current. The water turned cold; the bite was refreshing against the heat building in their veins.

Excitement burned through them, the promise of adventure beckoning from the stairs that rose out of the seabed, along the cliffside, and to the surface. The craggy stone was pockmarked and ancient by the look of it.

"We take the vial at the foot of the stairs. By the time we reach the surface, we'll be human-ish." Lyra reiterated the instructions they had been told repeatedly over the last twenty-one years.

Amber the vial,

drink at the foot.

Fare thee well, fins,

welcome your sins.

With a wicked grin, they uncorked their vials and threw back the jelly-textured liquid inside. Linking arms, they began their ascent. Nothing felt different at first, but after the first ten steps, Lyra noticed a change. Her scales began prickling, the familiar brush of the water more like the sting of a cut.

Then she felt the weight of it all. Her hair against her scalp, the heft of their arms against hers, and the suffocation of not being able to breathe.

But nothing compared to the slicing of one fin into two legs. So severe, it felt like she was being ripped in half.

In the blink of an eye, with a searing flash of golden light and a gasping breath, they breached the surface and stood on solid ground. It had happened so fast that her head spun and stars danced in her eyes.

It felt strange, heavy almost, but also light.

The air was not oppressive like the water had been. The water now lapped at the stairs below them. She missed its touch.

"Ennosidas' fins," she ground out between clenched teeth.

Marina pushed a hand against the riot of curls that fell onto her face. "What is this?"

Seraphina trilled a laugh. "This is life without water. Things sink up here."

They took the remaining steps at a much slower pace,

getting accustomed to moving their feet one after the other. With each step, Lyra felt the jostle through her bones. A thousand needles stabbing into the bottom of her fins—feet.

By the time they reached the top of the stairs of the small cliff, they looked positively abysmal—human, even. Their ethereal nature was subdued.

Viciously sharp teeth were replaced with blunt edges. Pointed fingernails filed to short stubs. And the attire was the worst of all.

"Humans wear this?" Lyra plucked at the yards of fabric clinging to her body.

Layers of skirts and a breath-stealing corset. The only good it had done was to push up the small mounds of her breasts.

"How do they walk in all this?" Marina complained while trying her best to push her ample breasts down from her chin.

Seraphina twirled, her skirts fluttering around her lithe body. A hint of her otherworldly grace was visible under the white light. "Well, I love it."

The light stole Lyra's attention. The moon was a giant orb of silver as it shone down on them, and she closed her eyes, basking in its glow. It was as bewitching as she had read it would be.

"Where are we?" Marina asked.

The town was of varying shades of gray. Strums of music floated down the cobblestone street, piquing Lyra's interest. But it was the air and the moon in the sky that kept tugging on her attention. To see it all in the flesh was overwhelming.

Something stirred within her at the sight of such awe-inspiring beauty. Her lungs filled effortlessly with air, and the feel of the breeze against her skin had her inhaling a large lungful. Reveling in its tender caress.

A tug had her lips curling up.

It was like this land was made for her …

No.

Lyra stomped it down. She was not here to admire.

Clearing her throat, she analyzed the distinct stone buildings and the rolling dark hills in the distance.

"I believe we're somewhere on the Emerald Coast."

Her smile turned feral.

That's where they had left her mother.

Maybe a little revenge was in order.

3
HUMAN HEART

Lyra blew a lock of auburn hair out of her face and stomped off onto the landing and into the street.

Seraphina walked steadily, bouncing on her toes. She didn't appear to be impacted by the pins and needles that stabbed Lyra with each step she took. Even Seraphina's hair had changed color. Gone were the silver strands, and in their place, a flaxen blonde.

Marina moved slowly, adjusting to the weight and pain, if the grimace on her face was any indication.

They tromped across the lane on their new legs. Their boots smacked against the stone. The feel of solid ground beneath her jarred with each step.

Crashing waves against the rocks nearby sang to Lyra's blood. Yet, it did not sound like the call of home, but of a warning. She pushed away the fear it brought and focused on not collapsing under the weight of it all.

"How quickly until we get used to it?" Lyra hissed, feeling the rattle in her knees and the bark of protest in her joints.

Seraphina shrugged. "Your incessant whining is tiresome. Think of something else or stay silent."

Lyra reached out to yank her by the hair, but a screech had them freezing. The sound was terrifying and unusual.

"What was that?" Seraphina asked as the whites of her eyes grew.

Lyra searched her memory through every book she had read about the land.

"It's some kind of animal—a flying kind," she muttered. "Look who's being tiresome now." She shot Seraphina a look. "Let's just find a tavern or something."

The buildings along the lane got closer together. Their wood and stone facades were plain compared to the spires and gold of Atlantis. And the smells—gods, the smells. Dirt, smoke, and something putrid like rotting meat.

Lyra clung to those things to keep her from admiring the rest of the surface world. The breeze brought in fresh scents, the bright moon, and the new and exciting animals.

"I hate it here," she grumbled, trying her best to convince herself. "Let's just pick our humans, eat their hearts, and get back."

Seraphina giggled, twirling her green skirt in her hand as she walked. "I think it's lovely. The air is pleasant."

Marina and Lyra shared a look, their noses scrunching in disgust. Lyra huffed a sigh and tried to ignore the frustration that Seraphina's excitement caused. She wished she could embrace this place, too. But that would make it back to Atlantis, and there would be hell to pay.

They should not like it here. It was unnatural to be out of the water. But as Lyra scanned their surroundings once more, she couldn't help but notice the plants.

Yarrow, butterfly bush, white clover, and Scotch broom.

Tiny leaves and dainty petals. The drawings in her books did not do them justice. Excitement lit her eyes. She had obsessed over these things before that wretched maid had thrown them out.

She shoved the thought away again. They were not here to admire the land. They were here to collect their tithes and return to—where they belonged.

A wooden sign creaked in the wind. The chipped and faded paint was that of a mug of ale clinking another, and marked the building as a tavern.

They had reached the front door when it flew open and music spilled out onto the street before them. A wiry man with a wide-brimmed hat and knee-high breeches leaned over in front of them and emptied the contents of his stomach.

Lyra didn't bat an eye as his vomit splashed up on the skirts of her dress. "*Lovely.*"

Seraphina burst into fits of giggles, the sound as lovely as bells chiming. Marina hushed her, and she covered her mouth with her hands.

Laughter and singing would be the quickest way for someone to realize they weren't human. No amount of magic could hide the otherworldliness of those voices.

Many a mortal had been dragged to their deaths because of their sound, and it's how they would lure them now—among other creative ways, if they chose.

Lyra strutted through the door with all the confidence she could muster, with vomit still staining the navy fabric. With her head held high, the femininity of her long neck was highlighted by her elegant updo.

Marina followed behind her, the violet gown iridescent in the candlelight. The color was lovely against her dark skin.

Seraphina was the last to enter. The emerald green gown was dangerously close to the color of her eyes. But the slight frown on her face was severe enough to make several lesser men avert their eyes.

Plucking at the pleats of her dress, Marina murmured, "I wonder who or what picks the dresses?"

Lyra sighed. "Why? Are you wanting something more alluring next time?"

Marina slapped her shoulder. "No, you witch. I'm just curious."

Lyra stared at where Marina's skin had struck hers. Feeling warm blood rushing to the surface was most unusual. "Let's get some wine. And then get on with it."

They made their way to the long wooden counter constructed as the bar. A stone fireplace made up the opposite wall, and Lyra couldn't help but marvel at the flames writhing and twisting as they consumed the wood. It was like a dance.

An unusual feeling washed over Lyra's skin. Almost like being watched. She scanned the room, searching for the culprit, but came up empty.

There were many tables around the wood-paneled room, all surrounded by humans of a variety of shapes and sizes. But most were standing. They had to weave through a throng of bodies. The mortals all seemed different, but similar in the way a species shares traits.

However, she was most disappointed by the lack of variety in their choices. Most of the people in this tavern were men—and ugly ones. Boiled skin, missing teeth, gnarled fingers—an abysmal selection.

"Um, excuse me, sir," she purred at the colossal man standing behind the bar.

His face was ruddy in the firelight, a stained linen button-down shirt pushed up over disgustingly hairy arms. Beady eyes roved over her face before dropping to her breasts and those of the two women beside her.

This was not the human she would pick. His blood was

probably as fatty as his diet. He spat on the floor, and spittle clung to the long black beard that reached his chest.

"Can I help you, sweetheart?"

Even his voice grated on her nerves. She had to school her features not to react to the sound.

"I would like a glass of red, please, and two more for my companions." She gestured to Marina and Seraphina.

Their eyes darted around the room, and if she was not mistaken by the twisting of their fingers, they, too, were nervous.

The barman looked her up and down again, a slight sneer marring his already grotesque features.

"That'll be three silvers, sweetheart."

Again with the sweetheart. This man was lucky she didn't rip his heart from his barrel chest.

But his words gave her pause, and she patted her hands on her empty skirts.

Of course, the magic didn't leave them anything useful. Not a pouch of coins or even a weapon.

They hadn't carried any coins or gold in Atlantis. Mermaids couldn't hold it there, so it did make sense they wouldn't have it here.

They were utterly powerless here, with no claws or teeth to protect themselves.

Ice slid through her veins—were they lambs to slaughter?

"I've got her," a rich, masculine voice answered from behind her.

Lyra's palms dampened with sweat, and she wiped the disgusting reaction on her gown before turning around to set eyes on her savior.

A quick sweep revealed polished black boots, charcoal breeches over muscular thighs, and an evergreen tunic hidden behind a black cape that still showcased a broad chest and shoulders. Lyra's eyes kept rising, and she had to tip her head back to get a look at his face.

His eyes were the color of a clear blue sky. Or what she imagined it would look like.

She had dreamed that it was what unending freedom would look like. Coupled with a jaw that could cut stone, and short, messy, dark hair. Her heart fluttered against her ribs, and something warm pooled low in her belly.

He was beautiful, unnaturally so.

This was the human whose heart she would consume.

He stared back at her with an unperturbed expression. Not at all distracted by her beauty or that of Marina or Seraphina, as the other men had been.

A peculiar sort of stillness settled around him as if the very world paled in comparison.

Lyra batted her eyelashes at him and plastered on her most alluring smile.

"Why, thank you, kind sir. How shall I repay you?"

Even her voice was not her own, taking on the same hollow-like quality that the most vapid of mermaids in their court possessed.

The kind stranger dipped his chin before reaching into his pockets. A sword pommel strapped to his waist gleamed in the firelight before it was hidden again by the falling of his cloak. Perfect—a weapon she could use. Maybe they weren't powerless here after all.

"No need. Consider it a welcoming present for newcomers."

His words were kind, but there was an edge to his tone as he leaned past Lyra to place the silvers on the bar top. His nostrils flared and his eyes narrowed, but then he stood tall, studying the women.

"That's very kind of you ..." Lyra trailed off, hinting at the desire of his name.

When he didn't reply, she looked up at him from beneath

lowered lashes, sucking her bottom lip behind her teeth. He was a giant of a man, really. Lyra barely reached the column of his neck. She felt small and helpless standing beside him.

And that feeling had her raising her chin. She would never feel helpless because of a mortal male.

"My name is Wilder."

Something about his name or how he said it had Lyra's lips tugging up into the most unusual smirk.

"Wilder," she breathed, testing out the way his name felt in her mouth.

She found she liked it very much, which was most unpleasant since no one would be speaking it aloud after tonight.

But before she could give him hers, he slipped back into the crowd and away from her. Seraphina giggled and whispered in her ear.

"Oh, the things I would do to him before sacrificing his heart to Ennosidas."

Before Lyra could stop herself, she snarled, "*Mine.*"

A loud bang had them whirling back around as the barman slammed three copper cups of red wine down.

"Here you go, ladies."

He trudged down the bar to help the next person vying for his attention.

Lyra studied the sloshing red wine in the glass before glancing over her shoulder to lock eyes with Wilder as he slipped out the front door.

He was getting away.

No.

She had wanted that human for a sacrifice, and she was going to have him.

"You two enjoy," she said. "I'll meet you back at the castle."

Seraphina rolled her eyes and grumbled, "Lyra always gets the nicest things."

Marina clutched Lyra's hand and gave it a squeeze. "Careful."

Lyra sauntered through the tavern without a reply. The stench of unwashed bodies and cloying perfume assaulted her senses with each step. She was surprised she hadn't noticed that before, but several women caught her eye on the way out.

They were sitting on the laps of men, brushing hair out of their faces or whispering in their ears. It was a strange sight to behold. That kind of behavior was forbidden in her kingdom.

She stumbled through the doorway and out into the clear air. Inhaling a lungful, she closed her eyes, feeling a thrill roll through her, like she had managed to escape.

"I hoped you would follow me," Wilder's voice came from behind her.

He was making this all too easy.

Lyra blinked open her eyes and feigned surprise.

"Sir! You have given me a fright."

Wilder leaned one shoulder against the stone wall of the tavern. Half hidden in shadow, he looked delectable. His cape was pulled around him, but it did nothing to hide his muscular frame.

She briefly wondered if his backside was just as well-built as his chest and thighs. The excitement in Lyra's veins scorched. She could make her sacrifice and have time for another if she felt like it, which would increase the fertility magic of her realm.

Or she could walk alone, enjoying her solitude while it lasted.

"So you're saying you didn't come out to find me?" His voice was seductive, and it reeled her in.

Lyra clutched her chest and forced a breath before approaching him.

Or she could try out these new legs and wrap them around his face first. She had never been intimate before, but the pounding between her legs made her want to try.

Lyra had never felt that way about Drystan. Most days, she

couldn't fathom his being her first encounter of intimacy. Ruining herself now might put an end to the wedding tomorrow, too.

What was that human phrase? Two birds, one stone.

"That's not what I said at all. Do not put words in my mouth," she spoke with insinuation, a smirk to her lips, and a sashay to her hips as she approached him.

Heat coiled in her veins, ready to strike.

His eyes flared a fraction.

It was working. He was falling under her spell already.

She stopped a hairsbreadth away from him, accidentally kicking the pack at his feet as she leaned in close to breathe him in. He smelled like how she would imagine the air from high up would smell, crisp and light. Not at all like the air coming off the muck on the street or the stringy weeds between buildings.

Wilder took her in, from her boots sinking into the mud, the navy gown splattered in vomit, and the pieces of auburn hair that dangled from her updo and grazed her collarbones.

If he appreciated what he saw, he didn't let on, which only spurred her on.

"Now why would you be out here waiting for me?" she asked, leaning towards him.

Her attention was so raptly focused on his face, the moonlight that lit high cheekbones, and up-tilted eyes. He looked nothing like the humans in the tavern. They were all marred with some kind of flaw. But not him—he was perfect. Beautiful, even.

It was almost a shame that he was about to die.

His arms moved from across his chest to his sides, allowing her another step closer. Lyra pressed her breasts against the space where his chest met his stomach. Her nipples pebbled as she strained to press harder against him.

The friction of the fabric was infuriating. She wanted to bare herself to him, or the caress of the air. Anything would be better than this confining fabric.

When he didn't answer her, she tried again, walking her fingers up his stomach and to his chest.

Right where his heart thumped beneath his ribs.

"Did you like what you saw—"

Wilder grabbed her hand and slung her around.

Her back and head crashed against the rough stone.

Sharp pain lashed down her spine, and her head pounded; stars erupted across her vision.

It took her a second too long to figure out what had happened.

One moment she had been standing there, pressing her breasts against his body, and the next she'd been slung and pushed against the wall, a steel blade angled at her neck.

Wrath twisted Wilder's beautiful features into something terrifying—something from her worst nightmares.

Elf. He was a godsdamn elf.

"Because I have been ordered to," he spat, pressing the blade to her throat as he answered her former question.

The edge nicked her pale skin.

The scouts had been right. But what could the elves possibly want from her? No one knew about her magic.

Her nostrils flared, catching the scent of her blood.

No—no, it was supposed to be his blood, his heart, she was consuming.

Lyra licked her lips and leaned forward against the blade, daring him to end her, and testing the boundaries of his orders.

Would she be the one who didn't return from the Tithe?

No.

Fury flooded her mind, clouding her vision and skewing her thoughts. Lyra needed to return to Atlantis—she had a fiancé to kill. And then her life would be better.

She would be free of her father and the court.

The only sound that reached her ears was the crash of waves against the stone. It echoed the roaring in her head.

Wilder's eyes narrowed, and he leaned away from her, moving the blade enough that it didn't slice through her.

She had called his bluff, and it had worked. So, he had been ordered to take her but not kill her.

"And *who* ordered you to?"

Wilder smiled, and it was savage, wicked even.

A small divot formed between her thin brows. She didn't know which side of him she preferred. The beautiful male or this wicked creature.

"You'll see soon enough."

His hand slipped around her throat like a large, tight necklace. Her blood heated at the scrape of his calluses against her flesh, causing her breathing to stutter through her lips.

Lyra didn't see his arm move before his fist connected with her jaw.

Blackness erupted, and she was gone, lost, floating in the spaces between the stars.

4
TAKEN

Lyra's head thudded against Wilder's back with each of his long strides. The constant swaying motion and the crunching of his boots upon the trodden grass roused her.

Blood roared behind her closed eyes, and it was an effort to peel them open. She was met with the sight of his backside, and unfortunately, it was as firm as she imagined it would be.

The thought made her roll her eyes, and then she hissed from the pain.

"I wondered how long it would take …"

The rich timbre of his voice rumbled through her where his shoulder pressed into her abdomen.

She squirmed in his hold, anger pulsing through her. Not at the humiliation of being carried like a sack of grain, but because this male—this elf—ruined a night she was most looking forward to. The unsatisfied itch curdled within her, souring her already tepid mood.

She took back all the lust she had originally felt—she hated him.

Lyra screamed, pounding her fists on the pack strapped to his back and kicking as if her feet were fins to swim away. A well-placed kick to the gut had Wilder dropping her to the ground. Trapped in the layers of twisted fabrics, she flopped to the ground like a floundering fish.

A blade appeared out of thin air and pressed against her throat.

"Try to escape, Princess, and I'll run you through."

Lyra stared up at him, not with arousal or lust this time, but with pure hatred.

"Where are we? And where are my friends?"

Wilder lowered the blade an inch and tilted his head.

"I didn't know mermaids were capable of having friends."

She bared her teeth at him in a display of violence before she realized the futility of that action. Her sharp teeth were gone, all the armor she was accustomed to having—gone.

She screamed with rage, tilting her head up to the night sky and bellowing with all the frustration that she had worked to lock away.

Wilder glowered but did nothing.

Her chest heaved, and she scrubbed at her face with a dirt-covered hand.

"Where are you taking me?"

She looked up at him but saw past his face to the sparkles behind him. Not sparkles—stars.

Millions upon millions of stars. Constellations and other tidbits of information surfaced in her mind.

The Northern Star leads away from home. Yarrow is good for pain when the legs become too sore, and unsalted water would be a necessity in this world if you were trapped here.

She looked around, peering into the sky for the big star. Unfortunately, it was behind her.

He was leading them towards it and away from the sea—away from her kingdom.

"Why are we going north?"

His eyes narrowed, and he sheathed the sword in its scabbard, then adjusted the straps of the pack.

"We're meeting with my guard, and then we'll be escorting you to the Wilds."

Lyra nodded, feigning acceptance, but began devising a plan of escape.

Wilder studied her a moment longer.

A sneer marred his lips as he opened his mouth to speak and then closed it, before finally opening it again to ask, "How did you know we were heading north?"

She didn't answer.

The cold seeped through the layers of her skirts, and she scrambled to her feet. Mud caked her hands, and with regret, she wiped them on the navy fabric of the dress. She scrunched her nose with distaste at the gritty feeling.

"What did you do to my friends?"

He shrugged. "I only had orders for you. I'm sure they're murdering mortals or doing whatever it is your kind do when they venture on land."

His answer surprised her.

She hadn't expected them to have been left alive. Relief cooled some of the burn of her anger. Marina's father would not have had to lose a wife and a daughter. And now they could tell someone what had happened to her.

Lyra wasn't a coward who hadn't completed the tithe—she had been kidnapped.

From her vantage point on the small hill, she could see far into the distance, to the dwindling glow on the horizon. The village was very far already, but still within sight.

She needed to make it back and sacrifice a heart before first light. How quickly could she run? Or would an elf's heart count towards the tithe?

Worry gnawed at her mind. She didn't know the answer to either of those questions. She'd have to kill him and a human—just to be safe.

Wilder crossed his arms and stared down his nose at her. Face twisted in a glower in the silver moonlight, he was still beautiful. His name was much more fitting than she would ever admit.

There was a wildness to his beauty, like the chaos of the universe was trapped in his body.

Glorious, untethered, and unending.

But then he spoke.

"Start walking, and no more questions. I don't think you realize the position you are in."

She frowned, not understanding his point. Yes, she had been kidnapped, but why shouldn't she ask questions? Or was it a threat of violence? Her eyes brightened then, the frown slipping away. Violence, she was accustomed to. It was familiar and not at all unexpected.

"You don't scare me. You called me Princess, so you must know who I am. Who my father is. Or my fiancé, for that matter?"

Surprise flickered in his eyes. Not from her words, but from the fact that she was speaking to him so brazenly.

"I'm not sure who should scare you the most," she continued. "My father? Or the male who views me as his property already? Neither appreciates people taking what is theirs."

With that, Wilder snorted and stepped towards her. His fingers closed around her upper arm, and he tugged her to him. The heat of his body chased away the cold that had slid through her. And in a move that surprised even her, she leaned into his warmth.

"With that mouth of yours, I take it you do not know who I

am. Allow me to enlighten you, princess. I am Wilder Vale, Crown Prince of the Wilds, the only son of Oberon, High King of the Elves."

Lyra couldn't help the disbelief that widened her eyes or the bitter taste of fear that poisoned her tongue.

She leaned away from him.

Gods.

Oberon was the most powerful of all the kings, second only to Fionn, god of the elves.

She unconsciously gripped the silver-and-sapphire shell on her necklace as she worked through his claim.

The absurdity of it all.

What could the King of the Wilds want from her?

King Auris' warning rang in her ears. They would use her in ways beyond her worst nightmares. She had to get out of here, and fast.

Although he was a nightmare, he didn't deem her as one with his narrow stance and arrogant sneer. It would be easy to catch him off guard right about now.

And with that thought, she did.

Swinging at him with an open hand, she raked her short nails across his face.

In shock, he released her arm. Lyra fled. Running on bumbling legs away from the Northern Star. Each step was excruciating, a thousand knives slicing her feet and legs.

Tears blurred her vision and stung her eyes. But she kept moving, kept running back to the safety of the water.

Air was stuck in the back of her throat as she breathed through her open mouth.

Mud and trampled grass squelched beneath her boots.

A hole in the earth had her ankle rolling painfully to the side. The searing pain cut her to the bone, and she cried out.

She was not fast enough.

Something rough wrapped around her other ankle and

yanked. She flew face-first to the ground before muscular arms flipped her face up and a solid body settled on top of her.

"Enough," he snarled in her face.

He looked savage. Fury rolled off him in waves and had her sinking farther into the earth to escape him.

Her heart fluttered like that of the tiny hummingbirds she had read about, and she panted through her mouth. Her breath stirred the hair around his face, and he recoiled from her, pressing a hand to her mouth as he worked to untie the rope that had wrapped around her ankle.

"Stop that."

He glared down at her, and his lowered brow cast his eyes in shadow. "Do not run from me again."

She felt the skin of her wrist burn and looked down.

A rope.

The rope that he caught her with had been tied around her wrist, the other side attached to him. Like a leash.

She snarled at the travesty, the very humiliation of it all.

Wilder leaned down, close enough that she could feel the stir of his soft breath. No one had ever touched her this closely before.

She hated this man.

"Like the leash? *Pet.*"

Fury speared through her, snuffing out every intelligent thought of self-preservation, and drove her head forward into his face.

The contact echoed loudly in the quiet night. Pain blackened her vision in spots.

If her head had been pounding before, using it as a battering ram hadn't helped.

Wilder grimaced.

Scarlet blood coated his teeth, and he wrapped a large hand around her throat, squeezing enough to make her breathing difficult.

"Do that again, and I will wring your neck." He squeezed a fraction more for emphasis, and her eyes bulged.

Lyra clawed at his hand, squirming under the weight of his body.

Fear doused her fury, leaving her hollowed out.

Wilder let go and grabbed her free hand, securing it with the rope. Lyra twisted and fought under him, but it was of no use.

"You've delayed us enough."

He rose and strode in the direction of the Northern Star that twinkled ahead of them.

Lyra felt the rope pull against her, and she scrambled to her feet. Standing still a moment longer, she looked to the south, to the sea and her home.

Would her father come for her? Would Drystan?

The answer was a resounding yes. They would. Not because they loved her, but because they owned her.

The rope tugged against her wrist, nearly knocking her off balance. She wobbled on legs she was still not accustomed to.

Wilder stared at her with a mixture of disgust and humor.

"I think Pet is the wrong name for you. How about, Legs?"

Lyra's teeth clacked together. She had preferred "Princess."

5
SURVIVAL

The night sky shimmered with stars and shades of black and navy. With each passing step, large plants loomed. Lyra struggled to remember the names of the things she was passing. So many books all warred for priority in her chaotic mind.

A stinging pain had her looking down at the rope that was tied around her wrists and then at the elf to which it was attached. He was foolish not to keep her in his line of sight. And with the looming tall things coming closer, she could find a place to hide.

Trees! They were called trees, and a multitude of them made up a forest.

An unusual feeling in her mouth had her smacking her lips together.

"Stop that."

"My mouth feels strange," she mumbled, continuing to smack her lips.

"It's dry because you keep breathing through your mouth."

Wilder jerked them to a stop and thrust a leather pouch at her. Lyra stared at it quizzically before grasping it between two fingers.

"What is this?" Her nose wrinkled in disgust at the feel of it.

"It's water. Your mouth is dry," Wilder replied, staring at her like she'd grown two heads.

Dry. That was the word. She had never known what that would feel like and could scarcely imagine it.

But now the air was dry, and her skin felt dry where it was covered in fabric. However, the ground was not dry. No, it had squelched with each of their steps.

Lyra continued staring at the leather pouch. "Do you think I'm that gullible? You've kidnapped me, so you're obviously not beneath drugging or poisoning me."

Wilder ripped it from her grip and twisted the metal cap. It opened, and he held it to his mouth. Lyra watched with a curious expression as the leather pressed against his lips. The column of his throat bobbed as he swallowed.

A few drops sparkled on his chin, and he wiped them away with the back of his hand. He had such large hands; the palms were pale compared to the tanned skin on the tops of them, and his fingers were long, like a musician's.

Wilder thrust it back out to her, and this time, she took it greedily. She was thirsty, but more than that, she needed a distraction from staring at his hands. She pressed it to her lips and tilted her head back, allowing the water to flow into her mouth.

It was surprisingly fresh. Lyra gulped down a few mouthfuls. Water clung to her chin as well, but she did not wipe it away. She delighted in its touch.

The water was a comfort, even if it wasn't the same as the ocean she had come from.

Wilder's attention narrowed on the droplets clinging to her

pale skin before he ripped the container from her hands. Their hands grazed, and Lyra stared at where his skin had touched hers.

An unusual feeling—that touch.

"Let's move," he grumbled.

The trees grew closer, and the glow of the small, distant village winked out of existence. He was moving quickly. If she were going to escape, she needed to do it soon. But how?

Lyra stared down at the rope around her wrist. If she had teeth, she could bite through it. Hell, even her nails would have worked against this pathetically human contraption. But stuck in this body, she had nothing.

She tugged at the rope around her wrist. It swayed and jostled under her ministrations.

Wilder turned around in an instant to glare at her.

"Haven't I made myself perfectly clear?"

Lyra held her hands up in surrender. But anger simmered in her eyes.

She would find a way.

Wilder saw the fight in her that was growing, a steady current of power swelling like a wave before it crashed against the shore.

"There is not a place you could run, a place you could hide, that I would not find you, Legs. And trust me, out here," he gestured around to the tall trees, "you don't want to leave my side."

"I'm not scared of you," Lyra muttered.

"You should be," he replied over his shoulder, already turning his back to her.

"And why, might I ask? Because you kidnap helpless females under your king's orders? Pathetic. I bet you haven't made a single decision in your entire life! You're a coward, little princeling."

Wilder shook his head. His dark mass of hair bounced with

the movement. "You talk too much." But his tone held a sharp edge of annoyance.

If she could burrow herself under his skin, maybe he would let her go to free himself of her.

"What is that you want? Jewels? Gold?"

He didn't answer, but she could see his shoulders stiffen.

"I am the Princess! Tales of my beauty are known across the realm. Surely that would be enough to entice you for a trade?"

Wilder laughed and shook his head as he halted to stare at her.

"There is nothing that you could offer me that I would trade for my duty to my kingdom. Save your breath. You'll need your energy for this journey."

Wilder tugged her forward, walking along the narrow path into the increasing darkness of the forest. The canopy of leaves blotted out the stars, and it was a struggle for her to see where they were going. He was leading her into the depths of darkness, and she was terrified. Yet his feet did not falter, and each step was meticulously planted.

With nothing else to do, she wielded her knowledge as a weapon. Lyra would talk and talk until it annoyed him enough that he didn't notice when she slipped the rope. Or until he gagged her, and in that case, she would fling herself to the ground and fight with everything she had.

Lyra would not go down without a fight. She had to get back to the water—where she belonged.

"Did you know these trees are a mix of juniper and hawthorn?"

Her voice seemed amplified in the sleeping forest, her tone purposely superior. Males hated it when you knew a thing more than they did.

Wilder grunted in response.

"And that tree there," she jutted with her chin, "is an ash tree."

"Quiet," he hissed. His head swiveled from side to side as if he were looking for something.

Lyra continued walking, but twisted her wrists under the rope, trying to loosen it. Wilder was too busy scanning their surroundings as they walked to notice the rope jiggling at his side.

"These fluffy things are ferns. They have fronds. I know you won't understand that word, so I will explain. Fronds or f-r-o-n-d-s are leaves. Compound leaves, to be exact. Shall I explain what a compound is?"

Twisting and tugging at the rope as she spoke. A flap of wings startled her. But Wilder continued, not at all bothered by the proximity of the creature and still looking as if he was searching for something.

"Oh, and that must've been an owl," she gushed.

The rope loosened a fraction, and she bit her lip to keep her excitement contained as she twisted some more.

"If you don't shut up, I will gag you." His shoulders almost touched his ears.

She really was getting under his skin, then.

A howl pierced the air, and goosebumps raised on Lyra's arms.

"That must be a wolf!" she whispered-shouted with excitement.

The sound stopped Wilder in his tracks, and he unsheathed the sword at his hip. The blade gleamed in the moonlight, and Lyra's mouth dried up.

While death would be preferable to the Wilds, she was not exactly ready. Sure, her entire existence until this point had been miserable, but it had been hers.

The wolf's howl tapered off, and Wilder tugged back on the rope to get her moving again.

"Do you know what other kinds of animals live in these woods?" Lyra asked him.

"I know nothing about the mortal land, and I don't care to. So shut up."

She twisted and tugged at the rope again as she talked. "How can you be a prince and know nothing?"

They walked farther on in silence, each step adding to the insurmountable distance to the sea. That knowledge was unsettling. She wavered in her plans once more.

It would be excruciating to run the whole way back. But would it be worse never to return? Maybe she could live among the mortals. She knew enough about the surface world to carve out a measly existence here.

"There are probably chipmunks in these woods, and moles, and gophers. Oh, and I bet there are cardinals. They are red birds. The color of their feathers is like fresh blood."

Wilder ground his teeth, trying his best to ignore her chatter and keep alert. But his ignoring her was what she was counting on. The rope finally gave way, widening enough that she could slip one hand out.

Her skin burned and was discolored where the rope had rubbed her raw. She held onto it and slipped the other hand out as they continued to walk so that he wouldn't catch on to her plans yet.

Lyra knew there would be only one tiny window of opportunity.

"There are other birds that are blue, and do you know what they're called?" She waited for a response she knew would not come. "They call them Blue Jays. How unoriginal. Why would they name a bird after the color it was called?"

"I swear to the gods, Legs. If you don't shut your mouth …"

With his words, she lowered the rope to the ground, bending over at the waist as they walked. Her leg muscles howled with the change of position. But he didn't notice the lowered rope on his side. Wilder breathed a sigh of relief when she didn't respond.

Lyra let go of the rope and held her breath, praying to all the gods that he wouldn't turn around. And he did continue without her, unfazed by the quiet or the rope that rustled against the forest floor behind him. It was not louder than her tromping footsteps had been, anyway.

Wilder adjusted the pack on his shoulders and kept marching along the path.

"Finally, some peace and quiet," he said. "This journey will not be half as miserable if you just follow my orders. It's already taking everything I have to …"

His words trailed off as he walked on without her.

Lyra smirked, and as he walked farther away, she slipped between two large ash trees and into utter darkness. She walked off the beaten path, running her hands from tree trunk to tree trunk to find her way.

It was nice up here on land, with so many more sensations than she was accustomed to.

She needed to get out of these trees and find her way back to the water. And if that took too long, and she ran out of time, she needed to hide so that he wouldn't find her.

Lyra stopped walking and craned her ears to listen. It was quiet. She couldn't hear Wilder's footsteps now. There was only the soft rustle of the leaves in the trees. She smiled to herself, feeling free for the first time and wondering how long it would take him to realize she wasn't attached to the rope.

A roar of fury had birds flying away and the forest coming to life.

Not long, apparently.

Wilder roared her name like it was a world he planned to conquer. Her actual name—not Legs.

Holding her breath, she crouched under the branches of an immense hawthorn tree. She slid along the base of the trunk to the forest floor.

She needed to stay still and quiet, and surely he would not

find her. This seemed to be a vast forest, and he was only one man—elf.

The forest grew quiet again, and she could no longer hear the echo of her name. He must have gone in the opposite direction then.

Lyra had a sudden sinking feeling like she would never make it back to the water. It was an eerie feeling, unsettling and bizarre. It prickled the skin of her palms and slithered through her gut.

A crunch of leaves beside her made her flinch. Her heart was a flurry of panic in her chest. Rough hands seized her arms and wrenched her to her feet. They were not the large, skilled hands of the elf.

"Ah, ah, ah. What do we have here?" The stench of ale had her leaning away from the bear of a man who gripped her.

Her eyes adjusted to the dim light outside of the tree's shadow.

The man looked monstrous. Scarred cheeks and one milky eye.

"My, my, that is a nice cunt," another voice chortled from the darkness beside them.

The sound was like claws raking at her skin.

Lyra's stomach plummeted to the ground.

A meaty, sweaty hand pawed at her face and roughly grabbed her by the cheeks.

"Such a pretty mouth to fuck."

Terror sliced through her, snatching the air from her lungs. She fought under his hold, biting and clawing at the man who held her. Her thread of power glimmered brighter in her chest.

But she couldn't. Not even now.

Wilder had warned her there were worse things in these woods. She should have listened.

Blindly biting, she clipped the finger of one.

"Fuck! She bit me!"

She spat the fleshy taste onto the ground. Her mouth filled with saliva as nausea roiled through her stomach.

Disgusting. These men were rotten.

Lyra wasn't prepared for the punch to the gut that had her doubling over. A groan escaped her as the air deflated her lungs. A searing pain tore at her scalp as he wrenched her head back up.

"Get the dress out of the way, Rupert," the man from the shadows spoke.

He stepped out of the night then and into the dappled shaft of moonlight spearing through the tree canopy. He was thin, with a hawkish nose and eyes that rivaled the darkness of the forest around him. He tugged at his belt to loosen it and leered at her.

Rupert, the bear of the man holding her, ripped at her dress. The fabric, though heavy to her, tore easily under his fist.

No.

No, this would not happen to her. The thread of power flared, and she pushed that thought away. These men would not take her maidenhead—or her soul.

Lyra fought harder. She would save herself—without losing herself to magic.

She swung wildly and ripped with her short nails at anything she could manage.

"A feisty one! Help me hold her," Rupert grunted when she tore at the skin of his hand.

The thin man grabbed hold of her from behind, holding her still with astonishing strength.

He licked up the column of her neck. The feel of his tongue had a scream tearing out of her. His breath smelled putrid, like festering, rotten meat.

"Oh, I like it when they scream," he moaned into her ear.

Lyra threw her head back, and with a satisfying thwack, he let go of her. The crisp night air pebbled her bare breasts, and she moved to escape.

A slinking sound had them all freezing.

Rupert stood frozen, holding the swathe of fabric that had made up the front of her dress.

Lyra blinked, and a blade protruded from his chest. The deepest crimson blood, nearly black, poured from him.

The shadow behind him rippled and pulled the blade out.

It grabbed Lyra by the arm, whirling her to its side.

Another swing had the blade cutting off the thin man's head. A disgustingly wet thudding sound rang out as his body crumpled to the ground.

"Are you alright?" Wilder asked, sheathing his blade again.

He materialized from the shadows as if he had stepped through them. It took Lyra a moment to realize *he was the shadow*. He had pulled up the hood of his cape and blended in with the night.

Lyra stood in shock and stared down at the corpses that he had cut down in the blink of an eye. She couldn't move, other than the rapid movements of her bare chest with each breath.

Wilder coughed and peeled off his cape. He held it out to her, but when she didn't move or acknowledge it anyway, he pressed it to her naked chest and tied it around her back for her.

"Legs, you still with me?"

When she didn't respond, he leaned down. Looking into her eyes, he cupped her cheeks. "You're in shock, but you will be okay. I'm here."

Lyra couldn't speak, couldn't move on her own, as Wilder tugged her away from the humans he had murdered on her behalf. He had come for her—had saved her.

No one had ever saved her before.

She followed him willingly but told herself it was only

because he was the lesser of two evils and that she had no other choice now. She couldn't find her way back to the water, and she couldn't survive with the mortals.

This was survival.

6
DUTY OR NOT

The mermaid was a fool.

A fool to think she could survive in these lands, in any lands alone. They walked in silence away from the corpses. She didn't make a sound, didn't ask a question, or point out anything she saw. And it unnerved Wilder.

Yes, she had been annoying before, but this was something else. This was trauma. He scanned her once more, opting to walk beside her now in case this was all a front and she planned on giving him the slip again.

When he had finally noticed her absence, he had never felt such anger or fear. He knew these woods, the terrifying creatures that wandered them, and the loathsome barbarians that had made this place their home.

This was the forest between worlds. Between the elf and human realms. His plan, now futile, had been to keep her scared of him so that she wouldn't realize the dangerous line they were walking.

Her breath came out in quick pants, her eyes still widened. Her scent had changed, too. It was now drenched in fear. He felt a semblance of guilt. This was his doing, after all.

When she shivered and clutched her chest, he knew adrenaline was taking hold. He knew what that felt like, so he did the only thing he could think to do—talk.

"How did you know all that stuff before?"

He didn't want the fear taking hold of her too strongly. Then she would pass out, and he would be forced to carry her again for the sake of his mission.

He hadn't liked how that had felt. It had been too intimate.

She was his enemy, and he didn't need to feel anything for her at all.

"Books," she muttered.

He could hear the fluttering that had taken hold of her chest and smell the fear that still pumped through her veins.

Wilder tilted his head at her voice. When she looked up into his eyes, the fluttering slowed and returned to the rhythmic, albeit quick, pumping.

"So, do you like to read?" he asked, scrubbing the back of his neck with an open hand.

She furrowed her brow before answering. "Yes," she hissed. "What kind of question is that? Why would I read so much if I didn't like it?"

He turned back to the path to hide the smirk that was blooming on his face.

"I take it you don't like reading, and that's why you know nothing?" She said the words as if it offended her that someone could not enjoy reading.

"I prefer having adventures to reading about them."

"That's called privilege," she snapped.

They walked farther on, but her pace had dwindled. Twigs snapped beneath her feet, and she stumbled more often than not. But he had done his duty. She was still alive, no longer quaking with fear, and following willingly. His father would be proud, and maybe that would suffice to get him a few days of freedom.

"Are there more humans like that around here?" Her voice was so small, so timid compared to the haughty arrogance she had been exuding.

Wilder's face fell into a scowl, and he scanned their surroundings.

"Undoubtedly." He sniffed and was hit with the scent of unwashed bodies and stale ale that seemed to permeate the men of this forest.

"How do you know?"

Lyra studied him a bit too closely for his liking.

There was something about her eyes. The emerald green color was most unusual, but also the sharpness in them. Like she could see more than what was physically there.

Wilder tapped the side of his nose and continued walking.

He hadn't bothered to tie her back up, but there hadn't been a need. For whatever reason, she had seemed to trust his words, or maybe she was smart enough not to run back into the forest after her ordeal.

"You can smell the humans?" she asked as she kept pace with him. Her steps became quicker when she was after information.

"I can scent you, too."

Lyra stopped. Her eyes grew wide, and he chuckled. He hadn't been lying when he told her there was no place she could run or hide. Now she believed him.

His next words were quiet because only a small part of him wanted her to know.

"You smell of the sea in a storm."

That wasn't the complete truth, but he didn't know how to explain that it was more powerful than that.

Wilder scanned the forest, breathing in the earth and moss-covered trees. He picked up the fleeting scent of feathers and small critters as they scurried silently around them.

Her scent sang to him, and he should have known the moment it faded to a whisper that she had escaped. But he had been relieved that its grip on him had loosened.

"You smell too," Lyra replied, stepping close to him again and shivering as the breeze floated by.

His brows hit his hairline. "I do?"

She grinned maliciously. "Yeah. Terribly so." She gripped her nose with her fingers and waved a hand in front of her face.

A laugh nearly bubbled out of him, but he tamped it down.

His enemy.

She was his enemy, he reminded himself again.

"Let's go, Legs."

Wilder stomped through the knee-high ferns, and Lyra scurried after him, throwing cautious glances around her.

"Where is your guard meeting us?"

Wilder didn't answer her, and a pout plumped her bottom lip.

"Why were you ordered to kidnap me?"

Wilder's broad shoulders seemed to grow wider as he flexed them under the weight of that question. He shifted his rucksack once more.

"You're back to asking questions."

"I am."

"My father requires your presence. I'm following orders."

"But why does he want *me*? And why, *you*? Don't you have a royal guard or paid kidnappers?"

That was a very astute question. But it led to even larger questions that he had.

"I don't know what he wants from you."

"And?" she prodded.

"And we do have a guard to complete this task. But I am the best," Wilder replied.

He didn't say it arrogantly, but Lyra still snorted.

"Best at kidnapping females? My, my, what a reputation you have, Princeling."

Her biting wit and sneer had Wilder hiding another smirk.

She was resilient. He'd give her that much. She had faced a horror most females don't walk away from, and it had only knocked her down a peg or two.

But it was her darting eyes that gave her away, and the constant twisting of the sapphire charm on the end of her necklace. Lyra could feign normalcy all she'd like, but he could smell her fear even now.

It made the smell of the sea sharper, like lingering salt on dried skin. But he would play along. The sooner she was back to normal, the sooner this would all be over, and he'd never have to see her again.

He truly didn't know the plans his father had for her. Wilder had only been instructed to escort the Princess, *alive*, to the Wilds. And that's what he would do. First, he had to get her there, and the safest way to do that was to meet up with his crew in Fresia.

"It's a two-day trek to the village where we're to meet them, and we have to skirt the human capital. I know it's impossible for you, but to keep us from running into any more ruffians— shut your mouth."

"Why do we have to skirt the human capital?"

"Because no creature sets foot in Badenvaria. Now, please— *silence.*"

7
NURSEMAID

H e guided them a few more miles before the pain became too much for Lyra. When she started whining, Wilder swallowed his complaints and found them a large boulder with a towering cedar beside it, a perfect makeshift camp.

"Can we start a fire?" Lyra asked, rubbing her arms with her hands.

"So we can alert every creature in this forest to our location?" Wilder's brow rose precariously high on his forehead.

Lyra's teeth chattered, which may well give away their position, anyway. He had nothing left to give her. She already wore his cloak.

Wilder was confused about how she was this cold to begin with under the multitude of fabrics that made up her dress. If he was not mistaken, that outer layer was velvet. It should have kept her warm on its own.

"It's n-not the t-temperature," she stuttered out, plopping onto the ground and rubbing her legs.

Gods. Of course, it wasn't the temperature. It was undoubtedly the shock from her kidnapping, her near rape, and the walking. She had never walked before.

Wilder's lips pressed into a grim line. It was unfortunate for her to be uncomfortable, but he did not know how to help her. And yet, strangely enough, he wanted to.

"I need yarrow," she mumbled between trembling lips.

"What's yarrow?" He tilted his head and squatted down to hear her better. The line between his brows grew deeper.

"It's a plant. It helps with the pain."

Wilder studied her. This could very well be a trick for her to escape again.

But when her gaze shifted from her legs to him, the truth was plainly written. She was in agony.

The emerald green of her irises had shifted to gray.

"Where can I find yarrow, and what does it look like?"

His question had a breath of relief slipping through her lips.

"It's a tallish green plant with small white flowers. It will be in grassy areas."

Her voice was a raspy whisper. She was fading fast. Wilder stood and looked down at her for a moment longer.

"Do not leave this spot. I meant what I said. I am the least of your worries here. I will get you to the Wilds *safely*. You have my word. But you must listen to me."

He didn't know how much weight that would carry with her, that his word was his bond, but with her abundance of reading, surely she had read that somewhere. She looked up and nodded, but her eyes struggled to stay open.

He moved to leave and then paused. "And do not make a noise unless you are attacked. In that case—scream. I will come for you."

Lyra's lashes fluttered at his words as she fought to stay conscious. He did not like that at all. His orders had been to keep her alive.

Turning on his heel, he rushed back onto the path. He had thought he had spotted something similar a few hundred yards back. A weight settled onto his chest when he got far enough away from Lyra that her scent no longer plagued him.

Plagued him—like she was a disease that could not be cured.

A disease that corrupted everything in its path.

He had been taught about the merfolk. That they were monsters. Vile, evil creatures that knew only war, death, and wickedness. Wilder jogged down the path they had traveled, spotting the small clearing up ahead. The yarrow must be there. It had been the only place they had passed thus far without trees.

Wilder broke through the wall of trees and into the small clearing. There he spotted row after row of small white petals on tall green stalks. This had to be yarrow.

Lyra hadn't instructed him on how much to grab. But it was two days to Fresia, and from there, at least another week to the Wilds. That was a long time for her to be in pain.

He yanked a handful of yarrow from the ground, and another, and then another.

Before he knew it, he had an armful of the thin stalks. The wispy petals tickled his chin, and dirt from their roots coated his trousers. But he ignored both as he hurried back to her. She had looked so pale when he left; her breath had stuttered from her mouth in pants. The pain must be excruciating.

The smell of a raging sea reached him before he saw her, and the sight had him stumbling. Her skin was the color of moonlight filtering through the fluffy branches of the cedar tree. She was lying on her side, her auburn hair a mass of curls upon the forest floor. Her face was solemn and peaceful in this state.

The pain had become too much, and blessed sleep dragged her down before he could return. He approached her on silent feet, not wanting to startle her awake if she truly was asleep. Her chest rose and fell in a steady rhythm, and he placed the yarrow beside her. She smelled of rain and the sea, the sharp scent of fear dissipating with every thump of her heart.

Wilder pressed his back against the boulder before easing down onto the ground. With only a small amount of magic in the mortal realm, he could feel the wear on his joints and the exhaustion that would be kept at bay in the Wilds. He rarely required rest, but here, it was a necessity.

Instead, though, he opted to keep watch for them.

The humans had stumbled upon her too quickly, and something about that didn't seem right, almost as if they had been looking.

Lyra whimpered in her sleep, and he jerked his head to her, ready to fight off the attacker, but there was no one. She was having a nightmare. Her brow furrowed, and she clenched and relaxed her jaw. Without thinking, Wilder placed a hand on her shoulder.

The weight of his palm had her stilling once more. The frown on her face slipped away.

8
No
RETURN

S leep was only a temporary relief. The moon was still in the sky when Lyra flinched awake.

The pain crashed back down and burned her eyes. She fumbled in the dark.

"The yarrow is next to you," Wilder said, his voice rough with disuse.

Her hand clasped around the thin stalks, and she pulled them to her. The best way to use yarrow was to brew the leaves in a tea. But without fire or time to waste, she opted to shove the whole plant into her mouth and began chewing.

It was bitter, but that didn't stop her from devouring one entire plant and grabbing for another.

Wilder watched on with amused curiosity. And she didn't care how ferociously she ate the plants. She allowed a bit of the monster within to slip through the cracks of her human facade.

Let him see it.

Even with her human teeth and blunt nails, she looked like

the mermaid that would have ripped his heart from his chest and devoured it whole.

Lyra groaned and pressed a hand to her stomach.

"Are you alright?" Wilder asked, sitting up straighter.

"I ate too quickly."

Lyra belched.

His eyes widened in alarm. He probably had never heard such a sound come from a female before.

"Better?"

"Much." She beamed at him.

Small white petals littered the cloak, still tied backward around her. Her auburn hair had fallen from the intricate updo she had it in, and it hung in loose tendrils down to her lap.

She looked wild now.

"What time is it?" Lyra asked, staring up at the sky.

"Late."

His answer didn't surprise her. She had only mere hours left of the Tithe before it would be too late. But even if she escaped from him now, she wouldn't make it in time. She had long since passed the point of no return.

Lyra shoved that thought away just in time for a new rippling pain to draw her attention to the muscles of her lower legs. She rubbed at them, trying to remember the name, trying to focus on anything other than the hopelessness that would consume her if she thought about it.

Her life was over.

Never again would she float along the current or admire her powerful tail. Gritting her teeth, she breathed sharply through her nose, trying to focus on the physical pain and not the emotional one. Her legs and those lower muscles. What was the name?

It was the same name as a baby cow. That part she remembered just fine.

"Calves," she mumbled to herself.

"Excuse me?"

"This muscle," she squeezed it, "it's called a calf."

Wilder's head tilted to the side, his brows pinching together.

"It is," he replied slowly, as if she were on the verge of a mental breakdown.

And she was. She was in pain, excruciating pain, and she was lost, with no hope of return.

Lyra looked at her surroundings, taking a deep breath again to clear her head.

She felt a buzzing numbness as the yarrow flooded her senses. It pried her from pain's grip slowly, releasing each tightened finger with an arduous pull.

"Did you know you could brew the leaves of this plant for tea? Or pulverize it into a poultice to stop bleeding?"

Wilder squeezed the bridge of his nose with two fingers.

"I did not—and I don't care to."

Lyra hummed her disagreement but lay back to look up at the stars twinkling between the boughs of the cedar tree.

Wilder had saved her, hadn't left her in the hands of those humans. He had also gotten her the yarrow to ease her suffering. Which was wholly at odds with what she knew about his kind. And if it was important to his king that she make it alive and uninjured, it meant that he wouldn't torture or kill her immediately.

She held onto that thought and pushed everything else away.

9
STARS

Wilder studied her more closely now that she couldn't see him.

Lyra was strange—not in a bad way, but in an unpredictable way. She stared up at the stars with quiet fascination. But she seemed to be amazed by everything, really.

The Wilds might send her into shock. It was everything this mortal land was, but better. The air was clearer, the stars brighter, and there was a richer vibrancy to the colors of the plants.

Lyra held her hand up in front of her, tracing the outline of her fingers. She smiled, and it was a bright, lovely thing. Wholly at odds with her sneer or smirk, it was genuine.

"What are you doing?"

"Tracing constellations," she breathed and tilted her head to the side to stare at him.

When he didn't reply, she went back to stargazing but shared her thoughts.

"This is Orwandil." She outlined the constellation also known as the Great Hunter. "He fell in love with a goddess. The gods became jealous and killed him with a giant scorpion. And in her grief, she immortalized him in the stars."

"We have an entire day of walking ahead of us. Sleep. I will not be carrying you," he ordered.

She glared at the stars, and he could see the muscles of her jaw quivering.

"Let's get something straight right now," she snarled. "While I am *technically* your captive, you will not command me to do anything. I will follow you to the Wilds because it is far too late for me to return to the sea, so I am trapped here." Her voice shook as if those words had caused her pain. "But do not think for one second, *Princeling*, that I will follow your orders if I don't want to."

Wilder stared at her with a mix of frustration and humor. She was infuriating, insufferable, really, and he had never wanted to put someone in their place so badly. He ground his teeth and opened his mouth, preparing to lay into her. And yet, she rolled onto her side and flipped her hair over her shoulder.

"Save it. I won't be listening to anything you have to say."

His jaw snapped shut so quickly that the sound echoed through the woods.

Wilder held his breath, attempting to hold back his roar of frustration. He closed his eyes and let the breath out.

It wasn't worth it. She was attempting to get under his skin, to throw him off guard so that she could escape.

But oh, was he going to have words with his father when he returned. Why in all the realms would he have sought this mermaid?

Wilder closed his eyes and worked on controlling his breathing to settle down his fury. He was only three breaths in when Lyra's slow, shallow breaths met his ears. And that only enraged him further.

It was dawn before he had cooled off. The sun was gilding the sky with rays of gold.

They had a long day of travel before them. If she traveled as slowly as she had last night, then it would tack on another half day of travel to Fresia, where his guard waited. They would not be happy about the delay.

They might have alerted his father to his elongated absence, but surely Otto had seen the cause of their delay.

And if not—King Oberon would be furious, naturally, but it was nothing he couldn't handle. He had plenty he wanted to say to him after this mission.

Stretching his arms up above his head, his neck and back popped. Closing his eyes, he took slow, deep breaths, centering himself in the world around him. Feeling the water in the tree roots, the life pulsing up through the branches and into the leaves. He could feel the birds awaken to sing, and the smaller animals scavenging for food.

And her. She was awake now.

Lyra watched him as he stood with his back to her, as still as any predator.

"It will be a long journey today. We should move."

He turned to find her flexing each foot.

"They don't hurt."

"Wonderful. We should be off."

His words were brusque, and she grimaced. The lines between them had blurred last night, and he was doing his best to rectify it now. But when she clutched her stomach, he grew concerned.

"What is it now, Legs?" Wilder studied her expression.

"Yes. Um, I need to empty my bladder," she replied.

Wilder's ears burned with mortification. How could he be so stupid?

"I'll stay here," he replied and jutted his chin towards the denser forest. "Don't go too far and yell if you need anything."

Lyra nodded and stumbled off in the direction of the larger trees.

10
UNRIPE

They walked in companionable silence for quite some time. Lyra's stomach growled, and as they passed brambles full of berries, she racked her memory to see if they were the kind she could consume. Wilder slowed their pace as she picked some and nibbled.

"Are you sure those are edible?" he asked with a quirked brow.

Lyra's eyes screwed shut at the sour and sweet taste. "Mhm —these are raspberries. Would you like one?"

Wilder crossed his arms and shook his head. He watched as she puckered her cheeks before smacking her lips.

"And?"

"Water, please," she spat. "They're not quite ripe."

Wilder huffed and handed her the flask of water.

She gulped it down greedily before handing it back.

"Don't you need to eat?"

Wilder shook his head. "I don't require as much as you, and

mortal food is repugnant. I left the bulk of my supplies in Fresia. I'll eat then."

Lyra glared. "How lucky for you."

He rolled his eyes and pulled his pack off. "Here—" He threw her an apple that shone a deep scarlet. "Don't eat too quickly."

She did not heed his warning and scarfed it down, core and all, as they continued their trek, keeping off the beaten path but with it still in their line of sight.

"What are the Wilds like?"

He snorted. "Why? Haven't you read all about them?"

"Why would I want to read about something I *don't* like?" she scoffed, and he glared.

Lyra rolled her eyes with a sigh. "No. We don't have any books about the elves."

She ran her fingers along the ferns in their path, avoiding his eyes. That wasn't true, but he didn't need to know that. It would be better to let him underestimate her.

But her reply was not at all what he was expecting.

"You know nothing of the elves—*at all*?" he asked incredulously, halting their progress.

Lyra shook her head, feeling annoyed by his questions. She was a liar and a good one, and she didn't like that he did not believe her.

Wilder's eyes narrowed, but he reluctantly began explaining.

"The Elf realm is separated from the mortal realm by a veil, or a ward, if you will. It divides the nonmagical land from the magical land. And the magical realm is split between two kingdoms—the Wilds and the Mannereds. Oberon, my father, is the High King of the Wilds and a direct descendant of Fionn. Long ago, our line fractured, some ancient family squabble that divided the realm in two. High Queen Titania rules the other half, known as the Mannereds."

That name—Titania. She had heard that name somewhere; a

long-ago voice whispered into her ear. His words baffled her, though.

"And you are at war?" Lyra questioned, feigning confusion.

Wilder shook his head. "We had been. The war between our realms stretches back as far as our recorded history. But we are at peace now."

There was peace between their kingdoms? Why had they heard of nothing but war between them?

"Since when?" Her mask slipped.

Before she could master her expression, Wilder noticed her pursed lips and lowered brows.

"What?"

"I have always been taught that the elves were at war with each other."

Wilder gazed sidelong at her.

"And without books, how were you taught this information?"

Lyra huffed. "Our scouts passed the information on."

He accepted that answer as truth and clarified his response.

"Your information is dated. The fighting ended long ago, and the alliance was formed within the last hundred years."

"I see," she replied simply. "What else should I know?"

"Well, our society is divided between noble houses that rule over their granted territories, but everyone swears fealty to my father. Regardless of their kind." He ground his teeth at that and continued. "There are seven noble houses, three of which are related to my family."

Lyra processed all that information and came up with more questions.

"What do you mean by 'their kind'?"

Wilder strode around a particularly large fern and ran his fingertips over the fronds.

"Not all the elves look like me. Some resemble trees, the sun, or the night sky. There are also trolls, fairies, and pixies, although they are rarer to see. There are also," he ticked off his long fingers, "sentient trees that are as old as the land, and wulvers." He spoke of the last creature with a snarl.

"And the Mannereds?" Lyra prompted, trying to understand beyond what she had once read.

Wilder shrugged. "All the elves there resemble me, and the land is much different. It's flat with manicured gardens and forests, hence the 'manner' part of their name."

It took Lyra a moment to realize he had cracked a joke, but when she did, she giggled.

Her laugh brushed against the thread of power coiled around her heart. It wasn't a complete tug on it, but enough that it stirred.

Wilder halted immediately and stared at her, enthralled. A gray fog clouded his blue eyes like heavy clouds in the sky.

That laugh, that sound. It was magic. Beautifully haunted, blessed magic.

He stared enraptured at her, willing to do or say anything she commanded.

Lyra clamped a hand over her mouth and stared at him with terror.

"I'm so sorry. I did not mean to."

Wilder shook his head, and the power that had encircled his mind, controlling every part of him, vanished. His eyes returning to the clear, crystal blue.

It was terrifying. Utterly terrifying how all-consuming her power was.

He would have killed himself if she had commanded it—with merely a laugh, she had gripped him so completely.

Which is why she worked so hard never to use it. Even a mere brush against it was euphoric. Her blood hummed through her veins, her muscles relaxed, and the anxiety that usually coiled around her gut vanished. It was addictive.

That power could enthrall anyone or anything.

But more than that, it could destroy.

Slaughter and annihilate. As she had before. The image of that male flashed behind her closed eyes, evaporating the feeling of euphoria and leaving her feeling bereft of any feelings besides misery.

"What was that?" Wilder breathed, his brow furrowing over his rapidly darkening eyes.

She couldn't—wouldn't answer.

And Wilder didn't speak to her again.

The sun rose high in the sky, its golden light shining down on Lyra. But even its appearance couldn't bring her out of her despair. She had been a fool, a careless fool yet again.

The magic wasn't safe; it was corruption. And although she hadn't meant it to, it had happened, and their tenuous alliance had crumbled.

Wilder had barricaded himself behind a wall of silence to keep her at bay. To keep himself safe from her. The monster.

The memory of the sea witch in the cave sprang to her mind. What was it the witch had said?

"A monster—a monster that would destroy the entire world."

No one would ever understand her. Not her father, and certainly not her friends if they ever learned the truth of what she hid.

Lyra walked in silence beside him, seeing past the wonder of the land and keeping her eyes on the path.

What good would it be to enjoy anything at all?

She had no one to share it with—and she never would.

II
SCHEMES

His father's plan had come to light.

It was Lyra's power he was after. She was a weapon to be wielded.

But against whom?

And why?

They walked the rest of the way taciturnly. They stopped to sleep and woke with the sun again.

Wilder hadn't spoken to her, not even as he handed her food or water from the pack. And she didn't utter a sound either.

It had taken them a little less than two days to reach Fresia. Having shaved off quite a bit of time, they made it right before nightfall.

The sun was turning the sky glorious shades of pink, orange, and yellow. But every second of their journey, Wilder contemplated what he had felt at that moment and what exactly that meant about his father's plans.

He didn't think it was likely that Oberon did not know about her gift.

That voice—that unholy voice.

It gripped him so completely that he had not known his name or even who he was. He was fully at her command. At her mercy. A puppet held by her fingers, or more accurately, her lips.

She would rule kingdoms—even worlds if it were as powerful as he had felt. Wilder didn't want to be anywhere near her or this at all.

His father wasn't a horrible elf and had even seemed repentant for raising Wilder the way he had in his youth. But no one should have that kind of power.

Maybe he'd be doing the world a service if he killed her now.

He glanced over at her and brushed a palm across the pommel of his sword. Lyra was twirling a small flower between her fingers. She stared at it with awestruck wonder and brought it to her nose. Closing her eyes, she inhaled its floral fragrance.

His mind stopped its incessant machinations.

A monster would not do that.

A monster would not find joy in the simple things.

Lyra had been horrified that she had accidentally used her power on him. And she hadn't used it to save herself against him or the humans.

What kind of mind game was this?

Everything he had read about mermaids was not what she was—or, at least, what she pretended to be. Their voices could ensnare a mortal, but it should not have been possible for her to enthrall him.

Magic was balance, but he felt in his bones there was nothing of her equal.

No one was ever as they presented themselves, and that was surely the case now. He was merely falling for her facade. He wanted to pummel something—he knew better than this.

This is why he followed orders and did not give them.

Wilder decided at that moment that he would continue to stay silent and that he would observe her for any signs that she was not who she pretended to be.

He would get to the bottom of this.

12
FICKLE BITCH

Lyra twirled jasmine between her fingers. She had plucked it when they walked through the small gate and into the village square.

It was very similar to the village he had kidnapped her from. Stone buildings, cobblestone lanes, and thatched roofs. But it didn't smell, or perhaps she was getting used to it. She brought the flower up to her nose again and inhaled. It was light and airy, exactly as the book had described it.

She flicked her attention to Wilder to see him staring sidelong at her before looking straight ahead again.

He had been stoic the entire time. But she could feel his eyes on her more often than not.

Her accidental use of power had shaken him to his core. She figured he was probably thinking of the best way to kill her right about now. Glancing down, she watched as he flexed his hand open before squeezing it back into a fist.

Yep. He wanted to kill her.

Surely he knew she hadn't meant to use it against him. She hadn't used it to free herself or even to save herself from the humans.

Lyra didn't want to be a monster. Didn't want to destroy this place or any place.

She missed the water, of course, but did not want to ruin the land so that she could return. No matter how much she yearned for the sea, she couldn't fathom laying waste to this place, with its lovely plants and tiny birds.

Clenching her jaw, she staunched the pull of the power within her. This was how it would start.

The magic was addictive. And she had worked her entire life to never use it.

Her stomach pitched, and her lungs tightened when a flash of the accident speared through her mind. It would corrupt her in the worst of ways, turning her into the same monsters she rebelled against.

A strange bird cawed from the large tree in the center of the square. No—not a bird, a person. They materialized beside the tree and walked towards them.

Wilder squared his shoulders and picked up the pace, embracing the shadow and clapping it on the back once.

"Look who finally graced us with their presence," a masculine voice teased.

He was Lyra's size, much shorter than Wilder, but broad through the shoulders and legs. Like a walking wall, she mused to herself. His accent was unique, too. Not the polished accent she had grown accustomed to from Wilder, but something— wild. Quick, but also like his tongue, was too wide for his mouth.

"Orders aren't always easy to follow, and I'm sure you saw exactly what I had to put up with," Wilder replied and shot her a look.

"Otto, this is Princess Lyra."

Otto removed the cloak that shadowed him.

Lyra was struck mute.

White skin, white hair, and gray-colored eyes, like the dark gray seas underneath the moon's glow. But beyond his physical appearance was vast wisdom.

An all-seeing kind of wisdom that peered at her from cloud-colored eyes.

Lyra wanted to wrap her arms around herself, to hide from his gaze.

"Pleasure, Princess—or should I call you Legs, too?" Otto replied and tilted his head.

The words annoyed her, and before she could stop herself, she lashed out.

"It's Lyra or *Your Highness*. I don't care which you prefer."

Wilder pinched the bridge of his nose and squeezed his eyes shut. Otto only grinned and addressed Wilder.

"The others are at the tavern, awaiting your orders. Even though I already told them what they would be."

Wilder merely nodded and gestured with his hand.

Lyra's stomach growled, and she reluctantly followed. Not that she had a choice. But she had hoped the tavern would mean food.

"I got you a plate already—Lyra," Otto threw over his shoulder at her with a wink.

Flames danced in the tall lanterns on either side of the narrow street. A small breeze snaked through the buildings, rustling the broadleaf ivy that clung to the crumbling stone walls.

It was nice here, cozy even. It was a place she would like to sit outside with a book. She rather liked that idea.

In Atlantis, her reading had always been confined to her room or the stuffy library with its nearly murderous attendants. She briefly wondered what libraries in the mortal realm would look like—or in the Wilds.

Lyra was so caught up in her daydreams that she didn't even notice the building they stepped into or the uncomfortable silence that greeted them.

Humans knew of the elves, but it seemed their appearance wasn't always accepted.

The evidence of that truth was made apparent by the boar of a woman by the window, shrewdly analyzing each step. Diners at the sparse tables split their attention between them and the two other people crowded around a far back table. Some didn't even dare to take a bite of their food until they had passed.

Wood creaked underneath her feet. It was everywhere: the walls, the ceiling, even a winding staircase at the far left of the room. All the same grayish wood. There was nothing of the sort in Atlantis. She studied each groove before meeting the penetrating stare of the humans.

Lyra made it a point to stare at each and every one who glared at her until they looked away. They knew the others were elvish.

Would they know what she was, too?

Otto plopped down on a spindly chair on the opposite side of a stained and rough wooden table. The two people gathered around it didn't startle at his presence or even look at him at all. Their attention was trained on her and the deathly quiet prince behind her.

"Took you long enough," a feminine voice purred from beside Otto. She leaned back in her chair. Her molten golden eyes never left Wilder's face.

Wilder nodded and pulled out a chair for Lyra before taking the one next to it. She stood there dumbfounded, staring at it. Had he done that on purpose to confuse her, or was it some kind of elvish tradition? She tried not to care but wound up annoyed.

"I am perfectly capable of pulling out my chair," she hissed under her breath.

Their eyes turned to her, and her back stiffened. Wilder rested an elbow on the arm of the chair and brushed a long finger over his lips.

"I am aware. Now sit."

Their gazes stayed locked in battle before she finally plopped down in the chair with an annoyed flourish.

The elf on the other side of Lyra pulled his bowl closer and away from her.

She wanted to snort. She wasn't an animal that would steal his food.

Otto pushed a bowl across the table and nodded to her. "This is for you."

Lyra looked at the chipped blue bowl and the steaming soup inside before looking at Wilder. Not for permission, of course, but for safety. She had never consumed prepared mortal food before.

Wilder met her stare before giving her a quick dip of his chin. "It's just stew."

"Got her trained already? That was quick," the man beside her chuckled, shoveling in another mouthful of the stew.

Lyra froze with her hand wrapped around the spoon. She gripped it tightly in her hand, deciding if she had the strength to stab him with the pointed end.

"Don't, Ridge," Wilder ordered, clenching his hands into fists.

Now that he knew what she was capable of, he seemed wary of her. But the elf—Ridge—didn't heed his warning.

"She doesn't seem dangerous for her kind, does she, Maelys?"

Ridge leered at her, his brown eyes the color of the tree bark they had passed through on their journey here. It occurred to her then that how she was seeing them in the mortal realm wouldn't be how they looked in the Elvish realm once they had crossed the veil into magic. She wondered if they would look similar to this or if they would resemble the land from which they were from.

"She seems kind of tame."

Lyra lashed out, stabbing at his hand with the pointy end of the spoon. Ridge snatched it from her and waved it with a taunt in front of her. She seethed, curling her empty hand into a fist.

She felt heavy eyes upon her skin and looked to see the female—Maelys, studying her before looking at Wilder.

"Quite tame, actually. I wouldn't have missed."

Lyra met her stare head-on and let a remnant of the monster show. She bared her teeth at Maelys.

It didn't do the trick. If anything, it had made her look foolish. Maelys snorted and then returned her attention to Wilder.

"What caused the delay?" She spoke clearly, but something about her phrasing led Lyra to believe that wasn't what she was asking.

"Lyra encountered ruffians," Otto answered for them. "And some issues with her new legs."

He took a bite of the stew and then raised his spoon, insinuating Lyra should do the same. Ridge set her spoon back down beside her bowl, and she flinched. He leveled her with a look that doubled as a warning: lash out again, and I'm keeping it.

"Exhaustion and hunger will make everything worse for you," Otto said. "Your new legs will require you to eat and rest."

Otto seemed older than the rest of them. She wasn't sure if it was because he was or if his gifts led him to be perceived that way. He was a seer, but she didn't know about the other two.

Lyra scooped some of the broth and meat chunks onto the spoon before taking a bite. It was some kind of game, by the taste of it. But she was surprised that it tasted so good. Meat, carrots, and corn with a melding of spices. Interesting. She didn't think she would like human food.

It was quiet at their table, quiet enough that Lyra could hear the disgruntled murmurings of the surrounding mortals. In particular, a man with a large bushy beard seemed very upset that there were elves in his presence.

"Elves in our dining hall. It's a travesty!" His voice rose loud enough for Lyra to hear him. She glanced over her shoulder in time to see the man beside the disgruntled one grab him by the collar.

"Pipe down," he hissed, shooting a terrified expression their way. "That is Wilder Vale. The prince."

The bearded man ducked his head and averted his gaze. "The swordsman?" His question was met with furious nods.

It appeared Wilder's name held weight here.

"Are we leaving first thing in the morning?" Maelys asked, loud enough for all to hear.

Wilder grunted in response.

So he wasn't only quiet with her—he was like this with everyone.

Lyra took a few more bites of the stew, opting to eat around the corn. It was quiet for some time while she shoveled in bites as quickly as she could swallow.

The heat of the stew seeped into her bones, warming her from the inside out. When she took to slurping the broth out of the chipped bowl, they began speaking again.

"There's been an issue acquiring rooms," Ridge said.

"How so?" Wilder bit out, looking at Lyra in disgust as she slurped even louder.

"They only had two available," Otto answered, taking another bite of the stew. "I see you will not allow anyone but yourself to guard Lyra." The gray of his irises became darker in the candlelight, and if Lyra wasn't mistaken, they appeared to be swirling.

Wilder ground his teeth, the muscle in his jaw quivering at the sharp angle. Something beyond the room situation was irking him.

"Last room on the left," Otto said.

"We leave at first light—get some rest," Wilder said before tugging her along.

The humans watched them as they tromped up the stairs. Wilder didn't speak to anyone at all as he led her down the hall on the second floor and to the last door on the left.

He flung open the door and shoved her inside. The space was much larger on the inside than she thought it would be. But not large enough to hold more than one bed.

Wilder glared at the single iron bed like it had insulted him before gritting his teeth. It was dark beyond the open curtains, and warm candles glowed around the space, making it appear cozy.

"You take the bed." He stomped over to the window and drew the curtains closed.

Lyra stood at the threshold a beat longer, feeling an array of emotions. She tried to cycle through them, but as soon as she identified one, three more sprang to mind.

It was awkward with this tension between them. She felt lost, confused, and even annoyed. *He kidnapped her.* She didn't want to be a hindrance. He was making her one.

Wilder peeked through the small gap he made in the curtains, monitoring the street before shutting it back up. He breathed sharply through his nose and looked at her once more.

"Well, why are you standing in the doorway? Go to bed."

Lyra's spine stiffened at the order and his tone. She had warned him of that already and dug her heels in.

But he misunderstood her stubbornness and took it for confusion.

"Do you need to use the bathroom?"

Lyra shook her head. Her mass of unbound hair swayed with the movement. She looked down at where her hair brushed against her body and realized she was still wearing his cloak—backward—over her ripped and stained gown. She must have looked like a vagrant.

Wilder followed her stare and cleared his throat.

"Do you require a change of clothes? I could see if Maelys packed some. We will be on the road awhile."

Lyra continued glaring at him. He glared right back.

"You did nothing but yap the entire way here, and now that I need you to answer a question, you decide to be mute." His nostrils flared as he clenched his teeth.

It infuriated her, that arrogance.

He threw up his hands and stalked past her and to the door, throwing a withering glare her way.

"That's a basin full of clean water. Clean yourself up. You stink," he ordered. "And do not move from this room."

Wilder didn't even wait for her to respond before he stepped past her and slammed the wooden door shut behind him. The resounding slam echoed through her head.

The food had warmed her bones, but now she felt the weight of the day. Exhaustion tugged at her. She should sleep, and then she could think through her next steps with a clear head.

Lyra looked around the room. There was nothing in here but a few charcoal drawings on the wall, a dilapidated bedside table, and a mirror. She hadn't seen what she looked like yet as a human, so she worked up the courage to walk across the room.

She was horrifying.

Lyra had never seen her hair down before. It hung in loose waves and random ringlets to her waist. It framed her frighteningly pale face. Her emerald eyes were dull and muted. She looked like a specter.

No wonder the humans had stared—she did not resemble one of them at all.

The door cracked open, and Maelys peered through.

"Otto had me pack extra." She waved a fistful of fabric at Lyra.

Lyra took the clothes and gave her a curt nod.

Maelys returned the nod with one of her own, but also a small smile that softened her features.

"You'll be more comfortable in those. See you in the morning."

The door closed with a click.

Lyra frowned and stood there dumbfounded before looking down at the fabric in her hands. There were two of them. One was soft green. She searched her mind for the name …

A blouse. It was a blouse.

The second one was longer and of the same fabric the water was kept in—leather. It was pants.

She sighed, holding the pants up in front of her legs.

Well, for someone all-seeing, he had made a mistake in the sizing. There was no way these were going to fit. She tugged at the top of them and marveled when the fabric stretched. Never mind then, maybe they would.

Two small pieces of fabric dropped from the leg of the pants when she held them up. Lyra glared down at them before picking them up. Her cheeks burned when she realized what they were: undergarments.

A thin, nearly sheer pair of bottoms that would barely fit her by the looks of them, and then a strange top that she assumed was for her breasts due to the similarity in shape.

Lyra tossed her new garments onto the bed and pulled off her boots before untying Wilder's cloak. She draped it at the foot of the bed before ripping off what remained of her dress.

It was sad, really. The stitching was so elaborate, the ruffles and pleats so exquisite, and she had ruined it. She traced a flower that was stitched onto the hem before throwing the dress onto the floor. She stood there naked and looked down at her bare legs.

They were shapely, not too thin nor too thick. She pointed her toes, and the muscles on her thighs bulged. Running a hand down them, she smiled. Lyra liked her legs. They were pretty.

A commotion in the hall had her covering her naked flesh with a hand.

She froze.

That was not how that felt before. She peered down at herself. Why was it in the front? She looked behind her, and her eyes widened. Her backside had not been that supple when she had a tail.

What kind of magic was this?

Another clamber outside the door had her scurrying over to the basin. She needed to hurry before Wilder decided that was enough time and burst back in.

Lyra dunked the small towel in the basin. The water was clear and lightly scented with fresh herbs. She wiped off her face and then the rest of her body.

Leaving the water in the basin cloudy with dirt, she scrubbed from her skin. When the water was no longer usable, she sighed, already missing it against her skin. It had been a comfort to feel the water and not the grime of the land.

With the undergarments in their assumed positions, she tugged the top over her head before grabbing the pants and slipping them on one leg at a time.

The pants did in fact stretch to fit her perfectly. Even if they were snug, suctioning to her skin. They highlighted every curve of her legs and backside.

The top fell right at the top of the pants, and when she moved, a sliver of her stomach showed. She was tugging the shirt down to cover the exposed skin fully when there was a knock on the door.

"Are you done?"

"Mhm," she called.

The door swung open, and Wilder appeared.

She waited for him to comment on her new clothes, but he didn't.

His face was twisted somewhere between a grimace and a

snarl. But he froze when he saw her. His eyes flared a fraction before he tucked whatever emotion he had felt back behind his carefully crafted mask. He kicked the door closed and ripped the cloak off the bed.

A pillow was tucked under his arm. Lyra watched as he threw it onto the floor between the bed and the door and lay down. He still hadn't said a word to her, but his actions were clear; it was time to sleep.

Quilts of varying patterns covered blue floral sheets. It was quite pretty for an old tavern such as this. As she slipped beneath the sheets and quilts, a sigh escaped her.

The bed was fluffy and held her tenderly as she settled in. It was strange. Nothing had ever held her before.

In Atlantis, the constant ebb and flow of the ocean kept her hovering just a hairsbreadth over the giant shell she used as a bed. Even with her multitude of kelp blankets to weigh her down, it was never enough and felt more smothering than anything.

It probably didn't help that the shell resembled the large mouths of ancient sea monsters.

Wilder cleared his throat, and all the candles in the room were snuffed out. Had he done that? What kind of elf magic was that?

A deluge of questions bubbled up, but she tamped them down. They hadn't spoken since her outburst with magic, and she doubted he would be willing now.

Lyra closed her eyes, inhaling the lingering smoke from the candles. She hoped sleep would take her soon. She'd welcome any kind of reprieve from the awkwardness that was growing between them.

But sleep was a fickle bitch.

13
BLOW THE
HOUSE DOWN

Wilder lay as still as his body would allow. Which was very, very still. His chest didn't move as he breathed through his nose. He was going to kill Otto. What the fuck had he been thinking, having Maelys pack an outfit like that for her?

Calling her Legs would be torture now because all he would ever think about would be the perfection of hers. And good gods.

A groan built in the recesses of his hollow chest. He bit his fist to tamp it down. When the arousal that had flooded his senses had passed, he swallowed and prayed that she couldn't hear it.

He was in a world of monumental muck. The gods had sent her to test him, dredging up his wildest fantasies and packaging them into a creature of his worst nightmares—the enemy.

He needed to focus on the bad to keep from seeing the good. She was dangerous, more than dangerous. She could bring about the destruction of the entire world.

Lyra shifted under the covers, and Wilder listened. Her breathing was not steady or slow; she was still awake. He had an uncontrollable urge to speak to her, but he bit his tongue. She was not his to assure or comfort. Let her figure this out on her own.

When she flopped onto her other side, he sighed.

"Sorry."

Wilder didn't respond.

"I'm not used to sleeping on something this soft."

He rolled his eyes. The wooden floor dug into his spine.

"How long until morning?" she whispered.

Rage surged through him. Hadn't he been clear enough that he wanted nothing to do with her?

The silence between them grew taught and when he could no longer bear it, he ground out, "Hours."

"What will the journey be like?"

He squeezed his eyes shut, letting the frustration flow through him in waves. He needed to stay angry.

"Maybe if you tried closing your eyes and mouth—you'd be able to sleep."

There. That should have been obvious enough to her.

A bird squawked outside, and the sound pierced through the silent room.

"What was that?" she said, sitting up quickly in bed.

Before he knew it, her feet were thudding against the wooden floor, and she was standing at his feet, clutching her chest. Wilder sat up on his elbows. Moonlight poured through the small gap in the curtains behind her and outlined her body.

Gods dammit.

He had just stopped thinking about her legs, and now here they were.

"It. Was. A. Bird," he ground out between clenched teeth, breathing sharply through his nose. Which only exacerbated his problem.

"That didn't sound like any bird I've heard before."

He could see her shoulders rapidly rising and falling.

"You haven't been here long enough to have heard every bird. Go back to bed."

Lyra stood there, twisting her shirt in her hands and staring down at him.

"Get in bed and go to sleep. We have a long journey ahead, and I'm not carrying you the entire way there," he ordered her again.

He lay back down and covered his face with both hands, listening to her bare feet against the wood floors as she walked away.

Lyra drew the curtain back and peered outside. Her breath caught at the same time he smelled them.

The blood-curdling odor of the wulvers.

Images of mottled fur and elongated canines pelted his mind.

It hadn't been a bird after all.

"*Wilder*," she shrieked.

He was already on his feet, ripping her away from the window.

A bolt crashed through the glass and embedded in the opposite wall. He had clutched her to his chest as they had fallen onto the bed. Her body vibrated with fear, but she ripped herself out of his grip.

"I told you it wasn't a bird!"

The door flew open. Maelys and Ridge were flanking Otto.

"We have company," Otto said, drawing the steel blade at his side.

Ridge gripped his bow, already strung, in his hand, as his eyes darted around the room before landing on the arrow lodged in the wall.

Maelys gripped two daggers in her fists and scanned the hallway.

Wilder was already shoving his boots on and throwing Lyra's at her.

"How many?"

Otto shook his head.

"Do we know which clan?"

"What is happening?" Lyra asked, struggling to get her boots back on.

Her fingers trembled so violently that he was surprised her voice had been steady.

Otto looked from Lyra to Wilder, gauging how much information to share.

Wilder took the boots from her and squatted down at her feet.

Shards of glass from the window crunched under his boots as he pushed hers onto her feet and then laced them up tight.

"Someone is after you."

"Me!" She pointed to her chest. "How does anyone know where I am? You've kidnapped me!"

She moved to stand up, and he wrenched her back down in a crouch.

"Stay away from the window!"

Lyra covered her mouth with her hands to keep from screaming, and he could see the whites of her eyes swallow her emerald irises.

"They've got the building surrounded," Otto muttered.

Maelys nodded and stalked to the end of the hall with quiet, sure steps.

"We're gonna have to make a break for it," Wilder said, looking from a frightened Lyra to a calm Otto.

"We'll make it."

"Well, that's a relief," Lyra muttered. "Why didn't you lead with that?"

Sarcasm dripped from her every word, and if they weren't in

such a precarious position, Wilder might have admired her tenacity.

"Wilder doesn't like to know."

Lyra frowned at him. "Why?"

Wilder huffed. "Can we not do this now?"

"Ten seconds," Otto added.

Wilder looked Lyra steadily in her eyes. Her throat bobbed as she forced a swallow.

"What are you doing?"

He didn't respond, but grabbed her under her arms and hauled her body to him.

"Close your eyes," he said against the side of her head.

He didn't even spare a second to see if she complied before he hurtled them out of the two-story window.

Lyra let out a mewling scream. He landed on his feet, Lyra's body clutched firmly to his chest. She stared up at him with wonder for a split second before it turned to rage, and she pounded against his chest.

"How dare you?" she seethed as Maelys, Otto, and Ridge hit the ground running right beside them.

"We don't have the time." He threw her over his shoulder and sprinted into the night.

Howls reached their ears, and Wilder's feet pounded harder against the ground.

He could outrun them on his own, even with their elongated limbs and advanced muscle tone. But it wouldn't be possible with Lyra thrown over his shoulder.

Wilder saw the crimson eyes shining in the darkness as the wulver launched itself at them.

Mangy black fur helped camouflage the creature, but its eyes —they always gave it away. Its claws were outstretched, and Wilder could feel the ghost of that pain lashing down his spine.

Otto and Ridge streaked ahead, followed by Maelys.

Ridge stopped and whirled, firing two arrows.

Wilder felt them whiz by and then heard the crunch as they embedded into massive skulls.

There was a booming crash as the bodies slammed to the ground. He hadn't realized there were two on his tail.

And the odor, he would never for as long as he lived, which would be a very long time, forget that smell.

These wulvers belonged to Igneous' Clan.

And they were after *her*.

He had suffered at their hands, and no matter how much he despised Lyra, he wouldn't wish that pain on even her.

They continued running through the forest, a blur among the still trees.

But the wulvers did not pursue them.

As the moon dropped lower in the sky, so did their pace before Wilder halted them.

Lyra slid off his shoulder and collapsed in a heap on the forest floor. Her hair was tangled, and her eyes were wild, but she did not seem frightened.

Quite the contrary, she was livid.

Wilder bent over at the waist, sucking down air to cool his burning throat and fatigued muscles.

Lyra clambered to her feet and shoved him.

"What," she shoved again, "was that?"

Wilder stood and gripped her hands in front of him to keep her from touching him anymore.

"Someone knew we would be there. The humans found you too quickly, and the wulvers shouldn't be anywhere near this village. Someone is after you."

Maelys, Otto, and Ridge shifted on their feet, watching the exchange with a hint of amusement.

Lyra gave Wilder one scathing sweep of her eyes before she crossed her arms over her chest.

"You have a traitor in your midst." She flung the accusation with precision before turning her glare to his guard.

Wilder took great offense at that. He had battled beside the three of them since he could hold a blade.

If there was a traitor, it was in his father's court, or hers.

"Or you have one in yours." He stood tall and smirked at her with all the arrogance he could muster. "Who else knows about your power?"

Lyra floundered for a retort and snarled her upper lip before shifting her attention to the crew and then back to him.

"Oh, trust me, they'll know everything that I know. I don't keep secrets from them. Tell them about your magic, Lyra." He flung his arms out wide. "That's why you're in this mess, isn't it? You wicked siren." He spat the words venomously and watched as they cut her up.

Her chest heaved, and her eyes were lined with silver as she stared at him.

"I don't use my magic," she ground out, balling her hands into fists.

Wilder snorted. "Funny, I seem to remember feeling differently under your thrall."

Maelys, Otto, and Ridge volleyed their heads back and forth but stayed quiet.

"It was an accident," she screeched. "I never use my magic. I haven't used it to save myself from you or the humans. It will consume me. It will destroy everything. And I hate it! I loathe myself for holding that power!"

Her words echoed around the silent forest.

Not a leaf rustled, nor a bird chirped in the early morning light.

Wilder felt her words like a punch to the gut. She hated herself, hated the part of herself that she had no control over.

Lyra stood in front of him, her lip trembling, but her shoulders squared.

"If your father seeks to use my power—*kill me*. Just kill me now and get it over with. I will never touch it."

When she dropped to her knees and bowed her head in front of him, his chest tightened unbearably.

What kind of horror must she have lived through? Before he could respond, Maelys' voice cracked like a whip.

"*Enough.*"

She stepped forward, wrapping an arm around Lyra. "That is enough."

Lyra's head rose as Maelys embraced her.

"We do not treat people this way, regardless of their kind or magic."

She pulled Lyra to her feet and led them away from the men.

"Let me tell you my story …"

Wilder could feel the hollowness in his chest devouring the rest of him.

For Maelys to share her story with Lyra spoke volumes.

There must be something in Lyra worth saving, worth fighting for.

14
HURT PEOPLE

Lyra felt warm in Maelys' embrace despite the chilly morning air.

"I am sorry," Maelys whispered.

Lyra's breath caught in her throat. She had never heard those words before.

"We have lost sight of who we are by following our king's orders." Maelys stared out into the forest, and a bird landed on a nearby branch and began singing. The song was beautiful, full of cheer and merriment. Maelys nodded and then looked back at Lyra.

"My story is like many. I was unwanted and unloved. Left in the human world to be raised alongside them."

"A changeling," Lyra muttered.

Maelys nodded. "My birth parents might have been monsters, but that action was the single greatest kindness that they could have ever bestowed upon me. My human mother— she loved me."

Lyra watched as a multitude of reactions flitted across Maelys' face. She took a seat on the ground, and Lyra sat beside her.

"She was a widow and had already buried two children when I was placed on her doorstep. She often told me that the gods had blessed her that night." Maelys snorted. "She had a healthy respect for the gods, not just Alfor, the human god, but Ennosidas, and Fionn as well."

Lyra knew each of the three gods that had split the world between them, but for a human to observe them was confounding. She was taught to recognize only Ennosidas and that the others would be angered at her attention. They were not meant for her. Even Ennosidas merely tolerated her observance since she was a female.

"I grew up strange, called to the magic of the land and animals. But I was alone, if not for my mother; only she had ever understood me. Saw my quietness as curiosity and not aloofness, my desire to speak with animals, kind, and not peculiar. It didn't make her many friends either. I was still a child when the men came and burned down our house. Screaming that the kind, loving woman who had raised me was a witch."

Lyra's throat burned at the emotion raging across Maelys' face.

"People fear what they do not understand, and they mask that fear with hate. You hate yourself, Lyra, because you do not know yourself."

Maelys' words dropped like a stone in water inside Lyra's chest, the ripples carrying outward until they swallowed her.

"It took me a long time to find myself," Maelys continued. "It helped that when I ran from the cottage that night, the magic led me to the Wilds. To Ridge, Otto, and Wilder. They became the family I lost, the family I needed. It's never easy to travel this life alone."

Lyra took a deep breath and squeezed her eyes shut. The

pain in her chest was a living thing, writhing, biting, and clawing. She didn't know if she was capable of letting people in.

"I have only ever caused pain," Lyra whispered.

Maelys tilted her head and stared at her.

"Have you ever tried not to?"

Lyra bit her lip and shook her head.

"We'll try together."

Maelys stretched out a hand in offering, and Lyra stared and stared at it. At what this meant. She didn't think for a second that Maelys would offer her story or her friendship under a ruse.

Lyra's gaze shifted from the offering to Maelys' eyes. They were golden. As bright as the sun that Lyra had dreamed of seeing one day.

Yes, they were her captors, but it was more than that.

Safety took precedence, and she tentatively took Maelys' hand and closed her fingers around it.

They walked all through the night and morning, but hadn't even made it halfway to the next town before Lyra's legs began to ache and throb.

The sun was well past its apex in the sky and was resting on the tops of the trees to the west. Each step was a stab and burn to her muscles, joints, and bones. With her last step, she grimaced, and a small cry escaped her.

Otto turned around and stopped.

She was slowing them down.

Wilder forged on ahead, barely visible from his lead position. Following behind him were Ridge and Maelys. The only person walking as slowly as her was Otto, but she had a feeling he'd been ordered to stay behind with her.

"Do you need a moment?" Otto was kind, and that was strange too.

She couldn't tell what his angle was. If he were a true seer, did he pity her for her past ... or maybe her future?

"Just let me catch my breath," she panted out.

A cramp seized her right calf, and she crumpled to the ground.

"Easy now!" Otto was immediately at her side, gripping her by the elbow.

"I'm alright. I'm alright. It was only a cramp," Lyra replied. Her cheeks burned. She felt pathetic.

"Here, chew on this," Otto replied, pulling a stalk of yarrow from his pocket.

Lyra took it without a second thought and shoved it stem and all into her mouth.

He untied his water flask from his belt and held it out to her. "Drink?"

She nodded enthusiastically and swallowed before chugging some of the water. Otto looked on with a small smile and a twinkle in his eye.

"What?" she asked, handing him back the water.

"He would carry you, you know? If you asked. He would."

Lyra shook her head, and a lock of auburn hair slid across her face. When Otto stayed quiet and the pain lessened, she slowly stood.

"I don't need his help."

Otto bit back a smile.

"Of course not."

"Why are you—"

"Being nice?" he finished for her.

Lyra nodded. She wasn't used to freely given kindness. There was always an angle to be played.

"Because everyone deserves kindness, even those who think they deserve it the least."

It was an effort not to flinch or snap back with something bitter, but she had promised Maelys that she would try.

"So you have seen me in your visions? What I've done and

what I am capable of?" She squared her shoulders, waiting for the disappointment she knew was coming.

"What you have done? Sure. And I don't fault you for it one bit. That was how you had to survive, Lyra."

The world fell silent, the wind stopped blowing, and the birds stopped singing. Was he being truthful? Or telling her what she desperately wanted to hear.

"We have all done things we are not proud of," Otto gestured to the figures far ahead that belonged to Ridge and Maelys. "What matters now is how you choose to live. Are you going to keep hurting because you were hurt? Or can you grow?"

She heaved a sigh at such a philosophical question.

"I guess it depends on what happens from here …"

Otto tapped the side of his head.

"I know what you are capable of, and with the right encouragement, love, and acceptance, it will be many great things."

Her eyes stung, and she had to grit her teeth to keep from sobbing. This stranger, this understanding stranger, had told her everything she had ever wanted to hear but would never admit. She didn't know how to react or even what to say.

This was the second time that she had felt seen today.

The elves differed greatly from all the stories she had been told. Stories about merciless monsters who leave their babies in the woods or swap them with human children, who fought in countless battles against creatures of pure nightmare and won, and their overall ruthless barbarism.

While some stories had been told as truth, she didn't see an ounce of that looking at Otto now.

"Stopping to smell the flowers?" Wilder barked.

Ridge and Maelys stood beside him like sentinels. His face was pinched with a snarl, and Lyra felt for all the world that he wanted to strike her.

"She had a cramp. Her legs are unaccustomed to the strain," Otto replied, unfazed by the fury wafting off Wilder.

"And what do you see needing to happen so that we can get there on time?"

Maelys bumped her shoulder against his. His eyes slid to hers, and she shook her head once. Lyra was stunned.

Otto looked from Lyra, who stood grimacing, squeezing her thigh, to Wilder with his rigid shoulders and hands squeezed into fists.

"You can slow your pace, and we'll be late. Or we can take turns carrying her. But we'll only make it on time when you carry her."

The color drained from Lyra's face. She thought she had made another ally, and then he goes off and does a thing like that.

Wilder didn't reply. He stalked to Lyra and pulled one of her arms over his shoulders before crouching down. In one swift movement, he had slung her onto his back as if she weighed no more than a cloak. Lyra clung to his neck.

"Don't choke me," he grumbled and started walking.

She loosened her grip and leaned away from him. His hands tightened around her thighs.

"If you lean too far back, I will drop you on your ass," he bit out.

He squeezed her legs for emphasis, and she sighed before leaning forward.

"I didn't think you would want me pressed against you." Lyra could have sworn his face shook slightly.

"We don't have the time for me to be dropping you and picking you up every few miles. So just hold on and stay quiet."

Lyra nodded and pursed her lips, looking out at the forest around them.

Now that she didn't have to watch where she was walking, she could enjoy the view.

Colossal trees with trunks the size of buildings in the

villages, bushy ferns with fronds larger than her torso, and a variety of animals. Birds, chipmunks, and deer.

It was magical. And she loved it.

Her body jostled against Wilder's, and she bit her lip as her cheeks burned. With nothing else to do, she started talking again. Whether he listened or not, she didn't care. She talked about the different birds, plants, and types of clouds she could see in the sky.

Wilder stayed quiet, but Otto, Maelys, and even Ridge joined in with her ramblings.

When Lyra asked about the land in the Wilds, both Otto and Maelys seemed thrilled.

"The forest there is crawling with an assortment of magical creatures, from unicorns to skin-walkers," Maelys said, her eyes bright as she gestured to her forehead like she too had a horn.

"Skin-walkers?" Lyra questioned, her eyes growing wide with fear.

"Nasty creatures," Otto replied, shivering. "They'll flay you alive to wear your skin."

"That's horrific!" Lyra cried.

Wilder snorted, but didn't add to the conversation.

"Are there really unicorns?" she asked, but tried to disguise the hope in her voice.

Maelys smirked and shrugged. "Some say there are, but we've never been able to see them, and we've tried for decades."

"Decades? How long have you all known each other?"

Ridge chuckled. "It's hard to say. I don't remember my life before them."

"Same," Maelys replied with a smile at him. A tiny speckled bird fluttered down from the trees and landed on her shoulder.

Lyra was stunned as she watched the bird nuzzle Maelys' cheek.

"Do you all have magic? I mean, besides Otto," Lyra said.

"Most elves do," Otto answered. "Maelys has an affinity for animals. Ridge with plants."

His words excited her. Merfolk didn't have powers anymore. At least the men didn't, which made mermaids with magical inclinations sought after.

"Can I see?" Lyra asked, looking from Ridge to Maelys.

They looked at each other before shrugging. Maelys whispered to the bird on her shoulder, and the bird chirped a lovely song in reply.

Lyra stared with quiet excitement, her eyes full of surprise and wonder.

"She says she likes your hair," Maelys said, looking from the bird to Lyra.

"I like her song," Lyra whispered.

The bird flapped away, and Lyra looked to Ridge, who was receiving a scathing glare from Wilder. But Ridge was unperturbed as he plucked a small flower bud from a nearby vine and held it in his hand.

The bud bloomed and then grew. The white petals unfurled with a small shiver.

"But if you pick a flower, won't it die?" Lyra asked, a bit saddened, if the flower would now wither away.

Ridge shook his head and offered it to her. "The magic will keep it alive as long as I will it."

Lyra slipped a hand off Wilder's shoulder and took the tiny flower in her hand.

This day was already becoming one of her favorites. Which made her sad. She was being held hostage by people foretold to be vicious monsters, but in the span of a few hours, she had been treated with more kindness and respect than she ever had by her own people.

"Thank you," Lyra whispered. "It's so beautiful."

Ridge continued to march alongside them and smiled at her gratitude.

"What is the land like there?" Lyra asked, smelling the flower.

"It's wild," he answered with a chuckle. "The Wilds are composed of an ancient, mystical forest called the Valewood, the Three Sisters Swamp, and rolling hills called the High Lands, where the castle is built into the highest hill."

Wilder's grip on her thighs slipped, and he hoisted her up higher on his spine.

"I can walk," she murmured to him.

He snorted and shook his head.

"Do you have something you'd like to say?"

"You mean to tell me that in all those books, you really never read or learned anything about the elves?"

He was calling her a liar again. Her chest tightened, and her lips drew back over her teeth as she squeezed his shoulders.

"I told you I didn't. There were no books about the elves in our libraries, and my teachers didn't elaborate on anything other than 'avoid elves at all costs; they're dangerous'."

Ridge, Maelys, and Otto laughed, full belly laughs, and Lyra's cheeks bloomed with color.

"Why is that funny?"

Wilder halted in a small clearing. A riot of small purple flowers with vibrant red centers danced in the breeze all around them. He let go of her, and she slid ungracefully to the ground. A sharp, slicing pain shot through her legs and up to her abdomen.

"Merfolk have murdered more mortals and creatures than the elves have in centuries of our war."

Lyra found herself looking at Otto for confirmation.

"He's not wrong. We're all dangerous. Just in our own way."

She stayed quiet after his response.

It made little sense. If her kind were responsible for more casualties, why would they frame the elves in such a light?

A flash of Wilder in the night, striking down those ruffians, sprang to her mind.

She had never seen a merman or mermaid cut anyone down like that.

"You don't have a retort for that?" Wilder asked, cocking his head to the side.

It grew quiet in their small circle, and she could feel different eyes on her, awaiting her response. And for once, she didn't have a biting retort.

"She did not know," Otto replied after a while, addressing Wilder. He swung his attention back to Lyra.

"Take a moment to rest, relieve yourself if you need to, and then we need to keep moving," he said and stomped away.

Otto watched Wilder walk away before Otto walked off in the opposite direction.

Lyra was missing something. Some kind of fundamental layer to this group of elves. Wilder was their leader. Otto, a close second. Even if there was an undercurrent of hostility there. But where did that leave Maelys and Ridge? Honestly, she was shocked that there was a female in his guard.

That would never have been allowed in Atlantis or any of its territories. Women were not allowed in positions of power—or positions at all. No women scholars, healers, or councilors. She felt a small kernel of something grow when she thought of what Maelys' position meant for females in the Wilds. It had a light, buttery taste. Was that hope?

Lyra didn't need to relieve herself, and her legs still felt peculiar, so she sat down in the small clearing. Maelys and Ridge walked away together, leaving her all alone. She lay down and stared up at the clear blue sky.

It was breathtaking. Like the clear, quiet waters outside of her kingdom, when the sun shone brightly through the still current. It was rare for her to get to experience a moment like this. No one was watching or judging her. No one reported to her father every word she spoke or decision she made.

How strange that she had traded one pair of shackles for another, but this one felt far less confining.

Long ago, she had felt a similar way. She had fled the castle and, right before she was dragged back, had felt a brief moment of peace. Much like she did now.

Unfortunately, that peace had turned to agony. And only her books about the land had given her solitude. Now, looking up at the sky, it was like everything she had always dreamed it would be.

Would it be ripped away from her as well?

15
PRINCE GROUCHY

Wilder rested against a colossal yew tree on the outskirts of the clearing, watching Lyra stare up at the sky. The hard bark of the twisting and bulging trunk bit into the thin linen of his shirt, but he welcomed the pain. Anything to keep his mind off the female before him.

"We have a problem," Maelys said from behind him.

He was startled, not realizing she had crept up behind him after she had walked off the clearing from the opposite side.

"What problem is that?" he replied, regrettably taking his eyes off Lyra.

"She's unusual, that mermaid," Maelys jerked her chin in Lyra's direction. "*I like her.*"

Wilder glowered at her. "She's more than *unusual.*" He shook his head in an attempt to clear the thoughts from his mind. "She's incredibly powerful. I worry about the plans my father has in store for her."

"You should ask Otto about that."

Wilder shook his head. "His sight around her is not as reliable as we've grown accustomed to."

"Since when?"

Wilder sighed and turned to look back at Lyra. "Since he didn't see the wulvers until they were upon us."

"What are our orders, then?" Ridge asked, materializing out of thin air on the other side of the tree. His appearance didn't startle Wilder. If anything, he was curious about what took him so long. He was never a step away from Maelys.

"Don't get too close. I don't trust her. No one should have power like that."

"There's something good in her. I'm sure of it," Maelys murmured. "And there's always a balance."

Wilder shrugged and stepped back into the clearing, heading for Lyra. "I'm not sure if there is—this time."

Otto was standing beside her, offering her a hand up. The sight of it stirred something in Wilder. They had to stop helping her and being kind to her. It wouldn't serve anyone well.

She had to become stronger, and to do that, she needed to walk. His father be damned. They'd make it to the Wilds when they made it to the Wilds.

"You're walking on your own," he said to Lyra in a way that brooked no argument.

She seemed resigned to his order.

"That's fine," she murmured, taking Otto's hand and standing with a wobble.

Otto's eyes darkened. "That will delay us two days."

Wilder jerked his chin down. "Then we'll be late." He turned on a heel and walked out of the clearing and into the forest once more. Maelys and Ridge close behind him.

Lyra and Otto followed behind them, but at a much slower pace.

An acidic taste wet Wilder's tongue. It was pain—her pain.

"Pinna is not too much further away," Otto said to Lyra.

Wilder strained his ears for her response but heard nothing.

Ridge hummed a tune as they walked, a flower unfurling and furling in his hand.

The sun was low on the horizon, a light chill settling over the land.

Birds followed them, feeling a pull towards Maelys. Wilder found himself glancing back at Lyra. There was pain on her face. A tightness to her mouth and a divot to her brow. The flower that Ridge had given her was tucked in her fist. But the multitude of birds that swarmed was keeping and holding her attention. That small glimpse of wonder in her eyes had his chest aching. He didn't like to be cruel.

But life was cruel. The quicker she learned that, the better.

They walked the winding path through the forest. Their footsteps were silent, and then there was Lyra's. Newborn animals walked with more grace than she did.

"How far did you say it was to Pinna?" Wilder heard her ask Otto.

"We should be there by sunrise," Otto replied.

Wilder could feel Maelys staring sidelong at him. He had ordered them to stay away—but that didn't apply to Otto.

Nothing ever seemed to apply to him. It wasn't because he was closer to Wilder than the others, but the nature of his gift gave him an advantage.

After all these years, Wilder still wasn't sure how it worked. Sometimes it was so strong, Otto could answer your question before you asked. Sometimes the vision changed in the middle. Wilder thought it had to do with the person's choice, or maybe the threads of fate were always changing.

That seemed to be the case with Lyra. Fate didn't quite know what lay in wait for her yet. And that made him even more wary of her.

He'd known as a child what his future would hold. The only son of King Oberon, he would assume the throne when his father ever tired of it. But in the meantime, he would serve his father and their court.

It wasn't a particularly difficult job. He trained with the guard, was often a liaison to the Mannereds, and completed every other task his father felt was beneath his power as king. And lately, that seemed to be more and more.

He hated the lack of freedom. His decisions weren't ever his own; his image had to be upheld within his court, and he could never tell his father no. Not that there had been too many times he wanted to.

Although some days he would have preferred to do nothing. To lie on the edge of the Valewood and listen to the ancient willow sing, to paddle through the Three Sisters Swamp with no need to hurry, to take a dip in the ocean for the hell of it.

Lyra lurched and then fell behind him, pulling him from his thoughts.

"Are you alright?" Otto was already at her side.

"It's these godsdamned boots," she whined, squeezing them.

Otto shot Wilder a look before turning back to Lyra. "Let me see."

Lyra froze, biting her lip and shaking her head.

"Let him see," Wilder ordered.

His concern for her was overwhelming, and he hated it.

With his barked order, Lyra huffed a sigh and began untying her laces. When she pulled the first boot off, his heart sank.

Blood.

Her boot was full of blood. Worn skin down nearly to the bone on her heel and a few of her toes.

"Good gods." Maelys pressed a hand to her mouth, her eyes widening.

"Why didn't you say something?" Ridge added.

Lyra shrugged.

"Why didn't you tell me?" Wilder asked.

Lyra met his stare head-on.

"You wanted no more delays."

This was all his fault. His coldness and cruelty had pushed her to this. He was rotten, to his very core, for allowing it.

"What do you need?" he asked, knowing she would know exactly what kind of plant would heal the open wounds.

"Marigold," she said, looking around. "It's a yellow flower with—"

"I know what a marigold is," Wilder retorted. "Ridge, Otto, help me find some. Maelys, stay with her."

Wilder didn't wait for a response before he set off to find her the fucking flowers.

16
Only smell flowers

Lyra sat on the edge of the forest trail beside Maelys, who shot her wary glances.

"So you like books?" Maelys asked, breaking up the uncomfortable quiet.

"Mhm."

It felt heavy.

They had seemed on equal footing before they stopped in the clearing, but now it felt *off*. Lyra thought back to their agreement to try.

"Do you speak to the animals or do you command them?"

Maelys' brows hit her hairline. "I don't 'command' them. Animals do whatever they want."

Lyra nodded, thinking through that answer.

A flock of birds settled in the tree nearby, and she studied them. Shiny black feathers, with a streak of reddish-orange on their wings.

"That's a red-winged blackbird," Lyra murmured to herself or Maelys if she was actually listening.

"They like you," Maelys replied.

"They do?"

Maelys picked at a leaf and shrugged before looking up at the birds. "Animals have a way of knowing what lies within the soul, and you smell like the wind off the sea. They like the wind."

Lyra's brow furrowed. That was similar to what Wilder had said she smelled like.

She leaned closer to Maelys and sniffed.

"Did you just *smell* me?" Maelys scrunched her nose with disgust and leaned away.

Lyra huffed with a shrug. "I tried to. I couldn't smell anything."

"Well, that's a relief! Don't do that—it's weird."

A frown marred Lyra's face. "Everyone else has told me what I smelled like. Why shouldn't I smell you?"

Maelys shook her head and chuckled.

"We're elves. We don't smell you on purpose. Our senses are stronger. But you trying to smell us—it's not the way."

"*The way?*" Lyra asked slowly.

"Yeah. You know? The way things are done. Decorum and all that."

"Oh," Lyra muttered.

A divot formed between Maelys' brows. "Surely there's a way of doing things where you're from."

Lyra snorted. "Yeah, whatever the mermen tell you to do, which usually means you are to be seen and not heard."

Maelys reeled back at her words. "What?"

Lyra looked around at the darkening forest and shivered.

"I mean, where I come from, the males rule everything. And the females do as they are commanded."

Maelys' mouth dropped open in shock or horror, or both, from the looks of it.

"I had heard stories, but I thought it was just propaganda."

Lyra pressed her lips into a grim line and shook her head.

"I was to be raised in my father's court and then married off to a prince in a territory he deemed a threat. All my sisters were married off to other territories for positions of power. We are bartered wombs and nothing else."

An angry gleam entered Maelys' golden eyes, turning the hue molten.

"Females can do anything in the Wilds and the Mannereds. Hell, the Mannereds are ruled by a female."

"You are lucky."

It was a surprise to Lyra as the words fell out of her mouth. Never would she have thought she would converse with a female elf. Not only that, she envied one. Maelys had to be high-ranking to serve so close to Wilder.

It grew quiet and pensive as they each worked through the information they had shared. Lyra wanted to know more about what a female elf's life was like here.

"Are you high-born?"

Maelys laughed. "No. Does that offend you?"

"Why would that offend me?" Lyra twirled the flower between her fingers.

"Because you are a princess."

Lyra covered her mouth to staunch a laugh that bubbled up. She squeezed her eyes shut, keeping well away from that glimmering thread in her chest. Once the feeling had passed, she took a steadying breath and looked back at Maelys, who was analyzing her.

"I don't think being a princess means much."

"It does in the Wilds. Being high-born holds weight. Are you sure you're using your position correctly?"

Her words rang like a struck bell. *Use her position?* How on earth was she expected to do that?

Had Maelys not been listening to what she just said? And Lyra was a prisoner—*at their hands!*

The pain in Lyra's feet increased with her rising anger. She could feel the blood pumping in her toes. Luckily, there was an intentional stomping through the forest. Wilder stepped through the trees, marigold in hand.

"We found little. It's not the right season. Will this do?" Wilder held up three golden flowers.

"I'll take anything at this point," Lyra replied, but then froze. *Not anything.*

Wilder thrust the flowers out to her, and she took them, managing not to accidentally touch him.

"Do you need anything else?"

"I need a way to grind the petals down to make a salve."

Wilder looked at Ridge, who nodded and turned away, heading back into the forest.

"How do you know all this?" Maelys asked her.

"I like to read."

Wilder crossed his arms over his chest. "That's an understatement."

Lyra glared at him from her seated position on the forest floor. But before she could make a scathing remark, Ridge appeared with two large, rounded stones.

"Will this work?"

"It's perfect. Thank you."

Wilder's brows rose high on his forehead. She realized she had not thanked him for finding her the flowers. And he would not get one now, the prick.

She set to work on the flowers, grinding the delicate golden petals into a poultice. She could feel their eyes on her as she worked, but she didn't look, didn't want to see their expressions.

When she had ground all the flowers down into a mushy mess, she began spreading them all over her heels and toes. It was cold and refreshing. Relief had her eyes slipping closed.

"Here," Otto said, and her eyes fluttered open. "For your feet."

He held out several scraps of fabric, and she took them with a smile.

"Thank you," she whispered again.

That was twice now she had said the words and meant them. Maybe she would be better at this kindness thing than she thought.

17
ANOTHER THREAD

Wilder watched as Lyra tied her feet up with scraps of fabric from Otto's tunic. He should have been the one to cut fabric from his cloak.

The cloak still smelled faintly of her. After she was finished wrapping her feet, she stuffed them back into her boots with a wince. It clawed at him.

Maelys picked up the discarded flower and tucked it into Lyra's hair with a smile. They clasped hands, and Maelys pulled Lyra to her feet.

"If it bleeds again—say something," he told her.

Lyra only nodded. He didn't like that either. He wanted to hear her words.

"Say it," he commanded.

She lifted her chin, meeting his stare with a livid one of her own.

"I will," she hissed.

He liked it too much when she showed her true colors, the

fire that writhed within her veins, the monster that lurked under the surface. It felt more authentic. Like only he could bring out that side of her.

He didn't want to know what that said about him.

But maybe he could push her to let the monster show, and then he wouldn't feel too bad about killing her.

It was when she was kind that it irked him. Power like hers shouldn't belong to anyone, but not the least bit to someone who was kind.

A monster having that power made more sense to him.

Monsters were meant to be vanquished.

Wilder glowered at her before pushing past and setting off again. He had his mind made up that they would walk until they reached Pinna. He did not want to sleep in these woods longer than necessary.

Pinna would be the last town they reached before the Wilds. After Pinna, they would cross the flatlands, a barren, sickly green wasteland of nothing that's on the edge of the Three Sisters Swamp. After the swamp was the Valewood, and then *home.*

To the rolling hills of the High Land.

They were still so far away. His decision to strengthen her felt like folly now. Because the longer it took them to get to the Wilds, the longer he had to be near her.

He could still hear her stumbling behind him. She and the riot of birds fluttering about in the trees.

Wilder turned to tell Maelys to tell them to leave, but she was not flanking him. No, she was walking beside Lyra and Otto. He balled his hands into fists. Had he not just commanded them to keep their distance? Ignoring the urge to yell at Maelys, he looked forward again and kept moving.

One step at a time.

They needed to get to Pinna, and then he could have a break from her, from them all.

Lyra tripped and collapsed with a delicate shriek.

Wilder wanted to rage.

This was going to take forever. He spun and ripped her from the ground and carried her over his shoulder like a sack of grain.

Fuck it.

Fuck it all to hell.

If he had to carry her the entire way there, he would. As long as he could be rid of her. Lyra stayed still, not heaving breaths or spitting an agitated remark. She must be afraid of him then.

Well, good. So long as she kept quiet, it would make his life much easier.

Ridge chuckled beside him, and he glared his way.

"Not a fucking word," he ground out.

Ridge held his hands up in a placating gesture.

The rest of the journey passed in a blur of trees and silence. It wasn't the reprieve he had hoped it would be.

After shifting Lyra to a more comfortable position on his back, he could feel her. Her chest expanded with air and then expelled, and her thighs clenched his waist when he walked with haste. Or she saw something interesting.

At long last, her head had fallen against his shoulder as sleep dragged her under.

In the distance, the lamps of the lanterns glowed. The flames flickered in the night, leading their way in.

It should have relieved him, but it didn't.

An unsettling feeling crawled through him, and he paused, sweeping the village for anything amiss.

"Would you like to know?" Otto asked.

Wilder shook his head and received a grunt.

"You're fine with knowing everyone else's future still, but not your own?"

"I like to think I'm in control of my own decisions and not just another thread in the tapestry of the universe."

Otto sighed through his nose. "Some threads are brighter than others. Like hers—and yours."

He didn't know what to make of that—and didn't want to.

Wilder swept a wind through the village and caught the odor of something that should not be there, wulvers.

"Matthias …" he ground out. "We're being hunted."

"Very good, Prince." Otto nodded. "Igneous is a few hours behind, but headed this way. If we stay, they'll catch us, too."

Wilder groaned. He had wanted a few hours of rest. As he shifted a sleeping Lyra to a more comfortable position, he envied her ability to rest. She slept like the dead.

"Find us some horses. I don't care if you have to steal them."

Ridge and Maelys vanished to find horses. Their footsteps were silent despite the leaves and twigs.

They stayed quiet. Listening and preparing for whatever could be lurking in the darkness. Lyra whimpered in her sleep, and Wilder hushed her, soothing her back to slumber.

"I have seen—" Otto began. Wilder cut him off.

"I don't want to know."

"It's not about you—*it's about her.*"

Wilder grimaced and then inclined his head.

"She will need you."

Wilder stared ahead, not daring to look at Otto.

"It will be your decision, of course. But your ability or inability to set your preconceived ideas aside will lead to great change or utter destruction."

"Funny how you said this was about her," Wilder snapped.

"You are tied together. There is not one without the other."

"What the hell does that mean?"

Otto smirked and shrugged. "Would you like to know?"

Damn him and his stupid riddles. He didn't want to be tied to *anyone.* He was already tied to the court and his responsibilities. There wasn't anything of himself left.

The thudding of hooves interrupted Wilder's reply.

"We could only find four," Maelys said, coming upon them astride a white mare. She tugged a black stallion behind her. Ridge sat astride a dappled gray mare and pulled along a golden mare.

Otto chuckled, and Wilder bit his tongue. Of course, they only found four. It was like the universe was doing everything in its power to continue to shove them together.

Wilder passed Lyra off to Otto so he could mount the black stallion. His body felt light, vacant, without her.

When Otto passed her back, he settled her in front of him so that she could continue sleeping. She didn't stir once in the handoff. His brow furrowed. She must have been exhausted.

His heart fluttered in his chest, the space between his ribs squeezed tight. Something was coming. And it was not good.

They set off immediately. The horse's speed jostled Lyra, but still, she did not wake. What pain she must have been in to sleep this hard.

18

DROWNED THE WHOLE WORLD

Lyra woke to the clomping of hooves against stone and the warmth of a body against her face. She flinched, and the hands around her tightened their grip.

"Easy," Wilder grumbled. "You'll tumble off the horse, and then I'll be forced to retrieve you."

Her hips ached, and her feet were numb. They dangled over the side of the horse, and she flexed her toes in her boots. At least it wasn't painful any longer.

Lyra glanced around at the path they were on. The trees were farther apart, but vast. This was a much older wood. It felt ancient, like the names of the plants and animals had come from a dialect no one spoke anymore.

"Where are we?"

She gazed up at Wilder, and she was stunned by the sheer beauty of him. His dark hair waved in the wind, and there was a sharpness to his gaze.

His lips moved then, but she was so caught in his snare that she didn't hear the words.

Releasing the reins, he flicked her forehead, and her mouth dropped open in shock. It didn't hurt, but it was humiliating.

"Did you hear me, Legs?"

"How dare you?" she seethed.

Her eyes narrowed on his exposed throat. She should rip it out for that offense. As if sensing her desire, he tilted his chin down.

"Maybe you should listen to the answer to the question you just asked," he said with a quiet calmness.

The fire within her raged. He was a stupid, abrasive elvish male. And she wanted to kill him.

She squirmed to get away from him. To put some distance between their touching bodies before she did kill him. But his grip on her tightened as he slowed the horse down.

"Oh no, you don't. You are staying on this horse. We have to get to the Wilds as soon as possible."

Lyra glared at him as her chest heaved.

"Whatever happened to making me walk on my own two feet?"

She was annoyed.

He couldn't make up his mind. It was like whiplash. He refused to carry her, and then he did. She must walk on her own, and then he's carrying her again.

Every one of his threats had been ignored, not by her—but by him.

"That was before. We're being followed still, and we're getting closer to the Three Sisters."

Lyra shivered.

A light mist grew around them, shrouding the forest in a breathing cloak. It made the emerging trees look haunting. At any moment, they could tug the cloak tighter around themselves and set off for the hills.

Lyra didn't like it, but she didn't hate it either. There was a sentience in this wood, but she hadn't figured out if it was kind yet.

When she began squeezing her legs, Wilder looked down at her.

"Do they hurt?" His voice was quiet, almost sincere.

"They're numb. C-could we perhaps halt for a moment so that I could stretch?"

"Will your feet be okay?"

Lyra shrugged and nibbled on her bottom lip.

Wilder nodded. "Make it quick."

He stopped their horse, and the rest of the group stopped alongside them.

Lyra bent at the waist to touch her toes before squatting down. She rubbed at her thighs and then her calves, trying to effuse warmth and blood back into them.

Maelys stared on with a curious expression. Otto monitored the wood, and Ridge peeled an apple with his dagger. The skin twisted around in a single peel.

"Here." Ridge tossed her the apple, and she fumbled it, but did not drop it.

"Thank you," she whispered, looking up at him with a small grin.

Wilder watched the entire exchange with a passive expression plastered on his face. He didn't seem to like it when the others spoke to her or were accommodating.

Lyra kept her eyes on Wilder as she bit down on the apple. She moaned at the delectable crisp flavor that hit her tongue, and he blanched.

"Get on the fucking horse," he growled.

She smiled sweetly at him, having gotten under his skin so swiftly, and held up her hand.

In one swift movement, he pulled her onto the horse. Not side saddle this time, though.

No, her legs straddled the wide beast, and she clenched her jaw at the sheer awkwardness of it.

Lyra missed her tail and the weightlessness of the water. The mists were a close second and a brief reprieve from the dryness of the air.

The thoughts she had long held at bay broke through, and her heart sank. She would never swim below the depths again. That world had been snatched from her.

Lyra didn't think she would miss it this much. She had nothing waiting for her back home but misery. Yet now, she didn't have a place to belong to.

Her head dropped between her shoulders, and she bit her lip as Wilder urged the horse on.

She was miserable.

And it was as if the world could feel her pain.

It started raining then, pouring as if all the water in the world had been held aloft and then dropped.

It soaked her to the bone, reminding her of all that she had lost. She closed her eyes as tears and rain streaked down her face.

"Gods dammit," Wilder grumbled.

That was at least a small silver lining. He was going to be as miserable as she was now.

Lyra let her anguish swallow her whole.

It rained all day and all night. Her hair was soaked through, and the thick auburn mass dripped down and splattered against her soaked pants.

It was unbelievably miserable, but still not even a fraction of what she felt writhing within her chest.

19
BODY
HEAT

It had never been so wet or cold before. Wilder locked his muscles in place to keep from shivering. This was insufferable.

They needed to find some shelter, and quickly. A tremor vibrated Lyra's body. As she turned to the side, he caught a glimpse of her blue lips. If he was cold in his nearly immortal body, he couldn't fathom how she must be feeling.

"Otto," Wilder called louder than the torrential rain.

"I'm on it." Otto galloped past them in search of somewhere for them to wait out the storm.

He couldn't remember the last time he had seen rain such as this. Raindrops the size of his fist. Lyra shivered again, and his chest cleaved in half. He let go of the reins, wrapped an arm around her, and pulled her against him.

"What are you doing?" She tried to pull away.

"Your lips are blue, and my orders are to bring you to the King alive."

"That doesn't explain why you are touching me."

Wilder's expression darkened as his brow lowered, and a smirk tugged his lip up. "You mean to tell me, in all those books, you read nothing about body heat?"

He could see the wheels turning in her brilliant mind. When her eyes widened, he knew she had figured it out.

"I would rather die at this point," she ground out.

"Believe me, Legs, I would love to let you. But orders are orders."

Thunder rumbled high overhead, cutting off her reply, and had her flinching into him.

"What was that?" she breathed, staring up into the sky. She had to squint against the rain pelting her face.

"That was thunder."

"Thunder," she tested the word out.

Wilder realized that Lyra had never heard thunder before. Deep below the surface, the sound never reached them.

"It's the heat from lightning that causes it."

Lyra nodded. "I've read about it."

Of course, she had. She had read about storms and plants, but not about body heat, which could save her life as a human.

Obviously, there were gaps in her knowledge, and he wanted to see where those were.

"You read about storms but not about other helpful survival tactics?"

Lyra shrugged. "I'm sure the texts about 'body heat' were deemed too crude for females to read."

"What do you mean?"

She turned to meet his gaze. "There were some books that females weren't allowed to read."

Wilder scoffed. He felt like he stepped into the deep end with this line of questioning.

What was taking Otto so long?

"I'm not lying," she murmured, turning around. "We couldn't

read things about politics, history, or anything remotely intimate."

Wilder pulled their horse to a stop as the words shocked him to his core. *They censored the knowledge of their females.* Who would do such a thing?

"And who decided what was appropriate or not?" He didn't know why he had asked. He already knew the answer.

"The King and the other males in power."

White-hot rage surged through him; stifling knowledge to half your population was a way to keep control. So the rumors about the mermen's cruelty were not fabricated.

Puffs of steam slipped through his lips and into the frigid air between them.

"Is that not what you do in the Wilds?" she asked, with a timidness that surprised him.

"*Absolutely not.*" The words came out much harsher than he had intended, but he was still lost in his rage. The buffoonery that was censoring knowledge because of one's sex or social standing was offensive to him.

Even his father, with all of his faults, would never agree to such a thing. The world demanded balance, and limiting knowledge tipped the scales.

Otto clambered towards them. His clothes stuck to his pale white skin, but his eyes were bright.

"I've found a small cave that will do. There have been no occupants for quite some time."

"Thank you," Wilder replied and followed after him.

The cave was tiny. Barely large enough to fit them sitting side by side, but it was out of the rain and in a favorable location to keep an eye out for an attack.

Wilder had torn down boughs of cedar branches to make a makeshift stable for the horses, although they didn't seem to mind the rain. He had watched as Ridge let Lyra help him feed each beast. It was amusing when she stared with wide-eyed wonder at their large teeth and tongues.

But now an uncomfortable silence filled the cave, and Wilder knew it was his doing. His silence wasn't unusual, but to not allow the others to speak was. He couldn't help it, though.

Lyra kept burrowing underneath his skin, and he needed to keep his distance—or better yet, get her to keep hers.

"How long will the rain last?" Her quiet voice echoed through the small space.

"Not too much longer," Otto replied, holding his hand out into the pouring rain past the rim of the granite overhang.

"That's good," she replied. "I have a strange feeling."

Wilder's ears pricked with the insinuation, and he looked over her head to meet Otto's stare.

"How so?" Wilder asked.

It was common knowledge among their people to always listen to your gut. That was how fate, the gods—hell, even the universe—guided you.

"It's an eerie feeling. Like something bad is going to happen," she murmured, tucking her legs up under her chin and resting her head against them.

"Has that ever happened before?" Otto asked.

Lyra squinted as she thought and then nodded.

"Mhm. The night Wilder rescued me from the human attackers."

Wilder lurched to his feet and stalked into the rain. With his sword gripped in his fist, he paced along the entrance of the cave. Daring anyone or anything out there to come close.

That's when he felt them—out there in the distance, watching. There were at least two from Igneous' clan and three from Matthias'.

It was highly unusual for wulver clans to work together. They had a history of violence that stretched back further than the Wilds and the Mannereds. But if they were smart, they would cut their losses now and flee.

Wilder had a reputation as one of the best swordsmen in their realm and had been cutting down monsters and men alike since he could hold a sword on his own. It was like breathing to him.

The sword in his grip had been passed down through his ancestors for millennia. It was as legendary as he was. The blade was composed of layered steel, forged in the volcanoes of a long-forgotten place that didn't exist on any map. The pommel was unremarkable, a series of silver runes carved into an ancient ash wood.

There wasn't a creature the blade could not cut down, magical and human alike. It glowed in the watery light streaming through the rain-leaden clouds as he paced.

Even if they weren't stupid enough to fear him, they would fear that sword.

20
BARNACLE

Lyra watched Wilder prowl back and forth in front of the cave. The pouring rain slid down his face and soaked his tunic, highlighting the outline of his muscled physique. His boots thundered with each step. And if it wasn't such a menacing sight, she might have laughed at his obvious discomfort, but then she remembered he was on her side, protecting her from whatever was out there. Lyra could look at the snarling mass of muscle in front of her and smile.

So she did.

"What?" Maelys asked, looking from her to Wilder.

"It's kind of funny," Lyra replied, a bright twinkle in her emerald eyes.

"How so?" Maelys cocked her head to the side, and her wet braid slid over her shoulder.

"Well, it's nice and dry in here. And he's out there in the cold rain to protect me, *the person he hates*, from unforeseen danger." Lyra pointed from Wilder to herself and grinned.

"Oh, that's diabolical," Maelys replied, but a smile tugged her lips up.

Ridge shoulder-bumped Maelys, and her smile dropped away. Battle lines had been drawn. Wilder must have told them not to speak to her or be nice. That was fine—just fine. It's not like she had a choice in being here.

It's not like this was her grand idea to leave everything she'd ever known and be whisked away to an enemy kingdom.

If she could grow her tail back, she would be gone immediately. Lyra paused at that thought. *Would she?* Her father would no doubt be furious with her for being captured. And Drystan, well, he had made it perfectly clear how he felt about her staying topside.

But everything she had read about the elves told her going back to Atlantis was the lesser of two evils. Yet, she didn't know if that was the truth anymore. These elves hadn't displayed the violence she had read about, and she was stuck here. She couldn't grow her tail back. Lyra decided she would not be miserable because of choices that were not her own.

No, she was going to win them over. But she didn't know how. Merfolk weren't known for their social skills. Marina and Seraphina had grown on her much the same way a barnacle did to a ship. Was that what she needed to do? Entrench herself so deeply in their lives that the only way they could be rid of her was to scrape her off?

Lyra frowned to herself.

She had never *tried* to make friends. If anything, her violent tendencies drove everyone else away except for Marina and Seraphina. But that wouldn't help her survive now—and she didn't know where that left her. Lyra hated this journey. It was making her confront things she never had the time to analyze before.

Otto cleared his throat and called to Wilder. "The rain will be stopping soon, and we need to move. *Quickly.*"

"I can take them," Wilder growled back.

"You can. But they will take her," Otto nodded to Lyra.

"I would like to see them try."

Otto stood, crossing his arms over his chest. "I have seen it, and *we fail*. Unless we move."

Wilder heaved a breath, squeezing his eyes shut, he tipped his head back to the sky. Lyra watched as the rain pelted his face and ran down his high cheekbones. She couldn't stop herself from watching.

"*Fine*. Let's move."

He grabbed Lyra by the arm and tugged her behind him, keeping himself between her and whatever dangers lay before them. It surprised her how much she liked that. Even with the blisters on her feet and legs barking in protest—it felt delightful. To be protected. She had never been protected before. Even if he was doing it out of a sense of duty, it was still nice.

THEY REACHED the Three Sisters Swamp sooner than they had planned. Having only stopped a handful of times to see to their needs or let the horses rest and graze. The elves and Lyra had feasted on bread and fruits that Ridge and Otto never failed to pull from their packs.

Lyra was starting to believe those bags were bewitched to never be empty. She marveled at the ethereal magic of this place. Trees rose out of the murky water, but their branches sagged as if they longed to return to the soil beneath the surface.

They didn't slow their pace even as they pushed themselves and their horses to the brink of death. Whatever was after them was dangerous enough that Wilder would put their lives at risk to get her to their borders.

A strip of raised ground no more than two horses wide cut through the marshy land. Mud kicked up as they galloped along. The wind tore at Lyra's hair, and the tangled and matted strands flapped like a wave behind her and right into Wilder's face. Her cheeks were rosy, not from the temperature but from the wind's burn. Anytime she blinked or moved her mouth, she could feel the rawness of her skin. It was tiresome, all this unnecessary pain that land dwellers were accustomed to.

"Once we're through the Three Sisters, it's a straight shot through the Valewood. Then you'll be safe," Wilder murmured in her ear.

Lyra couldn't help the shiver that his voice so close to her body elicited.

But she wanted to laugh at his word choice. *Safe.* She wouldn't be safe anywhere. Had never been. She didn't think that was going to change now.

A ripple in the water beside them drew her attention as she watched it rise and then fall. Her knowledge of swamps and the manner of creatures that dwelled within them was abysmal.

"Why is it called the 'Three Sisters'?"

"It's named for the original three," he replied with a dull sort of enthusiasm.

"I figured as much. But *who* are they?"

Wilder slowed their horse a fraction so that he didn't have to yell over the wind, and Lyra was grateful the sting against her flesh abated.

"You've never been told about the three sisters? About where you came from?"

Lyra shook her head. She didn't hold her breath on him replying, but when he cleared his throat, she tried to quell the excitement that built.

"Long ago, this world was ruled by three sisters: Mab, Tiandra, and Aradia. They were sisters by blood, but each a different creature. Mab was an elf, Tiandra a mermaid, and Aradia was human. They were the original balance."

It wasn't surprising she was never taught this story. Females being rulers was not a thing that would be allowed to be learned or discussed in Atlantis. But how Wilder spoke of balance intrigued her. It was as if it were common knowledge.

"Balance?" she asked, tilting her head to the side.

Lyra could feel Wilder's gaze on the side of her face as she looked out at the murky water.

"The universe demands balance. For every poison a cure, for every ruler an equal, for every power an opposite."

Her face hurt as she scrunched her nose in confusion. That couldn't be true.

There was no balance in Atlantis. And there was no equal to her power … she could feel it stir when she thought of it.

A vibration in the golden thread that called to her.

Lyra curled in upon herself as if she could hide. And when she didn't ask another question, Wilder prodded their horse along and increased their speed.

21
SLEEPING BEAUTY

After he had told her the story of the three sisters, Lyra had turned inward and remained that way. She didn't look up when they made it through the swamp, and from what he could tell, she didn't even look at the Valewood as they entered its southern border.

It confused him because the forest here was more majestic than the mortal forest she marveled at, and the eerie swamp she studied with ravenous curiosity.

He hadn't thought he had been rude to her; he even explained when she asked questions, but now, in her silence, he rethought every word he had spoken to her. He had told her their names, what species they were, and about balance. Nothing out of that was opinion-based or delivered with sarcasm. But she had disliked something he had said.

They passed a group of trolls that strolled with a sluggish gait around burrows. Their hunched and moss-covered figures blended into the forest completely. He was astonished that Lyra didn't react or comment on their presence. Maybe she didn't see them?

They traveled with speed through the Valewood, passing forest nymphs dancing through trees, their willowy limbs ethereal with their movements. He glimpsed a flock of pixies next, whose glittering wings tinkled and trilled their tiny bodies as they moved out of their path.

It had been quite a while since they had stopped for her to stretch or for the horses to rest. Maybe if they did that, then he could figure out what perturbed her. Slowing their horses, Wilder raised a fist in the air so that the others would stop. Lyra still didn't move.

When the horse came to a complete stop, he slid off first and turned to reach for her hand. To find her asleep.

This whole time, he had worried that he had offended her, and she was merely sleeping. He cleared his throat, and she stirred.

"Did you need to stretch?"

She tilted her head to the sky and yawned, stretching her arms up as well. He couldn't help but watch. The moonlight cast the profile of her face in white, glittering light as it filtered through the canopy of jewel-colored trees.

"Mhm," she murmured, covering her mouth with her hand and yawning again.

Wilder raised his hand higher in the offering. She stared at it before throwing her feet over the other side of the horse and sliding down opposite him. She grimaced in pain when her feet hit the ground. He almost rolled his eyes, but he felt Otto watching him. So he stalked away.

He made a mental note to ask Otto if he saw anything of value later, but first, he needed to clear his head and check the perimeter of their rest stop.

Wilder could hear Lyra trudging through the forest. An explosion would have been quieter. Leaves crunched and twigs snapped. He would need to teach her to walk with some stealth in the future, lest she give away their position every time.

When her walking stopped, he sighed and closed his eyes. Wilder listened to the forest at night and inhaled deeply. There was nothing out of the ordinary, thankfully. Nevertheless, he stood there and strained his ears for anything at all.

Someone had been following them, someone had known where they were and who they had. It didn't mean it was someone in his court who had spilled secrets. It could have very well been an informant in her court, maybe even the same one who had told his father who and where she was.

Neither clan had caught up to them yet. The forest stayed quiet. But they shouldn't dally too long. They were still days from the Wilds border—*to safety.*

Purposeful footsteps thudded behind him, and he turned to see Ridge, his arms crossed over his muscled chest.

"We're ready."

Wilder nodded and turned back towards the forest once more.

"What do you think is happening with the wulvers?" Ridge asked.

Wilder shrugged. "Someone got them to work together in their pursuit of Lyra. I don't know who could be capable of that."

Ridge's arms slipped to his side as he squeezed his hands into fists. "Titania?"

Wilder shook his head.

The Queen of the Mannereds had worked tirelessly for an alliance, and she was kind. He hadn't scented a rotten bone in her body when he had met her, which was unusual. Rulers in power often had ulterior motives. Not Titania. She had only wanted peace for her people and did what no ruler of the Mannereds had ever done before—formed an alliance with the Wilds.

"No, this came from inside. My order came directly from my father. So we need to find out who else knew."

Ridge's jaw clenched. "We have a traitor?"

Wilder turned and stalked towards Ridge, pausing at his side. "It appears we do."

Along with his powers of growth and life, Ridge had an affinity for sniffing out weaknesses. Wilder would use that to his advantage. Especially when it came to the livelihood of the court.

"I will find them."

"See that you do. But first, we need to get Lyra to the border."

Ridge nodded, and the violence that danced in his eyes waned. "I know how you feel, but there's something about her …"

Wilder's eyes narrowed. "How so?"

"I haven't been able to puzzle it out yet. But she's different from what I was expecting from a mermaid. She's … pure."

"*Pure*? You mean not evil?"

"Sure—not evil. Whatever you want to call it. But I sense no corruption within her. Despite her sharp tongue." Ridge chuckled.

Just because she wasn't evil didn't mean she wasn't a threat. But it was still comforting to know she wasn't completely corrupted.

"Let me know when you complete that puzzle."

Ridge nodded, and they turned as one and headed back for the horses. Tension settled along Wilder's shoulders as he strode back to Lyra.

No, she wasn't evil, but that power was unfathomable.

That wasn't the measly gift of song that was known for her kind. It had entranced him.

Lyra was so powerful, she could control rulers.

22
MAGIC SIGHT

As she handed the water skin back to Maelys, Lyra glanced around at their surroundings. If she had thought the human forest had been lovely, it was nothing compared to the Valewood. Magic poured from every facet of this place.

The air was crisp and light against her face, soothing the burn on her cheeks. It smelled of wild roses, citrus, and robust cedar. Green leaves glimmered like emeralds in the moonlight. It was a forest of jewels. Ruby flowers, amber trunks, and sapphire fronds.

Majestic, eternal, otherworldly.

The air filled her lungs easier and warmth stirred in her veins. This was magic. She hungered for it as she gulped down the air greedily. Closing her eyes and tilting her head up to the moonlight, she reveled in its electric embrace. This was a place unlike any other. She felt the stirrings of guilt—she had never felt this way about Atlantis.

That thought frightened her. She snapped her eyes open in

time to see Wilder slipping through the darkness. Moonlight poured through the trees, casting him in its glow. No—he was magic.

"We need to keep moving," he ordered. His voice was gruff and the warmth in her veins rose to a blistering degree. Arousal and anger mingled and melded. She didn't like to be ordered around—had never liked it. But something about the words coming from his mouth, that voice …

Well, you'd have to be dead not to find the allure in him.

"They're a few hours behind us," Otto answered Wilder from behind her. She flinched, having not heard him creep up.

"Good. Will they stay that way?" Wilder asked, looking right over the top of her head at Otto.

"If we keep on this pace? Yes."

Wilder nodded and stopped a mere foot in front of her. His face hardened again, and she knew he would be answering none of her questions. Without a word, he scooped her up and threw her onto the back of their horse. She had to bite her tongue to keep from crying out in surprise.

"*Was that necessary?*" She glared down at him. And if she was not mistaken, a hint of mischief gleamed in his eyes.

"Of course, Legs. Can't have you slowing us down or becoming injured."

She cast her eyes around the rest of them, all seeming to have somewhere—*anywhere*— else to look.

"Touch me again and I'll cut your hand off."

As if he couldn't help himself, he slid a hand up from her ankle to her calf. If she thought she had felt warm before, nothing could compare to the heat of his skin on her body.

But he goaded her on purpose, testing the boundaries she set. On instinct, she slapped his hand away. It stung, but she didn't stop there. Kicking out with her foot, she aimed for his face and met a hardened wall of steel. He caught her foot before it could make contact with his face.

"Do not do that again," he intoned. Fire blazed in his eyes, clashing with the fire in hers.

"*I warned you,*" she hissed.

Wilder let go of her foot and then nodded.

"I apologize."

The world paused. And then tilted.

Apologized? No male had ever apologized for touching her against her will. Her chest rose and fell with her pants as she stared at him.

"My actions were thoughtless. And they will not happen again."

Again, she was speechless. This male—this elvish male—was apologizing to her.

How strange. And utterly terrifying.

Lyra gave him a stiff nod and turned forward. Wilder gracefully mounted the horse behind her and gripped the reins in both hands.

Then they were off. Flying through the forest and farther away from everything she had ever known.

NIGHT TURNED TO DAY, and then night once more.

Otto had convinced Wilder that whoever had been chasing them was far enough behind that a few hours of rest was a necessity for Lyra and their horses. Lyra had piled together some leaves and moss for a pillow and was lying on her side, her back to Wilder and the rest of them.

She had been too tired to help Ridge tend to the horses and was now trying her best to sleep, but every breeze through the trees or rustle of wings in the night had her heart fluttering in her chest.

The damp earth seeped through her clothes and into her bones. It was a fool's dream, but she had hoped when they reached the Wilds, she could bathe. Warm water was a luxury she had once taken for granted. But never again.

The wind blew stronger, blowing her hair into her face, and she tucked her arms closer to her chest for warmth. With her eyes squeezed shut, she tried to block out the unease of it all.

One more day, Wilder had said, then they would be in his kingdom.

The coldness ceased, and the wind no longer cut through her. It took her a moment to realize why. Peeling her eyes open, she saw Wilder's cloak draped over her. Lyra breathed in the fabric. It smelled of him, but it was more intense here, where magic flourished. She was right to think he smelled of fresh air, but it was stronger than that. He smelled like the fresh air coming down from the tops of the hawthorn trees.

His scent settled her. And her breathing slowed.

It slowed enough that they must have thought she was sleeping because Otto had started speaking.

"Your father plans to make a deal with her."

Her ears strained as she tried her best to listen.

"What kind of deal?"

"There's an unbalance of magic he wants to set right. And he needs her help."

"Unbalance?" Wilder's voice rang deeper than usual. He must be angry—or disturbed. From how he talked about the balance, it must have been very important to them.

"The night you kidnapped her was a ritual for their kind. And it's disrupting magic."

Lyra held very still, trying not to lurch at the information that was uncovered. So he hadn't known about Tidal Tithe, just that she would be on land. But their information was wrong.

The Tidal Tithe was to replenish their magic, not disrupt it.

Otto's visions were incorrect. But she was not about to correct her enemy's mistake.

No—let them think the wrong thing.

"What kind of ritual?" Maelys asked.

"To gain power, they consume the hearts of twelve humans. The mermaids complete the ritual, and it fuels their fertility. Or it *had*—their births have rapidly decreased due to the imbalance."

That wasn't entirely incorrect, and that unsettled Lyra. But it was supposed to be *thirteen* maidens who made the sacrifice. It was a way to pay homage to their past of luring mortals to their deaths.

It was an honor—not an imbalance.

Ridge grumbled, "So why don't they just stop?"

"Because the wealthy are still producing spawns. They see no need. And they have a bargain with the humans."

"What kind of bargain?" Wilder asked. Lyra could tell by his voice he was surprised.

"I am unsure. Something is blocking my sight from Baden-varia. Like some kind of ward."

Wilder sighed. "That's the least of our problems now. We received this order directly from my father, and now we're being hunted."

"Have you seen who informed the King?" Ridge asked. "If we know who else is behind this, it will help narrow down the traitor."

"No. It's also blocked. Whoever informed him must know I'm searching and they're hiding."

That was interesting. So there was a way to keep Otto from seeing. She would need to figure that out if she ever intended to escape.

"Do you think it came from her court?" Maelys asked.

"Could be," Wilder answered. "Whoever wanted her gone

might have doubled up the mission to ensure that she would never return."

Those words didn't hurt Lyra as much as they should have. It was no secret that there wasn't camaraderie among the merfolk. But who could have been after her? It must have been an attempt to injure her father or Drystan. They were the only ones who had a stake in her survival.

Her father needed her to kill off the heir to Ithicais, and then all his plans of complete domination would be complete. And Drystan needed her to secure his future claim to the throne.

Maybe it was someone in Drystan's circle who had made this alliance with Oberon to get her out of the way to usurp him.

That seemed the most likely. No one liked her, but *everyone* despised him.

"Will she agree to the deal with my father?" Wilder asked.

Lyra quieted her mind and her breathing to hear Otto's answer. It was intriguing learning what her future self had in store for her current self.

"She will. And you will not like it."

23
NOOSES

Otto's prophecy had unease gripping Wilder. He didn't like knowing his future—ever. But a small part of him wanted to know. Especially since it had to do with her.

"Would you like to know?" Otto asked.

A smirk tightened the lines around his face.

"Knowing I won't like it is enough. I will not borrow my future problems this night."

Maelys chuckled and leaned into Ridge's side. The lines between them had blurred over the last few decades, and Wilder wondered where it would lead them.

"Tell me my future instead," Ridge suggested.

Otto smiled brighter. This was a favorite pastime of theirs. Learning things that would happen minutes or days away.

"Watch out for the lightning bug," Otto replied.

Ridge lurched up straighter, and Maelys leaned away, laughing loudly now. For as massive and powerful as he was,

Ridge detested any kind of bug. Had once shrieked like a small child at a spider that crawled across his boot.

A lightning bug lit up the night beside Ridge, and he swung his arms wildly, trying to knock the thing away.

Even Wilder chuckled at that. They had never failed to ease the tension that thrummed through him. This was his one small piece of self, this friendship with them.

Once Ridge had settled down, he pulled Maelys back against him. Wilder's chest ached seeing that companionship, the freedom they had in expressing themselves openly.

"How do things look for tomorrow?" Maelys asked, peeling her eyes from Ridge's face to look at Otto.

The gray in his eyes swirled like smoke.

"We'll need some more yarrow."

THE MOON SLIPPED beyond the trees as the sun took its place in the sky. Wilder had watched Lyra thrash about in her sleep for the last hour. He couldn't imagine what she must have dreamt about to fight like that. A small part of him hoped it had not been ruffians.

"It's the current," Otto murmured. "She moves as if she's still one with the tug of the sea."

Apparently, he had been about to ask aloud what it meant. It annoyed him that Otto's magic could still unnerve him.

"Have the clans caught up?" Wilder asked instead.

"Not yet."

But close, is what was thought but not said.

Wilder stood and walked over to Lyra and tapped her shoulder with his boot.

"Wake up, Legs."

Her eyes opened, and for a moment, her gaze was not filled with hatred or loathing, but with warmth and happiness.

Then she blinked, and it was gone. Like a wave breaking upon the shore, washing it all away.

She turned her head to glare at his booted foot and then rolled away and onto her side.

"Five more minutes," she grumbled, closing her eyes again.

Wilder looked back at Otto, who shook his head.

"We don't have five minutes to spare. Unless you want to be devoured by wulvers. I suggest you get up."

Her eyes flashed open, and she sat up on her elbows. Staring past him at Otto for confirmation.

"We gave you as long as we could," he replied.

She sighed and clambered to her feet. It aggravated him that she sought Otto out for confirmation and didn't believe him. But he hadn't given her a reason to turn to him.

Maelys and Ridge emerged from a giant oak nearby, a bushel of yarrow swinging in Maelys' hand. A small smile spread across her face as her eyes met Lyra's, and they nodded to each other in greeting.

No—he didn't like that either.

Lyra approached their horse and ran a hand down its neck. She whispered something in its ear, and it flicked them. Wilder felt eyes on him as he watched her and struggled to look away. Otto was staring at him from atop his mount. Maelys was analyzing him as she shoved the yarrow into her saddlebags. And Ridge had a tight-lipped grin on his face as his head volleyed between Wilder and Lyra.

Good gods, they were busybodies.

Wilder approached Lyra, ready to help her astride. She turned and held out a hand in warning.

He paused. She was too self-sufficient.

Wilder watched as she shoved a foot in the stirrup and

gripped the saddle horn. At the same time, Wilder could hear Otto slide off his horse.

That *should* have clued him in.

Lyra swung herself up over the horse right as a howl rent the still air. It was far enough away that it wasn't a threat. But the horse didn't know that. Wilder watched in slow motion as the beast took off like a shot, with a terrified Lyra holding on for dear life.

He turned in time to catch the reins that Otto had chucked at him and took off after her. A pit of dread had opened in his chest and swallowed him whole. She could be seriously injured or dead.

The thought had him pressing his heels into the horse's flank to hasten its speed. Wilder needed to set eyes on her and to know she was okay.

He hadn't made it very far when he found her sprawled on the ground, face up. The horse was not anywhere in sight. Her face was red, either from fear or anger. He couldn't tell. But as he got closer, he saw the silver lining her emerald eyes, and her bottom lip was quivering.

Wilder slid off the horse mid-stride and crouched beside her, moving a strand of auburn hair from her face.

"Are you alright?"

He breathed a quiet sigh of relief that she seemed physically unharmed, but he could see how she struggled to hold it all together.

"My ass hurts," she whined.

Tears spilled over the rims of her eyes and wet the hair at her temples.

"May I—may I touch you?"

Lyra nodded, but that wasn't quite good enough for him, especially since she had tried to kick him in the face the last time he had touched her.

"I need to hear the words, Legs."

Lyra screwed her eyes shut and heaved a sigh. "You may touch me, Wilder."

With a gentleness he didn't think possible, he scooped her up off the damp earth.

Small, slender twigs and thin, brown leaves clung to her as he clutched her to his chest. She was so fragile.

It was disturbing that something so meager wielded so much power.

When she rested her head against his chest, he felt something within him stir, but he shoved it away.

Shoved everything away.

If he cared to notice, his end had already begun. She was his ruin, but he was also hers.

It was like a noose, tightening around his soul with each moment they spent together.

24
WITCH'S CURSE

L yra *hated* Wilder. Hated him for how he made her feel at this moment.

Safe and cared for. It was despicable.

He was her enemy and had wanted to kill her, had been ordered to kidnap her. This was the part of her she had tucked away for good. A part of her she thought had been drowned and beaten away.

Her feet dangled as he carried her to the horse he had dismounted, Otto's horse. That howl had cost them an extra mount.

Wilder looked from her to the horse and back to her again. She could tell he was debating not just her pain, but her fear of getting back in the saddle. How extraordinary. He looked genuinely concerned.

And for once, she wanted to put someone out of their misery.

"It hurts, but I can ride," she muttered.

The pain was an annoying throb down her lower back and to her toes. She had been more annoyed than terrified when the horse took off until she fell, then was terrified. But he had put her mind at ease.

Wilder's lips pressed into a thin line and nodded. With supreme caution, he lifted her back onto the horse. Lyra gripped the saddle horn and grimaced. Nothing was broken, thankfully, but she was severely bruised.

"There's some yarrow in Maelys' saddlebag," Wilder said as he swung up behind her. "And we can take more breaks if needed."

Lyra shook her head, and a few leaves that had tangled in her hair fell between them.

If she had to spend any more time on the back of this horse, she would lose her mind.

"Let's just go. I'm sick of traveling."

This is what she got for wanting a life of adventure. She hadn't been able to stand still for longer than a few hours in the last week. That couldn't have been right?

An entire week had passed already. The world must be spinning faster on land. The days and nights dragged on under the water, but up here, without the weight of the entire ocean above your head, they flew by. Carried by the wind.

Ridge and Maelys, followed by Otto on foot, approached from behind. Maelys had yarrow outstretched in her hand and a carefully blank expression on her face.

Otto didn't even try to hide the smile that stretched across his face. Ridge scanned her over, and she felt the prodding of his assessment as if he could see beneath her skin, to the very core of her being.

"Otto thought something like this might happen," Maelys said, handing the yarrow to Lyra.

"A warning would have been nice," Lyra snapped, ripping the yarrow from Maelys' hand.

"He would have told you, but ..."

"It involved me," Wilder supplied. "And I don't like knowing."

Lyra stared at him with her mouth parted in surprise. That made sense. He did very much seem to make his own decisions and forge his own path.

"*In the future*, if it has to do with my well-being, you let me know," Lyra said around Wilder as she looked directly at Otto.

He stood with his hands in his breeches pockets, looking for all the world like he was on an afternoon stroll.

"Noted," he replied with a dip of his chin.

"Time?" Wilder asked Otto.

"We'll find your stallion up ahead. They won't catch us by the time we reach the border."

Wilder nodded and prodded the horse along.

Otto was right, of course.

They found the black stallion next to a massive ash tree. Otto mounted the beast and kept pace behind them. With each jostling step, Lyra's backside ached.

It made her breathing labored as she tried to hold her breath to keep from crying out. She pressed a hand to her chest and tried to breathe around the pain.

"Do we need to stop?" Wilder asked.

"No. I just want to be there already."

She wanted to be anywhere but where she was. In pain, pressed against him. It increased with that thought, but was different.

A searing burn lashed down her hip and leg, all the way down to her toes, and she screamed. Wilder yanked the horse to a stop.

"Gods, woman! What is it?"

"Something—something bit me!" she shrieked, scrubbing at her hip and thigh. She felt something crawling under her hand and flung herself off the horse.

Wilder was right behind her, staring at her with a confused and horrified expression.

Lyra didn't care. Something had bitten her, and it felt creepy and crawly. She ran in place as if she could dislodge whatever it was and ripped at her clothing.

"Otto—" Wilder barked as he continued to stare at Lyra as she flailed about.

"I can't see," Otto breathed, his face twisting in confusion.

Wilder gripped hold of her hands, keeping her still.

"Stop moving for one second so I can see," he ground out against her lurching.

There was a command in his voice she hadn't heard before, so despite the pain and the icky feeling, she halted. But she couldn't help the bouncing of her leg or the tremor down her spine.

"Gods," Wilder whispered, as something dropped from her and onto the ground.

It was about the size of an acorn and almost as dark as the fertile earth beneath their feet, but with eight long and hairy legs.

"It's a witch's curse spider."

Lyra blanched, her skin becoming as pale as the fog the sun had burned off earlier that morning.

She hadn't been able to read the book in their library about spiders. The image on the first page had given her nightmares for weeks.

"Is that bad?"

She began whimpering from the pain that burned down her leg and was spreading up through her torso.

Wilder looked at her, and she could see it written on his face.

"It's not good."

25
BALANCE

Fuck. He was a godsdamned idiot for not brushing her off after she had lain on the forest floor.

While not rare, the witch's curse spider wasn't common either. Usually, they stayed close to skinwalkers, feeding off whatever corpse they had skinned and left to rot.

Their bite wasn't lethal to elves, but you would wish it was.

The pain was unbearable, and he had seen five-hundred-year-old warriors beg for death and cry for their mothers. It took days for the venom to work out of your system—without the antidote.

There was a balance to everything.

Including spider venom. But the woodlark flower didn't bloom at this time of year.

There was only one place it would be—the castle.

Wilder watched as Lyra's face turned from pale to ghastly. She tugged up her shirt, and the blackened venom of the spider was visible as it coursed through her veins.

"Am I going to die?"

Wilder stepped towards her, tugging her shirt down and out of her grip.

"*No*. But this will hurt. I need to get you to the castle."

She wobbled on unsteady legs. The pain must be excruciating, but she didn't cry. Her voice hadn't even trembled when she asked after her fate.

"You will be alright. I'm going to touch you now to get you on that horse."

Lyra weakly nodded.

Wilder gripped her, throwing her back up on the horse.

"If you can't keep up—fall back," he threw over his shoulder to the rest of the group.

"Wilder—" Otto yelled before they took off. "You *will* make it."

Wilder breathed a small sigh of relief and took off.

She was on fire. Where her skin had grazed him, burned. He was astonished she wasn't screaming.

"It will be alright," he whispered to her when she whimpered louder.

Trees passed in a blur as he pushed them on. He needed that flower. Needed it right now.

With one hand on the reins, he held her to his chest. The heat coming off of her scorched his skin, but he didn't let go, didn't loosen his grip a fraction.

His skin sweat and then blistered where it touched her. Wilder ground his teeth against the pain. If it hurt him merely touching her skin, it was unfathomable what she must be feeling.

He chanced a look at her then. Her auburn hair clung to the sweat on her face, her cheeks scarlet, either from the heat or the wind burn, and her once lush and rosy lips were now ashen gray and dry as tree bark. Lashes fluttered against her cheeks as she squeezed her eyes shut.

"It's alright. You will be alright," Wilder repeated over the sound of clopping hooves and wind.

It was the only comfort he could offer.

The only thing he could think of to say, and he would make it so.

Lyra's head bounced against his chest, and her body went boneless as she passed out. Good, that was probably for the best.

When he passed through the wards of his kingdom, his breath came steadier. The light buzzing across his skin was a relief. He was close—so close.

The wildness of the moors opened up before him as he slipped from the forest edge to the rolling hills outside the palace gates. Mounds of evergreen grasses rippled in the wind between tufts of heather, and a light mist rose from the ground.

It was a mosaic of purple, green, and gray. He followed the well-kept path switchbacking through the high hills to the city gates.

Large hand-cut silver stones sparkled in the early morning light. A horn sounded at his arrival, and even from a distance, he could hear the squeaking of the wheel turning to open the gates. The castle rose beyond the great stone wall.

Long ago, it was only a wall around a colossal hill. But some distant ancestor had carved the stone out of the hill to create the magnificent castle. Peaks, battlements, and towers, all intricately carved from the gleaming stone.

Lyra whimpered, and he prodded the horse faster. He didn't slow as he passed through the gates or the cobblestone streets of the Lower District.

Thankfully, it was early enough that not too many people were out yet. He launched the horse over crates of food and barrels of ale, much to the chagrin of vendors setting up for the market.

Cries rang out through windows as children woke for the day, their mothers pulling closed the shutters as he passed. He would have felt guilty if not for the fading scent of the woman in his arms. Her pulse was slowing as the venom took root.

The wooden bridge that separated the Lower District from the Upper District came into view, and his grip on the reins tightened. He was almost there. The wood thudded as they passed over the bridge and navigated through the tree-lined streets of the Upper District. There were fewer elves on the streets here.

Flowers lined the windows instead of laundry. Shutters blocked out light and sound, leaving the occupants inside blissfully unaware of the prince streaking through the streets.

As he came upon the small courtyard that separated the castle from the people, he yanked the horse to a halt and slid off, taking Lyra with him. He carried her in both arms, racing up the steps and calling for a healer.

Healers were a rarity only the nobility could afford. The bloodline of the witches with the gift had faded. Fewer and fewer were learning the craft.

Wilder stomped through the towering archway and into the greeting hall. His muddy footprints were left behind on the polished black-and-white marble floor.

A flurry of servants rushed to help him. But no one could help him. He needed a healer. When a spindly elf with long limbs and the complexion of peat moss reached for Lyra, Wilder growled at him in warning.

"I need a healer—*now!*"

"I'm coming, I'm coming. Settle yourself," a voice of many answered.

An elder witch. She was neither young nor old; she simply was. And her voice wasn't hers alone, but all of her ancestors speaking through her at once.

"She was bitten by a witch's curse," Wilder replied, looking down at Lyra.

"Bring her to my workroom. I've got some woodlark brewing."

Wilder had a difficult time looking at the witch. She was the same size as Lyra, but her presence had the hair on the back of his neck rising. She didn't walk either. No, she hovered over the ground like a specter.

Her eyes were as golden as the sun, and they burned as such. Dressed in the finest lilac gown, she should have blended in with the rest of the nobility, but there was no hiding what she was.

"It's good to have you back, Prince. Your father was worried."

The witch attempted casual conversation. It was futile. He couldn't formulate a coherent thought until Lyra was awake and healed.

Passing statues of distant ancestors and heroic elves, Wilder breathed through clenched teeth. But when he passed a mirror, his reflection almost gave him pause.

He was back to his true self now and not the humanesque facade that slipped on him the moment he stepped outside of the wards. Briars grew from his scalp around the crown of his head, his ears were sharply pointed, and the otherworldliness wrapped around him like a familiar cloak.

The glittering gold wouldn't come off his skin, no matter how much he had scrubbed at it. His mother had once crooned that he was made of gold-flecked silver stone. He despised it. It made camouflaging himself at night difficult.

An ancient door made of ash wood creaked open as the witch approached, and torches flickered to life as they trudged down the smooth steps. It smelled of herbs and smoke down here.

The healer's workrooms were one of the few places he avoided. A monstrous fireplace crackled with green flames as the fire consumed driftwood from the shores on the east side of the kingdom. Bubbling sounded from the cauldron, hovering over the flames as the witch waltzed up to it.

She ladled a teacup full of violet tea and handed it to the prince.

"She needs to ingest at least half of that cup. Maybe more."

Wilder looked from Lyra to the cup. The witch nodded towards the worktable that was pushed into the corner.

"You can set her on that."

He carried Lyra's lifeless body to the table and set her down with a gentle reverence before taking the cup from the witch. She helped him angle Lyra's head just right. He blew on the tea to cool it down before he pressed it to her lips.

"Legs, I need you to drink this. It's the antidote."

Lyra's lips opened a fraction, and the skin cracked and bled. When she opened her mouth wide enough, he poured some of the tea in. The inside of her mouth was full of blisters from the heat. His chest ached.

Such pain, such excruciating pain she had endured.

Wilder stopped pouring, and Lyra heaved a breath before opening her mouth wider.

"More, Prince," the witch ordered.

He lifted the teacup and poured more into her waiting mouth. Lyra gulped it down, keeping her mouth open for more.

She reminded him of the baby birds being fed by their mothers, but he didn't think she would appreciate the joke. When he had poured the entire cup of tea into her mouth, her eyes opened.

Red-rimmed and glassy, she looked at him before turning her gaze to the witch.

"Thank you ..." she trailed off, not knowing the witch's name.

"Jordania," the witch answered with a hesitant smile.

"Jordania," Lyra replied before her eyes slid closed once more.

"She will probably sleep for the rest of the day, and then she will be hungry. Make sure she eats plenty of fruit. The acidity will purify her blood," Jordania ordered him.

Wilder looked relieved, his shoulders relaxing, and his breathing came easier.

"Thank you, *Jordania*."

It was the first time he had ever addressed a witch, and he felt the stirrings of guilt. She nodded before whirling away to a rack full of dried herbs.

Wilder eased Lyra off the table and back into his arms, the action familiar to him now. He walked out of the workroom and into the hallway. A servant was there and waiting for him. A young elf with white flowers in her light blue hair. She smiled exuberantly at him.

"We have a room ready for the princess, Your Highness. She is to be on the north wing—near you."

Wilder clenched his teeth. Of course, she was. When the servant's smile faded, he gave a dip of his chin.

"Lead the way."

She beamed at him then and scooped up the hem of her ruffled cream uniform. Her footsteps pitter-pattered against the marble as if she walked on her toes.

Wilder looked down at Lyra and noted the subtle changes. The scarlet of her cheeks was fading to a rosy red, the cracks in her lips were smoothing away, and the ghastly color of her skin now resembled the alabaster of the statues instead.

He was so enraptured at taking in these changes, he almost ran into the servant who had led him to a blue door right across the hall from him.

"Shall I attend to her, Your Highness?"

"*No*. Let her sleep," Wilder replied and nodded to the door.

The servant pushed the door open with a smile and stepped back, allowing him entry. He swept inside, heading for the large iron bed on the opposite wall. It was a grand room for a hostage, but that was the kind of king his father was.

Wilder placed Lyra on top of the downy comforter. He ripped a blanket off a nearby velvet chair and draped it over her.

"I'm going to bathe. Send for me the moment she wakes," Wilder ordered the young elf. "And don't touch her—she doesn't like to be touched."

26
DAISY

Cool air licked at her skin, and she was grateful the flames had extinguished. Lyra clenched her hands at her sides and felt the softness she had sunk into. She was lying on a bed, the softest bed she had ever felt. It made the bed at the tavern feel like a boulder.

Peeling open one eye, she was met with a stunning mural of wild, lush land and emerald trees. Tall, willowy women danced between tree trunks and orbs of golden light.

A throat cleared from beside her, and she turned to see Wilder. He had bathed, and his damp hair was brushed back, giving her a full view of the thick band of briars that wrapped from one side of his head to the other like a crown. The point of an ear peeked out behind his dark hair.

He was back in his true form. His fingers drummed upon the arms of a crimson velvet chair, and she marveled at the length of his fingers, the bulges of veins visible on his forearms. A black tunic with a standing collar enhanced the broadness of his shoulders and the length of his neck.

He was regrettably attractive and pristine.

And Lyra—she was filthy from their travels and her brush with death. She could feel the dirt clinging to the dried sweat on her face and arms. She almost cringed deeper into the bed, but didn't want to ruin it further with her muck.

"How are you feeling?" Wilder asked.

He shifted in the chair, leaning forward, and stared at her with all the intensity of an elvish male who was used to being answered.

"Fine," she croaked out, wetting her lips with her tongue.

Her mouth was dry like she had swallowed a handful of sand.

Wilder grasped the glass of water off the bedside table and extended it to her. Lyra watched as a droplet of condensation ran down the side of the green glass and lurched up. Taking it in both hands, she gulped it down and looked around for more.

He chuckled, standing from the chair and grabbing a pewter pitcher to pour her more.

"I'll call up for some food. I'm sure you're hungry."

Lyra nodded as she drained the entire glass again.

"I'll send for the servant to draw your bath."

Lyra's eyes flashed with humiliation and challenge.

"Are you saying I smell?"

"Terribly so," Wilder threw over his shoulder as he walked for the door. "Take it easy tonight. The king has requested an audience with you tomorrow."

Lyra looked from Wilder to the window opposite her room. The thick burgundy curtains were drawn up tight, leaving her no clues about the time of day.

Wilder leaned his back against the door and crossed his arms over his chest.

"It's just past seven in the evening. This room will be

guarded day and night, so don't even think about leaving. Bathe, eat, and then sleep. I'll fetch you in the morning."

He slipped out the door before she could remark about his use of the word fetch.

She flexed her toes and wiggled her fingers before ripping off the blanket and pulling up her shirt. There was not a trace of the venom that had blackened her veins. And her body felt strange. Lyra wasn't sure if it was from the venom or being around elvish magic. But she felt taller, stronger, somehow. There were no longer blisters on her feet, but her head felt foggy, as if the slumber she had awakened from did not want to release her.

Sliding out of bed, her feet landed on a plush, woven rug. It was like the mural on the ceiling, but close up, she could make out rabbits, birds, and even what she thought was a unicorn.

She glanced around the room, becoming curious. A long dresser, a tall armoire, and several doors she had no idea what could be behind. There was also a vanity placed to absorb the light that would stream through the windows if the curtains were not drawn.

Lyra headed that way first, hoping to glean some kind of inkling of where her room was. But as she made her way across the room on sure feet, a key slid into the lock and her door opened.

She rolled her eyes.

A tiny elf female with daisies in her periwinkle hair stood with an armload of fabrics. The female beamed at her, and the kindness in her smile had Lyra narrowing her eyes.

"My name is Daisy, and I'm here to tend to you, my lady. I'll draw you a bath first, and then we can go through these dresses."

She had never had anyone attend to her before, and she had preferred the movement the pants afforded. "I don't require your assistance. You may leave."

Daisy pursed her lips and gave a slight shake of her head. "I am under orders from the king."

Lyra placed her hands on her hips. "It is *unnecessary*." She hadn't expected a servant to argue.

"I'm sure where you came from it is. But here it is a *requirement*. Now—if that is all. How do you like your water?" Daisy dropped the pile of fabrics on the bed and then shuffled to the bathing room.

Lyra stared in shock before gathering her wits and following Daisy. She hadn't been rude, but she had handled Lyra with a firm hand. Lyra respected that.

Leaning against the doorway, she watched as Daisy turned a copper handle. Water started pouring from a pipe beside a large tub. Lyra leapt from the door to study the contraption.

"There's water behind the walls?"

Daisy straightened and took a step back. The action had Lyra's excitement sputtering out. She had frightened the poor girl.

"S-sorry, my lady," Daisy muttered.

"No, that's alright. You should be afraid. You don't know me or my intentions. I like my water hot—scorching even," Lyra replied before taking a step towards the mirror across the bathing chamber to give Daisy room to work.

It was a beautiful room. There was a worktop below the mirror with two of those copper things that Daisy had used to turn on the water. Lyra found herself curious and turned the knob. Water began pouring from the copper again. She stuck her fingers beneath the stream and smiled to herself. Now this was magic. Her movement caught her attention, and she looked at her reflection.

It was frightening. Dark shadows bloomed beneath her eyes, and her pale skin looked horrifying, like all the life had been drained from her. Streaks of auburn hair stuck to her forehead, and matted waves hung limply down her chest. She didn't look like a princess anymore.

A heavenly scent wafted from the steam rising behind her, and she turned to find Daisy pouring an array of vials into the tub. It seemed to be quite a lot of work to draw her a bath. Lyra found herself hoping that was common and not extra effort because of her current appearance.

"What is that?" she asked, watching as Daisy spooned something granular into the water.

"This is mineral salts," she looked over at Lyra, "it's good for sore muscles and weary bones after traveling."

"And what was that other stuff?" Lyra gestured to the array of vials near the tub.

"A variety of oils. Eucalyptus for energy, almond oil for dryness, and argan."

"What's the argan for?" Lyra asked when Daisy didn't provide an explanation.

"It's to help with your hair. It's quite matted, my lady."

Lyra appreciated her honesty and directness, even if her delivery was timid. The water filled the tub nearly to the rim before Daisy shut it off.

"I can step outside—" Daisy began.

Lyra had shucked her shirt and was pulling a pant leg off. There was an eagerness in her to return to the water that she hadn't expected. It wasn't that the water smelled amazing, but the grime of the last week clung to Lyra like a bad dream she could awaken from if she could only wash it off.

She moaned with ecstasy as she slipped one foot into the hot water. It was divine. Lyra sank deeper into the tub and could feel the anxiety and stress melting away.

When she dunked her head under the surface, she contemplated staying there forever. It was home, the water and her soul belonged to it.

Panic tightened her chest as fear gripped her; she could never go back. Lyra lurched out of the water, spluttering.

"Are you alright?" Daisy squeaked out, reaching for a towel and dabbing Lyra's face.

"I can't breathe underwater."

"Blessed three, no! You're not a mermaid anymore."

It didn't matter how kindly Daisy had said the words. Hearing them out loud was excruciating. A silent tear rolled down Lyra's cheek before dropping into the water. Her tears could return, but she could not.

She didn't want to cry.

If only part of her could return—then none of her could.

Daisy reached towards Lyra and then paused.

"Is it alright if I wash your hair?"

Lyra's brow raised as if tugged by an invisible string. Wasn't that her job? Why was she asking …

Wilder.

He must have told Daisy that Lyra didn't like to be touched. She wanted to roll her eyes. It was fine if others had touched her, just not him.

Lyra jerked her chin down, and Daisy proceeded.

Daisy was a goddess. Her fingers on Lyra's scalp were the closest to joy she had ever felt. It was so utterly delightful, Lyra closed her eyes.

"What is that song?" Daisy asked, her hands pausing.

Gods. Lyra had hummed and hadn't even realized it.

"A song from Atlantis," Lyra murmured. "I'm sorry."

"Don't apologize, my lady. It was beautiful."

Lyra's cheeks burned. Everyone was so nice here—it was throwing her off-kilter.

"Daisy," Lyra began.

"Hmm?"

"What does 'blessed three' mean?"

Lyra blinked her eyes open to see a small smile lighting

Daisy's face. "It's just an exclamation. The blessed three are the goddesses Aradia, Tiandra, and Mab."

"Oh, I see. And that's something elves say?"

Daisy nodded and proceeded to scrub the entirety of Lyra's skin and hair, not once, but twice, and then had Lyra stand. Water ran in rivulets down her body, and she marveled at the beauty of her skin now. A healthy flush and glow of vitality.

A small part of her had come back to life. But water had a way of doing that. Whether it was nourishing you from the inside out, the body always craved it.

Daisy held open a large white fabric and gestured for Lyra to step closer. When Lyra did, Daisy enveloped her in the fabric and gave her a gentle squeeze. She then stepped back and patted Lyra's body down before squeezing the excess water out of her hair with it.

"What is that?"

"It's a towel," Daisy replied, continuing to squeeze Lyra's hair.

If Daisy was annoyed with the multitude of Lyra's questions, she didn't let on. And Lyra found herself relieved. She didn't enjoy asking, but her curiosity rarely cared how she truly felt.

"And it dries off water?"

"Mmm, not all of it, but most of it." Daisy grabbed a dress, but this one was open completely in the front. "This is a robe," she murmured and then slipped it on Lyra before tying it around her so that it wasn't open any longer.

The fabric was soft against her skin, and the green of it matched her eyes. There was intricate stitching up the sleeves and shoulders of it.

"What is this fabric?"

"It's silk. Do you like it?" Daisy asked, stepping back and looking at Lyra.

"It's incredible," she breathed.

"I made it." Daisy beamed with pride. "That will help us

narrow down the dresses you like. Follow me," she instructed as she strutted back into the bedroom.

Feeling revitalized, Lyra bounced as she walked back into her bedroom. The dresses were piled in a heap on the bed, and Daisy grabbed the first one. It was the same silk fabric as the robe, but in a cheery yellow color. Lyra shook her head.

"No?" Daisy asked, looking from Lyra to the dress.

"Yellow isn't my color," Lyra answered.

"My lady, every color is your color."

Lyra blushed again but shook her head.

Daisy held up the next dress. It was garish. Large skirts and jewel-toned beads on the neckline.

Lyra shook her head again, and Daisy sighed. The next dress she held up was a grayish-blue silk gown with a low-cut neckline and a straight skirt. It resembled a flower petal.

"Yes," Lyra breathed and stepped closer to run her fingers down the length of the gown.

"It is quite beautiful," Daisy murmured. She didn't move to set it down but rather stood there patiently and let Lyra admire it.

"You can show me the next one now, Daisy," Lyra said as she stopped stroking the gown.

The next was a similar cut to the last but had dainty straps and was in the same color as a fruit she had read about. She couldn't quite remember the name, and she racked her brain, searching for it.

"What is this color?"

"Plum."

Lyra nodded. "Plum. I like this one, too."

When she yawned and covered her mouth, Daisy smiled at her.

"We don't have to go through the rest. I have an inkling of what you like now."

Lyra cocked her head, looking at the pile of dresses they had yet to go through.

"And what inkling is that?"

Daisy grinned and set the plum dress down. "You like things dark—that feel like the water."

Lyra snorted. Daisy had no idea how right she was.

"I'll ring for your food and bid you farewell, my lady. If you need anything else at all, pull that chain to the right of the door."

Lyra watched as Daisy hung up several gowns in the armoire before hefting colorful ones over her shoulder and leaving.

Pressing a hand to her stomach, Lyra felt hollow, but it wasn't from hunger.

27
NO KING OF MINE

Every disturbance in the night had Wilder staring at his bedroom door. Surely she wouldn't try to escape on her first night, especially after the toll the venom had taken on her body.

Another creaking noise in the hall had Wilder striding to his bedroom door.

Dust and Oron, guards Wilder knew and respected, were posted outside her door.

"Did you need something, Wilder?" Dust asked, trying to conceal the smirk on his face as he took in Wilder's night-clothes.

"Has she attempted anything?" Wilder asked, squaring his shoulders.

"No," Oron replied.

Wilder liked Oron the best; he was a male of few words.

"She fell asleep right after she ate. We'll let you know if we hear anything," Dust offered, with a dip of his chin.

"I appreciate that," Wilder replied, before slipping back into his room.

He had slept little while in the mortal realm, and though he rarely required much, he suffered from a bone-deep exhaustion. The meeting tomorrow would take all of his energy, so he would need to at least get a few hours.

But he couldn't get Lyra off his mind.

It took a few more hours, but sleep took him.

The following morning, Wilder paced outside Lyra's door. The guards had switched out already, and the morning duty took over their watches. Wilder didn't recognize these guards, and he was in no mood for conversation.

The blue-haired servant had curtsied as she passed him earlier before entering Lyra's room to help her ready for her audience with the King.

"How long does it take one female to get ready?" Wilder grumbled under his breath.

The guards on either side of the door didn't acknowledge his rhetorical question or react to his rising frustration at all. They were well-trained.

Lyra's door opened, and Wilder lurched to a stop.

He was done for. She was a creature of infinite beauty and his most achingly intimate desires.

A long gown of purple clung to her body and accentuated all of her curves. The long column of her neck looked even longer beside the thin straps that held the dress.

If he had been a painter, he would have tried all his life to paint her as he saw her now. She was exquisite.

Her eyes blazed brighter as she beheld him, and a small smirk tugged up her lips. She had left her hair down, and the auburn tresses floated up around her face. His magic reached for her and stirred the air.

Time stopped, and Wilder drew a slow, deep breath.

Lyra pressed her lips together.

"We're going to be late."

The small bit of delight on Lyra's face vanished. Like wind snuffing out a flame.

He turned, giving her his back, and strode down the hall. Leaving her, flanked by two guards, to follow him.

"Do you know the reason for this meeting?" Lyra called after Wilder.

He slowed then, if only so he didn't have to yell through the palace.

"One would assume it's the negotiation part of your kidnapping."

Lyra snorted, and he clenched his jaw.

"Obviously—but do you know why?"

Wilder thought back to what Otto had told him. His father was going to offer her a deal. He wouldn't like it, and she would agree.

This meeting was as life-altering for him as it would be for her, it seemed. He kept walking without answering her, and he could feel her impatience growing.

"Swell conversation," she muttered.

Wilder ground his teeth to staunch the well of emotions that bubbled up. She could get under his skin quicker than anyone he had ever met.

"Even if I did know, I couldn't tell you. I have or—"

"Orders," Lyra huffed. "You're so honorable in your duty, Prince."

He didn't know why that bothered him so much. Of course, he was honorable and followed the orders his father handed him. But that didn't mean that's all he was. He had thoughts and ideas of his own—even if he didn't listen to them.

The doorway to the throne room loomed ahead. Wilder straightened his spine and squared his shoulders.

He knew he would not like this, but he liked little of what he had to do daily. What was one more thing?

The guards on either side of the grand, arched doorway left their positions to pull the golden antler door handles open.

Wilder could hear Lyra's breath catch as the room opened up before them. His father's throne room was the Wilds personified.

Evergreen trees held up the domed ceiling. The floor was the same glittering stone that had made up the foundation of the hill the castle was built on, and it sparkled like the sun upon the sea.

Hundreds of elves turned to stare at them as they walked on the dark green runner that lay the length of the colossal room.

He turned and glanced at Lyra, who kept pace beside him. Her chin raised as she held her head high despite the malevolent glares from those they passed. Curses were hissed at her and, if he wasn't mistaken, a few of them spat at the train of her purple gown.

Fury surged through his veins at that offense. He caught the eye of a noble-born elf. Her ethereal glow and flowing gown were covered in glittering jewels. The glare he gave her had the flowers in her hair shriveling up and dying.

Wilder raised a hand, letting his magic flow. The wind carved a path through the room so that no one else could spit or hiss curses at her as they passed.

A page dressed in evergreen robes moved from beside his father's dais.

The throne sat high up on the wide stairs. Two massive emerald trees, with their trunks bent and split, created the seat of the chair and towering back. Bushels of heather frozen in time, and other flora native to the Wilds, sprouted around it. They appeared to have been carved from the land and dropped into the room.

It was transcendent and savage.

"His Majesty, Oberon, High King of the Wilds!" the page called.

Everyone in the room bowed. Wilder could feel his father's heavy gaze on him before it settled onto a still-standing Lyra.

"Bow," Wilder hissed under his breath. Lyra slid her gaze to him, and he watched as her upper lip curled back from her teeth.

"Do you not feel it necessary to bow to the King?" Oberon's voice thundered through the hall, similar to a thousand charging horses.

Wilder squeezed his eyes shut and took a deep breath. She was going to die within the first few moments of ever meeting his father. It had been pointless to work so tirelessly to keep her on this side of the ground when she was adamant to be laid beneath it.

"You're no King of mine," Lyra replied, her voice was so steady, as if she were merely discussing the weather.

Gasps swelled throughout the elves gathered.

"Leave us!"

28
THE
BARGAIN

The wind couldn't have flown faster than the speed at which the elves fled the throne room. Only four remained.

Wilder, Otto, Ridge, and Maelys.

Lyra gave them a quick once-over and tried to hide the alarm on her face. They were different here in their true forms. Maelys had been lovely before, but now she looked like a ray of sunshine.

Glimmering golden-brown hair, a smattering of freckles across her pert nose and cheeks, eyes sparkling. The very air seemed to swirl around her, giving her the appearance of floating as her blush gown rippled and swirled. A tiny blue bird was perched on her shoulder, nuzzling her neck.

Otto had iridescent skin and milky eyes that looked more through you than at you. Long white hair was decorated with black beads that had markings carved into them. His light gray tunic and matching breeches matched the color his eyes had been in the mortal realm.

Ridge was the most startling. More tree than elf. His dark skin was marked with black ink, a swirling pattern that hadn't been visible in the mortal realm. He had cropped hair that looked similar to the dark green moss that grew on the majestic trees in the Valewood.

Each of them had an otherworldly glow to them and sharply pointed ears that marked them as elves. As if they could have been anything else. Now that she thought about it, even their human forms hadn't seemed very human.

"Now that the prying eyes and ears are gone. Allow me to welcome you, Princess Lyra of Atlantis," Oberon said.

His voice had shifted. It wasn't the powerful booming of the King that had sat before her. It was softer now.

"Come closer, Princess."

Lyra's brow furrowed, and her eyes darted around the room. She couldn't decide whether he was being serious or if this was all some elaborate ruse. Hadn't this elf ordered her abduction?

Guards appeared on either side of the colossal throne, and a few descended to her level. They wore evergreen tunics and golden capes with stag horns embroidered on their chests.

Before she could decide whether she would like to walk up the stairs, a guard with dark hair and a sneer gripped her arm right above her elbow and began dragging her to King Oberon.

Lyra struggled against his grip, but he didn't let go.

"Unhand her," Wilder snapped. "She doesn't like to be touched."

Lyra turned to see Wilder snarling in the guard's face. Relief coursed through her, and blood pumped through her arm once more.

Oberon monitored the entire exchange and rubbed a finger across his jaw.

Wilder stood beside her and tilted his head towards his father.

"Please listen. For once in your life," he murmured.

Lyra had an argument on the tip of her tongue, but the crease that formed between his brows silenced her. He was truly concerned about this meeting. She hadn't been—until now.

"Fine," she huffed.

Oberon's brows raised when she agreed to Wilder's plea.

She gripped the train of her gown, refusing his outstretched arm, and stomped up the stairs. Her velvet slippers slapped against the stone steps.

The king rose and met her halfway. She steeled her spine to keep from trembling.

An elvish king, the High King, was standing mere feet from her. Talk of his power was legendary, as were the battles he fought in and the enemies he'd slain.

He was a direct descendant of Fionn.

She was nothing compared to him, and she felt it deep in her bones.

His eyes raked across her, and a small smirk curved his lips.

"I've heard whispers of your beauty and, for once, the rumors were not wrong. You are very beautiful—for a mermaid," he said, stepping closer to her.

Her hands squeezed into fists as she fought against the desire to take a step away.

He smelled of the earth, ancient and never-ending. There were leaves braided into strands of his long hair and a crown of golden antlers upon his brow. His emerald tunic and pants were intricately embroidered with golden thread in the swirling patterns of the trees and flowers of his kingdom.

For all the wealth she was accustomed to, it shouldn't have surprised her the luxury of this place, but it did.

Oberon leaned in close to her. "A little birdie has whispered to me of your power."

Lyra's eyes slid from the king to Wilder. "I have no power."

King Oberon tutted. "Now, now, there's no need to lie, Princess."

Lyra focused back on the king before her. She had to tilt her head to stare into his eyes, but with her clenched jaw and frosty gaze, she let him know it did not make her feel inferior.

"I do not touch it."

The king tilted his head at that. "Does it not live within you?"

Lyra's nostrils flared.

The maneuvering here was different from in Atlantis, and it was so quiet, not a shifting foot or the unending pull of the current.

"It does. But that does not mean it should."

"Interesting," he stroked his chin, "is that why you won't use it now? You could but speak the words and return home."

All this talk about her power had her heart racing, the golden thread of magic pulsing with each beat. Lyra could only shake her head.

"What could I offer you to wield it?"

Lyra swallowed and breathed through her nose.

This was dangerous, extremely dangerous.

One did not make deals with the elves. Hell, one should not even be conversing with them.

"Nothing." She shook her head.

She needed to get out of here. This had been a rotten idea. She should have taken her chance with the humans or lived wild in the forest over this. She should have escaped when she had the chance.

Oberon circled her before heading back to his throne. He sat with a graceful flourish before addressing her again.

"Ah—it's because you don't know how. You never learned."

Lyra's heart stopped, and the very air vanished from her lungs. But she had mastered her face into one of boredom, like she had done for years and years surrounded by her father's court.

She learned not to give anything away, even if he was right.

Lyra had never learned to wield and was afraid even now that it would kill her the moment she tried.

"What if I told you that I could teach you not only how to wield it, but that I could also grant you your true form and thus return you to the water?"

Her eyes narrowed on his face, his magnificent and wondrous face.

"*How?*"

He smiled then, knowing he held her interest. He offered her exactly what she wanted—a way home.

"There has been an imbalance of power for far too long between the humans and the merfolk. Help me right it, and I will grant you your freedom and your form back."

She feigned a chuckle and tugged at the silk fabric on her thigh. This was all a ruse. A cruel trick. She could never return, and she would never be free.

It wasn't possible. She hadn't completed the tithe—there was no going back. This is what every book warning her about the elves had said about their impossible bargains.

"I didn't complete the tithe," Lyra replied.

King Oberon crossed one long leg over the other and stared at her with the maniacal delight you see when someone knows they are winning.

He had her, and he knew it.

"You mean the tithe that is disrupting the delicate balance of magic? The very thing I want you to undo?"

Lyra ground her teeth to keep from reacting as she wanted to. Had she retained her sharp claws, she would have raked them across his neck. She locked her knees into place to keep the wrath from vibrating her legs.

Typical elfish arrogance to think anything the merfolk did was unnatural.

"The tithe balances our magic and increases the fertility of my people."

Lyra hadn't felt Wilder approaching, but when he brushed beside her, she took a breath. She had stepped forward without realizing it.

King Oberon stared at where Wilder's tunic brushed against her bare arm.

"It doesn't allow for anything of the sort."

Lyra's vision was clouded red. Her fury pulsed inside of her, right next to her beating heart.

A roaring filled her ears, and it was only Wilder's voice that broke through.

"Breathe," Wilder whispered, and brushed a cool breeze against her face as she inhaled.

"The tithe was a deal struck between the merfolk and the humans," Oberon explained. "It had nothing to do with fertility or keeping your magic balanced. In fact, the very bargain of only taking twelve human lives for the life of one mermaid had strengthened your magic beyond its normal bounds for a time."

His words were a blow to her heart.

A bargain? The merfolk had made a bargain with the humans and exchanged one of their own for a sacrifice?

Lyra shook her head. This could not be true. Females, although not in any position of power, were coveted because of their breeding potential.

"That's not true."

King Oberon smiled at her then, a gleeful, wicked smile. "Is it true that births have decreased throughout your population even though there is still a tithe every year?"

"Yes, but—"

"And is it true that one mermaid never makes it back from the tithe?"

"*Again*, yes. But—"

"But what? Everything I have said is true," Oberon said as if that put an end to things.

"Well, if you would allow me to speak, you would have known what my answer was," Lyra seethed.

Her chest heaved, and her nails carved little crescent moons into her palms.

Oberon's smile fell away, and his brow rose. "Do you speak to your father in such a manner?"

"*Always*." Lyra smiled then, showing a bit of the monster under her skin.

Wilder swallowed then, and she could feel him shift towards her. She was prodding this king of kings and didn't care about the consequences.

They had kidnapped her and were now coercing her into a bargain.

"I'm not sure what else you would have expected from me. You ordered your son to kidnap me, hindering me from completing the tithe and returning home. I was raced across the realm in abhorrent conditions," Lyra glared at Wilder before swinging her gaze back to the king, "ambushed by wulvers, bitten by a spider, and now you're telling me my entire life has been a lie? Did you expect me to rejoice in these circumstances and willingly accept your offer?"

The king opened his mouth to speak, but Lyra cut him off.

"I'm only in this predicament because you males think you can just take whatever you want and damn the consequences. I will not be a part of this. *So kill me now or set me free.*"

29
QUEEN MOMMY

Wilder couldn't believe what was happening. She had lost her mind, not only to speak to the High King this way, but to have cut him off when he was speaking.

Any moment now, his father would cut the very air off from her lungs, and she would die.

"She's not wrong," Wilder's mother said, walking down the long green runner towards them. Her burgundy gown resembled the calla lilies in her garden.

King Oberon shifted in his chair to get a look at his wife and smiled a genuine smile.

"I was wondering when you would interject yourself, my dear."

The queen smiled in return, taking his hand and standing beside the throne. Not behind the king, but directly beside him.

"Princess Lyra, this is my wife, Queen Aine."

Aine gazed down at Lyra, a smile fighting to make its presence known on her stunning face.

She was ethereal and warm. Not at all what some had pictured for the Queen of the Wilds. Peaceful and serene.

It had been a divisive time in his father's rule when he married her instead of whatever courtier his father had selected.

Lyra jerked her chin down in greeting.

"Darling," Aine crooned to Wilder.

"Mother." Wilder nodded.

"It has been a long time since anyone has spoken to my husband that way. I quite enjoyed it," Aine mused.

Lyra stared straight ahead, deadpan.

Wilder could tell she was trying to read this interaction beyond the words that were said. A small crease formed between her brows as she thought through each slight movement and tone of voice.

"We will not be killing you—today at least," Aine said, looking at Lyra. "To be frank, your life after this bargain could be better than the meager existence you had as the princess of Atlantis. So, if you were clever, *girl*, you would accept this deal. This plan might be foolish, but it's the only one being offered to you."

Wilder looked between his parents. It was not often they corrected each other, at least not in front of others.

His mother either hadn't known of this plan or did not approve of it.

Lyra crossed her arms the moment his mother called her girl, and he could feel the ire radiating off of her.

"You have yet to explain how she will help you restore balance," Wilder said.

Not just to diffuse what was about to be a descent into chaos, but to further understand what his part might be in all of this.

King Oberon looked away from his wife and studied Wilder and Lyra.

"She has unmatched power. Her voice could command gods

and weave fate. I need her only to speak the words to undo the tithe. That is all, no more, no less."

Lyra was shaking her head from side to side; her gown quivered with the movement, sending tiny ripples fluttering through the delicate silk. She was quaking like a newborn fawn.

"I cannot," she said.

"It is not that difficult a task," Aine replied, studying Lyra's unusual reaction.

"I do not use the power. It is absolute. It will corrupt and destroy."

King Oberon pondered her words. "It will if you continue to use it after our bargain."

Lyra screwed her eyes shut and took a deep breath. Her entire body moved with her inhale and exhale. When her eyes opened, she spoke.

"You misunderstand. It will corrupt and destroy me."

Wilder turned towards her then.

She had never said it was a death sentence before. She had only said it would consume her? But all magic did that. It was a rush of ecstasy every time you used it. Was that not what she had meant?

"How do you know?"

Lyra gazed at him. Utter hopelessness poured from her eyes.

It was a stab to the heart.

"The sea witch told me. The power will turn me wholly into a monster. She showed me visions. It was cold—chaos and death."

"The power will only corrupt if you do not know how to control it. That's how magic is," Aine replied, nodding. "I understand your fears. But the only way for you to return home is through this bargain. You need to learn how to wield it, just this once. And then you'll never have to use it again. If you do not, the very fabric of our world will be in jeopardy, and the gods will see fit to intervene."

Lyra bit her bottom lip, and Wilder could tell she was thinking it over.

"Intervene?" Wilder asked.

Oberon nodded, and his expression was grave. "Their intervention would not be welcome—or pleasant."

"What if we offered you one more thing?" Aine's brow rose in one elegant arch. "Your independence."

That word had Lyra's eyes glowing. Something about that had her risking it all. It was worth more to her than the possibility of death.

"So the proposed bargain is: you teach me how to wield my magic so that I can use my voice to break the bargain causing magical imbalance, and then you'll restore my form and free me."

Aine looked at King Oberon, and he looked at her. Something unreadable passed between them for a heartbeat.

Something was off about this bargain. Either his mother or his father knew something else that they would not share.

"If you break the bargain, we will restore your mermaid form and free you."

"Immediately," Lyra added.

Wilder smirked then. She must have known more about the elves than she let on if she was setting a time limit on their bargain.

"Immediately," King Oberon agreed.

Lyra glanced sidelong at Wilder before looking back at the king and queen. Her face blanched, but she nodded her head.

"I accept your bargain."

Queen Aine clapped her hands and beamed.

"Oh! Wonderful! You have made an excellent choice!"

Lyra didn't look like she felt that way at all, and Wilder had to agree. She had agreed to do the one thing she wouldn't even attempt to save herself.

"Your training will start this afternoon. Wilder will be your instructor," King Oberon decreed.

Wilder reeled back in shock. He did not want to be around her any more than necessary, and training would put him around her for hours each day.

King Oberon studied him with a daring expression, and his mother bit back a smile.

"Father, my orders were to bring her here alive. You never said anything about training her—"

King Oberon lowered his brow over his gleaming eyes. "I knew you could get her here, but why would I give you orders based on her decision that hadn't been made yet?"

He gestured with his head to Lyra. The other half of the equation.

"Surely Otto—or even Maelys—would be a better instructor," Wilder argued.

He did not want to do this. In the short week he had been stuck with her, she had burrowed herself beneath his skin.

"You will do it. It is your duty," his father ordered.

Duty.

His father knew what that word meant to him. The responsibility he had struggled with since he was a small child and learned that the survival of their court—the entire realm— would one day fall to him.

Wilder bowed his head, biting back the arguments that were ready to fly off the tip of his tongue.

"I know you don't like to hear about your future," Oberon started.

"Then don't tell me."

Wilder turned on his heel and stalked from the throne.

Otto, Ridge, and Maelys gave him a wide berth. He didn't care at all about the disrespect he had shown to his father or his mother.

Once again, his choice, his independence, had been ripped from him in the name of duty.

One more pound added to the ever-increasing weight on his shoulders. He hated this, hated what he had been born into.

He was envious that Lyra had a shot at freedom, for he knew he never would.

30
DAY ONE

Lyra stared open-mouthed after Wilder as he ripped open the throne room door and left her standing there, alone, in front of his stunned parents. She didn't know whether to laugh or applaud.

Why had he been scolding her for her disrespect, and only to blatantly do it now?

Queen Aine tutted and then heaved a sigh. "I told you this would happen. You should have included us in your scheming, darling."

She addressed her husband as if they were the only two people in the room. It was strange, this balance between them. King Oberon was the king, so he was in power. But he trusted and respected his wife if she was allowed to speak so freely.

"Princess," King Oberon addressed her now. "Maelys will escort you to your room to change and then take you to the training ground. We may have a partnership, but you are still the princess of Merfolk and here under my goodwill. Do not go anywhere without an escort."

Lyra tried to give him her kindest smile. She failed miserably.

Courtly demeanor was never her strength, and the fact that she had agreed to bargain with the High King was making her stomach roil. She had desperately wanted her freedom, but she hadn't thought this through in the slightest. Her breath came out in sharp pants.

"Fine," she replied.

Lyra turned and strode to Maelys without a goodbye or curtsy, following in Wilder's supremely disrespectful footsteps. She had to get out of here—and now.

Maelys blanched and curtsied to her king and queen, awaiting their dismissal, before walking with Lyra out of the throne room.

Once they had breached the doors, Maelys clutched her chest.

"That was tense," she said, shaking her head. "I thought for sure he would strike you down."

Lyra snorted. "I knew he wouldn't kill me."

Maelys yanked her to a stop and stared at her like she had grown two heads. "How?"

"Why go to all that trouble to kidnap and keep me alive just to kill me when no one was there to witness it?"

Maelys shook her head, and the bird on her shoulder clicked its beak.

"You're very sharp today."

Lyra grinned, and it was a thing of horror. "You have no idea."

After changing into pants and a bell-sleeved thin blouse, Lyra stood still as Maelys braided her hair back and out of her face.

"It shouldn't be too miserable today, but just in case you don't want your hair sticking to your sweat."

Lyra grimaced. If she knew anything about Wilder, he would make this miserable. Not just because of his spite for her, but because of the added responsibility that was thrust upon him.

She followed Maelys through the winding maze of the castle. So many hallways and staircases. Light speared through the windows, but they sped past them so Lyra couldn't place their location. She did not know where she was in this place or how to get out of it.

They walked down several hallways and stairs. Her legs burned after the second staircase and were practically impossible to use after the third.

The air became cooler, and the light was nonexistent except for torches hung every so often on the stone walls.

Maelys elbowed open a nondescript wooden door, and sunlight burst through. Lyra screwed her eyes shut and shielded her face with her hand. It was so bright compared to the darkened hallway they had walked down.

The air was crisp as it fluttered by on a gentle breeze. Maelys halted, allowing Lyra to catch her breath and grow accustomed to the light before they walked on.

Lyra glanced behind her, and the castle was gone. Or at least as far as she could tell. In its place was an immense hill.

Maelys turned to see her gaping. "The castle was built on the other side of the hill. There are tunnels and hallways throughout that we use. Like the one we went through, it leads to the training ground and the stables."

"Oh," Lyra replied, bewildered.

It was strange to be partially underground. Living under the water made sense to her, but why would anyone want to live underground? Wasn't that where they placed their dead?

Shaking her head, she followed Maelys through the patches

of heather and tall, wispy grasses. Large flat stones marked their path, and every so often, there was a pole.

"What're these things?" Lyra asked.

It resembled a lantern, but where there should have been a flame, there was nothing but a glass bowl.

"Fairy lights," Maelys replied, shrugging. "It is an orb of light to light your way in the night."

They used magic so freely here, it was astonishing.

"Do you know what my training will consist of?" Lyra asked.

It was easy to talk to Maelys—especially when she spoke back. She guessed the gag order from Wilder had vanished now that she had a deal with their king.

"It will be a mix of physical and mental activities. Similar to what ours was as children when we were learning about our magic and how to control it. "

Lyra did not like the sound of that at all. Her human form was weak. Walking through the castle and onto the grounds had been exhausting.

The strength she had felt last night had evaporated.

They crested another smaller hill and, from the top, they could see the large oval patch of grassless land beneath them. A waist-high stone wall surrounded it, and several tall, willowy trees marked the perimeter on the other side.

Lyra turned in place and could see the massive hill that blocked off the castle behind them. Where were all the elves? Did they live in the castle or in a town somewhere else? A small part of her hoped she'd be able to explore this land one day.

But looking out at the land before them, she smiled. It really was wild and raw. Beautiful and free. And she was joyfully envious.

Maelys looked back at Lyra from where she had descended the hill.

"You coming?"

Lyra sighed.

It wasn't like she had any choice in the matter. She followed Maelys through the stone archway that led onto the training grounds.

Wilder was nowhere to be seen. Maybe he was busy talking his parents out of his role in this plan.

As they entered the middle of the training ground, the wind picked up. Lyra turned in place, closing her eyes and feeling it rush past her.

She imagined she was a leaf floating through the air, and not a mermaid trapped in a mortal body, in a bargain she never wanted to agree to in the first place.

31
WEAK LEGS

Wilder knew Lyra hadn't spotted him yet from his sanctuary in the tree, even though Maelys had already. Lyra walked to the middle of the grounds and stood there, closing her eyes.

The well of magic in the core of his being surged, and he couldn't help but increase his wind.

Lyra spun in a circle, her head tilted towards the cloudless sky. He had never seen her hair braided back that way. But the serene expression on her face was his undoing.

He slid off the branch and dropped to the ground, his knees bent to absorb the impact, and then he stood to his full height, towering over her.

There was a gleam in her eyes when she saw him. He stood in her personal space, but she didn't cower or back away from the challenge.

No, she tipped her head back to meet his gaze. She squinted

against the sun's glare, and when she did, it curled up the corners of her lips. Similar to a smile, but not.

"I don't even know where to start with you," he said.

"Usually, you start at the beginning," she chirped. He closed his eyes and sighed. She would make this more difficult than it needed to be.

Footsteps crunched against the dirt, and they turned to see Otto, Ridge, and several guards breaching the grounds.

Otto gave a polite wave, bedecked in his gray linen tunic and pants, but had nearly half a dozen weapons strapped to him now.

Ridge walked through the archway next. He towered over everyone else, and his brown leather top and breeches were snug against his bulging muscles. Wilder squeezed his lips into a thin line to keep from chuckling.

The guards seemed to be the four he knew the best. Cedric, Oak, Dust, and Oron. They were the guards that Wilder, Ridge, and Otto trained when they joined the guard—and the only four Wilder trusted implicitly with his task.

Although Wilder oversaw the entirety of the guard, he delegated most of his tasks to them and had split their ranks into quarters, positioning each of them as captains.

Cedric and Oak were twins, but they couldn't have been more different. Cedric was broad and quiet. Oak was lithe and loud.

Dust was a fiery mix of color and personality. Both quick in wit and with his help. Oron was dark-haired and of a gloomy disposition.

"I thought you could do with some help," Otto said, stopping a few feet away from Lyra.

"Me?" she pointed to herself. "Or him?"

"Both," Otto chuckled.

"We were due for our midday training anyway," Cedric chimed in.

Wilder nodded. "That's good. Start with your normal warmup. I need to gauge where to begin with Lyra."

"And me?" Otto asked.

"You already know," Wilder replied, weary from the number of orders he was bound to give.

The guards and Otto peeled off and began jogging laps around the ring.

Ridge stood beside Maelys as they waited for Wilder's instructions.

"Maelys, get me a bow, two arrows, and the smallest sword you can find." She nodded, flashing Ridge a smile before disappearing.

"Ridge, we're going to need the witch on standby. And a table set up with plenty of water and fresh fruit."

Ridge crossed his arms and studied Lyra. "You'll probably need to start with morning exercise and afternoon sparring. I don't think she can take one long training."

Lyra straightened under the weight of their assessment. "*She* is right here. Don't talk about me as if I'm not." She crossed her arms over her chest and gave them both a look of disgust.

Ridge chuckled and walked away. "Good luck, Lyra. You're going to need it."

When he had cleared the archway and was trudging up the hill to the palace, Wilder began.

"Alright, your legs and muscles are new. I don't want to injure you immediately. Let's jog a lap and then stretch. We'll check your arm strength and your weapons capability before we move on to magic. You're such a *skillful liar*, I will have to see everything for myself."

He could see an array of emotions flit across her face. Annoyance, apathy, anger, and finally, fear.

"Why am I training physically and with weapons? The bargain was to use my magic."

Wilder glared at her as she conveniently skipped over her

admission of lying. "Your magic comes from within you. It's easier to wield when you can control yourself both mentally," he pointed to his head, "and physically." He gestured to his chest, where it was covered in the light tunic he favored for training.

What Wilder left off saying was that she was weak. And using her magic in her current state would likely injure or kill her.

"I can control myself."

Wilder reached out with two fingers and pushed her. She crumbled like a rotted tree in the Three Sisters. Not only did she not stay on her feet, but she also collapsed to the ground.

A cloud of dust plumed around her, and she coughed.

"That was unnecessary." Her eyes watered not from the pain; he couldn't scent any coursing through her. Perhaps it was from the dust she waved out of her face.

"You're weak, Legs."

Lyra clambered to her feet and charged at him, shoving with all her might, but she felt no bigger than a bird fluttering against him.

She huffed and struggled to shove him once more, and he chuckled. His laugh set her off, and she surged up with her knee, trying to kick the sensitive spot between his legs.

He blocked her with his hand, and she cried out.

"Ouch! That fucking hurt!"

"What was your plan there? Did you think I would allow you to hurt me?"

She rubbed her knee and then glared at him.

"You elvish males think you're so big and strong."

He smiled at her then, a sinister, bloodthirsty smile. "Because I am."

Lyra rolled her eyes and placed her hands on her hips. When her lips parted with what was surely a sharp retort, he cut her off.

"Start jogging, Legs. We have a workout to complete."

She bit her lip and looked to where Otto and the guards had started their warm-up. "How many laps?"

Wilder shook his head, crossing his arms over his chest. "Until I say to stop."

"No." Lyra plopped onto the ground, crossing her legs.

He tilted his head back to the sky to keep from screaming.

"You made a bargain with the High King."

Lyra wrapped her arms around her legs and squeezed them to her chest.

"Do you know what happens when you don't uphold a bargain?" he prompted.

She refused to answer and kept staring at the willow branches that waved in the rising wind.

"You. Die."

She closed her eyes and sucked a breath down. He squatted down so that they were face-to-face. "Suit yourself, but if you'd ever like your freedom, you'll follow my orders."

He dangled that word in front of her like a carrot.

Lyra took the bait. Pulling herself off the ground with forced slowness, she glared at him.

"Tell me how many laps, first."

He sighed through his nose. "Start with five."

32
COME ON LEGS

He was trying to kill her.

That surely had been the plan all along. Kidnap her, subject her to endless suffering on the way here, and then a slow, torturous death by running.

Her breath sawed out of her. Excruciating white-hot flames licked up her throat with every inhale and exhale. The spaces between her ribs were ripping apart, and it felt as if something was piercing her side.

"That's only three laps!"

She was going to kill him. She didn't know how or when, but he would pay for this.

Wilder stood smirking at her by the table Ridge had set up. The giant copper pitcher teased her with each pass by the table. Condensation had dripped down its side. The sweet temptation of cold water.

When she passed by him again, he looked her over. She was sure she looked close to death. Her skin had leaked, and her hair clung to it. Lyra wet her lips and then coughed raggedly at the breath that stuck in her dry throat.

"Never mind. Just stop. Get some water," Wilder said, holding out a hand to stop her.

If she wasn't mistaken, sympathy had softened his gaze.

Lyra bent over at the waist, resting her hands on her knees, and panting.

"Breathe in through your nose," Wilder ordered her. "And out through your mouth."

She listened to him despite herself, and it helped.

"Here, drink." He handed her a tin of water.

It was cold, blissfully frigid, and a relief to her blistering throat.

"You're more out of shape than I had thought," Wilder muttered.

"She has had legs for less than two weeks," Maelys added. "What did you expect?"

"Did you not do any kind of physical activity before this?" Ridge asked.

Lyra shook her head. "Not really."

But that wasn't completely true. She had learned how to wield a dagger. As a matter of fact, she missed her favorite dagger. She had planned to kill Drystan with it once she returned.

Drystan.

She wanted to vomit, thinking his name. Her training to kill him had been effortless compared to this. It was centered on her catching him unaware. Specifically, right after they had consummated their marriage, when he would be at his weakest. They had never planned for any alternatives, like her having to fight him.

Now that she was thinking about it, it was a terrible plan. What if he had injured her and it had become difficult for her to slit his throat? Then what would have been the plan? He wasn't very intelligent, but even she didn't think he would be stupid enough to fall asleep and make himself vulnerable around her.

Lyra set the tin back on the table, and looked back at Wilder. Maybe training with him wouldn't be the worst thing in the world. It would help her learn how to defend herself, and she would become stronger.

Merfolk would never have allowed such a thing. It would be scandalous to them. She would become stronger and capable of fending off attackers. Lyra relished that thought.

"What next?" she asked, now that her breathing had slowed and her resolve had settled.

Wilder seemed surprised by her change of tune. He arched a brow and studied her.

"We'll stretch. Then, do bodyweight activities. Followed by approaching your magic."

Lyra pursed her lips. "It isn't safe to use my magic."

Wilder grinned. "Why do you think guards and Otto are here? The moment you even think about turning it against us, he will kill you."

Well, that was comforting. But not at all what she meant.

When Lyra didn't reply, Wilder strode away from the table and out of the shade of the willows. He meant for her to follow, but she stood still, closing her eyes and enjoying the shade for one more moment. With her eyes closed and her breathing slowed, she listened.

She could hear the breeze through the willow trees, and it sounded like the strains of a song. The willow sang as the wind plucked its branches, and she could hear it as clearly as the current once sang in her blood.

"Waiting for you, Legs."

Lyra blinked her eyes open and found Maelys staring at her, a knowing smile on her face.

"You can hear the willow?"

Lyra gawked at her. "I didn't dream that?"

Ridge chuckled. "We can all hear it; we're elves."

Wilder whistled then, a low, screeching sound, and Lyra flinched.

"Let's go! It's only getting hotter out here." Bedecked in a light tunic and leather pants, she could see the sweat beading on his chest. A sliver of tan skin peeked out from where he had left the ties undone.

Yes, she was going to kill him.

And the best part was, he was going to teach her how.

33
MADE TO SUFFER

The sun was scorching as Wilder led Lyra through a number of stretches. She was more limber than he expected after watching her stumble through three laps around the grounds. But he didn't have high expectations about her strength.

"Do you know what a push-up is?"

She scrunched up her nose before shaking her head. They'd been out here long enough that he could see the flush of sun across her cheeks, and what looked like the beginning of freckles across her nose.

"I'll show you," he replied, sinking to his knees.

She bit her lip as she watched him.

He lay flat on his stomach, and the dirt clung to the sweat that had seeped through his tunic. In one swift motion, he pushed up. And just to burn off the building steam in his veins, he pumped out fifty more.

Lyra watched with the kind of boredom one would display watching grass grow.

He stood and gestured to the ground. "Just do as many as you can."

She flicked her braid over her shoulder, the picture of arrogance, and lay on the ground. It took him a moment to realize she was trying to push up, but couldn't. He could see her arms trembling through her light-colored blouse.

"Not so easy, is it?"

She turned her head and glared at him. "It's as difficult as it should be to someone with a larger brain than muscles."

Wilder tapped the side of his head. "This brainless, muscled prince is the one in charge of your training. So maybe fewer insults and more effort."

Lyra ground her teeth and shoved up.

So anger was an excellent motivator for her, after all.

"One," Wilder counted.

Her arms wobbled before collapsing out from under her.

"Again," he ordered.

She bared her teeth and pushed again, not making it half as far up as she had the last time.

"I don't even know why we're trying to break the bargain that gave your merfolk more power. It's obvious they need it if all of their females are as weak as you are."

Lyra pushed harder, completing one entire push-up.

"I don't know why we don't just wage war instead. Your people wouldn't be able to put up an adequate fight."

She went down and then pushed back up again.

"How you managed to survive this long is quite the mystery," he mused.

Again, she went down and back up. There was a tremble to her arms, and her face was as red as the apples that grew in the nearby orchard, but he kept pushing her.

"It must be an inverse relation, this strength to smarts for you. You must be incredibly smart because you're no stronger than a fairy."

Up and down, she struggled through another set.

"That's five. *Good*. You can stop now."

She collapsed face-first to the ground.

"You did that on purpose," she said into the dirt, before rolling over onto her back.

"Very smart, indeed," Wilder teased. "Up you get."

She found her way to her feet. Dirt clung to her chest and her forehead, but she made no movement to wipe it away. Small hairs had slipped her braid and were stuck to the moist skin on her neck.

"Do you know what squats and lunges are?"

She blinked at him. "Torture? And death?"

"Close!" Maelys called from her position beside the table.

"Both on the first day?" Ridge asked. "That seems like a lot."

Wilder waved them off. She needed to be pushed. No one had ever dared to do it before. And a part of him was curious to see where her breaking point was.

He demonstrated both. Lyra's eyes widened. When she gulped down a swallow, he smirked.

"Start at that end of the grounds and do a single line of lunges, then turn around and do a line of squats. When you get back where you started, you can take a break and get some water and some fruit."

Lyra stared at him like he had grown two heads.

"But that's really far …"

Wilder nodded. "You'll have to read a lot more to keep your brain larger than your muscles when I get through with you."

When she didn't move from her rooted position to the ground, he realized this was going to be like the pushups all over again.

"Come on, Legs. I'll do it with you."

He strode for the fence at the far end and could hear her footsteps lightly crunching behind him.

When he started lunging, she groaned out loud.

"So how did you survive so long, being so weak and puny?"

She started lunging. The grimace on her face nearly made him laugh, but he kept going. Lunging very slowly so that she could keep pace.

"I had teeth and claws," she retorted. "Is this supposed to burn?"

"It doesn't for me. But, yes. You've never used your muscles before."

When she didn't reply, he looked over to see her mocking him.

"I don't have to do this with you. I can just walk and yell," he offered, stopping and standing upright.

"Good. Why don't you go stand over there and breathe someone else's air?"

Wilder shrugged and walked away, leaving her struggling to bend into her third lunge.

He leaned against the table beside Maelys and Ridge.

"This is unbearable to watch," Maelys murmured.

"Then don't. Go spar with Otto and the guards," Wilder replied, jutting his chin to the other side of the grounds, where swords clanged against each other.

"I'll spar with you," Ridge offered.

"That's better," Maelys replied, and they set off arm-in-arm.

Wilder watched as Lyra struggled through one set of lunges. She stopped on the far end and leaned over the stone wall. She didn't move for quite some time, and Wilder gave up on waiting for her.

"Move!"

When she didn't move or snap back, he pushed off the table, cursing all the gods as he walked over to her.

"Is there a problem?" he asked when he was close enough that she could hear him.

"I hate you," she groaned.

"There's that sharp tongue. You just have one more set to do."

She shook her head, and that's when Wilder noticed the vomit clinging to the end of her braid. She had leaned over to retch. Dread soured his tongue as he bit back a groan. He shouldn't care that she was in pain. That was the point.

Training was pain.

"I can't do it." Angry tears spilled over the rim of her eyes. He felt a piece of him wither away to ash. He had pushed her too far, and now she was crying. Her anger smelled like a thunderstorm.

"I want to be strong. I do, I swear. But I was never raised to *train*. I was raised to *suffer*. I only know suffering, and I can't take it anymore."

Wilder froze, and ice slid through his veins. *She had been raised to suffer?*

"Lyra," he breathed. "I'm not doing this to punish you." *That was a lie.* "I'm not inflicting this on you to relish in your suffering." *Not a total lie.* "Training will make you better—stronger, even." *That was the truth of it.* She would eventually grow stronger. "But we can call it quits today if you've had enough. Today was for learning where your boundaries are, and pushing you to them—but not through them."

She nodded then, wiping the tears off her cheeks.

"Do you need help?" he asked, a shade quieter.

"No. I can at least make it to the table on my own two feet," she muttered. But when she straightened, her legs trembled.

"I won't carry you. But take my hand," Wilder bade her.

She stared at it for a heartbeat before looking up into his eyes. When her fingers clasped his, her eyes widened. A slight shock went through him, like the energy in a budding storm.

Lyra focused on where their hands touched and swallowed. He didn't know what that meant, but he had the strangest feeling fate had tied them together.

Whether he liked it or not, his future was inexplicably tied to hers.

34
TEETH

He had been kind, in a strange, domineering kind of way. Lyra didn't know what to make of it. He pushed her to strengthen her not only mentally, but also physically.

No one had ever tried to make her better. Not even the teachers who instructed her growing up. Every lesson was wrought with feminine fragility or the repetitive rhetoric that knowledge was wasted on her.

It was exhausting constantly trying to prove her worth, so she eventually stopped and became the helpless, useless mermaid they always said she was. But with a dash of violence. Because sometimes you just need to remind them you have teeth.

Wilder knew she had teeth, and he was trying to sharpen them.

Each step was agonizing, a ripping and burning lashing up her thighs and down her calves. The sound of clashing swords and grunts grew louder than her heaving breaths.

Lyra stared in awe as Maelys sparred with Ridge. She moved like light through the water, quickly and with a twinkling rhythm. It was beautiful.

"How?" Lyra breathed.

Wilder followed her line of sight and smirked.

"Years and years of training."

She would never be that good or powerful. Not even if she had a lifetime of training.

"I could never."

Wilder was gruff with his answer. "You will."

Lyra glanced sidelong at him. There was a stiff sort of resolution to his jaw, and a line was carved between his brows. He really thought he could make her into something like that. He believed she was capable.

What a strange place this was. A king who took advice from his queen, and females as warriors.

The table still felt far away, even after a few more struggling steps. And Lyra swallowed down a cry.

"It'll be dinner by the time we make it there," Wilder said under his breath.

"You weren't training this hard as a newborn," Lyra snapped back. "I'm essentially a week old."

He reeled back at her words and then shook his head. In one swift motion, he had thrown her over his shoulder and strode towards the table.

"We carry our babies here."

Lyra snorted, and the power within her gleamed. It was dull because of her exhaustion, but his humor had surprised her. She cringed away from it. This hadn't happened so often before. She could count on one hand the number of times her power had flared before she came to land, and now it happened twice.

Wilder placed her on her feet and held onto her elbow, ensuring she wouldn't crumple to the ground. He placed water in one of her hands and an apple in the other.

"Drink and eat. Then we need to approach your magic," he said.

Lyra stared at the food and drink in her hand. He had no idea how disappointed he was about to become. She wasn't ready to touch her magic, but he didn't have to know that.

She nodded and sipped at her water before biting into the apple. It was delicious. Juice dribbled down her chin, and she wiped it away with the back of her hand.

"I need to make sure Otto and the guards are ready. I'll be right back," Wilder said as he walked away.

His footsteps were silent on the dirt, and the blood pounding in her ears muted any other noise. He walked with all the grace and menace of a great white shark. He was fearsome. It had her steeling her spine.

Wilder approached Otto, who was locked in a battle between two guards who looked related—but not.

Lyra watched as Wilder halted beside them, and they paused. The guards bowed and left, but Otto grinned at Wilder and inclined his head.

She was too far away to hear their exchange, but Wilder drew the sword at his side and braced his feet. The sword wasn't ostentatious, but there was an indescribable glimmer of power that radiated from the blade—or maybe it was just the male who held it.

Lyra mimicked his stance and felt steadier on her feet. She had not known the power of a good stance. Wilder leveled his sword at Otto, and he did the same. They circled each other, and Lyra found her heart racing again.

The clash of their swords rang through the air, and she gasped. So much power was behind each of Wilder's blows. If this was him sparring, she couldn't imagine him in an actual battle. No wonder those mortals hadn't stood a chance.

Otto blocked each of his advances, but a split second too slow. It was as if his visions weren't coming as fast as Wilder's thoughts. It was beautiful, like a dance. She longed to learn the footwork. But as soon as she thought it—it was over.

Otto stood weaponless, and Wilder held both swords. She gaped like a fish, not seeing how he had done it. He tossed Otto his sword back and then gestured for him and the guards to follow.

Lyra watched as they approached her. A small voice inside her whispered to grab her thread of magic to show these males what she was truly capable of. She slammed the door on it.

It didn't matter what they thought of her. It would kill her to use it. Take all that she was and could be and turn it to ash.

She couldn't—*wouldn't* touch it.

It all became too much. The sun on her skin, the heat, the burning in her overused muscles. As if sensing her dread, Wilder stopped in front of her.

"We're just going to work on feeling the power inside of you. Where it is, what it feels like. I don't anticipate you wielding today."

She swallowed and nodded. Her eyes burned, and she blinked it away.

"She won't," Otto said.

Wilder shifted his gaze from her to Otto. "Can't or won't?"

"Both."

When he looked back at her, she could feel the weight of disappointment in his steady gaze.

"I'm just asking you to try."

Lyra bit her tongue and glared at him, using her anger as a shield so that he wouldn't see her fear. She didn't answer, and she didn't think he ever would.

She closed her eyes, feigning effort, and opened her hands palm up to the sky. But she didn't reach for her power, that golden thread that seemed thicker now around her heart. Nope, she stood there. Faking.

When she blew out a forced breath and opened her eyes to a glowering Wilder, she pressed her lips into a thin line.

"I tried," she shrugged.

He worked his jaw side to side.

"That's fine. We only have tomorrow and the day after, and the day after ..."

Her chest ached. She felt lost—scared, even. One time, she had plucked that thread.

She could still feel him pawing at her, and then nothing. It had felt like eternal darkness, and then she was in the sea witch's cave.

This was going to be different. At least, she hoped it would be. But she still couldn't see past the fear.

Daisy was the nicest creature in the entire world as she helped tug Lyra's shirt over her head. It had also taken Lyra sitting on the floor for Daisy to pull her boots and pants off. And then the darling girl helped ease her into the tub.

It was an abundance of kindness and care, and the moment Lyra slipped into that blissfully warm and heavenly-scented water, tears burned her eyes.

She had watched Daisy meticulously dole out the oils and the bath salts. It seemed ridiculous the effort that went into a bath. But the moment the ache and burn in her muscles evaporated, she realized it had all been well worth it.

There was a light clattering of doors shutting and fabric rustling. She leaned her head against the copper tub and closed her eyes, breathing in the heavenly aroma of the oils.

"Do you have a preference for this evening?" Daisy called through the closed door.

"This evening?" Lyra asked, sinking deeper into the water.

"Your dinner with the king and queen."

Lyra's eyes flashed open, and water splashed over the rim of the tub as she jolted up. No one had told her that. She hated the very idea of it. What would she even say to them?

"'Tis a great honor, my lady."

Lyra snorted. "I'm their *captive*. I fail to see the honor in that."

It was silent for a heartbeat. "Well, when you put it that way," Daisy chuckled. "The navy gown would be stunning with your complexion."

Lyra sighed. It didn't matter; none of it mattered. Scooping up a handful of water, she watched it ripple in her palm. She missed the sea. Missed Seraphina and Marina, if she was being honest. She was accustomed to their curtness, not this kindliness.

But she would need to break the bargain between humans and merfolk if she ever wanted to see her home again. Which meant using her magic. Her throat burned.

"You'll prune if you stay in there any longer," Daisy chided.

Closing her eyes and holding her breath, she sank beneath the water, not hearing anything anymore.

Daisy wasn't having any of that. A splash in the water had Lyra opening her eyes. The oils and salts burned, but she could still make out Daisy's annoyed expression.

When her lungs screamed from the lack of oxygen, she breached the surface, wiping the water from her eyes.

"Out you get. I still have much to do with your hair and trying to hide the burn on your cheeks and forehead," Daisy sighed. "Beautiful ivory skin fried like bacon."

She held a towel out, averting her eyes as Lyra rose from the water and stepped out. Daisy wrapped it around her, and she felt the strange strains of comfort.

Daisy truly was a soft-hearted soul. After she dried off and donned her robe, Lyra followed her to the vanity and plopped onto the velvet stool. It took her a moment to realize how easily she had walked across the room with the absence of pain. Those oils and salts were magic.

In her absence, Daisy had pulled open the curtains and laid a navy blue gown on her bed. Golden sunlight streamed through the open curtains, setting the room ablaze.

Lyra studied herself in the mirror. There was a flush to her cheeks and forehead, a new splattering of freckles across her nose. But there was a sharpness in her eyes. Being challenged all day by Wilder had awoken something in her she long thought dead.

Daisy hummed to herself as she worked. Strands of Lyra's auburn hair were pinned in an elaborate updo.

"Daisy, have you worked in the castle long?" Lyra attempted conversation.

"Since I was a child."

"And do you like it?"

Daisy smiled and nodded. "Very much so."

Lyra sat still and quiet, watching Daisy work. She smiled to herself, like she really did enjoy her work.

"Do you have any family?"

She met Daisy's eyes in the mirror and saw them sparkle.

"I have two younger sisters."

"Oh."

"How about you?"

Lyra shifted in her chair. "I have six older sisters."

"Blessed three! Such a big lot. Are you close?"

It was an effort for Lyra not to grimace. "Not really. They're much older than me and all married and gone."

Daisy frowned. "How terrible. I couldn't imagine not having my sisters. They're my best friends."

Lyra flinched at a pin Daisy placed, and she froze.

"Oh! I'm so sorry! Let me fix that." Daisy pulled the pin out and placed it back in her hair, but at a different angle. It was painless.

Lyra touched where the pin was and didn't feel the sharp stabbing sensation she had felt every day of her life in Atlantis.

"It doesn't hurt."

Daisy chuckled and resumed working. "It's not supposed to."

Lyra's mouth dropped open, and she sucked a sharp breath in through her teeth. Years and years of unnecessary pain. For what reason?

She wanted to rage, to scream to the gods. But what use would that do?

They had allowed this, after all.

Daisy turned Lyra so that she no longer could see her reflection as she dabbed something on her face.

"What is that?" Lyra asked when a cloud of it wafted up from her face.

"Makeup," Daisy replied.

"What does it do?"

"It enhances."

Lyra frowned and Daisy tutted. "Stop it, you'll crease."

Relaxing her face, Lyra closed her eyes and absorbed the gentleness in Daisy's touch. It was nice to be touched without pain.

"There. Beautiful as ever," Daisy said, spinning her back towards the mirror.

A princess stared back. It was still her. The emerald eyes and sharp cheekbones, but she looked softer somehow.

She pressed a hand to her cheek to make sure it was still her.

"Thank you," she breathed.

Daisy smiled and patted her shoulder.

"Let me help you into the gown. There are ties at the back."

Lyra rose from the vanity, untying her robe and letting it drop at her feet. Daisy held the gown open, and she stepped into it, feeling the buttery softness of the silk.

This one was as stunning as the last one. It was strapless, and the ties at the back cinched tight, showcasing her narrow waist. Patting the fabric around her waist, she breathed and found she could do so normally. Not at all restrained, as she had been in the navy gown in the mortal realm.

Daisy set a pair of embroidered slippers in front of her. They were the same shade of navy as the gown, but there were swirls of stars in gold and silver. The tiny heel raised her without making her unsteady. She felt as if they had been crafted for her.

"I don't have any jewelry for you, I'm afraid," Daisy mumbled.

Lyra turned the sapphire shell necklace that never left her throat.

"That's alright. The dress is stunning enough," Lyra replied.

"The dress would be just fabric without you."

Lyra couldn't help the smile that stretched across her face. Her gratitude was cut off by pounding on the door.

"That will be your escort," Daisy said.

Her periwinkle hair shimmered in the dwindling light as she hustled to the door and swung it open. She collapsed into a bow. "Your Highness."

Lyra rolled her eyes; she couldn't imagine bowing and scraping to *him*.

"Is she ready?" His tone wasn't rude, but it wasn't nice either.

She stalked to the door, coming up behind Daisy and resting her hands on her hips.

"How about a '*Hello, Daisy*'?"

Wilder stood frozen, staring at her. His gaze grazed along her exposed collarbones and the low-cut neckline of her gown before meeting her eyes again. She felt naked under his inspection. And she wasn't the only one.

Daisy cleared her throat. "She is, Your Highness. Do you find her acceptable for dinner with the king and queen?"

Wilder hadn't stopped staring at Lyra. "Very acceptable."

He cleared his throat and took a step back, allowing Lyra to pass through the threshold.

"Great work, Daisy. You've achieved the impossible."

Lyra froze and glared at him, but Daisy beamed at his compliment.

"The *impossible*? And what would that be?" Lyra hissed, stepping close to him.

"Making you look anything but monstrous," he whispered into her ear.

He didn't know how right he was.

Although he hadn't meant it as a compliment to her, she appreciated it all the same. Especially, having been pampered and doted on by Daisy—she was still a creature of the sea.

"And don't you forget it, Princeling."

35
Books &
Elixir

She was a thing of beauty. No, she was the epitome of beauty.

The navy gown hugged her curves and pooled at her feet. As if the ocean wrapped her in its dark and lovely embrace. They walked side-by-side to his parents' private dining chamber. This dinner was not expected to be pleasant, and he was already dreading the vitriol that would spew from her mouth the moment she felt offended.

"Try to be pleasant, and this evening will pass swiftly," he said to her.

Guards walked in front and behind them. His usual escort increased due to her. It felt unnecessary now after having seen her at training. She was the furthest thing from a danger. It would be more likely she would injure herself if she tried to hurt anyone else.

"I will be if they are."

He cut his attention to her once more, and he noticed how her gown was lavishly intricate. She no doubt would fit in with the courtiers here. Except there was the glaring absence of any jewelry. Besides the sapphire necklace she never took off. She was without earrings, a necklace, or bracelets. He frowned at that.

"*Fine*. I'll try my best," she grumbled, misreading his frown.

He shook his head. "That's not—never mind."

The guards stationed on either side of the black, arched door held it open for them. He had been in this room more times than he could count. His mother preferred an intimate dinner, just the three of them, and not the extravagant dinners in the dining hall that his father enjoyed.

There was a time he wondered why that was, but as he got older, he realized his father needed that show of power. To have courtiers fawning over him.

Wilder did not care what the courtiers thought of him, at least, not anymore. It was empty, their praise and love. It would turn to hate and repulsion within the blink of an eye.

But it was Lyra's first time in their private chambers, and although he had grown accustomed to the room, he remembered the magic of it.

Gleaming evergreen marble, lavish moldings, paintings spanning centuries of monarchs and his ancestors, and books. The books were, without a doubt, his favorite part of the room, and would be Lyra's, too. Colossal bookshelves that required rolling ladders lined an entire wall. She thirsted for knowledge, and while he told her he would rather live the adventures, he enjoyed a good story.

Lyra jerked to a stop, her mouth dropping open as she stared at the wall of bookshelves. Wilder stopped with her, one hand in his pocket, and enjoyed her mute surprise.

"You eat in a library?" she asked, when she could formulate words.

He chuckled and straightened the lapels of his black jacket. "This isn't the royal library, just my parents' private chambers."

She gawked at him now. "This isn't the library?"

Wilder shook his head and gestured for her to keep up.

"This would take me a hundred lifetimes to read," she whispered.

He shrugged. That was kind of the point. "Elves have considerable lifetimes."

And from what he remembered, the merfolk did too, but murder and sabotage ran rampant in their courts, and lives were often cut short.

"Darlings," his mother greeted them.

She was already sitting on her usual side of the table. Her gown was the same lilac shade as the twilight hour, an ode to her favorite time of day. It was when she did her best thinking, she claimed.

King Oberon sat at the head of the table, watching them approach with a keen eye. Wilder could feel him gauging the distance between their bodies, the near matching of their ensembles, but if he cared—he didn't let on.

"Lyra, Wilder," he greeted them with a boorish tone.

Lyra inclined her head in greeting to them both but did not deign to reply.

Wilder held the chair opposite his mother out for Lyra, and as she took her seat, he whispered low into her ear, "Be *pleasant*."

She rolled her eyes and grabbed the napkin beside her golden plate. She flapped it obnoxiously before placing it in her lap.

Wilder heaved a sigh and took his place opposite his father.

"How was your first training, my dear?" Aine asked her, a smirk quirking her lips.

"Abysmal," Lyra complained.

His father shot him a look as Aine chuckled.

"I hope Wilder wasn't the cause of such despair."

A dangerous gleam entered Lyra's eyes, but she blinked and it was gone.

"No, unfortunately, he is an excellent mentor. Especially with this being my first time."

All eyes turned to Lyra as she took a sip from her water goblet.

"First time?" Oberon asked.

Lyra nodded and set the glass back down. "I've never done any physical activity before. It's not allowed."

He had never seen his mother look that way. Her nostrils flared wide, and she clutched the diamond choker that wrapped around her neck. She was horrified.

"It's not *allowed*?"

"Nope." Lyra pronounced the "P" like a pop. "There is no need for physical activity outside of labor in the home. Females don't have jobs."

"That is quite a strange societal construct," Oberon said.

Lyra glanced around the room before answering him. "One could say that."

"And what would you say?" Aine prompted with a tilted head and arched brow.

Lyra shrugged. "It's not for me to say."

"You mean you're not allowed an opinion." Lyra frowned at that. "Tell me, child, why do you want to go back?"

And there it was, the most obvious question.

"Because it is my choice," Lyra replied. "I didn't have one in coming here. And I don't enjoy being where I'm not wanted."

Wilder couldn't stop the laugh that rumbled out of him. "And you believe you're wanted *there*?"

"Wilder!" his mother admonished

But Lyra didn't balk at his retort. This was a language she understood.

"It's my *home*. It's where I belong." She glared at Wilder but twisted the napkin in her lap. "I miss the steady pull of the current that matched the beating of my heart, my friends, and the familiarity." She looked down. "And unfortunately, I missed my wedding. I do hope my fiancé isn't too furious with me, since it wasn't *my* fault. "

Aine's head volleyed back and forth through their exchange. But his father didn't look away from Lyra.

"There's so much fire in her for her to be from the water," he said.

Wilder only nodded. She had surprised him, carving out an opinion of herself in their minds in a few brief moments.

Yet, he still didn't know how he truly saw her or felt. But something about how she had talked about her home led him to believe she wasn't being truthful—*again*.

At last, their dinner was served. Roasted meat over a bed of fresh greens. It wasn't an extravagant meal, but it was delicious.

Lyra dug in with the ferocity of someone who hadn't eaten in several days. When she stopped chewing long enough to sip her water, she studied the bookshelves before digging back into her food.

After they finished their meal and were waiting for dessert, the silence was broken again.

"Lyra, do you like to read?" Aine asked after catching her reading some spines behind her.

A blush bloomed high on Lyra's cheeks, causing blood to roar in his ears. It quieted in time for him to hear her reply.

"Very much so."

Aine nodded and smiled. "Wilder, be a dear and escort her to the library after dinner. Let her pick out anything her heart desires."

Wilder's shoulders rose with his agitated breath, but Lyra beamed at his mother.

"Thank you, Your Majesty."

Aine waved her off. "There's no need for formalities. Lest we not forget why you're here." She shot a look at Oberon, who was conscious enough to look bashful. "We will do our best to make your time here pleasant, no matter the circumstances that brought you here."

So, his mother was still not on board with this plan. It was unlike her to be this open about her disagreement, which told him everything he needed to know about her attitude towards his father.

Wilder was relieved. It was about time she had shown her backbone more quickly when the mood arose.

He had only wished she had done the same—for him.

"How did you know about the Tidal Tithe?" Lyra asked, sliding her gaze to Oberon.

He blinked at her direct question. "An informant."

"Of which court?" She circled a fingertip along the rim of her water goblet.

He smiled at her and gestured for the servant to bring out dessert.

A slice of cake was placed in front of each of them, and Lyra stared at it.

"It's cake," Wilder supplied.

"But we just ate."

He cut a piece off the corner of the chocolate cake with lavender mousse and put it in his mouth. Lyra watched with a blank expression as he swallowed it down.

"This is dessert. It comes after dinner."

She looked around the table to see Oberon and Aine eating their slices.

"Don't tell me you have never had dessert before?" Aine asked, dabbing a smudge of the mousse off the corner of her lip.

Lyra shook her head and picked up her fork.

"Hang on," Wilder said, and set down his fork. "I want to watch this."

Lyra glared at him but waited until he was settled. She lifted a bite and sniffed it before placing it in her mouth.

Her eyes grew as wide as saucers, and she covered her mouth with a hand.

"*Oh my gods.*"

Aine, Wilder, and even Oberon chuckled.

"Why don't you just eat this?" she asked, shoving another forkful in her mouth.

"It's not very nutritious and won't help you recover after training," Wilder answered.

"Not to mention it's catastrophic to the waistline," his mother added.

Lyra waved his mother off with her empty fork. "Who cares about waistlines when there is cake?"

Aine smiled, a broad, genuine smile at Lyra. "That is an excellent point."

After Lyra had devoured not only her cake, but also Wilder's, which he slid towards her, Oberon poured his evening elixir. He lifted the bottle in offering to Wilder, who nodded. The amber liquid was smoothly poured into the crystal glass.

A guard with black hair slipped into their chambers and handed Oberon a slip of paper, which he took with a nod. The guard strode out of the room without a word.

"What was that about?" Wilder asked, taking the glass from his father.

"We'll discuss it later."

Lyra looked on curiously as Wilder took a sip from the crystal glass.

Aine tutted, "Now that's one thing you don't want to partake in."

"What is it?"

"It's an elvish liquor," Oberon replied. "And you don't know you don't like it until you try."

He poured her a tiny splash and slid it over to her. Wilder watched with an amused expression, trying to decide if she was going to spit it in his father's face or cough like she was drying out.

In a move that surprised them, she sipped it and then paused, before draining what was left with a grin.

"Now that is heavenly," she breathed.

Wilder stared with a bemused expression.

"May I have another?"

Oberon obliged, but stood, gesturing for Wilder to follow him. "If you'll excuse us, ladies. We have matters to discuss."

Lyra sipped her glass and stayed seated. Aine must have taken pity on her, for she began speaking as soon as Wilder stepped away. "So tell me, dear, what is Atlantis truly like?"

He followed his father to his office, through the stacks of books on art, history, and philosophy. His father's office had always been a flurry of activity, depending on the mood he was in. He remembered a time when his father was obsessed with mortal art, a time before that he wanted to know about every creature that lived in their realm. It wasn't as chaotic as it had been as of late.

A small pile of books on Badenvaria history and genealogy texts on Merfolk were on the edge of his desk, and hinted at his current interests. Wilder took a seat in the distinguished leather chair behind the carved mahogany desk and gripped the glass in his fist. He didn't know what this meeting was about.

But if he had to guess, it would be about *her*.

"What did the message say?" Wilder nodded towards the slip of paper his father tucked into a desk drawer.

"You were ambushed after you took her?" His father's deep voice rumbled across the desk.

"That is correct." Wilder leaned back in the much smaller chair and twisted his glass between his hands.

"Wulvers?"

"As I'm sure you've already read Ridge's and Maelys' report, why is there a need to question me as well?"

"Because you can distinguish between their clans, and they can not. So who was it? Igneous or Matthias?"

Wilder sighed. "It was both clans. They seemed to be working together."

Oberon nodded and studied his son, looking for what, Wilder did not know.

"How did they know where we would be?"

Oberon gave him a flat look before taking a sip, choosing not to answer.

"Who gave you the information on Lyra? You didn't answer her, so I'm betting it was one of her people?"

Again, his father did not answer him.

"I know it was not one of mine. So it had to have been whoever you hatched this little plan with. We need to find out if we have a traitor in our midst."

The king slammed his empty glass on the desk. "You do not give me orders. And I will do nothing of the sort. They probably caught her scent and followed her in. There is no traitor."

But Wilder had ensured Lyra's scent was covered. After the humans came across her so quickly, she had not only slept beside him, but he had wrapped her in his cloak and ridden beside her.

Something about his father's demeanor told Wilder everything he needed to know.

His father was hiding something, something big.

"What was the cost?"

"I am the king. I certainly will not answer to someone who does not hold their duty in the highest regard."

Wilder didn't look away from his father's glare, no matter the intensity.

"I have more than proven myself as a dutiful and loyal servant to the crown. And I will have no part in this—find someone else to train her."

Wilder stood, discarding his still full glass on the desk and storming out.

After everything they had gone through to restore their relationship as father and son, now he dared to speak to him that way. Ordering him about as if they were in a room full of courtiers.

This had been the exact reason he never wanted to become king. That power and responsibility distorted you. Twisted your values and good nature into something corrupt and unrecognizable. What he had seen it do to his father.

He reached the dining table to find Lyra and his mother gone. But he heard their soft voices and followed them to the stacks on the other side of the room.

"I've read this one a dozen times in the last century," his mother said. "It's the story about Ophelia and how she vanquished the dragon, Turig. Have you read it?"

He peered around the stacks, not wanting to interrupt them and curious as to what Lyra was like when he wasn't around.

"She? Stories about heroines were forbidden," Lyra replied.

His mother sighed and pressed the book into her hands. "Keep it, then. I want you to have it."

Lyra shook her head. A few strands of her auburn hair had fallen from the updo and brushed against her back. "I couldn't. It's one of your favorites."

"I insist. Besides, I can always get another, and you need it."

Lyra smiled at his mother, and it was a genuine, beautiful smile.

"Lyra, I'm to escort you back to your room," Wilder interrupted.

"Stop by the library first," Aine reiterated, smiling at Lyra before turning to Wilder. Her smile dropped away when she saw him. No doubt, noticing the rigid shoulders and clenched jaw.

"Good night, Mother," he said before she could press him further.

36
ROMANCE SECTION

Something had shifted for Wilder during his talk with his father. Lyra could feel the ire wafting off of him. It was disappointing that he was so miserable now because she had had a lovely time conversing with Queen Aine.

It was strange having a conversation with another royal female so freely. Not only that, but the queen's intellect and benevolence were endearing. The evidence of that was now being squeezed against Lyra's chest.

The books around her were different and fragile, not like the stone or bewitched ones she was used to. It smelled of old parchment and oiled leather. She brought it up to her nose again and inhaled.

She could feel Wilder staring at her, but he did not comment. The only sounds in the empty hall were their footsteps and those of the guards escorting them.

It was quite annoying to be followed everywhere. Had it always been this way, or was it because of her?

Wilder didn't look inclined to answer that question, or any questions, from her right now. His brow lowered over his eyes, and his jaw flexed as he worked it side to side. Whatever had happened between them had upset him for this level of brooding.

"I can go to the library by myself if you'd prefer to be alone," Lyra muttered.

Her words snapped him out of his thoughts, and he whipped his head to her.

"You're not allowed to roam anywhere alone."

"I'm miles and miles from anyone and anything I know. I don't think I'll be running off into the night," she replied, tilting her head towards a darkened window. "Besides, I'm much safer in here than I am out there."

He didn't reply to that, but after her time with Aine and the excitement thrumming through her at getting to the royal library, she would not let him stifle it.

They followed the guards through winding hallways. Paintings of landscapes shifted to those of grand balls and gruesome battles. Lyra slowed to look at each one.

A particularly large battle scene between elves caught her attention, and she stopped.

Bodies of elves from the Wilds and Mannereds littered the battleground. Their lines clashed against each other. The Wilds had black armor and were an array of different species. Elves like Ridge stood out against the elves that looked like Otto or Wilder.

The Mannereds were wearing white armor, and they all looked similar. Pale skin and hair in varying shades of gold.

"What is this?"

Wilder had halted beside her, but did not speak as she inspected the painting.

"A painting."

"Obviously, but what is it of?"

"The Eclipse Battle. The last battle between the Wilds and the Mannereds."

She looked closer now and could see King Oberon leading the charge, his large antlers piercing the sky above him. He held a broadsword pointed at a Mannereds female. She was stunning. Her white armor was over a gown that blew in the painted wind. Her blonde hair had a hint of red to it, and there was a fierceness on her face that Lyra had seen on her own when faced with a challenge.

"Who is that?" Lyra pointed at the female.

"Queen Titania of the Mannereds."

"She fought in battle?" Lyra asked, turning to gape at Wilder.

He snorted and gripped one of his jacket lapels in his hand. "Not only did she fight—she led. Then she brokered the treaty between our kingdoms. There would not be peace without her."

Wilder spoke of her with such respect that Lyra questioned what else he must have thought about her.

"She's pretty too ..." Lyra goaded him.

"For an ancient, sure."

"What's an ancient?"

Wilder pressed his lips in a thin line, and a divot formed between his brows. "She's very old, like older than my father. I believe she began ruling 500 years ago. Other than briefly, when her daughter went missing. Titania has held continuous authority over the Mannereds."

"Missing?"

"Yes."

Lyra rubbed the corner of the book. "Is she still missing?"

Wilder squinted as if he were trying to remember. "I'm unsure."

Lyra wanted to know more. Was she kidnapped like her? Was she murdered?

"Who would know?"

Wilder stared at her, his upper lip curling back into a snarl. But she had more questions.

"Is the Queen's daughter as pretty as she is?"

He didn't answer.

"Is the daughter your age? How old are you?"

He glared. "216."

She snorted. "So, pretty old?"

Wilder brushed past her without saying a word.

The guard who trailed them cleared his throat and nodded for her to continue walking. Lyra sighed. They were headed to the library, and books held all the answers. She brushed her fingers over the golden embossed title on the book Aine had given her and sighed.

If she was going to be trapped here, at least she had books to bring her comfort. Maybe they had books about the sea kingdom so she could feel close to home.

She was so lost in thought that she ran smack dab into the middle of Wilder's back. He whirled, catching her before she could tumble to the ground. But his grip on her arm hurt.

She grimaced, and he loosened his grip.

"Watch where you're going," he snapped.

Lyra glared at him, rubbing the back of her arm. "It was an accident, you prick."

The guard behind them coughed into his golden cape to cover his obvious laugh, and Lyra smirked. At least someone found her funny. He ducked his head under Wilder's glare.

"Keep it up, and I won't show you what's behind that door," Wilder said, pointing at the door in front of them.

She wanted to roll her eyes. More accurately, she wanted to knee him in the balls for baiting her this way. But like a fish on the line, the library reeled her in.

"Fine," she huffed.

Wilder nodded to the guards, and they pulled open the enormous iron doors. Her heart stopped. Her very breath evaporated in her lungs.

It was glorious. Like all her pleasant dreams, come to life before her.

The room stretched on forever, colossal shelves housing tomes of every size, shape, and color. It was the best thing she had ever seen. And she could explore it, could pick any book off any shelf, and read it.

Wilder nudged her forward. "I don't have all night. You can explore more tomorrow. Pick out a book and let's be on our way."

But picking a single book could take ages. She didn't even know where to start.

He sighed, reading her expression for what it was, and began showing her around.

"This section is history. That one over there is mainly maps, the one down there is nature things, but I'm sure you're interested in the romance."

Lyra stared at him as if he spoke a foreign language.

"Romance?"

"Yeah, you know, love stories."

She had no idea what he was talking about.

Wilder's lips tightened in a grim line before he spoke. "You weren't allowed to read those. Were you?"

She did not know what he was talking about. Who would want to read about someone else's love?

Lyra avoided his gaze until Wilder tilted his head back to the painted ceiling. It was dark blue with lighter swirls of powder blue. Constellations and stars painted in glittering gold. It was beautiful, an academic version of the night sky she had seen during their travels.

His throat bobbed as he swallowed and scrubbed a hand down his face.

"I'm going to regret this—I know it. But you'd find it, eventually."

If it bothered him this much, she was definitely going to be reading it.

She followed him through the stacks. Sconces of yellow flames danced as they swept past. Her gown glowed each time they passed a swell of light, and she bit back a smile. The elves knew how to dress. She'd give them that.

Even Wilder, in his black jacket and matching pants, cut a delectable figure. The embroidery of ravens in a shiny navy thread almost went unnoticed. But now that she had, she couldn't stop noticing the creatures taking flight across his broad back.

"Here," he said, coming to a stop in front of a shelf that housed many books bound in varying shades of red.

She scanned the stack and pulled one out at random. The spine read, *The Knight in Shining Armor.* Flipping open the first page, her eyes darted across the page.

It didn't seem like romance, more like a woman in distress. How ironic, she had very much been in distress. She flipped to the middle of the book and read a passage. She couldn't understand what was happening.

"What does *'velvet-wrapped steel'* mean?" she asked, using her finger to hold her place and looking up at Wilder.

His face turned an exquisite shade of crimson, and he ripped the book from her hand and slipped it back on the shelf.

"Pick another," he grumbled.

But she was intrigued now. As he turned away from her, she slipped it back off the shelf and hid it underneath the one his mother had gifted her.

Turning on her heel, she walked away from where he headed and read the titles on the spines. *Savage Love, Secrets of the Wench, Sorcerer's Mistress.*

Only one of those titles had anything to do with love. Wilder tapped his foot behind her, and she grabbed *Savage Love.*

"Are you finished?"

She waved the book in front of his face but was careful not to let him read the title in case that one was ripped away from her, too. But she hadn't seen any males roaming the stacks, checking on the books that were selected. And Queen Aine had said she was welcome to read "anything."

He turned and walked towards the exit, leaving her scurrying behind him. She wasn't annoyed with him anymore. She had not one, but three books in her hands, and she could not be any happier.

Wilder discarded her at her bedroom door without so much as a goodnight. It bothered her, to be sure. She thought they had been encroaching on a tentative alliance at the very least.

But as the guards held her door open, she crept inside in time to hear him stomping down the hall. She dressed down for comfort and slid between the covers.

Alone in her room, she started the book Aine had gifted her. It was an epic story to be sure, but not what she was looking for at the moment. *The Knight in Shining Armor* had the most promise since Wilder was keen on her not reading it. The candle beside her bed was perfect for reading without straining her eyes as she opened the book and began.

A small vase of flowers had her inhaling the fresh aroma of the tiny chamomile flowers. With her soft nightclothes, a cup of steaming tea on her bedside table that Daisy had left, and the book in her hands, she was feeling less and less like a prisoner. Propped up against the pillow, she flew through the first chapter.

It seemed like this damsel was a prisoner as well. But the people who captured her were not as kind as her captors had been.

Lyra kept reading, hoping to get to the part about *"velvet-*

wrapped steel," but when a knight appeared to save the young woman, her eyes grew heavy.

She plucked a flower from the vase and slid it between the pages to mark her place. Lyra took one last sip of her tea and blew out the candle.

It wasn't long before sleep dragged her down into its depths. The ease of it was like slipping into water.

She hadn't realized how much she missed the ocean, but she dreamed of it.

37
A GOOD
TRY

He couldn't even find the words to tell her goodnight as he left her staring at him beside her bedroom door. All he could think about was her body under that dress and the question she had brazenly asked him.

Did she truly not know what it meant, or was she attempting to annoy him once more?

Velvet wrapped steel. He snorted. Such an inappropriate phrase from such a beautiful mouth.

It had been a shock to hear, and pulled him out of the brooding his father had elicited. But now that he was out of her presence, the anger resurfaced. He needed to get these frustrations out of his system, and there was only one place to go.

Wilder didn't even bother changing his attire before strutting out of the castle and to the Venus. A bottle of elixir and a release or two would put his obsession with her to rest and numb him from his father's cruelty.

The cobblestone streets were abuzz with activity as

everyone was preparing for Ostara. They were still some weeks away, but it was a beloved holiday and one of his favorites as well.

As he passed from the quiet, manicured streets of the Upper District and across the wooden bridge that led to the Lower District, he couldn't help but feel a twinge of dissatisfaction. It's not that it was a stark difference, but it was unfortunate that there was a separation between the noble-born and the non-noble-born.

A child with tattered clothes sat beside the bridge munching a piece of bread, and Wilder placed a gold coin beside him. The child reminded him of Ridge when they were young. Gangly from repetitive growth spurts, his mother found it difficult to keep up with his needs. Even now, Ridge wore shirts and pants that were a size too small because that was what was familiar to him.

The child looked up with bright eyes, and Wilder pressed a finger to his lips.

"I wasn't here," he whispered. And the child nodded in return.

Wilder turned the corner, and the Venus appeared ahead. He felt a buzz through his veins as his heart pumped quicker in his chest. His chest swelled, and his breath came easier as he sighed with relief. Finally—he could be rid of the constant thoughts of her.

He uncorked the tonic that prohibited unwanted births, and choked on the honey-textured liquid as he swallowed it down.

"Is there anything I can help you find?" the nymph at the door asked him as she ran a hand up his forearm. She was curvaceous, with long, evergreen hair and a pert nose. On any other night, he would have accepted her offer.

As the crowned prince, any of his desires would be accommodated here—but being a frequent visitor didn't hurt either.

"Are there any redheads tonight?"

She froze with her hand on his forearm. Her golden eyes narrowed before she shook her head.

"I'm so sorry, Your Highness. I don't think I know anyone with red hair."

Wilder scrunched his brow in confusion. Surely, red hair wasn't that uncommon.

"That's unfortunate," he drawled, feeling a tightening in his chest.

"Is there anyone else you desire?" she purred. With no other options, she would have to do, he supposed. But he didn't think her alone would be enough.

He scanned the crowded main hall and locked eyes with an elf that resembled the sun. Golden hair, golden eyes, and darkened skin. Her body was a close match to Lyra's. He raised his chin in greeting, and she sauntered over to him.

The two of them would have to do to get her out of his system. They walked arm-in-arm to his usual room at the end of the second-floor hall. It was darker here. He didn't care who saw him, but he didn't like the eyes on his back. He didn't like people to see the scars.

They wasted no time with formalities, and as soon as they entered the room, the nymph and the elf began undressing. Wilder took a seat in the armchair and watched as they showed tantalizing skin. He didn't even know their names. Not that it mattered, but they knew his.

The golden elf caressed the body of the forest nymph, and Wilder watched as she sucked a nipple into her mouth. He couldn't help but imagine what Lyra's breasts would taste like.

They turned to him as he stood and slid off the jacket before placing it on the armchair. With a jerk of his chin, they got on the bed.

It was disappointing—Lyra would have argued.

They lay naked together, kissing and caressing, while they

waited for him. He wasn't ready, not yet. He pictured alabaster skin and auburn hair where he saw evergreen and gold.

Wilder closed his eyes and imagined the smell of a storm off the ocean instead of cinnamon and cloves. It was futile. But they were ready and waiting for him. He slipped off his boots and pants, and they descended on him.

Gliding delicate fingertips down his chest before the golden one wrapped a hand around his length. The forest nymph licked up his neck before kissing his mouth. The golden one sucked his entire cock into her mouth while she massaged his balls.

It was of no use.

They weren't Lyra.

They took turns sucking him off before he could scent that they were completely aroused. He bent the golden one over the side of the bed while the forest nymph lay down in front of her. It was appealing to watch as she sucked her clit into her mouth and swirled her tongue. The forest nymph moaned and writhed as he pounded into the golden one. Her ass was close to the same shape as Lyra's, so he focused on that to bring about his completion.

After he had brought them their satisfaction and they lay nestled asleep together, he slipped out of the room and down to the bar.

Maybe a stiff drink would work.

38
GIRL FRIENDS

Lyra rose with the birds chirruping outside her bedroom window. She had slept peacefully. Stretching her arms out wide, her fingers grazed the teacup on her bedside table, and with a little nudge—she knocked it to the floor.

It shattered.

The sound echoed through the room.

Her bedroom door flew open, and two armed guards shoved into her room, swords drawn.

Covering her mouth with her hand, she pulled the sheets up to her chest.

"Excuse you!"

The blonde guard had the decency to look apologetic, but his dark-haired companion did not.

"Heart-eating siren," he hissed.

She would have been offended if it weren't so godsdamned funny.

"Cyrus," Blondie whispered. "Watch your tongue."

The mouthy, dark-haired one, Cyrus, glared at Lyra and stalked out of her room.

"My apologies, my lady. I will send someone to clean that up," Blondie said before pulling her door closed.

Interesting, so they would rush in here the mere moment they assumed she was trying to escape. She wouldn't be able to unless she did it very, very quietly.

A light knock on the door pulled her from her plans of escape.

"Your Highness," Daisy trilled through the door.

"Come in!"

Daisy pushed open the door. Her periwinkle hair was braided up into a crown, with tiny chamomile flowers placed throughout.

"I love your hair," Lyra gushed and then froze. Where in the world had that come from?

Daisy paused, patting her hair and then smiling. "Thank you, Your Highness."

She walked closer and saw the shattered teacup. Lyra feigned distress.

"I'm so sorry. I was stretching, and it was an accident."

It wasn't a lie, but all the best lies were like that. A bit of truth wrapped in.

"Not to worry. I'll have this squared away in no time. In the meantime, I'll draw you a bath."

"Oh, I can do that myself," Lyra offered, sliding out of the other side of the bed. She had watched Daisy do it enough times that she thought she could manage.

"Oh no, that is most ill-mannered. A lady never draws her bath."

And with that, Daisy scurried into the bathing chamber and got to work. Lyra walked with a sluggish gait and yawned and stretched.

By the time she had reached the bath, Daisy had already doled out the salts and was adding the oils to the steaming tub.

"What did you do?" Lyra asked, wondering what luxurious oils were added this time.

"Excuse me?" Daisy spluttered, whirling around. Her face pinched, wrinkles marched across her brows, and her lips were drawn so thin they were practically gone.

"Which oils did you use this time? It smells lovely—but different."

Daisy's pinched face relaxed. "I used citrus and yarrow. To help with your energy and pain."

"Thank you."

"My pleasure. I'll clean up the cup and set out your training clothes for today." Daisy strode with haste out of the bathing room.

Standing there alone, Lyra gazed around the room. The little voice inside her whispered that something wasn't right. She sniffed at the oils. Nothing about them smelled unusual or dangerous. And she didn't peg Daisy as an assassin. She dipped her fingertips into the warm water and closed her eyes.

What was she searching for?

But when there was no burning or dissolving of her flesh, she shrugged the encounter off to Daisy being nervous around her still.

Lyra shrugged out of her nightclothes and slipped into the water. It was still comforting after so much time on land to submerge herself in its weightlessness. She closed her eyes and imagined herself floating through the current, twirling through kelp forests, and near the reef.

It was splendid with its magical colors and plethora of life. That was the only part of the ocean that wasn't dark or twisted. Then again, she liked that part, too.

She was dark and twisted.

Once she was wrinkled, an aspect of this body she detested, she rose from the bath. But there wasn't a towel in sight.

"Daisy," she called.

"Yes, my lady?"

"There's no towel."

Daisy burst through the door.

"Oh goodness me! I'm so sorry!"

She was as flustered now as she had been when she left. The cabinet beside the tub held stacks of fluffy white towels, and Daisy pulled one out and shook it open.

Lyra stepped into the open towel, wrapping it around her.

"Are you alright?" Lyra asked, noting the pink hue to Daisy's cheeks and her widened eyes.

"I-I am, my lady. Thank you for asking," she stuttered out.

Lyra nodded, but didn't believe that answer at all. That was fine, though. It wasn't as if they were friends who confided in each other.

Soft chocolate-brown leather pants, a gauzy bell-sleeved blouse, and a strange, thick band of leather waited for Lyra on her bed. It was similar, but different from what she wore for training yesterday. An assortment of leather straps lay in a heap by the thick band.

"What is all this?"

Daisy looked at the pile.

"It's your new training clothes." She pointed to the thick band. "That goes around your waist to protect you. And those go around your wrists and forearms."

Lyra scrunched her nose. So many constraining items.

But Daisy didn't wait for a response. Holding up the pants, Lyra stepped in. The inside of them felt strange, cool, and soft.

She sucked in a sharp breath.

Daisy chuckled. "I know it feels strange. It wicks the moisture away from your skin when you sweat."

Lyra marveled at the magic. She was trying to respect

Daisy's level of modesty, but once the pants were up around her waist, she dropped the towel and stood topless. This time, Daisy didn't seem bothered as she tied the straps on the side of Lyra's hips.

When Lyra had shifted so that Daisy could see better, the scars on the inside of her arms became visible, as did the strange circular-shaped one below her left breast.

"My heavens," Daisy whispered. "What happened?"

The question surprised them both, and Daisy covered her mouth with a hand and took a step back.

"I'm so sorry. I didn't mean to pry."

Lyra shook her head. The question wasn't offensive. But she couldn't imagine why Daisy would care.

"The arms? My fiancée gave them to me," Lyra replied, tucking an arm over her breast to hide the scar there.

"That sounds dreadful," Daisy whispered, clutching the neckline of her ruffled dress.

Lyra snorted. "He is."

Daisy's eyes grew wide, and then she burst into laughter. Lyra watched as the girl now clutched at her stomach and wiped tears from her eyes. It surprised her how much joy it brought to make Daisy laugh.

"That was marvelous, my lady."

Lyra nodded. "I'm glad. You need not be afraid of me."

Daisy's mouth dropped open and she spluttered, "I-I'm not. Why would you think that?"

"You seem flustered around me today."

Daisy grabbed the linen shirt off the bed, but twisted it between her fingers. "It's not you, my lady."

Lyra stared long and hard at Daisy. "Then who?"

"I shouldn't say."

Pulling the shirt over her head, Lyra tried to read Daisy's body language. She had trembling hands, and her eyes kept darting to the bedroom door.

"Daisy—who?"

The young servant looked traumatized. With a heavy sigh, her head drooped between her shoulders. "It's the guard—Cyrus."

Lyra's blood ran cold. She had thought there was something off about that male.

"What has he done?"

Daisy shook her head. "No, he just, well, he leers. It's repugnant."

Lyra nodded. "If he ever does anything. And I mean anything—you let me know." There was enough malice in her words that Daisy's eyes bulged before her lips spread into a grateful smile.

"Thank you."

Lyra grinned wickedly. She felt a kinship with Daisy. The young servant was kind and deserved only good things. If Cyrus ever did anything wrong, he would meet Lyra's monster.

Daisy wrapped the leather around Lyra's waist and cinched it tight. It didn't make breathing difficult, but she could tell how it would protect her from a blow. The wrist guards went on next, and they made the sleeves of her blouse look like bells. It was feminine—but fierce.

"I like this," Lyra murmured.

"You look like a warrior."

Lyra couldn't explain how that made her feel. But it made her breathing easier and her shoulders square. Was it pride?

Right after Daisy had finished braiding her hair out of her face and into a coronet, there was a knock on the door. It seemed light compared to Wilder's pounding.

"Lyra," Maelys called. "Are you ready?"

Daisy and Lyra shared a look. Wilder was her escort and mentor for training.

"Yes. I'll be right out," Lyra replied.

Daisy smeared some kind of clear jelly on Lyra's face and rubbed it in. It was cool and smelled light and earthy.

"What's that?"

"It's to protect your skin from the sun. You've already had several freckles bloom, and your forehead is still burned."

Lyra raised her brow and found that the skin didn't pull as tight as it had this morning, which was a relief. And she despised the brown spots that had appeared on her skin of late.

"Thank you."

Daisy patted her shoulders. "Off you get! Have a lovely training."

Lyra grimaced and reached for the door before stopping and turning back to Daisy.

"I hope—I hope you have a wonderful day."

Daisy blushed and then nodded. "You as well, Your Highness."

Maelys was wearing the same training attire as Lyra, but her blouse was burgundy, which looked lovely against her golden brown hair. It was pulled up into a high ponytail, but the ends were braided. Ivy and heather woven into each plait made her resemble a forest nymph. She belonged here, in this place, and was crafted and molded by it.

"I'll be your trainer—for the foreseeable future," Maelys said as Lyra walked through the door.

"Where is Wilder?"

As if her words conjured him up, he stumbled down the hall.

His black hair was disheveled, sticking up in places over his briar crown. The jacket he had been wearing last night was draped over one shoulder, and the undershirt had been ripped open, exposing red and purple marks on his chest.

He had glassy eyes and a smirk on his lips. But, my gods, the smell. Elixir and something sweet.

Wilder slammed face-first into his door, and Lyra gasped. Maelys rolled her eyes and crossed her arms.

"Are you just getting in?"

Wilder slid his face across the door to peer at them. His hand was still grappling for the doorknob he couldn't seem to find.

"What time is it?" he asked, slurring his words.

Lyra had never seen someone so inebriated before.

"It's nine in the morning," Maelys replied. "Were you at the Venus?"

Wilder grinned broadly, his hand finding the doorknob at last. He opened it underneath himself and stumbled into the room before kicking it closed.

Lyra turned her head to look at Maelys, who was shaking her head and laughing as they set off down the hall with two guards trailing them.

"What's the Venus?" It must be some kind of tavern if the stench of liquor hinted at anything.

"It's a pleasure hall in the Lower District."

The answer had Lyra blushing bright scarlet. She had heard whispers of such things from the mermen who had wanted to become scouts—it was a huge motivation for life in the mortal realm.

The humans were much freer with their sexuality than the mermaids, but not nearly as free as the elves.

But Maelys' unabashed answer to her question had sparked an idea in her mind.

"What does 'velvet-wrapped steel' mean?"

Maelys bit down on her lip. "Why?"

Lyra sighed. "I read it in a book last night, and Wilder ripped it out of my hands and refused to answer."

Maelys shook her head with a chuckle and her braided ponytail swung side to side. "It's a euphemism for cock."

The golden thread in Lyra glowed at the emotion that coursed through her. She had to cover her mouth with both hands to keep the laugh from bursting out.

A choking coughing sound from behind had them both

turning to look at the guards following them. It was Blondie from earlier, but the mouthy one had been replaced.

Which was a good thing.

Lyra needed to take this embarrassment out on someone, and after her conversation with Daisy, she would be more than happy to fight with him. But Blondie made eye contact with Lyra and lingered.

She turned back around and pressed her lips into a thin line. He wasn't unattractive by any means, but he was an elf, and she was still a mermaid.

"We're going to be doing things a bit differently than Wilder does them since I'm in charge now." Maelys' voice interrupted Lyra's thoughts of elvish suitors.

"That's fine," she answered in a distracted tone.

Maelys bumped Lyra with a shoulder. "You didn't even bother to ask how it would be different before you agreed."

Lyra glanced sidelong at her. "Well, unless you plan to string me up by my toes or run me naked through the streets—nothing could have been worse than training with Wilder."

Maelys laughed louder, and a smile tugged Lyra's lips up at the corners.

"You got me there. I wouldn't say it will be worse. Maybe equally horrible, but in an entirely new way."

Lyra huffed. She had a feeling Maelys was going to be creative with her torture disguised as training.

Fine, that was just fine.

39
LITTLE
FISH

Wilder felt like his head had just hit the pillow when he flinched awake. He didn't know what had startled him, but the dryness in his mouth was unbearable. He had needed the release. Even through the irritation that had arisen thanks to his father, he couldn't ignore the sexual frustration that had consumed him after seeing her in that godsforsaken dress. If he thought the tight pants were torture, that was murder through and through.

He squeezed his eyes closed as his room tilted and spun. A pounding behind his eyes had him sitting up and pressing a palm to his temple. He didn't remember making it to bed.

Sighing to himself, he threw his legs over the side. He was still dressed in his dinner attire. The floor was frigid against his bare feet. Well, at least he had pulled his boots off by himself.

Stumbling to the bathing room, he rinsed his mouth out with water and stripped down. The smell of the females clung to him and made his stomach roil—or was that the liquor?

He had a quick bath to get rid of the scent and clear his head. The sun was coming through the windows at a slant. Which meant Lyra would be at training already. He rubbed his eyes with his hands.

Flickers from last night swirled through his mind. Wilder had told his father he had quit and would not be training her anymore.

He groaned. Well, at least that meant he would see her less and less.

But who would be in charge of her training now, and would they measure up to the task at hand?

Wilder tilted his head back and hissed when the cold of the marble pressed against his neck. The arched ceiling rose into the shape of a glass star that had light pouring down onto his face.

Lyra had a momentous task in front of her, and Wilder was the best there was. If he gave up on her, she would fail, and it would be his fault. He drummed his long fingers against the rim of the marble tub before huffing.

He focused on the water that rippled with each drum and the warmth that eased his headache. What if something bad happened?

Lyra wasn't ready to use her magic. She could get hurt. He had to see her training for himself before he decided what his future held.

The ancient stone was smooth against his feet as he padded out of the bathing chamber and into his room. With the black velvet curtains still drawn, his room was cast in utter darkness, but he could move blindly around without knocking into the chaise by the windows or the posts of his iron bed.

He pulled open the doors to his armoire and rummaged around for his white linen tunic and brown leather pants. Donning both, he brushed the tangles of his dark hair back, attempting to hide his briars as best he could. His head pounded behind closed eyes as he struggled to pull his boots on.

Wilder set off for the training grounds at a forced leisurely pace. But it was empty when he stalked down the path and through the stone archway. He whirled in a circle, thinking maybe his inebriated state was playing tricks on him.

No one was here.

They had been, and recently by the smell of it. The scent didn't lead back towards the castle, however, but into the thicket near the grounds.

Wilder followed Lyra's scent, and it made his chest ache. No other female had come close to her last night, and that was a problem—an enormous one. He followed the trodden path through birch and rowan trees as a light breeze ruffled the leaves and his hair. He heard them before he saw them.

Maelys was singing loudly and off-key, followed by Otto's deep baritone. The stomping on the ground, he figured, was from Ridge. He didn't hear a sound coming from Lyra. And Cedric, Oak, Dust, and Oron weren't here at all.

He scaled a large ash tree. Its wide branches were sturdy enough to hold him, and the foliage concealed him. He was also downwind, so none of the others below could scent him.

"Alright, Lyra. I want you to close your eyes and listen," Maelys ordered.

Wilder was disgruntled when Lyra obeyed without argument.

"I don't want you to reach for your magic, or touch it at all. I want you to study it only. What does it look like?"

Lyra's bottom lip quivered, and her breathing stuttered.

Maelys reached out and clasped Lyra's hand.

"I'm right here with you."

Ice flooded Wilder's veins, watching the companionship of that embrace. They could have been sisters with the way Maelys was treating her.

Ridge shifted on his feet, relaxed shoulders, and then tugged at one of Otto's beads in his hair. Otto smirked but swatted at Ridge's hand.

"What does it look like?" Maelys asked again.

"A thread of gold," Lyra responded.

Otto's face lit with surprise, and Maelys beamed with pride.

"Good. Very good."

Lyra inhaled through her nose, and her eyes whirled wildly beneath her closed lids. Wilder was enraptured, watching her stand as still as a stone—but work so hard. She hadn't even tried to touch her magic when he was around.

"What does it feel like?"

Lyra didn't answer. Her face pinched with what looked like pain, her breath slipping through her parted lips in pants. Maelys squeezed her hand, reminding Lyra that she wasn't alone. In response, her face relaxed, and her breathing slowed.

"Lyra, don't be afraid. What does it feel like?"

Wilder could see Lyra's eyes move behind her closed lids before they froze—as did the rest of her. Her arms and legs seized before she toppled like a felled tree.

Maelys crouched beside her and brushed a hand against her arm. "Are you alright?"

Lyra's body shook with chaotic tremors.

"Let's get her back to the castle. She needs a healer." Ridge's voice was strained. Maelys turned wide eyes to him and swallowed forcibly.

With those words, Wilder dropped to the ground beside them.

Ridge whirled, sword drawn. Otto held two daggers in his palms. And Maelys positioned herself in front of Lyra.

"I will take her," Wilder growled.

"Good gods. Was that necessary?" Maelys spat. "Why are you hiding in the shadows?"

Wilder glared at her. "You took my position. I wanted to see how it was going without me."

Maelys pointed a finger at his chest. "I was ordered to since you abandoned your duty."

Her words stung more than he would ever admit. His duty was all he had, even if he resented it most of the time.

Wilder shrugged off her words and continued past her and to the now still Lyra. He swept her off the ground and clutched her to his chest.

"Had she come that close before?" he asked, looking at the freckles that blazed against her porcelain skin.

"No, that was the first time," Otto replied.

"And the rest of her training?" There was a bruise blooming on her cheek. It made his blood boil. "Someone struck her?"

Ridge chuckled. "No. She did that to herself."

Wilder stopped and turned towards him. "How?" The word came out like a growl.

"She thought she was going to be fancy with a wooden sword, and it slapped her in the face when she failed to catch it."

The answer had extinguished the fire within him. She would do that. But the anger he had felt when he thought someone had hurt her—he pushed that thought away.

He began striding through the thicket and then through the rolling hills of heather. When he breached the castle, he didn't slow until he hit the hallway of the healer's chambers.

The witch was standing in the doorway, waiting. Twirling an ivy leaf in her hand, she sized him up.

"Did the little fish touch her magic?" she purred.

Wilder flinched and clutched her to his chest.

"She doesn't need me. She needs rest. Take her to her room and have food ready. A ferocious appetite will turn her fearsome when she wakes. She's not used to the power and isn't strong enough to wield it."

Wilder turned without answering and carried Lyra up to her

room. He didn't like the witch calling her "little fish." But he was relieved that this unconscious state wouldn't last.

Maelys, Otto, and Ridge followed them. Their purposeful footsteps alerted him to their presence.

"I see why she never touched the thing," Maelys mumbled.

"It's because she hasn't touched it. Now it's too powerful for her to wield without collapsing," Otto said.

"Why has she never touched it?" Ridge asked.

"Besides the obvious, that is merfolk not believing their females equal? A sea witch instilled a deep, misguided fear in her," Otto answered.

Wilder's ears pricked. "Misguided?"

Otto nodded, his face turned grave. "Her father ordered it so that Lyra wouldn't wield it against them."

"Did her father order her kidnapping?"

Otto's eyes turned glassy. "No."

"Then who did?"

"I can't see."

SHE SLEPT FOR TWO DAYS. Wilder only left her side to eat. But now he was being summoned by his father for the second time, and this time he could not refuse.

Maelys and Daisy volunteered to stay by her side in his absence, and with near-rabid insistence from his mother, he agreed.

The throne room was empty when Wilder stalked through the doors and to the foot of the dais. His father lounged on his throne, but there was a stiff countenance to his jaw and shoulders.

"You've summoned me?" Wilder came to a halt at the foot of the stairs.

His father shifted in his chair and rubbed the bridge of his nose.

"I apologize for my behavior after dinner."

This had his mother written all over it. Queen Aine had worked tirelessly to bridge the rift between them. What had happened kept that from ever being possible. But he wasn't about to tell her that.

Time healed all wounds, and as an elf, he would have an immeasurable amount of time to forgive what had happened to him.

It still had not mattered to him that his father had changed. What mattered was the time it took for him to do it and the pain Wilder had endured.

He gave a curt dip of his chin before spinning on his heel.

"I was not finished," King Oberon's voice boomed through the empty hall. Wilder froze, but did not turn around. "If you believe Maelys leading her training will delay things, you will be required to step in."

Wilder looked over his shoulder at his father, but still did not reply.

"We are running out of time, Wilder. The gods will intervene if magic is not balanced."

He quirked his brow and turned.

"What are the stipulations of this bargain between you and this unnameable creature?"

King Oberon glared at him with all the authority of the High King.

"If you don't see fit to include me in this in its entirety, I will not play a part in any facet."

His father shook his head. "You have no idea of the powers at work here, son. If you think you could do a better job, I implore you to challenge me."

It was a jab used time and time again.

Wilder didn't want the throne, had never wanted it, and his father knew that. And was merely being cruel.

So, with that, Wilder strode from the throne room.

40
GOLDEN GIRLS

The frigid water and tentacles that appeared in her nightmares were muted somehow. Before, they were suffocating and all-consuming. Her distance from the sea must have weakened them.

Lyra blinked her eyes open. She was back in her room. But where Wilder had sat the last time she woke from unconsciousness, Maelys was now there.

"You're awake! How do you feel?" she asked, scanning her for injury.

Lyra pressed a hand to the hollowness that threatened to consume her. Her stomach growled so loudly it shook her body.

Maelys smiled and reached for the plate on her bedside table, handing it to Lyra. Meats, cheeses, small crackers, and grapes.

"Daisy is in the kitchen getting you something heavier."

Lyra nodded and dug in. It wasn't enough food to sate her, so she licked the plate clean.

"Do you remember anything?" Maelys asked with a gentle nature.

Lyra shook her head and gripped the fabric on her bed as she squeezed her eyes shut.

Her power. It had called to her, screamed so loudly that she couldn't ignore it any longer, and she had reached for it.

She dropped the plate onto her lap and looked at Maelys with a mix of anguish and horror.

"I am so sorry," Lyra whispered.

Maelys shook her head and grabbed Lyra's hand.

"Nothing happened to us. We were worried about you. You just collapsed."

Lyra sighed and leaned back against the pillows. She didn't understand why they were worried or why they seemed to care.

"You worried about me?"

Maelys reeled back. "Of course we were."

"But—why?" A tiny part of Lyra hoped it was for her and not what she could do for them.

"Because we care about you, and you were hurt. What do you mean, why?"

Lyra felt a burning in her eyes and a tightness in her chest. They cared about her.

"I just didn't know. And my power. Well, you should know something about it."

Maelys cocked her head to the side. "Okay …"

"It will make me a monster. It will corrupt me, and I know, I know all magic does that, but there was a prophecy about mine."

"I need to tell you something. And I need you to promise me you'll listen."

Lyra turned and looked at Maelys, really looked at her. She sucked her lower lip into her mouth, and her eyes narrowed with an unbearable intensity.

"I'm listening."

"The fear of your power ... it was fabricated. By your father and a sea witch."

Lyra's eyes slid closed as Maelys' words wrapped around her and squeezed.

"Otto saw it all. So you don't have to be afraid. If we can teach you to control it, you'll be fine. You won't lose—"

"No."

Maelys flinched at the command in Lyra's voice. She hadn't even used her power, and it still made Maelys flinch.

Which is why Lyra would never use it ever again. It wasn't just the power that frightened Lyra, but what would happen when she used it.

She was a murderer.

Even if her father and the sea witch had fabricated the prophecy, it wouldn't have mattered. There were countless stories of creatures abusing their power and becoming nightmares. Even just now, Maelys, who had been consoling her, flinched in fear at her loud tone.

"Lyra ..." Maelys began. "Think of the good you could do. You could not only restore balance, but also think about what you could do when you returned home. A lot more—"

"No," Lyra said again, quieter this time. "No one should have that power. Especially not me."

But Maelys' words sank into her heart. When she returned home, would she have it in her to bring about change? She shoved that thought away.

She knew she wasn't strong enough. And even if she became strong enough—she had to fulfill her bargain first.

Maelys stroked a thumb over Lyra's knuckles. "I won't press you again."

Lyra's breath caught in the back of her throat.

"I'm sorry," Maelys muttered. "I don't know what it's like."

Lyra's chest felt light, her breath coming easier.

"Thank you." She had expected no one to understand. Even

her father had tried to carve the power out of her when she made it apparent she would never use it.

Her door banged open, and Wilder strode through.

"You're awake."

Lyra studied him. He seemed sobered at least, but his hair stuck up between the brambles of briars as if he had been tugging on it. His eyes lightened and then darkened under her gaze.

"I am."

Maelys looked between them both but didn't contribute.

"Oh, goodie, the door is already open—" Daisy came waltzing in, almost running into Wilder with a tray of food. She sidestepped him and closed her mouth.

Wilder looked between the three females and then nodded before turning on a heel and walking out.

"What in the world has gotten into him?" Maelys muttered, bewildered.

Lyra plucked at her downy comforter and shrugged. Her eyes were on the very full tray that Daisy had brought in. Her mouth watered, and she cleared her throat.

"Daisy?"

"Oh goodness me! Sorry," she replied, striding to Lyra and handing her the tray. "Hope you're hungry!"

Lyra shoved handfuls of berries and small cheeses into her mouth as Daisy and Maelys talked.

"I have never seen him in such a tizzy," Maelys muttered.

Daisy hovered beside the bed until Lyra patted the corner, and then she plopped down.

"It seems as if he's worried about her," Daisy replied, nodding to Lyra.

Maelys reached to grab a grape, and Lyra swatted at her hand. Unperturbed, Maelys grabbed one anyway and popped it into her mouth. "You might be onto something." She spoke with her mouth full. "He was very protective of her on the way here."

"Under orders," Lyra clarified.

Maelys threw her a look that said otherwise.

"He stayed by her side the entire time she was fighting off the spider venom, and when he left to bathe, he gave me specific instructions to alert him the moment she woke if it happened while he was gone," Daisy added.

"What are you two trying to say?" Lyra volleyed her head between Maelys and Daisy.

"It's obvious, isn't it?" Maelys asked with a smirk.

Lyra rose when the sun was already well into the sky and enjoyed the serenity of nothingness. She had a day off from training and hadn't decided yet what the day would bring.

A soft knocking on the door had her shifting her attention from the light streaming through the window to Daisy's face.

"Still in bed, I see?"

Lyra yawned and stretched her arms up above her head.

"I didn't have training this morning."

Daisy grinned and patted the cream ruffles of her uniform.

"Well, then. What would you like to do today, so that I know how to dress you?"

Lyra frowned, and her nose scrunched. "I'm not sure. Maybe the library? Oh! Are there gardens here?"

Daisy walked to the armoire and began rifling through it. "There are the queen's gardens and the northern gardens. Both are expansive."

"Which do you prefer?"

Daisy froze with her hands on a sky-blue gossamer gown. "I don't know. I've never walked through the queen's gardens."

"Could you go with me, then?" Lyra asked, sitting up against the pillows.

"I would like that very much."

Lyra swung her legs off the side of the bed and stood up. "Then it's settled. You'll go with me."

They walked arm-in-arm through the queen's gardens, and it was magical.

There were all manner of flowers and trees, of which most Lyra didn't even know the names. Some trees had giant leaves in the shapes of stars and flowers whose petals were so thin, they were clear and gleamed iridescently when the light hit them.

Daisy stared in wonder just as much as Lyra. They were trailed by two guards Lyra had never seen before. Which was a relief. She didn't want the dark-haired one, Cyrus, to ruin Daisy's time.

Their emerald-green uniforms matched some of the leaves perfectly. And several flowers were the same shade of gold as the embroidered stag horns.

A cool breeze swirled through the garden, and they basked in the afternoon sun. Giggles up ahead reached their ears, and Daisy plucked at her servant's uniform.

"What's the matter?" Lyra asked when Daisy straightened her collar for the fourth time.

"There are courtiers up ahead. Ladies to Queen Aine."

Lyra's brow furrowed. "So?"

"They're high-born," Daisy hissed under her breath as they came closer.

"Does that matter?" Lyra asked, not lowering the volume of her voice.

They rounded the corner where the ladies had congregated around a bench. Only one sat on the bench, draped in crimson silk and glittering jewels. Two more were standing close by in similar shades of pink.

The ladies went silent as they passed. Daisy ducked her chin and tried to pick up the pace, but Lyra tugged her back.

"Ladies," Lyra greeted them with a dip of her chin.

Only one had the decency to return her greeting. And when she did, the two others shot her a look of disdain.

Lyra rolled her eyes and continued.

"That's the prince's pet," the one on the bench whispered, fanning herself with a large ruffled fan.

"I hear she's a mermaid that the king is training to kill humans," another whispered.

"Well, I heard the prince *loves* her. He asked for a redhead at the Venus."

Lyra couldn't help the snort that shot from her.

The prince, in love with her? It would be more likely that the king was training her to be an assassin.

Daisy stared quizzically at her as they continued. "Are you training to kill people?"

"No!" Lyra gasped. "You know why I'm here, don't you?"

Daisy shook her head.

"I'm training to use my magic to undo a bargain."

Daisy's eyes turned as large as the yellow flowers they were passing. "A bargain? Isn't that dangerous?"

Lyra shrugged. "I guess I'll find out. I don't really have a choice anymore. I entered into a bargain with the king."

"Oh, Lyra. That is most disconcerting to hear. Bargains are tricky to undo."

"They are indeed, Little Fish," a female voice purred from underneath the branches of a large willow.

A woman appeared, breezing through a sweeping curtain of branches. Her charcoal gown appeared to change colors in the sunlight and was cut straight across her collarbones.

Daisy gasped and dipped her chin. "Lady Jordania."

Lyra stared at this new lady—Jordania.

She was unusual, not shallow as the other courtiers had been, but there was something about her, something powerful.

"Little Fish?" Lyra asked, cocking her head to the side and narrowing her eyes.

"It's my nickname for you, mermaid. How has the land been treating you?"

Jordania stopped in front of Lyra, and that's when she realized what she had felt. Jordania was a witch. A powerful one.

"I don't like the nickname, and the land has been … unkind. But the people have been nice."

Jordania gave Lyra a sweep of her eye and then grinned. "Nasty bite, those witch's curse spiders."

Lyra looked at Daisy for an explanation. "Lady Jordania is the healer here. Prince Wilder brought you to her after your spider bite and then again after your accident in training."

"Then I guess a thank you is in order."

Jordania brushed a thick lock of chestnut hair behind her ear. "There's no need."

Her ears were blunt, not pointed like the elves. Silence stretched taut between them, and Daisy shifted on her feet.

"As a witch, you're not like the elves, are you?" Lyra asked.

"Very astute, Princess. No, I am not elvish, but I'm not human either. I'm something—in between." Her voice changed when she said the last part. It was old and young, hers and many.

It made goosebumps rise on Lyra's flesh.

"What was that?"

Jordania smiled. "Sometimes my magic slips through when it's called." The thread of gold in Lyra flared. "You're almost ready, Little Fish. Use yours when it calls."

Then Jordania was walking away, her sweeping charcoal gown flowing behind her like a trail of smoke.

"That was … strange," Lyra said, her brow raising high.

Daisy shivered. "I know she's nice and all, but goodness, she scares me."

"Is she nice?" Lyra pursed her lips.

"Very. She's been nothing but kind, but when her voice does that powerful thing, it startles me."

Lyra tried not to let her shoulders droop.

What would Daisy think of her if she used her magic?

"Ready to check out the library?" Daisy asked.

Lyra nodded and followed her back through the winding pathway and into the library.

But Jordania's words plagued her all day. "Use yours when it calls." Would she recognize it when it did?

41
SHOWGIRL

The following week passed in a blur. Training, reading, sleeping.

Lyra had read unbelievable things in *The Knight in Shining Armor*. Intimacy and ecstasy, pain and rapture. She still couldn't quite comprehend it all.

Actually, she wished there had been pictures so she could understand the positions. Sex in this body would differ greatly from the single position that her mermaid form allowed for.

A tail can't split, and with the main organ in the front, there was really only one way to do it. Unless you got really creative, but being upside down for that long didn't seem enjoyable.

As she and Maelys walked down to the grounds, she noticed a difference in her gait. Her legs felt stronger somehow, and her breathing came easier, even while keeping up with Maelys' quick pace. The last two days had been scorching. It was changing seasons here. She hadn't ever experienced that before.

"Ostara will be upon us soon," Maelys said, raising a hand to block the blistering sun. "Do the merfolk celebrate?"

Lyra sighed. "The males do. Females are—"

"Forbidden," Maelys finished for her.

They shared a look, and Lyra managed a small laugh without feeling her power flare. It hadn't been as noticeable since the incident. Like that light stroke had taken the edge off. *The Knight in Shining Armor* had mentioned something similar.

"How do you celebrate here?"

Maelys smiled. "A lavish feast, a ball, and, of course, the pleasure halls will brim with revelers." She wiggled her eyebrows for emphasis.

"Do you go—to the pleasure hall?"

"Of course! Most of us do during the holidays. Exploring your carnal desires is welcome and even encouraged for males and females. We're more than vessels of life—but life itself."

Maelys said it with such glee that Lyra couldn't help but marvel. She hadn't been raised on anything other than females being vessels *for* life.

"That sounds—interesting."

"We should go. I'll take you," Maelys offered.

Lyra grinned and nodded. "When is Ostara?"

"Two weeks."

Lyra bounced on her toes as she walked now, excitement thrumming through her veins. She had time to read a few more of those romance books she picked out with Daisy and learn some things before she lost her maidenhead. Her father would be murderous if he knew. And Drystan—well, he would call off the entire engagement.

That had her smiling even bigger. She could take her life into her own hands with this decision.

Something about that hadn't excited her as much as it should have. She glanced sidelong at Maelys, admiring the quiet grace she exuded, and sighed.

When they arrived at the training ground, Lyra was surprised to see Queen Aine and a retinue of ladies in pastel dresses. Queen Aine wore a gown of the purest white. The small cap sleeves fluttered like wings, and she walked with such a floating flourish, it appeared that she was hovering above the ground.

Ladies flounced about her, holding large parasols in gowns that mimicked the wildflowers that had bloomed on the fields. Powder blue, blush, and buttery yellow. They all seemed too delicate to be here, where Lyra and Maelys were bedecked in leather and weapons.

"Lyra, darling!" Queen Aine called from her chair by the willows. "We've come to see your training."

Dread filled Lyra's stomach. Her training was abysmal.

She couldn't hold a sword, fire a bow, or even throw a punch properly. She wasn't a warrior like Maelys. Lyra didn't know who or what she was.

Maelys chuckled from beside her. "I hope they weren't expecting a show."

Lyra elbowed her in the ribs and immediately regretted it when her elbow throbbed.

"Pretend we're not even here!" Queen Aine called when they came closer. "We wanted to get a look at you."

Lyra grimaced. "I'm not sure there is much to see."

"Oh, nonsense! You've been training with the best. Surely you've mastered *something* by now."

Lyra shot a salacious grin at Maelys. So her failure wouldn't be solely hers to carry, but Maelys' as well.

Maelys blanched and turned to look at Lyra. "Uh, we're still working on getting her land-legs, Your Majesty."

"Very well, then," Queen Aine replied with a dip of her chin. "Carry on."

Lyra and Maelys turned as one and headed for their starting spot for their warmup jog.

"Here goes nothing," Lyra whispered. "Don't embarrass us."

42
GIRL POWER

Wilder materialized from the shadows of the willow tree and stood behind his mother. There hadn't been a second he had missed of Lyra's training the past week, and although Maelys was trying her best, she just couldn't get anywhere with it.

A strong breeze blew in from behind him, and his mother stiffened.

"Wilder," she addressed him without turning around.

It hadn't been windy all day. He looked around the training ground, spotting Dust and Oak grinning at him. Either one of them could have stirred the wind on purpose. Meddling fools.

"Mother," he replied.

"Has her training improved?"

"No."

She clicked her tongue, and the ladies around her shifted nervously, hoping her annoyance wasn't with them. It didn't matter where his mother went.

There was always a gaggle of those preening courtiers vying for her favor. It annoyed him on her behalf—he didn't know how she could stand it.

"And you don't think it would benefit the kingdom for you to step in?"

There it was.

The very thought he had been avoiding the past week, watching her fail over and over. Magic demanded balance.

What the merfolk and humans had agreed to was an abomination. It was a wonder the very fabric of their world wasn't unraveling because of it. The sooner they could undo it—the better.

"I will not get involved," he said under his breath.

His father was keeping secrets, dangerous secrets. If he didn't respect Wilder enough to share the details, then Wilder would not be involved in this scheme.

"I see your pride is still intact," his mother said, turning to gaze at him at last. "Would you consider your pride above your duty to this kingdom?"

Wilder could feel his anger rising. Every second of every day since he had returned, he had put this kingdom above his own needs. For her to insinuate such a thing was an incredulous offense.

"Nothing to say?" She arched a well-manicured brow. "Fine, then. What if I told you her survival depends on you helping her?"

Wilder rolled his eyes. Why she thought he would care about the life of a single mermaid was beyond him. But when he didn't answer, she pressed on.

"You should ask Otto what the outlook is. I know you refuse to hear your future, but you should at least hear hers."

It took a lot of power and focus for Otto to see far into the future. Which meant it was important to him—or his mother.

"Why do you care, Mother?"

Aine looked across the grounds to where Lyra was laughing with Maelys as she tried to skip.

"Such innocence in a creature we've been told was monstrous. Don't you think?"

Wilder had followed her gaze and found himself entranced by her all over again.

Lyra wore a sleeveless training top, and it showed off the delicate lines of her arms. Her auburn hair gleamed scarlet in the sunlight, and his chest tightened.

"I would like to see her live. Find out what she is capable of, and the rest of her kind. The females there deserve more."

He couldn't argue with that. The mermen of her kingdom sounded like the monsters everyone claimed. Keeping their females uneducated and weak. It was a wonder they didn't keep them locked up.

Lyra and Maelys began stretching, and Wilder tried to avert his eyes. But her hair blew around her face in the breeze, and she closed her eyes, tipping her face up to the clear sky.

His mother was right; there was an innocence to her. He had noticed it when she had smelled the flowers or marveled at the birds in flight. Not a second of her time on land had been taken for granted. Even though she claimed it had all been against her will.

Queen Aine sighed and watched as they broke away from stretching, and Lyra was attempting to draw the string back on a bow.

Dust and Oak were now standing beside Maelys and giving Lyra instructions.

They had been at this for the last two days. Wilder had picked up exactly what was hindering her from pulling the string back, but the others hadn't. They said pleasant words of encouragement and clapped when she pulled it back an inch.

But Lyra was a fire that needed to burn.

Their kindness was water dousing her flames. She hadn't

been raised with kindness; therefore, she didn't know how to react to it.

She needed air to fan her flames—hot air.

Queen Aine winced when Lyra's fingers slipped off the bowstring, and it slapped her forearm.

A bright red welt bloomed on her porcelain skin, but it was the silver scars on her biceps that Wilder noticed when she held her arm up to look.

There wasn't a thought in his mind, only the roaring of blood in his ears. He stalked past his mother and her retinue and across the grounds.

"I have it," Maelys said as he approached.

His glower silenced her.

Gripping Lyra's arm, he turned her biceps towards him to get a better look at the silver scars. *Talons.* Talons had left those on her flesh.

"Who did this?" he growled. Lyra tugged on her arm and glared at him.

"It's none of *your* business," she spat back, ripping her arm from his grip and darting her eyes around at the people gathered.

She had been trying to hide her scars, and he had pointed them out in front of everyone. He was a fool. A stupid, thoughtless fool.

"Pick up the bow." She flinched at his tone, but obeyed. "Grip it tightly."

"Wilder, she's been—" Oak started.

"Silence."

Oak's head lowered as he pressed his lips together.

Lyra trembled; the ferocity coming off of Wilder in waves was alarming her.

"You pick up that bow and pull the gods damn string back. Stop fucking about. You're not weak or helpless. If you don't learn how to defend yourself, you will end up with more scars, or *you will die.*"

Her lip trembled, but there was a storm building in her emerald eyes, and the way she clenched her teeth seemed to staunch the fear coursing through her.

Fury pumped through her now, and he could smell it. It shifted her scent from the ocean to something darker, like tempestuous storms.

Lyra closed her eyes and pulled on the string.

"You are not weak," he said. The string came back farther. "You are not helpless." Farther and farther she pulled it, letting her anger give her strength.

"Let go," he whispered.

She did.

The arrow flew, thudding right outside the lines on the target. She hadn't even been close to the bullseye, but that wasn't his goal. His only goal had been to get her to pull the fucking string back.

Lyra opened her eyes and stared, wide-eyed at the target, and then at the bow in her hands. The happiness in her gaze was enough to stop his heart from beating. But he nodded and turned on his heel.

"Stop coddling her," he ordered Maelys.

Maelys glared at him but didn't argue.

He had gotten further with Lyra in two minutes than she had in days. Satisfied with himself, he stalked off the training grounds and back to the castle.

He needed to find a way to get Lyra out of his system—and quickly.

43
SIDE QUEST

Lyra was still smiling to herself after a long day of training. She had fired the bow two more times. Neither time had she hit the target again.

But that hadn't mattered. She had fired it, and that was a success in her book.

She walked beside Maelys on the way back to the castle. Sweat and dirt clung to her, and she was looking forward to the bath that Daisy would draw.

"You did well today," Maelys said as they walked up to the doorway on the hill. "I hadn't realized that being mean to you would get you past that threshold."

Lyra pursed her lips. "It probably wouldn't work if you did it. It's just *him*."

Maelys smiled and nodded. "I've noticed that about you two. He's the moon and you are the tide."

Lyra stilled, having never heard of that expression before.

"What does that mean?"

Maelys opened the door but stood outside it. "It means he pulls you higher—and you grow, like a swelling tide."

Lyra snorted. "You mean pushes? He is quite pushy."

"No," Maelys shook her head, and her eyes softened, "it looks like he's pulling you in."

She understood what Maelys was saying, but the words made little sense.

There was no way he was pulling her in—he seemed repulsed by everything that she was.

"My lady!" Daisy called down the hallway. She ran towards Lyra, waving her hand. "You've been summoned."

A pit of dread yawned open in front of Lyra and swallowed her whole. A summons right after training could not be a good sign.

"Right now?"

Daisy skidded to a halt and waved the folded bit of parchment paper in front of her.

"Right now."

Lyra looked down at her dirty training clothes. Hopefully, the king wouldn't take offense.

"Do you want me to come with you?" Maelys asked.

Daisy shook her head. "She's to come—alone."

Maelys shrugged. "I'll follow you to the door at least."

"Thank you."

They walked in silence to the private chambers of the king and queen. What could be so important that they didn't require her to bathe and change beforehand?

They reached the ornate hallway, and two guards peeled off the walls and walked behind them. The temperature in the hallway plummeted.

Lyra worked to still her trembling fingers. The eyes in the paintings seemed to follow her as she passed, and dread coiled around her gut. She hadn't tried to escape—as far as they knew. She showed up on time for training and tried her best. Hell, she even shot the bow today. What could this be about?

The doors of the private chambers swung open as she approached, and she left a very uneasy-looking Maelys and Daisy at the threshold.

"Lyra, darling, have a seat," Queen Aine murmured from a chaise lounge by the bookshelf.

She reclined against the cushions and had an air of aloofness about her as she patted the end of her seat. Lyra walked with hesitant steps.

"Has something happened?"

Queen Aine looked up from the book she was reading.

"I thought we could have a little chat."

Lyra breathed a sigh of relief and took a seat on the plush chair.

"It was quite spectacular watching your training today."

"Thank you," Lyra murmured.

Queen Aine had always been pleasant towards her, but she didn't know how much of it was genuine. Most royalty, she knew, always had ulterior motives.

"I've been thinking a bit about this situation with your magic …"

Lyra stilled. Her magic was still a source of contention.

"I think you would have a stronger connection to it if you felt more comfortable with your surroundings. Perhaps a tour of the kingdom?'

Lyra frowned.

"Do you think that will help?"

She nodded. "I do. Magic is tied to the heart, and your heart belongs to the sea. Does it not?"

Lyra thought of her home, of the rhythmic current that her heart mimicked with each beat. The queen could be on to something.

"And you want my heart tied here?"

Queen Aine tittered. "I would never expect you to feel at home here. But if you were more familiar with your surroundings and the people here, it would be easier for you."

Lyra weighed her words and found them agreeable, so she nodded.

"Great, I'll make all the arrangements. Oh, and one more thing." Queen Aine picked up another book beside her and handed it to Lyra. "I thought you might like to learn a little bit about our customs here and how exactly bargains are made and broken."

She reached for the book, but Queen Aine did not relinquish it immediately.

"If you're after something you've never truly had, you'll have to do things you've never done, darling."

With that, she let go of the book and released Lyra from her gaze. She picked up the book she was reading and resumed.

Lyra sat frozen as the queen's words gripped her completely. It was as if the queen knew all her thoughts and motivations, all the things she kept tucked tightly to her chest.

"You may go."

Lyra rose and strode for the door, but before she could reach it, she turned.

"Thank you, Your Majesty."

Queen Aine waved her off with a kind smile.

Maelys and Daisy were right where she had left them when she pulled the door open.

"Well?" Daisy asked, twisting her fingers.

"She gave me a book," Lyra waved the book, "and wants to set up a tour of the Wilds so that I will be more comfortable here."

Maelys reeled back in shock. "When?"

Lyra shrugged. "I don't know when. She just said she'd make all the arrangements."

Their footsteps seemed loud in the empty hallway.

"Hopefully not during Ostara," Daisy added. "It's your first one!"

Lyra was partial to agree. She didn't want to miss her first holiday. It was exciting to have something to look forward to.

Wilder crossed through the hallway in front of them but didn't acknowledge them at all. Actually—maybe being away from him would be better. It was uncomfortable being close to him. She had felt things, things she would never admit to feeling. There was something about him that always felt familiar, like she knew him, the real him. And he understood her, pushed her in a way no one had.

It didn't help that she couldn't deny his physical attributes; he was handsome, exceedingly so. Lyra found herself thinking about him more often than not. Sometimes she wondered if he thought about her.

44
BUBBLES

Wilder sat in the smaller, uncomfortable chair in his father's private office. The entire way here, he had pondered the meaning. A summons at this time of day was alarming. Was it because of how he had treated Lyra during training?

Regrettably, it wasn't kind, but it had worked. He was relieved it had worked and was proud of her. She didn't seem perturbed by his anger; if anything, she understood him. Even with the stress of this meeting, he couldn't get her out of his head.

But now sitting in front of his father, he was relieved their meeting was overseen by his mother, who had just met with Lyra. Her lingering scent greeted him when he walked into their chambers, and his heart thumped erratically in his chest.

She was everywhere, all the time. In the hallways, the library, the gardens, he couldn't escape.

"Your mother has decided that she doesn't like our current

state of affairs," Oberon muttered. He sat hunched over like a scolded child. While Aine stood beside him, with an arm draped over the back of his chair.

"We have only one son," she snapped. "And I will not allow you to drive him away because you can't regulate your own emotions."

Wilder's brow arched. He had never heard her speak to his father that way. Not even after their incident.

"Yes, yes," Oberon waved her off. "With that being said, you are to escort Lyra on a tour of our kingdom."

Wilder flicked his eyes from his father to his mother. He couldn't decide who was doing this, but it reeked of his meddling mother.

"Is that an order?" he asked, leaning back in his chair and crossing his arms.

"It is," Aine replied. "I watched her today—most carefully. She needs more motivation, like what you gave her. A bond between the two of you could encourage her to comply."

"So you want to use me as what? A bargaining chip? Make the pitiful princess fall for the prince to get her to do your bidding? Good gods, Mother!"

It wasn't like his mother to be calculating, especially since she hadn't been on board with this plan from the beginning. Which meant this was his father's doing.

He turned his head with a predator's slowness to the male who had sired him. Wilder still couldn't understand how his father could look at himself in the mirror. How all the greed and vanity weren't as blatantly obvious to Oberon as they were to him.

"Yes and no," Aine replied. "I think being around people who are strong-willed and kind will help her grow. She doesn't know any different from the monsters she was raised by, which could be what is inhibiting her from wanting to help. And I want her to finish your father's bargain so we can be done with this."

And there it was. Oberon still hadn't told Aine how he learned of Lyra's power or the deal between the humans and the merfolk, and it was bothering his mother as much as it had him.

"I have already said that I will not partake in this bargain without knowing the terms."

King Oberon leaned forward and straightened his shoulders. This wasn't his father addressing him now, but the king.

"I have had it with your waywardness, boy. You will escort the princess."

"Is that an order?"

"Yes," Aine said.

Wilder slid his gaze from the king to his mother.

"Wilder, please. Even without knowing all the details, it is vital that we restore balance before the gods intervene."

It was unusual that they hadn't already. This bargain had been in place far too long to go without their notice. This must all be part of the conniving, grand scale that was fate.

"When do we leave?" Wilder asked, accepting defeat.

"Tomorrow," Oberon ordered.

"Does she know?"

Aine shook her head. "You'll need to tell her."

"Oh, and another thing," King Oberon added. "You will be taking no one with you. Just you and the princess. I've arranged for four of the noble houses to host you for two days each."

"Lyra had trouble on the way here," Wilder muttered. Flashes of him having to carry her across emerald fields and through the shadows of towering trees surfaced in his mind.

"You can take the carriage, of course," Aine offered. "But I doubt she'll enjoy being stuck in there alone."

There was a light in his mother's eyes when she said that.

A gleam of meddling he was all too familiar with. She couldn't be trying to push them together?

Their kingdom would never accept a mermaid on the throne, and her kingdom—well, let's just say the tithe was not even the top concern when it came to his still-beating heart.

"You should go tell her now. So she has time to prepare for the journey," Aine said at last. Wilder groaned internally. Another journey, another order, another choice taken away. He didn't know how much longer he could do this, could be the obedient prince.

He rose from his chair without so much as a farewell and stalked across the castle to her room. This was typical of his life, flitting from order to order, never having plans or goals of his own.

The door to Lyra's room was shut, but he could hear movement inside. Two guards beside the door bowed as he approached, and he nodded in return, even to the dark-haired one he detested.

He couldn't even remember the male's name, but there was always a sort of smug arrogance about him.

Wilder rapped his knuckles against the door. There was no answer. He knocked louder and waited. When there was still no response, he tried the handle. It was unlocked.

He paused with the handle in his grip. It was most impolite to just barge in without an invitation, but she was their captive.

"Do you want us to go in first, Your Highness?" The blond guard asked. Wilder approved of that guard. He had always been genuine.

Wilder shook his head and pushed the door open. It was empty, but not still. The window was opened, and a breeze billowed the sheer curtains.

He froze, thinking the worst. That she had somehow snuck out the window and scaled the castle wall to escape. There was no way she could have done that. Her legs weren't even strong enough to do a complete lap of lunges yet.

The water turned on and off in the bathing room, and he

sighed, trudging over to the closed bathing room door and calling through it.

"Legs?"

There was no response. Only the turning off and on of the water.

"I know you can hear me."

He leaned in close. Her scent was stronger here. The smell of her mingled with the bath oils Daisy added.

"If you don't respond, I'm coming in. And I doubt you want that," he said louder.

He waited a heartbeat, and when she still didn't respond, he pushed into the room and stilled.

Lyra was in the bath, but she wasn't ignoring him. She had half of her head underwater, specifically her ears. A delicate foot rested against the lip of the tub, and she used her big toe to turn the water off and on.

Her naked body was hidden by clumps of pink bubbles. Yet, he could see enough. She was glorious.

A goddess with moon-white skin and soft curves. With the faintest freckles scattered across her cheeks and nose. He wanted to memorize each and every one.

If he thought he couldn't get her out of his mind before, it would never be possible now. He wanted to know every inch of her skin, wanted it so badly he might bite her in places so she would never forget where he had been.

Auburn hair wreathed her angelic face. Her sea-glass eyes were shut, and it was the light humming coming from her that had his mouth parting.

She was singing, but not with her power—just singing. It was the most beautiful thing he had ever heard. No wonder so many were lost to the sea, trying to find the source of such a melody.

He wondered what he would sacrifice to keep such a treasure.

Everything.

He might sacrifice everything.

Lyra blinked, and it wasn't horror that sparked in her eyes. No—it was something darker.

"Prince." She pulled her head from the water so she could hear him. "Is it common to surprise ladies while they're bathing?"

He thought back to a few days ago when he had shared a bath with three females. But that wasn't what she meant.

"I fear that title is lost upon you, Legs."

Lyra smirked and brought her legs out of the water. Her pale knees glistened in the light streaming through the window. A droplet of water raced down her thigh to places he would love to explore.

"I'm sure you would think that. But I'm not the one stumbling in late in the morning from pleasure houses." She said the words as if they offended her, but her attention darted over to a very well-loved book on the stool next to the tub. *The Knight in Shining Armor.*

"You take offense to going to a pleasure house, but see nothing wrong with reading about activities that take place there?"

This line of questioning was a horrible idea. His arousal was clouding his judgment, and her body was becoming visible from the dissipating bubbles.

"Is that a rhetorical question?" she asked with an arched brow.

Wilder shook his head, trying to clear the visual of her skin on his.

"I came to tell you we leave for a tour—tomorrow morning. Begin preparing."

Her happiness vanished like smoke in the wind.

"Are we staying for Ostara?"

"We should be back in time."

"Oh," she said. Her head drooped a bit, and she looked at the water. "That's a relief."

The sadness in her voice gripped him.

"It's not on my order that we leave so soon. You can thank my father for that," he replied.

Wilder wasn't there when she looked up. He was already striding through her bedroom and addressing the guards.

"Call for Daisy and see to it they have everything she requests for the journey."

The dark-haired one looked annoyed. "Everything, Your Highness?"

Wilder came close to lashing out and punching the male in his smug face for questioning him. "Everything."

45
OOPSY DAISY

Lyra's bath water had grown cold when Daisy barged in, all in a tizzy. Her periwinkle hair had been tugged in places from her braid, and her eyes were bright.

"You leave in the morning. *At first light!*" she screeched.

Lyra nodded and sighed.

"Prince Wilder instructed me that you'd be leaving in the morning *and* staying with four of the noble families." Daisy's chest heaved as she grabbed a towel and held it out to her. "We have to prepare at once. You're pruning. Get out!"

"Ugh, Daisy, calm down. You're fluttering about like a wild bird."

Daisy shook the towel out and frowned. "You would be moving a lot quicker if you knew what this meant."

Lyra rolled her eyes and stood as her bedroom door flew open.

"A tour in the morning?" Maelys yelled as she struggled through the door with an armload of clothes.

"What is the *big deal?*" Lyra asked, wrapping herself in the towel.

"The big deal is that you're staying with the *noble* families. The king's brother, and at least one of the cousins," Daisy muttered, grabbing Lyra's robe off the hook and handing it to her.

Dressed in her emerald silk robe and clutching a cup of tea, Lyra sat cross-legged on her bed as Maelys and Daisy shoveled as many dresses as they could manage into a trunk.

"You'll be staying with the king's brother—Warick."

Lyra scrunched her nose. "Warick?"

Maelys shot her a look. "He is the court gossip. Anything spoken about anyone *ever*, he knows about."

"Oh dear, we'll need the lilac gown then," Daisy muttered to herself.

"Is there a lot of gossip?"

Maelys snorted. "Depends on which century—but yes."

Bathroom cabinets slammed as Daisy rummaged around. "Tell her about the etiquette!"

Lyra wanted to roll her eyes. She was a princess, etiquette she knew.

Maelys began pacing and rubbing the bridge of her nose. "There's just so much to cover in such a short time."

"I don't think it's that big of a deal. It's not like I'm trying to win their favor."

Daisy stumbled through the bathroom door, wrapping a dress around something. "It is very much important!"

Maelys had stopped her pacing to gape at her. "You truly don't care about this at all, do you?"

Lyra shook her head before falling back onto the bed. She didn't care about anything lately, not with the stress of using her magic outweighing everything else.

"I have to fulfill this bargain, and then I'm going back home. What does it matter?"

Daisy and Maelys kept her up until late in the night, explaining just how important it was.

46
TRUCE

Wilder stood at the foot of the carriage and straightened his jacket for the fifth time. His knee-high boots squeaked as he shifted on his feet. Where was she? He had instructed Daisy last night that they needed to be off first thing in the morning, and now the sun was already well into the sky, along with its heat.

The doors to the castle slid open, and several servants came out grunting under the strain of a large trunk, followed by a flustered Daisy.

"I still think I forgot something! Who leaves for a tour and doesn't have an itinerary?"

Her voice reached an octave he didn't think was possible, and his eyes squeezed shut.

"Daisy, I'm sure it's fine," Lyra said. Her voice was soft and lovely.

She stepped out of the dim castle and into a ray of golden light. He involuntarily stepped forward at the sight of her. A light pink traveling dress brought out the flush on her cheeks and the rose of her lips. Her auburn hair hung in loose waves down to her waist, except for a small braid over her crown that had wisps of small white flowers tucked into it.

She resembled the wild buttercups that grew alongside the brambles of Valewood.

Wilder ascended the few steps to the castle door and extended his elbow to her.

She looked up at him beneath lowered lashes and nibbled at her bottom lip.

"What are you doing?" She looked around as if she were expecting someone else.

"I'm escorting you to the carriage."

She stared at his outstretched arm as if it were a spider.

"Is there a problem?" he asked, not understanding.

"Yes," she said, placing her hands on her hips and squaring her shoulders.

"What is the problem?" He sighed and felt the fight leave his body. Of course, she was going to make this difficult.

"Why are you being—*charming*?"

Wilder smirked and raised his arm a fraction. "Don't mistake my actions for anything but duty. You're on an official tour. I am just doing what is expected."

That wasn't entirely true, but he was not about to tell her he wanted to be close to her, to touch her.

"Well, in that case," she muttered, and slipped her arm through his.

They descended a single step before his mother called.

"Wilder!"

He groaned but turned them to face her.

"Yes, Mother."

"There's been a change to your itinerary."

Queen Aine was wrapped in a gown of crimson, with a high collar resembling feathers that stood up behind her even taller updo. A golden folder was gripped in her fist, which coincided with the tightened expression on her face.

Wilder reached out to take the folder, but his mother stared intently at him.

"May I have it?"

She handed him the folder, but when he took it in his hands, she did not let go.

"Follow the itinerary to the letter."

Lyra looked between Queen Aine and Wilder, trying to understand what was passing between them.

"Yes, Mother."

"I mean it, Wilder. To the letter."

Wilder arched a brow but nodded his agreement.

Queen Aine looked at Lyra and smiled broadly.

"You look wonderful, dear. Have a marvelous time!"

She didn't even wait for Lyra to respond before she gathered up her gown and strode back inside.

Lyra looked from her retreating form to Wilder and then to the folder.

"That was … strange."

Wilder cracked open the folder and stared and stared.

Do whatever you would like to do. Be free. But be back in time for Ostara.

A smile tugged the corner of his lips up, and he whirled them back to the carriage.

"Change of plans. Take us to the Three Sisters," Wilder ordered the servant driving the carriage.

Lyra looked bewildered. A small divot formed between her brows.

"What is happening?" she hissed under her breath as he held open the door and nodded for her to take a seat inside.

"A royal engagement is off, and a week of freedom has just landed in our laps," he replied, taking a seat opposite her.

The carriage was one of the extravagant ones his father

preferred. Plush navy benches, gold filigree around the windows, and a mural of a wilderness scene on the ceiling.

He could tell she didn't know where to look as her eyes swiveled from one side of the carriage to the other. To the pair of doves carved beside her head with an olive branch extended between them, to the miniature unicorn nibbling next to a babbling brook on the ceiling.

Lyra tilted her head back and gaped. Wilder chuckled, and she snapped her mouth shut.

"What do you mean, freedom?"

He leaned his head back against the wall and took a deep breath.

"My mother has canceled our entire tour and has instructed me to do as I wish."

Lyra gaped. "She can do that? Wait—we can do that?"

He closed his eyes and smiled.

"Where are we going then?"

The carriage began driving them around the back of the castle and through the side gate to bypass the bustling city streets.

"We're going to the Three Sisters. I would like to canoe through it."

Lyra scrunched her nose up. "And then what?"

"And then I would like to take a nap under the ancient willow."

She nodded, but her brow was still furrowed.

"And then what?"

Wilder snorted. "I'm not sure. Not everything has to be planned."

Her frown deepened. "So we're just going to do whatever you want, whenever you think of it? With no plans?"

"Exactly," he replied with a sigh.

With each wheel rotation away, the constant weight that burdened him dissipated.

Lyra leaned against the door and stared out the window as the carriage bumbled along the uneven path between the hills. Wilder looked with her, beyond the hills and to the looming smudge of the swamp.

"Why would you want to canoe through a swamp?" she muttered.

Wilder cracked an eye open to see her trying to puzzle out his desires.

"The swamps are some of the oldest parts of our land."

"Okay."

There was a slight hesitation in her answer.

He stared at her, waiting for what would undoubtedly come next.

She cast her eyes from the window to him and pursed her lips. Any second now, the deluge of questions would burst from her. He felt it.

He needed only to wait.

Her shoulders rose and fell, and she twisted her fingers into her gauzy pink skirts.

His eyes slid closed, and he rested his head against the coach wall.

"But what's the point?"

He couldn't fight the chuckle that slipped through his lips.

"Who says there has to be a point?"

"Well—no one, but why do you want to go to the oldest part of your lands?"

"Because that's where magic is the strongest."

"Why?"

He shrugged his shoulders.

"Is that true?"

He shrugged again. A stinging slap on his knee had his eyes flying open and falling upon a very disgruntled-looking Lyra.

"Are you incapable of having a civilized conversation today?"

she seethed. There was a faint glow in her eyes as the rage flowed through her veins.

"Are you incapable of going five seconds without asking a multitude of questions?"

She shrugged, and it was so irritating. He squeezed the bridge of his nose and screwed his eyes shut.

"I don't know. I don't know why the oldest parts have the most magic. All I know is that it sings to my blood, and I crave it. I rarely, if ever, get time to myself, and for just a few days, I will have the freedom that I so greatly desire. So, please, for once in your miserable life, can you try to be pleasant? Please?"

She crossed her arms over her chest, and the mounds of her breasts squeezed almost completely out of the top of her dress.

"I was being pleasant. You were being an ass."

He rolled his eyes, placed an ankle on the opposite knee, and rested an elbow on the window opening. The picture of arrogance and nonchalance.

"My apologies, Legs. I will absolutely endeavor to answer every single question that pops into that inquisitive mind of yours, even if I am trying to rest."

She fluffed out her skirts and raised her chin.

"Thank you for apologizing," she said. Completely dismissing any wrongdoing on her part.

He had half a mind to kick her out of the carriage and journey on without her, but that would no doubt see him being dragged back to the castle by his father's personal guard.

So instead, he bit his tongue and gazed outside. A few days trapped with her and her questions would be worth it for the freedom he so desperately wanted. He could handle this. Could handle her.

"Now, you said it sings to your blood. What's that like?"

His jaw quivered under the strain, and only after he had counted to five and breathed slowly could he answer.

"I think it's pretty self-explanatory."

She arched an eyebrow.

"I don't even know how to describe it," he ground out. "It's euphoric."

"Interesting," she muttered.

"You think so?" he asked, tilting his head.

"No, not at all. I was trying to be pleasant," she replied with a smile.

He chuckled and felt the irritation leave him.

"I appreciate your candor."

Her smile broadened, and he was struck mute by her. She really was stunning when she wasn't trying to irritate him on purpose. But there was a small joy in that, too. She pushed him, challenged him in a way no one had before with her quick wit, and he found that sometimes he might even admire it.

"What are you thinking about?" she asked, her brow furrowing again.

"I'm thinking ..." he stumbled out. "How about a truce? If only for our tour, so that we can both enjoy our small slice of freedom."

Lyra leaned forward and gripped the edge of her seat. "What kind of truce?"

"I promise to answer all of your questions. Nicely—might I add? If you can promise not to intentionally annoy me."

She pursed her lips, and he could see the wheels of her mind spinning.

"So you're agreeing to be pleasant company if I can promise to do the same?"

He nodded. "Exactly."

"Like ... friends?"

He continued to nod and now even smirked. "Yes. We can be friends."

Her emerald eyes flared like sea glass before narrowing on him. "Why is this so important to you?"

He huffed and leaned back. "Like I said—I very rarely get

free time. So, doing whatever I want for several days instead of following the multitude of orders my father doles out—well, it's not something I want to pass up. So yes, I will be your friend if you will allow me to just enjoy this."

She had been glaring at him until he said "freedom," and then her gaze softened like she, too, understood what that meant.

"Fine. I understand the desire for freedom."

Wilder extended a hand out to her, and she took it. A light buzzing tingled over his flesh, but he ignored it and shook her hand, just once. When he let go, so did she, but of course, she went one step further and wiped her hand on the seat, making a face.

He sighed. "You're not off to a good start."

She froze and looked down at her hand before grimacing. "Sorry—old habit."

He laughed, and she looked up in shock before chuckling alongside him.

Maybe this wouldn't be terrible after all.

47
THE FOURTH

Lyra watched as Wilder's eyes brightened with his laugh, and then his shoulders relaxed. What unbearable pressure must he be under if he had offered her a deal to enjoy the next few days? It must be very important to him, this time off, for him to have been willing to be vulnerable with her, of all people.

She couldn't help but feel sorry for him. He didn't take his duty lightly, and it showed in the tightened lines around his eyes and mouth. She hadn't noticed it until after they made their deal, when he had suddenly appeared youthful and relaxed.

He had always been beautiful, but now—now it was heart-achingly apparent.

"So, a canoe ride through the Three Sisters?"

He nodded and continued to smile.

"I've never ridden in a canoe before."

His eyebrows rose with surprise. "Are you serious?"

"Mhm. Haven't had the chance. Fins and all." She shrugged.

Wilder stared at her, and a divot formed between his brows.

"We'll be on the water. You should be fine."

Lyra shrugged and continued to watch the rolling, highlands drift by outside her window.

"You're not worried, are you?" Wilder asked, struggling to understand what she was not saying.

When she didn't respond, he leaned forward and tapped her knee.

"We called a truce, Legs. What are you not telling me?"

Her eyes burned, and she bit her lip before returning his gaze. She didn't know if she was capable of doing it, of being his friend. But for any amount of freedom, she would try.

"Truce?" she whispered.

He sat back and nodded.

"I miss the water."

His mouth opened before snapping shut and then opening again.

"We'll go to the sea on the east side of the kingdom, then. There's a place there I think you might appreciate."

She sat up straighter at his words, and her heart fluttered against his ribs at his offer. The sea. She would get to see the sea.

"We can?"

Wilder nodded as if that settled the matter, but then muttered. "Of course. This is your opportunity for freedom, too, Lyra."

She smiled, feeling the weight on her chest lessen. She would get to smell the ocean. Maybe even dip her toes into the water to feel its lost embrace.

This wouldn't be an entirely awful trip, then, after all.

They traveled in silence for some time. Lyra tried to keep her multitude of questions to herself and allow Wilder some time to breathe.

It had been a good idea—this truce.

But she had so many questions now. Like, why had they

avoided traveling through the kingdom? She would have liked to have seen it since she was unconscious on the way in. But maybe that had been the point? They didn't want her to know everything. She was still the enemy.

She made a mental note to ask Wilder if they could travel through the city on their way back in. Lyra found herself extremely curious about how the elves lived in relation to each other.

They were all different. Whereas the merfolk were all the same.

The sun rose higher outside her window, but the land around them became cooler. A slight fog crept up from the ground, and there was a thickness to the air here. Trees loomed with widened trunks like the shape of a fan, and the carriage slowed.

Wilder sighed, and when the carriage came to a full stop, he clambered out of the coach and outstretched his hand to her.

Lyra stuck her head out before wrapping her fingers around his. It felt strange here, but a good strange—familiar somehow.

"Do you feel it?" he asked when she held his hand and did not take a step to the ground.

She nodded. It felt as if the land were alive and watching her.

"You're safe here," he murmured. It put her fears to rest, and she took a step and then another.

It was like a wall of dense green. It clung to the trees, floated in patches on the clear water, and fluttered in the wind. Nothing but a deep, vibrant green. The green of new life and the dark green of ancient life twining together.

The ground beneath her slippers squelched, and she grimaced.

She was not prepared for a trek through the swamp, and when she wobbled on her slippery shoes, Wilder grabbed hold of her hand to steady her.

"I'm not dressed for this new adventure," she muttered, tugging on his hand when she almost fell again.

"I'll hold on to this just in case," he replied, lifting their conjoined hands.

They walked towards the river a few steps before he stopped. Standing beside her and gripping her hand, he breathed deeply. She watched as his eyes slid closed and his shoulders heaved with a deep breath. His skin seemed to glow a deeper gold with each of his breaths, like the magic was filling him from within.

When his eyes opened, they seemed brighter than the sky above the low-hanging clouds.

"There's usually a canoe off the bank, but we'll walk until we find one," he said to her before turning to the servant who had driven the carriage. "We'll be back in a few hours."

They set off together hand in hand, and it didn't feel strange to her. Almost as if they had done this before, but it was refreshing nonetheless.

She swung their hands as they walked and looked around with curiosity. Wilder had a lightness to his gait compared to his usual tromping, and a small grin pulled up his lips.

Lyra tried not to marvel at the changes in him, but it was difficult. So she opted for conversation.

"You said the swamp was named after the three original sisters?"

Wilder smirked at her question. No doubt prepared for her encroaching onslaught of curiosity.

"Yes. But some claim there was a fourth sister and that her story was lost to time."

Lyra jolted to a stop, and their conjoined hands yanked Wilder to a halt as well.

"A missing sister?"

Wilder chuckled at the look of horror that contorted her face.

"Not just a lost sister, but a lost brother, too."

"Alright, now you're making stuff up. How does history forget two gods?"

Wilder's brow furrowed, and they continued walking again.

"I didn't say they were gods. How did you know that?"

Lyra shrugged. "I merely assumed. The three original sisters were all goddesses, weren't they?"

"Eventually."

"So, who were the missing ones?"

Wilder pressed his lips into a thin line to stop himself from chuckling.

"Wait. You're telling me you haven't read about this yet?" He teased.

She shook her head, and her auburn locks glimmered in the light filtering through the dense canopy of trees and the darkening clouds.

It was a rather peaceful day.

They passed an old Sweetbay magnolia on the bank. It had the largest white flowers she had ever seen. The petals were wider than her hands, and she reached up to delicately trace the bloom.

Dainty wildflowers circled the tree. Their blossoms in shades of blue and violet.

Wilder picked her one. Lyra blushed and then frowned.

"Won't it die now?"

Wilder stepped beside her. "The flowers here survive on air and not water."

A knock sounded from behind the tree.

"What was that?" Lyra asked.

Wilder peered around the wide trunk. "We're in luck."

The bow of a canoe bumped against the trunk with the bobbing current.

Water lapped up onto the shore, rocking the boat as he tugged it closer for her to step in. He held her hand, and as she stepped into the hull, she gripped his fingers tightly to avoid falling overboard.

"Easy, Legs," he murmured.

When Lyra had settled on board, she fluffed out her dress and then her hair. Wilder settled in front of her and used the oar to launch them from the shore and into the lazy water. Water rippled around them, and she stared at it with longing.

"The missing siblings?" she prompted him.

He paddled them deeper into the swamp. The moss on the trees seemed to reach for them, and he cleared his throat.

"So you know of the three brothers. Alfor, Ennosidas, and Fionn. When they arrived in this world, the land was already inhabited by the sisters. Mab, Tiandra, Aradia, and the fourth sister whose name is no longer known."

Lyra tried to quiet the roaring in her mind as she dipped her fingers in the water. Those females had been wiped from their history completely.

A bird flew overhead, its rustle of wings interrupting his words as she stared after it.

She peered at him, waiting for him to begin again, and he gazed back. An unreadable moment passed between them. She felt as if she knew him. Not in this moment, but in another time, another life. There was something about him she knew as intrinsically as she knew herself.

"And?" she prompted.

Wilder shook his head, clearing his thoughts, and paddled some more. She could see his shoulders ripple beneath his charcoal tunic.

"The sisters sent their fourth sister as a delegate to speak to the newcomers. She was the oldest and wisest of them all. But the brothers did not receive her kindly. They were here to conquer and claim. It did not matter to them that the world was already occupied."

Lyra gulped, sensing the conflict in the story was approaching.

"But the fourth brother ..."

She gripped the edge of the boat, and her knuckles turned white.

"They were soulmates," Wilder explained. "Their souls are tied together through the tapestry of fate that weaves the entire universe."

Lyra's eyes widened with surprise, and her lips parted with a gasp. "Soulmates?"

"Of course," he hummed. "The three other brothers planned to strike her down and then kill the rest of the sisters, exerting their power over the realm. But the fourth brother could not raise a hand against her any more than he could against his brothers. He took the sister for his own, their bond slipping into place, tying them together forever. When the oldest sister did not return, her sisters became worried and came looking for her. They found three brothers and expected the worst, of course."

Lyra nodded and worried her bottom lip. "And then what happened?"

Wilder paddled their boat underneath the roots of a giant cypress tree. The branches of the ancient tree stretched far and wide. He looked up as they passed underneath, and Lyra followed suit. Seeing thousands of years of life resting above her head.

She swallowed audibly and then sighed with relief when they passed through unscathed.

"They appeared and told their siblings what had happened. This land demanded balance. That magic was balance. And in doing so, created the foundation for our world. Each brother, a sister. Each partnership, a land. Ennosidas and Tiandra ruled over the merfolk. Alfor and Aradia, the mortals, and Fionn and Mab, the elves."

Lyra's eyes sparkled in the watery light, and a rush of emotions coursed through her. The world demanded balance, and yet—she was not raised that way. The ocean was ruled by men. Knowledge of Tiandra had been stripped away.

"What of the fourth brother and sister? Where are they?"

Wilder smiled a sad smile and looked around at the swamp, and then up into the sky.

"I was always told that they became the sun and the moon. Watching over the world that they had saved. Sharing an eternity in the sky."

It was bewitching and gut-wrenching, this story of his.

"But do they ever get to see each other?" Lyra whispered, her eyes burning again.

"Of course," Wilder replied. "But it's just an old legend. Who knows if it's true?"

He shrugged and kept paddling them down the winding, lazy river. Lyra leaned her side against the wooden bow of their canoe and watched as the Three Sisters came alive around them.

Turtles were perched on large river stones, napping in the sun that filtered through. Otters splashed along the banks, chattering as they played. An egret gracefully dunked its bill in the water and walked with long strides through the marsh.

It was full of life and buzzing energy, even if the water seemed anything but. It was idle and calm.

"I see why you like it here," Lyra muttered.

Wilder nodded and prodded them farther along. He seemed happy here and settled.

"I think you will enjoy the willow more."

She watched a turtle slide off the rock and into the water with a splash.

"Why?"

Wilder watched her, and a knowing smile tugged on his lips.

"It's a good place to read. Under the branches that sway in the breeze. It blocks out the entire world."

Lyra grinned back at him. "It sounds lovely."

48
CATCH ME

They lay together under the branches of the ancient willow. It sang to them as Wilder napped and Lyra read on a quilt that they had spread on the soft grass. He had his arms underneath his head, and his chest rose and fell in line with the branches that swayed back and forth around them.

It was as he said it would be. The long branches blocked out the outside world, but there was still enough light that she could see the words on the page.

Lyra had started the book about magic and bargains that Queen Aine had lent her. It read like an educational text, but she was still fascinated.

There had been a lot more to bargains than what she knew. Particularly, how her part would not rely only on her using her voice but on being in the places where the original bargain had been struck between the merfolk and mortals.

The book had explained it like a braided cord, and to undo it, she would have to undo the knot and unweave the plait.

Her heart and brain hurt thinking about it, so she switched to something more inspiring, the other book Aine had lent her. She found the chamomile flowers that had marked her place and slid back into the story of Ophelia, the heroine who vanquished a dragon.

Although the beginning had not been as gripping as the romance novels she preferred, the story had picked up. It was strange reading about heroines.

But as Ophelia plucked up the courage to face her fears, Lyra felt the power of the story hum within her blood. There was so much that was possible when you believed in yourself.

Maybe that was why the mermen had blocked access to these kinds of stories.

"What are you reading?" Wilder's deep voice rumbled through the quiet.

Lyra stopped reading and kept her finger in her place. "It's the book your mother lent me."

She looked at him as he continued to lie there with his eyes closed, but turned onto his side to face her. She thought he had drifted back to sleep and had turned her eyes back on the page again when he spoke.

"What is it about?"

Lyra couldn't help the grin that spread across her lips. No one had ever asked about the books she read, or really anything about her interests.

"It's about Ophelia vanquishing the dragon Turig."

"Do you like it?"

She looked up from the pages to find his sky-blue eyes locked onto her face.

"I do, very much."

Wilder smiled, and she felt her heart squeeze.

"Turig the great and evil. Turig, the slayer of knights, the widow maker."

"You've read it?"

He nodded. "It was my favorite bedtime story as a lad. My mother read it to me every night."

Lyra beamed. "So, the part when Ophelia dons her father's helmet …"

"Oh, it's pivotal to the climax, of course," he finished for her.

"Exactly!" she screeched. "It's genius."

Wilder chuckled and pushed up onto an elbow. His high cheekbones were darkened from their brief afternoon in the sun, and the color suited his dark hair.

"I thought you preferred to be outdoors," Lyra muttered and turned to look at her book to keep from staring at him.

"I enjoy balance. A rainy afternoon requires a good book and a cup of tea."

The very idea of that was like heaven to her.

Thunder rumbled in the distance, and Lyra looked up, alarmed.

"Are we safe here?"

Wilder looked behind them and into the distance, where the storm built. When he shrugged, she snorted.

"That's comforting."

He fiddled with the blanket near her bare feet.

An odd sensation shot through her feet and her body as the blanket brushed against her skin, and she squirmed.

"Don't do that," she tutted.

Wilder's brow arched nearly into his hairline.

"Legs?"

She gazed at him, and her brow furrowed. "Yes?"

"Are you ticklish?"

Lyra stared and stared. She didn't know that word, but didn't like the sound of it either.

"What is 'ticklish'?"

Wilder's grin turned wolfish, and he waggled his long fingers against her toes.

Lyra squealed and ripped her feet from his reach and tucked them underneath her.

"Don't do that!" She laughed and tried to hide her limbs under the layers of her skirt.

He was upon her with a boyish smile that made him look much younger. He prodded her ribs with light fingertips, and she laughed raucously.

She had fallen against the quilts, and he straddled her. She squirmed beneath him, and his eyes turned molten with delight.

"Have you lost your mind?" she squealed.

Tears slipped from her eyes, and his laugh boomed from his chest and intertwined with hers.

Luckily, he didn't torture her for long and stopped his incessant tickling so that she could catch her breath. Her laughter trilled around them long after she had stopped.

He gazed down at her. Their breaths mingled in the space between them, and when she glanced at his lips, she wondered what they might taste like.

Wilder leaned forward, and Lyra raised her chin as he lowered his.

Their faces inched closer and closer. And she wanted to kiss him. She wanted him, and that terrified her.

This was only a temporary truce.

When Wilder's eyes closed, Lyra flicked his nose.

His eyes flashed open, and she smiled so widely at him that her nose scrunched up.

"Did you flick me?"

Lyra slid out from beneath him and grinned.

"I did." She put her hands on her hips. "And what are you going to do about it?" she teased.

Wilder got to his feet and flashed her a mischievous smile.

"I'm going to hold you down and tickle you until you can't breathe," he vowed.

Lyra dashed out of the branches of the ancient willow.

"You'll have to catch me first."

49
THE KISS

Wilder watched as she streaked through branches and the tall, verdant grasses. It was like a dream.

He could feel this memory etching itself into his mind.

Flashes of golden light and auburn hair. She had left her mark here, and the land would remember her forever, as would he.

He dashed out after her; the chase heating his blood.

They ran and laughed.

He tickled, and she squealed.

But then the downpour started. Lyra raced for the willow, and he was right on her heels.

The rain awakened his senses. And she was intoxicating. Her scent sang to his blood as much as the land did.

"I thought you said we were safe here?" She shivered, rubbing a hand down her arm.

The rain had soaked her. The fabric of the light pink dress was now as dark as her lips.

"We are safe. It's just rain."

When she shivered again, he wrapped an arm low around her waist.

"What're you doing?" She leaned away from him.

Wilder grinned down at her. "Did you forget what I taught you about body heat?"

She looked up at him, and her gaze darkened. Her eyes darted to his lips once more.

Wilder had to know what she tasted like.

"I like these," he murmured, tracing a finger across the freckles on her nose.

"I hate them," she breathed.

Wilder tilted his head. "Why?"

"They're unsightly."

He shook his head. "It just means you were kissed by the sun, but they remind me of the stars."

Lyra leaned into his warmth, and he had to swallow the groan that built in the back of his throat.

His face lowered to hers as she raised her chin.

"Wilder," she whispered.

His lips were a hairbreadth from hers. "Yes?"

"Kiss me."

He complied with her order.

Pressing his lips with a gentle reverence to hers, he had to work to keep the fire in his veins at bay.

The feel of her against him was consuming him, and he couldn't get enough.

He wrapped a hand in her wet hair and angled her face up to him.

She sighed in a happy, satisfied way.

And with that, he deepened the kiss, slipping his tongue inside her mouth and finally getting a taste. She was everything he dreamed she would be.

Wild and eternal. As sweet as the ripest berries, and as strong as a well-aged elixir.

Her kiss was invigorating and breathed life into his very soul.

Lyra gripped a fistful of the tunic covering his chest and pulled him to her. Wilder let her, feeling her need build. Her arousal twirled in the storm wind around them and raised goosebumps on his flesh.

She wasn't a mermaid but a siren, and he was falling under her spell. He now knew why the mortals went willingly if it felt anything like this.

They parted, gasping for air before she rose on her toes. Wrapping a hand around his neck, she tugged him back down and kissed him reverently. He couldn't remember why they had even hated each other to begin with.

She was perfect. His lips parted, and in a move that surprised him, she slipped her tongue inside his mouth with a slight flick. He felt the vibrations of that movement all the way down to the bulge in his pants that stirred.

He had never been aroused by just a kiss, and yet—she had. He wanted only more of her.

When they broke apart again, the lust in her gaze rivaled the storm clouds that had passed over them. The rain slowed before stopping. Tiny droplets of light shone all around them as the sun broke through.

Lyra shivered again, and Wilder pulled away.

"Let's get you back before you catch a cold."

She frowned before he wrapped an arm around her and tugged her flush to his side. She bit her lip to hide her smile, and he worked to slow his rapid heart rate.

Lyra had burrowed even further under his skin, and he found he didn't mind one bit.

They walked, wrapped around each other, to the carriage and set off for the sea.

As the carriage bumbled through the rocky hills and the tall forests, Lyra slept in Wilder's arms. He watched her as she slept, and it reminded him of the first night they had spent together. Yet now she did not stir with nightmares.

She was enchanting, even during her slumber. It wound itself around him, making him feel things he hadn't thought himself capable of before.

He didn't know if it had been the kiss they shared or if it was him feeling free for the first time in a long while.

Wilder enjoyed listening to her talk about the books she read and the new surprises the land had afforded her. It was obvious she missed the sea, but the land called to her all the same. It was as if she were from both places.

That was unusual for him. He could only ever be from the Wilds. It was at the very core of his being—the magic of this place. Even with all its faults, he loved it.

Lyra sighed in her sleep, and he gripped her to his chest, hoping to calm whatever ailed her. Without thinking, he brushed his lips against her temple. He hadn't meant to kiss her again—but he had.

It had felt natural, like a habit. She smelled of crisp rain.

He sighed, and his breath fluttered the soft petals of the white flowers still tucked within her braid.

It was strange.

For someone who didn't like to know his future, he enjoyed looking at her.

50

DEBAUCHERY LESSONS

Lyra opened her eyes at the first whiff of salty air. The carriage still bounced along the uneven path, and she felt Wilder's arms tighten around her with the latest jostle. His head rested against the coach wall, and his eyes were closed. She had never slept so peacefully before, and she thought it might have something to do with him.

He relaxed further, slumping against the cushions when she eased herself out of his arms. Lyra looked out at the rocky shore as they drove parallel to it. She did not know where they were or how long they had been on the road.

The day had passed in a blur. From paddling through the swamp to lounging underneath the ancient willow. Or had it been two days already? She wasn't quite sure.

They had stopped on the way for her to bathe in one of the hot springs and change her clothes. Daisy had outdone herself packing all manner of clothes, shoes, and books.

Lyra would forever be grateful to Daisy for packing a

handful of novels between layers of gowns and nightclothes. It was a small kindness, but Lyra couldn't stop smiling when thinking about the care Daisy had taken to ensure the books were safe.

Stretching her arms up over her head, the violet gown she had donned rippled against her skin. The dress itself reminded her of the water at night.

She leaned against the window and watched the sea smash against the rocks. Sprays of sea foam burst into the sky as she sighed.

Lyra had felt like a rock being pummeled by life. Now, she felt like the water being pulled along by the tide.

Wilder stirred in his sleep. Opening and closing his hand as if he were reaching for something. Lyra looked over her shoulder at him. Sensing his need, she placed her hand in his, and he drifted back off to sleep.

She traced small circles over the top of his hand. Long fingers and tan skin stretched taut over bulging veins. They were elegant and yet powerful. She had watched him kill humans with these hands. And had also watched him pluck a flower for her.

She didn't want to think about what she was feeling for him. Although her intention had been to burrow under his skin, he had somehow managed to get under hers. And that kiss.

Her heart leapt at the memory of his lips on hers, his body against hers. Lyra ghosted her fingertips along her lips and felt the warmth pool low in her belly before she shook her head and reached for her book. She had to get him off her mind before it consumed her completely.

Lyra opened her book with one hand. But it took her a while to sink back into the story. It was another romance, like *The Knight in Shining Armor* had been, but different.

The romance had started from the very first page in this story, and she was having a hard time relating. She thought of romance as something that needed to build and grow, not something that was instantaneous. But these characters had fallen in love the moment they set eyes on each other, and their story was a happy one.

That was something else she was having a hard time relating to. There was no challenge, nothing to overcome. It didn't feel authentic. Life was a struggle.

The man in the story was ravishing his new wife. Worshipping her with his tongue as she lay splayed wide open on their bed. Lyra shifted in her seat and brought the book up closer.

Her hand tightened its grip on Wilder's, which in turn roused him. She was too engrossed in the book to realize he was watching her. She continued reading about how the husband brought his wife euphoric pleasure, her eyes darting across the page as she nibbled on her bottom lip.

It was intriguing, and she felt a heat pool in the bottom of her belly, but she couldn't quite figure out the logistics of it. Was he actually eating her? And if he was, why did she like it?

"Good story?" Wilder asked.

Lyra squeaked and slammed the book shut. She tried ripping her hand out of his, but he clung to her.

He chuckled, raising a brow and looking from her to the book she tucked under her leg.

Lyra cleared her throat before addressing him. "You're awake."

Wilder patted his chest with his free hand and looked around quizzically.

"I am?"

Lyra rolled her eyes and huffed a breath.

"What were you reading?"

She pursed her lips and shook her head.

Wilder gazed across the flush of her cheeks and the fluttering pulse on her neck.

"Do you want to tell me? Or do you want me to find out on my own?"

"Wilder," Lyra breathed, shaking her head. "Don't."

He moved so fast. She blinked, and he already had the book open in his hand and was holding her at bay with the other. Lyra clawed at his chest from across the bench, trying to reach the book.

"His tongue traveled over her bundle of nerves," he read aloud. His eyes widened, and his cheeks blazed with color. "Oh, Legs. My, my, what have you been reading?"

Lyra's face burned as hot as the sun that was rising in the pastel sky.

"Wilder Vale, you put that book back right now!" she hissed, still trying to rip the book out of his hands.

He continued reading the explicit scene, and Lyra howled with mortification, giving up on reaching for the book and opting to cover her ears to keep from hearing.

Only when she saw his lips stop moving did she uncover them.

The smile on his face didn't budge as she glared. Wilder shook the book in her vicinity, and she snatched it out of his hands.

"The romance section?" he asked with a laugh.

"Yes," she spat. "There is nothing wrong with what I like to read."

He looked taken aback. "Of course, there isn't. Why would you say that?"

"Because you're being ridiculous," she snapped.

"I am teasing you."

"Exactly! You promised to be nice."

Wilder laughed a full belly laugh and wiped at the tears that slipped over the rim of his eyes.

It infuriated her. How dare he? She moved to slap him, and

he gripped her hand before reaching for her and cupping her face.

"Of course, I'm teasing you. That's how we are with each other. This is our nice."

It wiped the scowl right off his face. He could tease her, and she could give it right back without worrying about coming across as rude or abrasive.

Wilder understood her in a way few people did.

"Does it bother you when I tease you about your books?" He asked, trying to read her expression.

She nodded, and he tilted his head.

"We're not allowed to read things like this where I'm from …"

Wilder's head bobbed, and he heaved a sigh. "It makes sense you're protective of it, then. It's important to you, and you were worried it would be taken away."

His words rang true even if she hadn't realized that was why she felt so strongly about it.

"I will not take your books from you again, and I'm sorry I made you feel that way," he murmured, tucking a strand of her auburn hair behind her ear.

She rested her head against his chest and relaxed into his embrace.

"Thank you. But you're making it awfully difficult to hate you after our truce is over."

Wilder smirked, but Lyra's smile had fallen away. She knew what his lips felt like on hers and had enjoyed it. But Wilder had more experience than her in that regard and in others.

Which meant he very well might know the logistics of some other things.

"Do I need to apologize for something else?"

Lyra shook her head but toyed with the cover of the book in her lap. "No, it's—never mind."

He tilted his head, trying to figure out what she was so hesitant to tell him.

"Lyra, you can tell me. We are friends right now."

"Friends who kiss?" Friends who had kissed. Friends who had held hands. How far did that title stretch before they entered dangerous territory?

He smirked at her, and it was so devilish she squirmed in her seat again.

"It's just that I don't understand the logistics of *it*." Lyra looked down at the book in her hand.

His eyes widened, and he pursed his lips. "The logistics of that scene I read aloud?"

Lyra squeezed her eyes shut, trying to staunch the embarrassment that bloomed high on her cheeks. "It's just that, well, that isn't something that my mermaid form would have allowed for and, um, okay," she inhaled sharply, squaring her shoulders, "can you show me how it works?"

Wilder had leaned forward as she was speaking, and now he stared at her with darkened eyes.

"Are you asking me to show you how *that scene* would play out?"

She nodded, biting her lip again.

"And this isn't something you've ever done before?" His eyebrow arched high on his forehead.

"Not that particular thing, no," she lied. "If you don't want to, it's fine. I assumed with the kiss that—" She couldn't believe she had actually asked him. But the kiss they shared had been so natural—so perfect.

"I'll do it," he blurted out. "But the moment it's too much or you want me to stop, you say so immediately. Do you understand?"

Lyra nodded with enthusiasm, but felt an explosion of butterflies in her stomach twining with the heat that was already there.

Wilder inhaled and ran his fingers through his hair.

"Are you sure you want it to be me?" She watched as his throat bobbed with a swallow.

Lyra let her gaze roam over him. From his thick, muscular thighs to the broad expanse of his chest to his blue eyes that were clouding with arousal.

"Yes. I'm assuming you have experience that would be beneficial."

He chuckled, and it was so deliciously dark that Lyra squeezed her legs together.

"I do. Do you not?"

Lyra grimaced. "I do. Just not with this," she lied again.

Wilder shifted in his seat. Leaning forward, he rested a large hand on her knee and gave it the slightest amount of pressure to get her to spread her legs.

He sank to his knees before her and gripped the hem of her gown.

Lyra leaned back against the seat and spread her legs farther to give him room. Her pulse pounded in her throat, and she found it difficult to breathe normally.

Wilder lifted her gown with a forced slowness.

"You tell me the moment you want me to stop." He stared as he revealed more and more of her bare skin.

Lyra nodded, her breath caught in her throat when he pushed her gown up to her waist. There was only a thin layer of fabric between her sex and him.

Wilder hooked his thumbs beneath her undergarment, and Lyra lifted her hips. She closed her eyes as he slid it over her thighs and down her calves.

"Open your eyes," he ordered.

She peeled her eyes open.

"I'm scared," she whispered.

Wilder stopped at once. "We don't have to do this."

"I want to," she breathed.

He nodded and grazed a hand up her calf and then over her thigh.

She was bared to him, splayed open like the character in her book.

Wilder brushed his thumb over the top of her entrance, and her hips bucked involuntarily. A gasp slipped through her clenched teeth.

"Easy," he murmured. "That was the 'bundle of nerves' in that scene. Did you feel it?"

Lyra nodded, and her head thudded against the wall. Her breath came out in uneven staccato bursts.

Wilder leaned forward, and she could feel his warm breath against her skin. Her eyes slid closed, and he stopped with both hands on her legs.

"I want you to touch yourself."

Her eyes flew open. "W-what?"

He gazed at her with heavy eyelids. The arousal must be coursing through him as much as it was through her.

Wilder grabbed her hand from where she gripped the bench and placed it on her sex. "Show me what you like."

Lyra froze with her hand covering herself. "But I don't know what I like."

He put his hand over hers and moved it a fraction. The pressure was exquisite. "Just do what feels good."

She moved her hand in languid strokes, her attention never leaving him. His tongue darted out and licked his lower lip. "That's it—get yourself ready for me."

Lyra glowed under his praise and picked up the pace. She hadn't realized she could do this on her own. But as she watched him watch her, she craved his touch—his mouth.

"Wilder, please," she moaned.

"Do you want me to take over?"

Lyra nodded, but that wasn't good enough.

"Tell me what you want me to do."

"Touch me," she panted.

He leaned closer to her, and her eyes slid closed, expecting his touch.

"Watch me, Lyra. Watch what you want me to do."

She watched as he kissed her sex and then slid his tongue over her. A moan slid past her lips, and it was an effort to keep her eyes from closing from the pleasure that coursed through her.

"This is your clit," he murmured against her skin before licking her again. She rose to meet him, craving an increase in pressure. "How does it feel?"

He licked her again, and she gasped. "Good."

"I'm going to do it faster now. Just relax and do what feels natural."

Lyra bit her tongue to keep from crying out.

He lapped at her at the same time as he swirled his thumb around her most sensitive part.

She gripped him by the hair to steady herself as he sucked her clit into his mouth.

The heat and pressure were undoing her.

It was like a wave swelling and cresting before it crashed against the shore. Something was building within her, and she knew that at some point, she would explode.

"Oh, gods," she cried out as he circled her with his tongue and thumb.

"Are you okay?" he asked, leaning away from her.

She still had hold of his head and tugged him back down to her. "Don't stop," she panted out.

Wilder's grin was positively salacious as he lowered his mouth back to her.

The outside world faded away. She no longer felt the jostling of the carriage or heard the roaring of waves against the cliffs.

No, it was only her and him. And his mouth on her. Blood pounded in her ears, and pleasure roiled through her.

"Don't stop," she moaned again.

Wilder worshiped her body with debauched fervor.

She felt a tightness in her legs before her body went rigid against his mouth. Waves of euphoria rolled through her as she rode it out.

He lapped it up and didn't stop until she went boneless against his mouth.

He pulled her undergarment back up and lowered her dress. But she was too focused on trying to breathe normally once more.

"Is it what you expected it to be?" he asked, sitting back against his bench and staring at her with an amused expression as he licked his lips.

Lyra hummed her agreement as she reached for him. "It was even better."

51
THE
COTTAGE

The summer cottage perched on the rocks was now Lyra's favorite place in the whole world. Made of sun-bleached gray stone and a pitching roofline, it was very modest for a royal family's abode.

"It's very cozy," she said, taking in the plush, muted furniture and velvety soft rugs that were spread about the main living space.

A quaint kitchen was tucked in the corner. But the entire back wall was made of glass, showcasing dramatic views of the seaside cliffs. *An entire horizon of the ocean.* She took a step towards it, staying just an arm's reach from the window.

"I built it."

Lyra gaped like a fish as she whipped her head in his direction.

"You built *this house?*"

He nodded and leaned against the picture windows. "I

needed a place to escape to after everything, and I was calmer by the sea. That, and it's far away from the court and my father."

"What happened between you two?"

Wilder didn't answer for a moment. She could tell he was thinking it over and tugged at the hem of his tunic to get him to look at her.

"It can't be any worse than what I confided in you." She blushed. But when he gave her a heart-stopping grin and raked his eyes over her body, she felt the heat pool in her once more.

"That was a good thing. This—is definitely not."

Lyra sighed and shrugged. "If you don't want to tell me, fine. But don't think it's because you can't. I'm all ears."

He ground his teeth and raked a hand through his dark hair. The light shimmered on his briar crown, and he looked ethereal in the afternoon light.

"Fine. I'll tell you. Tea?"

She smiled at him. "Sure."

Wilder moved to put the kettle on, and not even its whistling could break her attention from the sea.

Her mind was in chaos, trying to puzzle out what he struggled with that would cause him to venture out here and build a house. He pressed a small blue teacup into her hand, and she took a sip of the lemon mint tea.

"That is divine," she breathed, inhaling the steam.

He took a seat in the leather armchair in front of the windows and nodded for her to do the same in the matching armchair.

She plopped down and set her cup on the low-lying table.

"I struggled with the weight of my position for a long time."

Lyra nodded. She found it hard to understand, as there wasn't a lot of weight to her position. Females were to be seen— rarely—and never heard. However, there was a lot of pressure with carrying her magic.

"During the peace negotiations, my father got it in his head that a marriage between our courts was the answer."

"Marriage?"

"Between me and Odette—the princess of the Mannereds."

Lyra felt an uncomfortable twisting in her gut.

Wilder took a sip of his tea before setting the cup down on the table. His hand clenched into a fist.

"I couldn't stomach the idea of being the heir to one throne, much less two. So, like the coward I was, I fled."

Lyra gasped, covering her mouth with both hands.

"I wasn't always chock full of duty." He clenched his jaw. "I had planned to live among the humans, but was kidnapped by wulvers instead."

Her gut twisted tighter, and she felt bile rise in the back of her throat. She had seen one of the wulvers outside a village they had passed through. They were nightmarish. Mottled fur and spindly legs.

"It took a decade or so for Oberon to broker my release. And I was tortured every day of that time."

She couldn't bear it. A heavy weight pressed down on her chest, making it difficult to breathe. Squeezing the arms of the chair, she met his gaze. "*Why*—why did it take so long to free you?"

Wilder shrugged and picked a speck of dust from his pant leg. "Oberon was making a point at first. I was a coward and deserved to be punished. I'm still not even sure what was promised to free me, but I have a feeling it came at great personal cost to him, for he hasn't let me live it down a single moment of my life since."

"I had sensed things were—off between you two, but not with your mother."

He shook his head then. "No, she has tried to repair the rift between us. I don't have the heart to tell her it is irreparable."

"I can't imagine."

Wilder snorted. "If *anyone* could imagine, it would be you."

She thought back over her life. The contempt she felt for her father and the pain she had endured at his hands.

"I am sorry for your suffering," she mumbled.

"And I am sorry for yours."

They sat in silence for some time, sipping their tea and absorbing the stillness of the moment.

"How often do you come out here?"

Wilder frowned and tugged at his black tunic. The evergreen embroidery on his sleeves was nearly black, but Lyra could make out the stitching of a forest.

"Not enough. I felt guilty for fleeing, so now, all I know is duty. Which doesn't offer a lot of—"

"Free time," she finished for him.

"Exactly," he murmured, taking a sip of his tea.

"That's unfortunate. I don't think I would ever leave this place."

He nodded, and she leaned back in her chair, watching the waves roll in and the surf crash against the rocks. She felt as if she should tell him the story of her horrors. Of being tortured by her father after she had run away.

But now didn't feel like the time.

"I'm surprised you're not already in the water," he said, watching her stare with longing at the sea.

"I'm frightened."

Wilder tilted his head. "Of what?"

"What if it's not the same?"

He chuckled, and the sound was a balm to her fraying nerves. "It probably won't be. But you're going to get in the water, anyway. Might as well enjoy it—changes and all."

He was right, and that annoyed her. She huffed a sigh and took another sip of her lemony tea.

"Do we have any other plans?"

Wilder shook his head.

"I figured I'd do some fishing to catch us something for dinner. I need to check the garden and see if there's anything still edible to scrounge together. There used to be someone to tend to these things while I was away, but it doesn't look like they've been here for quite some time."

"What do you think happened?"

Wilder pondered her question. "It was an elder elf. I'm worried he's passed and no one bothered to tell me."

Lyra pursed her lips and turned her gaze back to the sea to avoid the emotion that flickered across his face.

"I'm so sorry."

He sighed. "It happens. We're not immortal, even if sometimes it feels that way."

Lyra nodded and plucked at the silk fabric of her gown. "I'm going to see if Daisy packed anything for swimming." She stood and felt the weight of his stare on her. When she met that gaze, she was surprised to see his eyes had darkened, the bright blue now the dark blue of the ocean outside.

"Let me know if I can be of *any* assistance."

His voice was practically a purr, and she fought the shiver that crawled down her spine.

Lyra didn't know if she could handle his mouth on her again. It had been better than she imagined, and this body welcomed a heightened sense of pleasure.

Her mermaid form didn't allow for those kinds of positions. But to do it again crossed some kind of invisible line. This was only a truce, but it was feeling like it had shifted to *more*.

The servant had discarded her trunk in the bedroom on the right side of the house. A narrow iron bed sat in the corner, and an ancient, carved wooden armoire was on the opposite side of the room.

Carvings of ivy and small butterflies twined up the door. Her trunk was at the foot of the bed, and she had to shove the plush comforter out of the way to open the lid.

Rifling through the plethora of dresses, tunics, and shoes, she was annoyed that there wasn't anything suitable for swimming. But that hadn't been Daisy's fault. She was supposed to be on a royal tour, meeting the Lords and Ladies of Oberon's court —not traipsing through the countryside and swimming in the ocean.

She'd take the latter any day, though. It wasn't unfathomable to think Oberon's court was as twisted as her father's.

Lyra kept pulling out dresses until she came to the bottom of the trunk. A thin blue cotton dress with ruffled cap sleeves and a shorter hemline lay at the bottom.

It would have to do. It was the only dress that might hold up against the saltwater. The thin chiffon and gleaming beaded gowns would be ruined.

Lyra slipped out of the violet silk and donned the blue cotton dress. There was a small mirror beside the armoire, and she stood in front of it as she braided her hair back in one long braid that grazed her lower back.

She padded on bare feet through the cottage. Paintings of wildflower-covered meadows and roiling oceans dotted the whitewashed walls. It was cozy here, and she felt like she was seeing a glimpse of who Wilder was on the inside. And she found she very much liked what she saw.

He was already outside and had swapped his black pants for light linen trousers that were rolled up over his ankles. The extravagant tunic was replaced with a plain white short-sleeved one, and he gripped a fishing cane in his hand. He looked like part of the landscape.

As hard as the stones and as glorious as the ocean. Lyra took a deep breath, but something tightened in her chest and slithered through her veins as she found her way outside.

He outstretched his hand to her, and when she took it, her heart pounded in her throat. Wilder tucked her in close to his body. They walked as one over the rocky landscape and to the sandy shore.

Millennia of waves had pulverized large boulders into black sand. They stood at the water's edge, and Wilder placed the cane on the ground before toeing the water. He bared his teeth, and she giggled.

"Cold?"

"Frigid," he ground out.

Wilder urged her further, and when the water caressed her toes, she closed her eyes. It was arctic but also lovely. She inhaled big gulps of briny sea air and tilted her face to the cloudy sky. He stood behind and wrapped her in his arms.

"Are you okay?" he whispered.

Lyra leaned against him and rested her hands on his.

"I will be. Are you okay?"

She could feel him nod and then press his head to the side of hers.

"I will be too."

The water rushed up higher on her bare feet, reaching up to her ankles. The familiar feel sent a shiver that spasmed through her body.

"Are you really going to go swimming?" he asked, shivering alongside her.

"Mhm," she murmured. "And you're coming with me." Grabbing hold of his arms, she pulled him with her and splashed deeper into the waves.

"Lyra!"

She laughed at the frozen look of horror on his face.

"It's cold!"

Lyra splashed him, and his eyes darkened further, and he took a step towards her and then another, with his arms outstretched.

"Don't even think about it," she replied, retreating a step.

A larger wave caught her off guard and slammed against her

back, knocking her off her feet, but the frigid water took her breath away. Her dress was soaked, her braid wet from the crown to the end.

Wilder laughed so hard he clutched at his ribs. Lyra flung herself at him, and they fell together into the surf. Water surged around them, and he spluttered, cradling her to his chest.

"That was unnecessary," he drawled, but a smile stretched his lips wide.

"Now you're cold and wet too," she replied, looking up at him beneath lowered lashes.

Wilder pulled them to their feet, and they stood firm against another wave that crashed around them.

"Feel better?" he asked.

Lyra nodded and then shivered. She was better, much better.

Wilder lowered his head to her, and she raised her chin.

When their lips met, she felt a familiar warmth spear through her, chasing away the chill of the water.

52
FISH CAN'T HEAR

Wilder led them to a small pond near the cottage to catch their dinner. Lyra didn't have the heart to tell him that this was second nature to her and that they didn't need the pole.

She had swapped her cotton gown for another, similar one she had found at the bottom of the trunk. This one was a dark gray that had a hem of ruffles.

Wilder wore a dry white tunic and linen pants. Every so often, when the light hit him just right, Lyra could've sworn she'd seen red crisscrossing his back.

"What do you think?" Wilder asked, as they crept through a hedgerow and the pond appeared, flanked by large willows and fragrant cedars.

"It's nice," she replied. "And there are fish here?"

Wilder nodded. "There used to be quite a bit. But I haven't been here in ages, so I'm sure the occupants have multiplied greatly."

Lyra glimpsed the turtles on the banks and the bubbles that

popped at the surface. Again, she didn't have the heart to tell him he was wrong.

The turtles might have decimated a good portion of the fish, and the lack of birds didn't bode well either.

The reeds waved in the breeze as Wilder cast their line. Lyra sat on the ground beside him. The grass on the bank was soft, and there were colorful wildflowers blooming throughout. Such charming peace exuded from this place.

"So you've seen what most of the Wilds have to offer. Will you tell me about Atlantis?" Wilder prompted, taking a seat beside her and keeping an eye on his line.

"There's not much to tell."

"Friends? Siblings?"

Lyra sighed through her nose. "The closest things to friends I have are Marina and Seraphina. The two women who were with me the night you kidnapped me."

"Oh, right," Wilder bit back a smile.

"I guess you could call them friends. But they're not friends in the same way that you have Maelys, Ridge, and Otto. And as far as siblings go, I have six older sisters."

"All females," Wilder said in surprise.

"It's ironic King Auris only sired daughters when they have no place in our kingdom except as bargaining chips or pawns," she mused.

Wilder furrowed his brow and recast his line.

"What do you mean?"

"All of my older sisters were married off to bordering territories when I was still quite young. My engagement was even planned from infancy. But there was a large age gap between me and my next oldest sister."

"How big?"

"Eight years. When I was ten, she was married off."

"That's so young."

"Mhm." Lyra sighed through her nose. "I'm not exactly sure

why I wasn't married off as soon as I turned eighteen, as well. Except maybe it was because I was my father's favorite—or that I needed to become stronger to survive my fiancé."

Wilder turned to her then. "Is he that bad?"

Lyra gestured to the scars on the inside of her arms. "He's the worst sort. More muscle than brains, he is cruel, and the only thing he truly loves is himself. He turned his mother over for reading 'illicit material.'"

"I just can't imagine why they would want their females to suffer," Wilder murmured.

Lyra shrugged. "Control, maybe? I don't know. There's no mention of the three sisters, either. They stripped that tidbit from all our books, paintings, and rites. But then again, we can't partake in that, anyway."

Wilder shook his head, and Lyra sighed.

It fell silent before he asked, "How are Seraphina and Marina different from my friends?"

Lyra frowned, thinking back over her bond with the two of them.

"I would say I'm closer to Marina than Seraphina. But we were raised much differently. Her father was kind despite her being a female, and therefore, she's always been a bit different."

"How so?"

"Well, she—she asks a lot of pointed questions."

Wilder snorted, and Lyra glared.

"It's not like that. She has this way of riling me up and getting me into trouble." She didn't know how to explain it to him other than to give examples. "When I was fifteen, I found a book on elves that a library guard hadn't put back in the right place. Well, actually, Marina is the one who found it and showed me, and the one who caused a distraction so that I could slip out unnoticed. I devoured that book."

Wilder smirked. "We have no books about elves," he mimicked her.

She grimaced. "Sorry about that."

He shook his head and smiled. "Continue."

"I read all about the wars between your kingdoms, the different types of magics, and even your holidays. Ostara sounded exciting, and I dreamed of dancing in a ballroom."

She sighed and closed her eyes, remembering how it felt to spin around her room in Atlantis.

"Seraphina and Marina were the only two who knew about the books. One of them tipped the maid off who cleaned my room. She found the book and the others I had stashed and turned them over to my father. I was punished, and the books were destroyed."

Wilder ground his teeth and shifted narrowed eyes to her. "That's dreadful."

She nodded and sucked her lips into her mouth. "Months later, when I ran away, one of them told my father where I had gone. It's things like that. I've come to realize they're not genuine. At least, not in the sense that yours are. Maelys would have never ratted you out, and Otto or Ridge would have given you sanctuary."

"They are good friends."

He cast the line out again, and a cloud floated across the sun, casting them in shadow.

"Maelys tended to my back when I was returned from Igneous' clan. Otto and Ridge refused to leave my side until I was healed and even sometime after that."

"Your back?" Lyra questioned, sitting up straighter.

"I don't like people knowing, usually."

"May I see?"

He sighed and leaned forward. "Just don't—scream."

His words had her stomach flipping. *What could be so bad he thought she would scream?*

Lyra pulled the hem of his shirt up and did, in fact, want to scream. Puckered red skin in varying lengths and depths, by the coloring, crisscrossed his back in a gruesome pattern. Scars the width of her finger looked angry and swollen. While longer scars bordered on violet in color and violent in nature.

It made her chest ache and bile burn the back of her throat as she thought about what tremendous pain he had undergone.

"Who did this?" she asked as calmly as she could, but there was no hiding the tremble in her voice.

"Mainly, Igneous—the alpha. But at times, he allowed others to join in."

She dropped his shirt and clenched her hand into a tight fist. She wanted to kill them. Kill them all for the violence they had waged across his skin.

Their experiences had been similar, although they had coped in vastly different ways. He wasn't a monster like she had been told the elves were. Not even close.

Monsters don't apologize or admit when they are wrong. But it was more than that; she realized his past and his father's opinion of him were his driving force in life.

Every decision he made was weighed against it. Much like her every decision was weighed against her father's promise of freedom.

They were two sides of the same coin.

"It makes sense now," she said.

"What does?"

"Why you seemed so familiar to me the first time I saw you."

He turned and grinned at her. The emotion in his gaze was unbearable as it cracked her open and threatened to spill every emotional thought she had brewing.

Lyra cleared her throat. "Um, you won't catch any fish with that."

Wilder frowned, looking at his pole. "Why is that?"

"The turtles have eaten most of what was in this pond. That's why there are no birds."

"So now what?"

"I'll catch us something from the ocean," she offered.

Wilder followed her back to the seaside and watched as she held her dress up and waded into the surf. It was familiar to her, watching the ripples under the surface and then spearing a hand in.

It didn't take her any time at all until she was walking back to the shore with two cods.

"Impressive," he said with raised brows.

"I'm starving," she replied with a grin.

"Let's pick some vegetables and I'll cook us dinner."

She stared at him, and he stared back. "What?"

"You can *really* cook?"

He laughed and took the fish from her. "Of course, can't you?"

She shook her head. "We don't 'cook' underwater."

He laughed harder. "So, what can you do?"

Lyra shrugged. "I can put together a salad, I suppose."

The garden was in complete disarray. Weeds and overgrown herbs, vegetables, and even a few fruits.

Wilder had deposited the fish in the kitchen and stood staring with a perplexed expression at the chaos.

"I don't even know where to start," he muttered, more to himself than to her.

But Lyra stood staring in wonder. It was perfect and magical, this garden.

"I see some kale," she gestured to the mass of furled green, "and some carrots, it looks like."

Wilder waved to the garden. "Then have at it."

She giggled and began foraging for their meager salads.

Back in the kitchen, Wilder prepped their fish, skinning the scales and removing their innards.

"We just eat them raw," Lyra added as she hovered over his shoulder, watching.

"You also lived under the water and had razor-sharp teeth."

"That's true."

"Do you miss it?" he asked, without looking at her.

"Sometimes. I miss the water and my sharp teeth and claws. But I don't miss the rules and the dreariness. Everything is so full of life and color here."

"What's the court like?"

"Abysmal," she uttered. "Scheming, corruption, and cruelty. I'm sure we're aptly described in your books."

He nodded then. "Like we were in yours." Wilder threw the fish into a pan that rested atop a flame.

"I have seen nothing of the sort from the elves."

Wilder snorted. "We're far from perfect, and you would have quickly realized that had we gone on an actual tour."

"I suppose even the humans could say that, too. Everyone has their issues."

"Very wise, Princess," Wilder replied with a smile. "What have you read about the humans?"

"Not much. But my experiences with them were terrifying."

He ran a hand down her spine before pulling her to him and pressing a kiss to her head. "I am sorry for that."

"You saved me."

"You were only there because of me. Not all humans are that way from my experiences, but from what I have heard about Badenvaria—well, you never want to go there. No creature leaves there."

She nestled into his side and breathed in his familiar scent.

A small part of her wished they could stay here—like this forever.

It was the closest she had ever felt to being home.

53

FLOUNDERED

The next few days passed in a blur of long morning walks along the surf, late afternoon dips in the ocean, and evening dinners of fish and whatever vegetables they could find in the untended garden.

They moved between the cottage, garden, and sea. Not to mention between each other. Lyra knew the truce was coming to an end, but she didn't want to think about that or what it meant for them.

It was their last night in the cottage before the servant would arrive to take them back to the castle. And it was bittersweet. Neither of them could admit that they had no real desire to go back. Including Lyra, who had been most excited to celebrate her first holiday.

Wilder was bent over the wood stove, their evening catch frying in the cast-iron skillet. Lyra felt utterly at peace while she arranged the kale into some semblance of a salad. Her breath came easy and her heart felt full.

"What is that song you're humming?" His voice tugged her lips up before his words resonated.

Lyra turned towards him, a question on her lips.

"You didn't realize you were humming, did you?"

She couldn't remember a time she had ever hummed on purpose in Atlantis. Wilder flipped the fish over and chuckled.

"You've been singing since we left the ancient willow."

Lyra frowned and shrugged. "I didn't realize I was, and couldn't even tell you what the song is."

"It's lovely," he murmured.

"Thank you." Her cheeks burned under his praise, and she tried her best to tamp it down.

"Did you not sing before because of your magic?"

Lyra studied the kale in front of her to keep from recoiling from his words. Her magic. That was the last thing she wanted to discuss, and she could feel it stronger now, the thread more like a corded rope around her heart.

"Yes."

"And now?" he asked with a quizzical raise of his brow. She could tell he wanted to discuss it further, but she couldn't find it in her to open that box.

"The magic feels different."

"How so?"

Lyra huffed. "I don't want to talk about it."

Wilder picked up the skillet and deposited the fish onto dark green plates before spooning some of the herbs from the pan onto their plates.

Lyra brought the bowl of kale over beside him and scooped out handfuls next to the fish.

"Wine?"

"Sure," Lyra replied, and he uncorked a bottle.

All of their dinners had been this way, casual and relaxed. It was exactly what she had needed and was healing to her in a way, but now with the conversation turning towards her magic, tension bloomed.

They took their seats at the walnut dinner table. It was pockmarked and grooved with age and love. Lyra set their plates down, and Wilder poured their wine, but they both remained quiet.

"What are you thinking about?"

She rubbed a finger along the rim of her glass. She was thinking about so many things. How much she'd enjoyed her time here, how much she had enjoyed him.

But now that he brought up her magic, the bargain loomed like a monster under the bed. And there was something darker surfacing in her mind, something that didn't sit right about the grand scheme of things.

"Something has been bothering me since I agreed to the bargain with your father."

"And what is that?"

"What did the humans get out of this bargain?"

Wilder shifted on his chair, and by the fluttering of his jaw, she could tell he was just as annoyed as she was. "My father never said. He's been ultra-secretive about this whole thing. It's why I refused to take part."

Lyra nodded and pushed the food around her plate. This evening was taking a turn for the worse.

She should have been honest with him and told him about her fears, but she couldn't.

"Did you really not ever notice that the tithe was something more? Did your father?"

Lyra shrugged, relieved that he didn't circle back to her magic. "Births had declined, but it was blamed on the mermaids for having lives outside of reproduction. That's why my father implemented all the rules."

Wilder's jaw clenched. "Your father is the reason for all the sanctions against females?"

Lyra sighed and met his gaze once more. "Yes."

"And did he notice when those rules weren't increasing the birthrate?"

"Of course not," she spat. "That would require him admitting he was wrong." That would never happen; she didn't even think her father knew those words.

"How do you think he's going to feel when you undo the tithe, proving him wrong?"

She didn't answer.

If she were honest, she hadn't thought about what would happen after she broke the bargain. Lyra had only focused on the severity of the first steps.

"Are we going to talk about this?" he asked as they picked at their dinners.

Her face scrunched up with disgust, and it wasn't from the food.

"I don't think there is anything to discuss."

Wilder glared at her and took a sip of the white wine. "You are under a bargained oath with my father to use magic. If you don't, you will die. You know this."

A shadow passed over her face as she glared right back. Again, it came back to her magic, like always.

"We are still under a truce until tomorrow, and I would like to keep it that way."

Wilder slammed the glass down. "We are going to talk about this."

She shoved her plate away and crossed her arms, but didn't move from the table. "You are ruining this."

He met her glare head-on without flinching.

"Why did you even agree to use it if you never planned on it?"

Lyra ground her teeth. "I do plan on using it. I'm just not ready yet."

"I find that hard to believe. You haven't even tried."

She couldn't do this.

Couldn't stomach telling him that she was afraid of being a failure, afraid that she would let everyone down—let him down.

Lyra stood and turned to flee the dining room, but Wilder was upon her, wrapping a hand around her wrist.

"Tell me you're going to break the bargain and that you will stay here—with me."

"I will say no such thing." She pulled against his grip, and he let go. When she didn't move farther away, he cupped her cheek.

"You will die if you don't break the bargain. And I—can't let that happen."

He had said it. Said what was so glaringly obvious between the two of them and what she had been struggling to keep at bay. And it terrified her to hear it.

Scared her more than losing herself to magic or failing and dying. She couldn't bear the thought of letting him down.

Lyra's fear hardened her heart.

"I don't want to stay here with you. I don't belong here or with you."

Wilder reeled back as if the words had struck him.

"You do not want me. I am not good." The words tasted bitter in her mouth. "No one has ever loved me because I am hard to love. I am impossible to be around most days. There is something wrong with me—so save your time and your energy."

"That is not true," he argued.

"It is. It is true. I don't belong here. I can't stay."

And there was the truth of it.

She still did not believe she was worthy of their kindness or their loyalty.

54

You can't unring a bell

They rode the entire way home in silence. Lyra regretted what she had said to him, but she had been petrified of the longing in his eyes and the magic that had coiled within her.

She couldn't feel that magic anymore though; it was as if her magic had vanished.

And it was for the best that he knew now who she was, so he could save himself from her.

She couldn't stop watching him as she pretended to read. It hurt to look at him, but it hurt even more to look away and miss a single fleeting moment.

There were already so few left.

Lyra had made up her mind. She must return to the water.

When she returned to the castle, she would work day and night to understand her magic so that she could break the tithe and return home.

Where she belonged—with the other monsters. She didn't

deserve the kindness that the land had offered her, and it was killing her.

Wilder sighed through his nose, and Lyra raked her gaze across him, trying to find the source of his discomfort.

When his eyes met hers, she looked at her book as if she hadn't been looking at him at all. The words blurred together, and her chest tightened with each passing moment.

The castle gates came into view, and Wilder thumped a fist on the ceiling of the coach.

When the wheels creaked to a stop, he flung open the door and stepped outside.

"Truce over," he said, slamming the door shut behind him.

Lyra's eyes burned, and she buried her head in her hands.

She had screwed this all up—royally. And it hurt.

It hurt like the slicing of her tail into two legs. It hurt like her missing the sea, but feeling like she no longer belonged. It hurt like her magic, siphoning off her life.

The carriage proceeded, but instead of passing through the castle gates, it took the long way around again. It looked like she wouldn't be getting to see the city after all.

She couldn't find it in her heart to care. She had cared too much already, and it had brought her misery.

Lyra gave herself time to grieve. Not a long enough time, but more time than she gave herself for the ocean. She reached out to touch the water dripping down her cheeks.

A single tear clung to her fingertip and then fell onto her emerald gown. She studied it, the water that sprang from her eyes, reminding her of all that she had lost.

As the carriage pulled up to the castle at last, Lyra wiped her tears away and shoved the rest of her anguish down.

She had a bargain to uphold, and she needed to get to work.

55
OSTARA

On the morning of Ostara, Lyra stood in the center of the training ground, facing the man-shaped target made of wood and straw ten yards away.

Maelys crouched down beside her and grasped a handful of dirt before letting it slip from her fingers back to the ground. The wind blew some of it at an angle as it slipped from her hand.

The dagger Lyra gripped in her fingertips was surprisingly warm, probably because of the number of times she had thrown it already.

"Breathe …" Maelys ordered as Lyra's breath came out in quick pants.

"I'm trying," Lyra growled back.

"No—you're panting. Breathe."

Lyra's eyes slid closed, and she inhaled. The tension left her shoulders, and her arms relaxed.

"Picture your target and only your target. Don't let those animals distract you," Maelys ordered.

And they were distracting. Dust and Oak squared off with their fists wrapped in a thick fabric, but that did nothing to muffle the sound of them pummeling each other.

Ridge and Otto battled with wooden swords. The thwacking sound of wood on wood echoed around the space. And Wilder—Wilder stayed perched on the stone wall of the fence, surveying everyone and everything around them. It wasn't the others that distracted her.

No, it was the glare from the male she missed.

Wilder snorted at what Maelys had said, and Lyra flicked her attention to him. He returned her stare with a scowl. The scent of the purple flowers wrapped around her and softened the usual dirt and grass aroma.

Wind whipped a strand of dark hair across Wilder's face, and a cloud floated across the sun, casting the ground in momentary shadow. It hadn't been the same between them since the disastrous ruin of their truce.

Lyra still couldn't stomach the feelings she shoved down every morning. She missed him—exceedingly so. And he did everything in his power to piss her off.

"Focus, Lyra," Maelys said, drawing Lyra's attention back to the target. "Pull back and throw it."

They had switched to smaller weapons because of Lyra's lack of muscle. Lyra was comfortable with daggers as she had used one in Atlantis, but she still was not accustomed to her legs, no matter how often Maelys made her use them.

Lyra huffed a breath and slung the dagger at the target. The hilt slapped against the wood target's midsection before it clattered to the ground.

"Are you pinching the tip when you throw?" Maelys asked, shaking her head and rising to retrieve her thrown blade.

"I think so," Lyra replied.

"She's not," Wilder called from the fence. He wrapped his arms around one knee while the other leg dangled.

"I didn't ask for your opinion!"

Ridge peered over at them, trying to gauge if they were quarreling or teasing. When Wilder started chuckling, Ridge focused back on the battle at hand.

Lyra stood with her hands on her hips and glared at Wilder.

"Are you going to help or continue with the unusual staring?"

Wilder rolled his eyes and hopped off the fence. With long strides, he walked towards Lyra, and her mouth dried up.

Such calculated steps, like a predator about to pounce.

It reminded her of him chasing her around the willow, and again at the seaside cottage. It made her throat burn with all the words she swallowed down.

He reached for her hand and turned it palm up to the sky. His fingers wrapped around her wrist, while his other hand touched her fingertips.

She had to strain to keep from trembling at his touch.

"Your fingers are damp," he murmured.

"It's hot," Lyra replied, annoyed with his less-than-astute observation.

Wilder shook his head. "I'm trying to say your grip is slipping because your fingers are damp." He reached down, grabbed a handful of dirt, and rubbed it on her fingers.

"Try it again," he ordered, jutting his chin towards the target. "Square your feet and throw on your exhale—not your inhale."

Maelys rolled her eyes and handed Lyra the blade.

"Do what he says—but ignore him," she added, crossing her arms over her chest.

Lyra slid her feet further apart and inhaled, gripping the blade with her dry but dirty fingers. She sent the blade flying on her exhale.

The dagger sank into the target, at what would be a person's knee.

Her eyes brightened upon hearing the blade slide into the wood.

"I did it!" she squealed, clapping her hands.

Maelys whooped and hollered with her, and the two females jumped up and down, hugging each other.

"No need to thank me. I only instructed you how to do it," Wilder said, crossing his arms over his leather-clad chest.

Maelys reached out an arm and shoved him. He didn't move an inch and glared at the dirty handprint she'd left on his training leathers.

"Imagine how much further along she would be if you would deign to help without being asked," Maelys said with a malicious grin.

"Yeah!" Lyra said, whipping her head between the two of them.

Wilder turned on a heel and stalked back to his favorite seat on the stone fence. "I'm not getting involved. Work on her magic now."

"For someone who doesn't want to get involved, you sure are bossy," Maelys replied.

He didn't answer and hopped back on the fence with feline grace.

"Alright, let's try some magic. I have an idea for today— Ridge!"

Ridge and Otto halted their assault on each other.

"Did you tell her the plan?" Ridge asked, cracking his knuckles. The leather tunic he wore was two sizes too small and showed off a broad strip of muscled abs.

Lyra didn't like the sound of that.

"What's the plan?" Otto asked with a smile, as if he didn't already know.

His long white hair was tied out of his face, and several new beads were tied around the ends. Lyra couldn't tell what was carved onto them, but they looked geometric.

Maelys nodded at Ridge, who focused on the dirt in front of them. A green stalk burst from the ground, and the flower bud at the center stayed green as if it was about to bloom, but not quite.

"Tell it to bloom," Maelys said to Lyra.

Lyra's mouth dropped open, and an unintelligible spluttering came out.

"You can do it. It's a plant, not a person, or a living creature. It's just a plant."

Ridge frowned at Maelys. "I mean, it is alive—"

"Shhh!" Maelys snapped. "We need Lyra to try. She'll be too scared if she thinks she'll hurt someone. You can make the plant grow back, can't you?"

Ridge nodded with enthusiasm. "Oh! Yes, yes, I can. Tell it to bloom. You got this."

The magic wouldn't budge, and it hadn't since she had returned from their tour.

"I can't," Lyra whispered, closing her eyes.

She had tried. Desperately tried to wield it, but of course, now that she wanted to use it, she couldn't.

Something had broken inside of her, and whatever it was had broken her magic as well.

"I know you're scared, but you made a bargain with the king. You have to," Maelys whispered.

She could feel them shift around her, could feel the weight of Wilder's stare on her face, could hear Dust and Oak stop to watch.

"I know, but I can't," she choked out. Tears dripped down her face, and the cool wetness startled her enough that her eyes opened.

"Don't push her," Otto said. "She needs to feel ready. And she's not."

Maelys sighed and looked skyward. "Well, that's all I have for you today, then."

Lyra nodded, sucking her bottom lip into her mouth.

"Let's join the festivities," Ridge said, slinging an arm around Maelys. "I'm ready to eat."

He patted his abdomen, the muscles visible through the leather.

His eagerness brought a smile to Maelys' lips.

"We have to get ready, and then we'll meet you guys at the ball," Maelys said, slipping out of his reach and grabbing Lyra's hand. "Don't wait for us. We'll find you!"

Maelys pulled Lyra off the grounds and past Wilder, who watched on with a disgruntled expression. Lyra frowned in return and hadn't a clue what was about to happen.

"What do we wear to this?"

"Daisy is getting everything ready for you," Maelys replied.

"Okay … but you didn't answer the question."

Maelys' smile turned feral. "Just wait and see!"

A GOWN of ocean waves was hung beside the windows of Lyra's room. Swirls of pearls were stitched to resemble sea foam on the nearly black navy skirts, and the bodice appeared to be the deepest, darkest depths of the ocean. It was enchanting.

"Do you like it?" Daisy asked, twisting her hands in front of her.

Lyra stroked a saltwater pearl and stared with awe at the straps of silk that would hang off her shoulders.

"No."

Daisy and Maelys gasped.

"I love it," Lyra finished, turning towards them with a beaming smile. "It's perfect! Thank you both so much."

The joy she felt was familiar—like the feeling she had with Wilder during the tour. It was sweet but also bitter. Lyra knew it wouldn't last and that she would leave all of this behind.

Daisy clutched her chest, and the ruffles of her servant's dress fluttered with the movement.

"That was not nice."

Maelys gripped her arm and nodded. "I didn't care for it either."

Lyra frowned. Wilder would have thought it was humorous.

"I was merely teasing. Of course, I love it. It's gorgeous."

Daisy stepped towards her and placed her hands on her hips.

"You need to bathe, and I still need to do your hair and makeup, so let's get to it, or you're going to be late."

"What are you wearing?" Lyra asked Maelys.

"I had something made, too. I'm going to get ready, and I'll be back to escort you," Maelys replied over her shoulder as she sauntered out the door. "Good luck."

Lyra didn't know if it had been for her or Daisy.

Hours later, when she had been scrubbed, plucked, and pinned within an inch of her life, she knew it had been for her. Daisy helped her step into the gown and then cinched it up tight around her waist.

The sleeves were off her shoulders, making her neck look longer and her breasts larger.

"You are a goddess," Daisy muttered, stepping back to admire her work.

Lyra couldn't help but spin, and when she did, a smile stretched her lips wide.

"I feel like one, too."

The door opened, and Maelys appeared, looking like a forest nymph. Her gown was layered with varying shades of green, and small flowers were scattered around the hem and grew up to her waist. Like she had stepped through the forest and into the castle. Her golden-brown hair was curled, and a flower crown rested on her brow.

"You look—"

"You are—"

They started at the same time.

"Stunning."

"Gorgeous."

They beamed at each other and laughed. They each embodied the land from which they came.

Maelys the Wilds, and Lyra, Atlantis.

"Are you ready?" Maelys asked.

Lyra looked at Daisy for confirmation.

"As ready as she'll ever be."

Maelys nodded. "We'll be back after the feast and first dance to get ready for the real celebrations."

Daisy's face turned an astonishing red. "I'll be here."

"You don't go to the ball?" Lyra asked, realizing Daisy was still in her servant's uniform.

Daisy shook her head. "Only the court goes to the ball."

Lyra's brow furrowed. She did not like that at all. "That's not fair."

Maelys nodded. "I've been after Wilder about it for ages. But he has no say in it."

Lyra approached Daisy. "I can stay with you if you like?"

Daisy shook her head and gripped Lyra's hand. "And waste all my hard work? Absolutely not! Go enjoy yourself. You deserve some happiness, Lyra." It made her heart ache, and Lyra had to ball her hands into fists at her side to keep from clutching at her chest.

"Thank you, Daisy. You're too kind."

"There's no such thing."

"We'll be back soon," Maelys trilled from the door, and Lyra followed. This ball better be spectacular, or she was going to feel awful for leaving Daisy behind.

Every single flat surface was covered with flowers. The picture frames lining the hallways, the bases of statues, and even the banisters were draped with flora. Lilies, tulips, baby's breath, hydrangeas, heather, foxtail, and many more she did not know the name of.

Small flames flickered in tiny tea lights. And the smells. Gods, the divine smells. Citrus and floral, and something sweet. It was immaculate.

"Is it like this every year?" Lyra asked as they waltzed down the hallway.

"Pretty much."

The flower petals on Maelys' dress fluttered behind her, and Lyra admired how exquisite it was.

"And this is like a real ball? With dancing?"

Maelys glanced sideways at her. "Of course. Why?"

Lyra shrugged, and her gown flowed and waved like a waterfall. "I don't know how."

Maelys pursed her lips. "Ridge and I can teach you. It's easy."

Lyra nodded, but unease coiled around her. There was no way she was going to make a fool of herself tonight, especially in front of Wilder.

They reached the doorway of the grand ballroom, and Maelys stopped. Peering at the open doors and the nonexistent line.

"We're probably the last two to arrive, since there is no line. They'll announce you and then walk in. That's it."

She must have noticed the unease on Lyra's face. The tightness around her eyes and the grimace on her mouth.

"I'll go first. And I'll wait for you. I promise."

She squeezed Lyra's hand before letting go and walking through the open door and waiting on the stair landing. It was a long walk down the stairs, and Lyra clenched her teeth as the page called out Maelys' name.

"Maelys Briarlace!"

Applause broke out, and Lyra watched as Maelys disappeared down the stairs. Her golden-brown hair gleamed in the crystalline light, and Lyra worked to calm her breathing.

She felt as if she were entering a battlefield. The first time she was surrounded by this many elves, they had hurled insults at her.

Taking a deep gulp of air and squaring her shoulders, Lyra walked through the doors.

The room fell silent. She could hear her dress hiss across the polished marble floors.

"Princess Lyra Auris of Atlantis!" the page announced.

Lyra traced her fingertips on the carved stair railing and looked out into the crowd to meet the glares of the gentry. Murmurs of her parentage were apparent in the sneers that she faced. She was an outsider here—an enemy.

But a shadow moved through the crowd, a blur of black striding with purpose. Those who didn't move out of his way quickly enough were shoved by his wind.

He stood beside the page and murmured in his ear. The page's tawny skin burned red before he announced to the room. "Escorted by Prince Wilder Moon Vale."

Lyra froze and looked down at him. A smirk curved at the corner of his lips as he gazed up at her. His black jacket was embroidered with silver and sapphire—an identical match to her gown. But where hers were swirls of ocean waves, his were whirls of the wind.

He leveled his chin, daring her to refute his arm. And she did not.

Taking the steps one at a time, she reached his side and looked up into his sky-blue eyes that met hers without malice.

"Escort?" she murmured, her brow furrowing.

"Protection," he replied, and stared past her and into the crowd that was still watching them.

Lyra nodded and took his arm, allowing him to lead her to the dais that King Oberon and Queen Aine sat on.

Wilder leaned towards her and whispered into her ear, "You look stunning."

His voice was like a caress to her nerves.

"Thank you."

Wilder walked her through the crowd, head held high, as they approached the king and queen.

Aine smiled down at her. "Lyra, darling, we're so delighted you're here to celebrate with us."

Lyra grinned in return and dropped her chin low.

King Oberon's face was unreadable. His antler crown gleamed when he nodded to her and then to Wilder. A cloak of crimson rested on his shoulders, and Lyra felt a thrill roll through her when she realized what it reminded her of—blood.

Queen Aine stood from her throne, and the murmurs that had bubbled were silenced. Her dress was like the night sky, navy and black, embroidered with diamonds that mimicked constellations.

"Let the festivities begin!" Queen Aine announced.

Strums of music began, and the crowd dispersed to the edges of the dance floor. Dancers took their positions in the center. Lyra stared on with a yearning she felt looking out at the sea. Swirls of color twined and flowed as the dancers twirled around the dance floor.

Wilder glanced down at a bouncing Lyra.

"Would you like to join them?"

Lyra bit her lip and tore her gaze from the gracefulness in the center of the room.

"I don't know how," she murmured.

Maelys was spun around by Ridge. His dark skin complemented her evergreen and floral gown. Like the gown itself had been made as the female equivalent of him.

"I'll show you," Wilder replied, tugging her to the dance floor.

Lyra's heart rate increased, and her palms became damp. She had dreamed of this moment for most of her life, and it was finally happening.

They strode through the crowd arm-in-arm. Elves stepped out of the way and threw snarls at her. But she didn't care. She was getting to dance on a holiday, something that was strictly forbidden for females.

Her attention was solely on the dance floor ahead of them.

Wilder grazed his hand across her waist before settling it low on her back. Her other hand was gripped in his. He looked down at her feet and then back up into her eyes.

"Just take a breath and follow my lead."

He scooped her up, and her feet hovered above the ground before he was twirling them in line with the other dancers.

Lyra felt a wave of happiness from the top of her head to the tips of her toes as she flew around the dance floor. A smile stretched wide across her face, and a laugh bubbled up between her lips.

Wilder leaned back to look at her as he swept them across the floor, and an answering smile bloomed on his face.

"Enjoying yourself?"

Lyra blushed and squeezed his hand. "I have always wanted to do this."

Wilder nodded. "I know."

Her brow arched, and her smile dropped away. "You did?"

He nodded and spun her around. "You told me."

Lyra frowned, not remembering such a conversation. "When?"

"At the cottage."

She remembered that it was when they had been cooking

their first meal together. A flood of memories from the cottage, the willow, and the swamp tormented her.

"Oh." Her voice was quiet, and Wilder frowned.

"Why do I feel like you're upset?"

Lyra shook her head, and her auburn hair shuddered with the movement.

"Then what's the matter?"

The music was drawing to a close, and in a move that surprised her, Wilder swept her higher off her feet before dropping her parallel to the ground. His face lowered to hers, and his eyes were on her lips.

Her heart pounded against her ribs.

"What was that for?"

"It's the end of the dance. It's called a dip."

Lyra sucked in a breath as he tilted her upright. The music took off once more, but they stood still, staring at each other.

"Why are you doing this?" she asked, tucking a wayward strand behind her ear.

His brow lowered over his bright eyes, casting them in shadow. "Doing what?"

"Being nice. I—hurt you," she muttered, looking anywhere but at him.

"Everyone deserves kindness, Lyra."

She nodded, biting her lip and staring at the surrounding dancers again. The colors of their attire were like a painting—they were so vivid—and their movements mimicked a painter's strokes.

"Care for another dance?" Wilder asked.

Lyra whipped her head to his and saw a flicker of emotion cross his eyes. Behind him, Aine and Oberon watched them from their thrones.

"Please."

Wilder scooped her up, and they set off again, this time at a much quicker pace.

"What is this dance called?"

"A waltz," he replied, close enough to her ear that a shiver wracked her body.

Lyra pressed herself closer to him and could hear the groan come from the back of his throat.

"I'm sorry. For what I said at the cottage," she said. She missed him. More than she ever imagined missing anything. He felt like home to her.

Wilder froze, and dancers had to spin out of control to keep from colliding with him.

But she had wanted to tell him the moment she had said those cruel words, and now was as good a time as any.

"I was frightened by what I was feeling, and I lashed out."

He shook his head and took a step back. "Don't."

"Why?"

"You were right. You don't belong—"

She felt the stab to her heart as if a dagger had pierced through her flesh, muscles, and bones.

The pain burned up through her throat, constricting it and making speech difficult.

"I see," Lyra snapped, raising her chin to keep her lip from trembling.

"We're from different worlds," Wilder clarified, trying to assuage her obvious misery. "It was just a truce."

She nodded, but her eyes turned glassy from the tears threatening to fall.

"May I cut in?" Otto asked, appearing beside Lyra with his hand outstretched.

He looked regal in a jacket of burgundy that made his white skin seem silver.

"Of course," Lyra replied, taking his hand in hers.

"Lyra—" Wilder began.

But she cut him off. "It's done."

She set off in a waltz with Otto, but no matter how much she concentrated, she couldn't quite find her footing as she had with Wilder.

"Are you having a pleasant time?" Otto asked. A small smile graced his thin lips.

"Quite."

Otto chuckled. "Could have fooled me."

"Sorry—I wasn't expecting to fight with him." Lyra grimaced.

"I was."

She rolled her eyes but stepped on his toe. "Sorry."

"Don't be. It won't always be like this," he murmured, and his voice was soft.

"It gets better?"

"Do you really want to know?"

Lyra thought about Wilder's feelings on hearing his future and shook her head.

"Just tell me one thing?"

Otto nodded. "Of course."

"Does it hurt?"

There was a grimace on his face that made her stomach sink.

She heaved a sigh as the music drew to yet another close.

"Physically or emotionally?" she asked low enough so that the crowd could not hear her.

"Both. But not forever. And you become stronger, Lyra. Stronger than your wildest dreams."

There was a small bit of comfort in his words that she clung to.

"Go find Maelys. She's ready for you," Otto ordered before slipping back into the crowd.

Lyra searched the room for Maelys and swept past the glares and sneers of displeasure.

Oberon and Aine were murmuring between themselves, heads bent together. Lyra caught Aine's eye before the queen turned.

That was unusual. And Lyra felt as if they had been speaking about her.

"There you are!" Maelys called, two goblets of wine in her hands.

"I was looking for you," Lyra replied, taking the glass Maelys handed her.

She was ready to flee from this place, and if she hadn't found Maelys soon, she would have left without a word. Everything hurt, and her time here was up.

"You weren't looking hard enough," Maelys teased. "How was the dancing?"

"It was fine. You and Ridge looked graceful."

Maelys laughed, and it was such a lovely sound that Lyra smiled despite herself.

"Years of practice. You and Wilder looked better than we did."

Lyra's heart fell into her stomach, and with it, her smile.

"You ready for the real fun?"

It took her a second to realize Maelys was not joking.

"What happens now?"

Maelys looked around for listening ears and smiled with devilish delight.

"The pleasure house."

56

VOYEURSIM

"Absolutely not," Lyra said, holding up the scrap of sheer fabric that could be compared to cobwebs.

Maelys already had hers on, and every inch of her body was visible beneath the sheer, pale pink lace.

The setting sun sent a beam of golden light through the wide-open window and highlighted every morsel of her curvaceous frame. And Lyra couldn't fight the blush that ignited across her cheeks and down to her chest.

"Wear anything else, and you'll stand out like a daisy among roses."

Lyra held up the sheer green fabric and stared at Maelys. "This is invisible!"

Maelys smiled and pulled the dress down between them. "That is the point! Ostara is the holiday that celebrates birth and new life. Hence the naked part."

Lyra looked at Daisy for confirmation. And she bobbed her head in agreement.

"And why aren't you dressed like that?" Lyra shot back.

"I don't celebrate," Daisy replied.

A slight frown marred Lyra's face. "Oh, why not?"

Maelys bumped Daisy's hip with hers. "Because Daisy has someone special, she celebrates with." A waggle of Maelys' eyebrows cleared up the insinuation.

"Ahhhh. And you don't?" Lyra asked Maelys.

A smirk was Maelys' reply.

"Ugh, fine," Lyra sighed, throwing her head back and screwing her eyes shut.

Maelys and Daisy didn't even move as Lyra shucked her robe and slipped on the sheer dress. Lyra shivered as the cool fabric slid over her sensitive nipples before clinging to her waist and fluttering right above her ankles.

"Goodness," Maelys breathed, her eyes widening. "You'll have an abundance of suitors."

Daisy bit her bottom lip and hummed. "Yes, but it's missing something. Oh!" She scrambled across the room and into the bathing chamber.

Lyra and Maelys stood listening to Daisy open and slam cabinet drawers before an exclamation of victory rang out.

"I put this away on your first day here. I thought you might want a piece of home," Daisy said, striding across the room with a bracelet clasped in her hands.

The chain sparkled like moonlight, and at the very end of it was an iridescent saltwater pearl. It must have been from the southern seas because the pearl gleamed with a slight emerald hue.

It was spellbinding, and Lyra found herself enraptured with the dainty thing.

"Daisy—it's perfect," Lyra whispered, reaching out and cupping the pearl, before clasping it around her wrist.

"It's perfect!" Maelys clapped her hands together. "Alright, we must be off. I'm sure it'll be standing room only now."

Lyra's stomach gurgled, and she pressed a hand to the hollowness. It wasn't hunger that had her stomach churning, but nerves.

Maelys was halfway out the door before she realized Lyra wasn't right beside her.

"Are you coming?"

Lyra sighed through her nose and followed with quick footsteps. She had better enjoy her time here now before it was all gone and she was back under the sea.

Besides, tonight would ruin her for Drystan, and she would no longer have to suffer the thought of their brief marriage.

As they wound their way through the halls, it was as silent as a tomb. But flickering lanterns outside the castle windows revealed the revelers making their way into the city for the festivities.

"I'm sure there will be some food in town we can snack on," Maelys murmured. Lyra still gripped her empty stomach. The sheer fabric was barely felt between her fingers and her bare flesh.

"Where are we going?"

"The Venus," Maelys replied.

Lyra's palms sweat, and she had nothing to wipe the dampness on.

"Are there any rules? Or things I should know about?" Lyra asked.

"They'll give you a tonic at the door. Take it. It will prohibit pregnancy. You don't want to conceive an offspring tonight," Maelys chuckled. It was ironic, given that this holiday was about new life.

"Anything else?" Lyra asked.

"Try to find someone who sparks a fire in you. Leave all your inhibitions at the door. Tonight is about exploring yourself and what you like."

Lyra nodded but worried her bottom lip. "I don't know what I like," she whispered.

Maelys slammed their quick pace to a halt and grabbed Lyra's arm. "Are you a virgin?"

Lyra nodded and averted her eyes.

Maelys squeezed her arm. "Then don't think you have to do anything at all. 'No' is a full sentence. If you don't want to, you don't have to. And if someone has a problem with that, they will become my problem."

Lyra's shoulders drooped. "But what if you're indisposed?"

Storm clouds gathered in Maelys' eyes. "I will make the time."

"Thank you," Lyra whispered.

Maelys smiled, but it was subdued. "Why didn't you tell me before? This might be a bit much for you."

"Because it was embarrassing. The elves are so free with their sexuality, and it's fascinating. I feel inadequate."

Maelys snorted, and they began walking again. "If you want to explore tonight—go for it. No one will judge you."

Lyra squirmed, and her face pinched with confusion. "Why? Doesn't that mean I lack skill?"

Maelys rolled her eyes. "Males like to be the first to conquer new territory. It's a character flaw in their gender."

Lyra laughed, and her nerves vanished. She wouldn't be viewed as an oddity, but as a treasure. Which was relieving after her rejection by Wilder.

The walk through the city streets was a sight to behold. Flowers and streamers hung everywhere. Broadleaf ivy that tangled its way up the building had fresh-cut flowers placed between its vines.

The lanterns flickered and danced in line with the drums that beat through the pathways. People danced, laughed, and kissed as they basked beneath the moon's glow. Lyra's blood warmed, watching such life and passion swell and surge around her.

Maelys swiped cinnamon bread off a cart and threw the vendor a wink.

"Send the bill to the prince," Maelys called to the male, who smiled.

"Of course, Briarlace."

Lyra took a bite of the bread and moaned. "This is incredible." She took another bite.

"It's laced with arousal herbs, too." Maelys waggled her eyebrows, and Lyra laughed.

They continued walking through the throng of elves. A male with midnight skin and eyes the color of the sea pressed two glasses of wine into their hands.

"Happy Ostara," he whispered, and the seduction in his voice sent a shiver down Lyra's spine.

The glass was painted in vibrant colors, and the shape reminded Lyra of a large egg. The lanterns glowed brighter as they crossed from the Upper District to the Lower District. Most of the city seemed to congregate here.

Females dressed in similar sheer dresses, all in pastel colors. Lavender, yellows, greens, blues, and soft pinks. It was like wading through a spring painting.

The males were all bare-chested, their skin glittering with a shimmer that reminded Lyra of the night sky.

The music grew louder as they neared the center of the Lower District. A makeshift stage had been erected in front of a large, bubbling fountain. The doors to all the homes and buildings were thrown wide open as people came and went freely.

"That's the Venus," Maelys shouted over the drums and nodded to a dim building covered in garlands of spring flowers.

It wasn't as bright on the outside as some of the other buildings, but through the sheer curtains on the many round windows, Lyra could see the golden glow of candlelight.

"Let's go," Maelys said, tugging Lyra across the cobblestone street and to the arched front door.

Eyes watched them as they went, and a few males followed them through the threshold. A female with flowers woven into the long braids of her hair and a lazy grin on her angelic face handed them each a vial as they crossed the threshold.

Maelys threw it back without hesitation. Lyra stared at it a moment longer before pressing it to her lips. It tasted delicious. Honey and something floral.

The female took the vial back and gestured with her chin. "The common rooms are all available, but some of the specific rooms are at capacity."

Maelys grinned. "We'll find our way. Thank you."

She tugged Lyra behind her and into the main room. A soaring ceiling and many leather couches and chairs were spread haphazardly in the cavernous space.

People congregated at a large bar, sipping various wines and ales. While others chatted on couches before heading up the sweeping staircases on either side of the room. From the outside, Lyra had not pictured such a grandiose space.

"Let's get a drink and see if anyone sparks your desire," Maelys whispered in her ear. Several males stood behind them, waiting to see where they went.

Maelys sauntered up to the bar and was greeted by the towering barman behind the carved wooden counter. Tiny tealights flickered on the wooden top, flanked by bowls of water that had floating petals inside.

Everything seemed so meticulously decorated for the holiday.

"Spring wine, please, Carmine."

Carmine nodded and placed two lavender crystal glasses in front of them. "Enjoy," he murmured with a smile.

An elvish male approached Lyra, and she stiffened as he slid in beside her.

"You're new," he purred. Something in his voice reminded her of Drystan.

"No," she replied flatly.

His brows hit his golden hairline, but he didn't argue or rebuke her answer. He nodded and removed himself from her vicinity. Lyra sighed with relief, and Maelys smiled.

"Good, follow your instincts."

Lyra turned around on the stool to watch a couple lock hands and walk up the stairs together.

"I gather the rooms are up there?" she asked Maelys.

"Yes," Maelys replied, taking a sip of her wine. "There are communal rooms for the more adventurous partners who are keen to share. Single rooms for those who aren't. And then there are desire-specific rooms."

"Desire specific?" Lyra asked, a frown tugging her brows together.

"It's easier to show you. Come on." Maelys slid from her chair and sauntered to the foot of the stairs, leaving her empty glass behind on the bar.

Lyra's heart pounded behind her ribs, but she followed. She could feel eyes tracking her every step, and when she glanced in the direction of those eyes, she met several lustful stares.

Her blood warmed, and she sucked her bottom lip into her mouth.

A flurry of noises hit her ears. Moans, shouts of pleasure, and rhythmic thumping. It was a feast of arousal, and she felt the delicious heat pool in the lowest part of her belly.

A pulsing built between her thighs, and the friction of the sheer fabric grew against her pebbling nipples.

The hallway was long with several open archways. Maelys walked to the first door and leaned against the opening.

"Communal room," she said, nodding inside.

Lyra walked to the front of the door and halted. There must

have been ten partners inside this room, all in salacious positions.

Thrusting, riding, pulsating bodies all in the throes of passion. Males with males, females with females, males and females.

Lyra couldn't imagine such heightened pleasure. *The Knight in Shining Armor* had not adequately prepared her for such deliciously scandalous behavior.

That book was tame compared to the appetites in this room. Lyra gripped the opening and stared with enraptured wonder.

"Wanna see another one?" Maelys breathed, and Lyra nodded.

They walked to the next door together, but Lyra's jaw was still dropped in surprise.

"Look, this is set up for a specific theme," Maelys said, leaning against the doorway and crossing her arms. "See."

Lyra peered around the doorframe to see a female tied to a giant wooden frame. Several males feasted on her body, and she writhed with an exclamatory moan.

"Why?" Lyra whispered as the female twisted in the chains, trying to grab the hair of the male feasting between her legs.

Maelys grinned. "Pleasure."

Lyra shivered and rubbed her hands up and down her arms.

"Do you enjoy that?"

Maelys nodded. "Occasionally. My appetite changes frequently."

"What are you in the mood for tonight?" Lyra asked.

Maelys looked behind Lyra at the footsteps of someone coming down the hallway.

"Ridge," she said.

"I thought I might find you two up here," he chuckled in response.

He walked to Maelys and wrapped his arms around her. "Showing Lyra the sights?"

"Of course." Maelys gazed up at him, and he looked her up and down.

"I got us the blue room," he whispered into her ear, and she closed her eyes.

Lyra shifted on her feet, feeling like an intruder in their moment.

"You guys have fun. I can keep exploring," Lyra said, and Maelys' eyes flashed open.

"I don't want to leave you."

Lyra shook her head, and the long strands of her auburn hair tickled her lower back. "I'll be fine. This is something I need to do on my own." Lyra winked and stepped past them. Pleasurable screaming erupted down the hall. "I'll yell 'fire' if I need anything."

"Stay away from the very end of the hall, and you should be fine," Maelys replied over her shoulder, and Ridge pulled her to another hallway.

Lyra turned to ask why, but they were already gone.

What could be so bad that Maelys warned her away? She had to find out now.

Lyra stared into each open doorway. Such freedom and exploration. She squeezed and twisted her fingers as she continued walking. Her heart pounded in a steady, hard rhythm in her chest with each step.

The hallway dimmed as she neared the end, but a shadow peeled off the wall and turned towards her.

"Are you lost?" a masculine voice asked.

Lyra halted, and he stepped into the light from the sconce hanging on the wall.

He was tall, with a chiseled, tanned chest. His face was hidden behind a gold filigree mask. There was something intoxicating about his mouth as he smiled at her.

It reminded her of Wilder's. The warmth that pooled low in her belly ignited like a flame.

"Not anymore," she purred, following her instincts as Maelys instructed.

He tilted his head and smiled. Delicate, pointy canine teeth gleamed in the light, and Lyra took an involuntary step forward.

"Come with me," he offered, stretching out a hand.

His fingers weren't as long as Wilder's, and fleeting disappointment washed through her, but she shook it off and accepted his hand. He escorted her farther into the darkness, but as they passed an open doorway, Lyra halted.

"Lyra."

Someone had whispered her name—like a plea. And it wasn't the male at her side.

No—it was coming from the doorway to her right.

A male plowed into a bent-over female. His long fingers wrapped around her throat to pull her upper body to him. Another female licked up his neck before gripping his black hair and pulling his face to her lips.

They kissed and sucked at each other's tongues, and Lyra stared, completely enthralled. The female he thrust into with deep, powerful strokes, writhed and moaned as she accelerated towards her climax.

Something about his fingers on her throat and the pleasure he was bringing to both his partners had Lyra entranced.

They were all so beautiful, so pleased, and aroused.

And she was jealous. Delightfully so.

As the pounding between her legs intensified, she took a step closer to the room. Her hand slipped from the masked man's hand.

The male in the room halted, much to the dismay of his two partners. He tore out of the grip of the female on his face, and his sizable cock pulled out of the other female.

Lyra stared and stared and stared.

As Wilder faced her.

"Lyra."

It *was* her name she had heard.

He was completely bare to her. The shaft of his cock glistened with the pleasure of the female he had been fucking.

"What are you doing here?" he growled, and every muscle in Lyra's body seized up.

The masked man put a hand on Lyra's shoulder and stepped closer.

"She found a partner, and you look otherwise engaged."

Wilder could have frozen the sea with the look on his face as he glared at the masked stranger.

"Remove your hand at once or forfeit your life."

The weight of his hand on her body vanished.

Lyra's arousal dried up, and anger took its place.

"Who do you think you are, dictating my experience on this holiday?"

Wilder hastily stepped into his pants. The black fabric hung low on his waist, highlighting the sharp 'v' she knew led to mouth-watering places.

In two bounding strides, he was upon her. His eyes devoured her in the sheer dress and turned molten.

Before Lyra could blink, he wrapped his massive arms around her legs, threw her over his shoulders, and strode like a madman down the hall.

57

POSSESSIVE

Lyra squirmed her naked, sheer-clad body against Wilder's bare shoulder, and it took everything in him not to caress the backside against his neck. Her fists thudded against his back, and he clenched his jaw.

"Put me down!"

"*No.*"

Various sensual scenes played out in the rooms as he strode past, which only heightened the arousal that wound around him.

He was stupid.

The smell of her had added to the climax that he had been approaching before it all became too much.

Wilder should've known it wasn't a figment of his imagination and that she had been there. Then he wouldn't have been caught off guard by her appearance.

Godsdamn Maelys for bringing her here.

Wilder reached the edge of the staircase and took the stairs down two at a time. He couldn't get out of this place fast enough.

The occupants of the Venus stared at the absurdity that was the crowned prince carrying a female out of the hall and not into a room.

"You are being ridiculous!" Lyra cried, still squirming to get out of his hold.

"And you should not be here," he replied as calmly as he could manage.

The door beckoned ahead, and he breathed a sigh of relief when he stepped out and onto the still-teeming street. Wilder turned down a dark alley and slid Lyra down his body and to her feet. With hands placed on either side of her face, he backed her against the stone wall of the building.

"Now tell me. What was the princess of Atlantis doing in a pleasure hall, of all places?"

Lyra stared up at him and swallowed. If he wasn't mistaken, she looked nervous.

"What a stupid question. You know exactly what I was doing there."

"Which was?" he drawled the words out.

Lyra huffed and crossed her arms over her breasts. Wilder's eyes dipped to her bare flesh for a moment before raising back to her emerald eyes.

"I was trying to celebrate the holiday," she replied quietly. "It was going to be my first time."

The way she phrased it, not the words, but the tone had his ears pricking.

"It's your first time celebrating the holiday," Wilder clarified.

She had told him already that she had never celebrated the holiday. And he couldn't understand why she was phrasing it that way now.

Lyra averted her eyes and stared at the elves that walked past the entrance of their quiet alley.

Wilder grabbed her chin to make her meet his eyes.

"Are you telling me you walked into the Venus intending to lose your virginity?"

She glared with the same ferocity he had seen in thunderstorms.

"Yes," she spat.

Wilder groaned and pressed his forehead against hers. He hadn't known she was intact. She had told him in the carriage that she had experience.

"You can't."

Lyra shoved against his chest. "You can't tell me what I can and can't do with my own body."

"You are correct."

Lyra floundered for words, not at all expecting him to concede.

"You can do whatever you want with your own body, but take it from someone who has experience in these matters: your first time should not be a quick fuck at a pleasure hall with a male who's paid to be there."

"And what should it be?" Lyra asked with a timidity that made his chest ache.

Wilder couldn't help himself and took a step closer to her, brushing a wayward lock of hair out of her face.

"It should be with someone who cares about you. Who would take all of your fears and desires into consideration and devote their time to your pleasure. Someone who would worship you."

Lyra looked at his lips before gazing into his eyes.

"I don't know anyone who cares about me."

And it felt like a punch to the gut. She wasn't wrong—he had made that clear.

"Please," he whispered. "Give it time." He took a step back.

Lyra rested her head against the stone wall. "Time is not something I have, Princeling. Thanks to your father."

The tension that had been building between them turned to ice. The sheer fabric of her dress and her position leaning against the wall made the flesh below her left breast and the scar that was there glaringly visible. A gnarled, angry red scar the length of his finger.

"What is that?" he asked.

His mind was emptied of all thoughts except fury.

"Are you an imbecile? It's another scar," she sneered, her fury entwining with his.

"Who did that to you?" Wilder's voice was like ice, and for the first time since his youth, he lost control of his magic.

A whirlwind spun through the alley.

Lyra's hair whipped in a chaotic tangle around her face, and the straps of her sheer gown fell off her shoulders.

"Wilder—stop," she pleaded, looking around. "It's an old scar. I was a child."

"Who touched you?" he roared over the straight-line winds that pushed him closer to her.

Lyra's face was inches from his, but her eyes were miles and miles away. To her cruel home beneath the sea.

"My father."

His magic halted, and the winds died.

Wilder sucked in a breath and felt his body vibrate.

"Why?" He reached towards her, stroking his hand from her cheek to her neck.

"Because of my magic."

It gutted him. She had been abused and was now being manipulated over something that was out of her control—her magic.

He felt no better than the monster that raised her.

"I thought—" her voice cracked. "I thought if I were no longer intact, that when I went back, I wouldn't be of value anymore. I would be free."

Wilder squeezed his eyes shut. She was cursed, and not because of her magic, but because she was a female.

"It was part of your bargain with my father. You will be free. I will make sure of it."

Lyra nodded. But her gaze was haunted as she stared up at him. "I don't need your pity."

It was his turn to argue, to shake his head, and to explain his feelings. But he couldn't. He was living his own nightmare, watching her struggle through hers.

She slipped out from under his arms and disappeared down the street. Leaving him all alone to ponder what the hell had happened between them and the mistake that he had made.

58
ORDERS
ROUND TWO

Wilder woke with a throbbing headache. No amount of elixir could clear her face from his thoughts after last night, no matter how hard he had tried.

The pounding on his door did not cease.

"Come in," he snapped, sitting up and gripping his head.

He was shocked when his mother waltzed into his room. Her gossamer lilac gown resembled a cloud with the number of pleats and puffs on the sleeves.

"Rough night?" she tutted, coming to sit at the end of his bed.

The jostling of the mattress matched the roiling of his stomach, and he turned an astounding shade of green.

"Why are you here, Mother?"

Queen Aine looked around his humble rooms with a keen eye, and he felt her scheming coming to a head. Whatever she said next would annoy him—he just knew it.

"I watched you closely all night," she said, turning to look at him.

If he had been a youth still, his cheeks would have flushed with embarrassment at hearing those words, because there is no way she watched him all night, or she would have seen what he got up to at The Venus.

"And?" he drawled, pouring himself a glass of water from the pitcher on his bedside table.

"You will escort Lyra to the Mannereds."

He stopped thinking, and the glass he was pouring overflowed.

"Gods," he snarled, and set the pitcher down, annoyed at the mess.

"You leave immediately."

Wilder glared at her.

"What is this about?"

"You're the key to unlocking her magic. Well—you and the sea. A controlled environment like the Mannereds will make her feel close to home in a way that will speed up the process. Your father is growing impatient."

He glared at his mother, feeling the exhaustion and nausea build.

"You're scheming. Why?"

Queen Aine shook her head and picked at his down comforter.

"I still don't know the details of this bargain, and it's making me uneasy. We need it finished, and now. So, I will use whatever means necessary in our arsenal to see to it."

And there it was, his mother's ruthless cunning that had secured her as King Oberon's partner.

Wilder sat up and leaned back against his headboard.

"What has you frightened, Mother?"

"Otto can't see."

He nodded. "That's not unusual. He hasn't ever seen clearly around Lyra."

Aine shook her head. "No. He can't see anything about this bargain your father made."

"Still? Who would have the power to hide from Otto's sight?"

"I don't know," she whispered. "And he's still refusing to tell me."

"We leave now?"

She nodded. "I just instructed Daisy to pack her things. They'll be ready soon."

Wilder leaned his head back and groaned.

"And there's something else," she muttered.

His eyes flashed open. "What?"

"I watched the two of you—"

"No."

Queen Aine flinched. "No?"

Wilder shook his head, glaring at his mother. "No. I will not speak of it—or her."

She smiled then, and her brow arched high. "As you wish."

59
ON THE ROAD

Wilder watched as Daisy clung to Lyra. He couldn't quite grasp how the two of them had become so close in the few short weeks she had been here.

But then again, Daisy saw Lyra much more than he had. And there had been nights when he could hear the two of them staying up until late in the evening, talking and laughing.

"I'll have more of the chamomile oil for you when you return," Daisy murmured into Lyra's hair. She had left it down, and the auburn waves floated up in the wind.

"Thank you, Daisy," Lyra replied, squeezing the smaller female before letting her go. "Wish me luck!"

Daisy eyed him with a look that said she was well aware he was eavesdropping.

"Good luck. You're going to need it."

Wilder rolled his eyes.

"Alright, let's go. You're putting us behind with all this female blubbering."

Lyra whipped her head to his, wrath glowing in her emerald eyes. "Just because you're not capable of any emotions deeper than arousal doesn't mean you should spout your stupidity so freely."

Maelys barked a laugh so loud he thought she was going to tumble off her horse. She covered it with a gasping cough. But the damage to his pride had been done.

He eyed her with contempt, and she shook her head, clutching the reins to her horse and his tighter. Ridge watched the entire interaction from atop his mount with an obviously forced neutrality.

"You wounded me, Legs," he said, clutching his leather-clad chest with faux sincerity. But he leaned in close to her. Close enough that his breath tickled the curls at her neck. "But you should know my emotional intelligence is immense."

He enunciated 'immense' with innuendo, and her eyes bulged.

Maybe this trip wouldn't be so bad if he could continue to get under her skin. But the likelihood of the reverse was greater.

Especially when she glared at the carriage and put her hands on her hips like a petulant child.

"I am not riding in that."

She tapped her booted foot on the ground, and her sky-blue undershirt billowed around her shoulders, giving a feminine quality to her training leathers.

"You have before and were fine." He pointed to the carriage door.

"I wouldn't say 'fine'," she mumbled under her breath.

His ears picked it up perfectly, but he couldn't help but goad her. "What was that, Princess?" Before she could retort, Oak, Dust, and Otto appeared. Their horses flicked their ears and swished their tails. Wilder looked around them for Oron. But Otto shook his head.

"Oron's sister is due to give birth any day now. King Oberon had him replaced with Cyrus."

Lyra stiffened, her hands balling into fists at her sides. Who the hell was Cyrus?

As if his name conjured him up, the dark-haired guard that Wilder detested walked down the front steps of the castle.

"Am I late?"

Oh, this did not bode well.

"You are. Where is your mount?" Wilder asked.

"King Oberon assigned me to carriage duty, Your Highness."

The hair on the back of Wilder's neck rose. Especially when Cyrus took a step towards Lyra and she slid her feet apart in a defensive stance.

This was already a disaster.

Crying females, disrespectful and late guards, and now arguments.

"Fine," he growled. "Cyrus, you can ride my horse for the time being."

Lyra looked smug when Cyrus glared. But then Wilder spoke again.

"Lyra, you're in the carriage—with me."

Her mouth dropped open, but Wilder had already turned on his heel and was opening the carriage door for her.

"Let's go, Legs. We're losing daylight."

She stood still, casting her eyes from person to person. Maelys shrugged and offered her an encouraging smile.

"Come on, Lyra. It's an adventure."

Lyra huffed and stomped to the carriage. When Wilder extended his hand to help her up the small step and into the cabin, she pushed his hand away.

He laughed, but inwardly it had stung that she wouldn't allow him to touch her, even now.

"Maelys, Otto, and Ridge, you three take up the lead. Oak, Dust, and Cyrus follow behind the carriage."

Wilder was thankful that the carriage was bewitched to follow the lead horse, so that there wasn't another person to be responsible for on this journey.

It was going to be difficult enough to keep Lyra from arguing every step of the way and to keep himself from killing Cyrus the next time he displayed such casual arrogance towards any person in his guard.

Otto closed his eyes and sighed. "We should reach the Mannereds on time, but I do foresee trouble."

Wilder heaved a deep breath. Of course, there was going to be trouble.

60

CHANGE
NEEDS
ACTION

The castle walls and then the city opened up outside the carriage window. Lyra had half her body hanging out to get a better look. She hadn't been able to explore as she had liked during the disaster that had been Ostara or the tour before.

It was silent in the Upper District. Large trees dotted the pathway, and the stone of the buildings gleamed in the early morning light. There were flower boxes on some of the large windows. The bright colors of violets and poppies added much-needed color against the grey stone.

There were also very few elves out, and the ones she saw lounged on balconies sipping piping hot tea. They all resembled Maelys in a way, with fair skin and ethereal beauty.

But as they continued, the street became narrower, the buildings closer together. The sun no longer gleamed on the gray stone due to the buildup of lichen and algae.

It was busier in the Lower District, too. People were

already out and about, setting up markets or going about their daily chores. A few were camped out on street corners—begging.

The elves here resembled Otto or Ridge.

Tree-bark-like skin or the outward characteristics of magic.

Lyra frowned and sat back in her seat.

"What's that face for?"

"I didn't realize class divisions existed here."

Wilder tilted his head, and a divot formed between his brows.

"Societal classes," Lyra clarified. "I don't know why I expected any differently. Especially given their names 'Upper and Lower'."

Realization dawned on Wilder's face, and he nodded.

"It's repugnant."

Lyra blanched. She hadn't expected him to agree with her, especially given his countenance and the disagreement they had had the night before.

"I've mentioned it to my father too many times. He won't do anything about it. And contrary to your opinion, I am not him."

"Then why don't you?"

"What can I do? I'm just a Prince."

Lyra shook her head and sighed in exasperation. "You're a male. There is a lot you can do—if you're not changing it, you are choosing it."

She could see that her words had made their expected blow, but he didn't react in the way she expected him to.

Ire glowed in his eyes. "I could say the same about you."

"Me?" she squeaked. "I'm just a female. And your captive, in case you have forgotten."

"Oh, that's moronic, and you know it." He crossed his arms.

She couldn't believe her ears. He had the audacity to think she wasn't a victim in her circumstances. The male who kidnapped her!

"We both know with a tug on that thread of magic in you—you could change everything."

Lyra's mouth snapped shut.

"You have power—limitless power—and you choose to do nothing. Gods, Legs, you could command the plants to grow, the wind to blow, and the moon to rise, and it would happen. With a snap of your fingers, the atrocities committed against your own kind would cease to exist. So don't lecture me on my privilege."

Lyra shook her head, her eyes lined with tears. "It's not that simple," she whispered.

"Then enlighten me."

"If I use it—I will never stop. It will corrupt me and twist me into something that not even your worst nightmares could depict. Something as simple as commanding it not to rain. What if that makes a plant die, and the animal that needed that plant will now die, and the predator that would eat that animal might starve? I could disrupt entire ecosystems!" Wilder scoffed. "But you want to know why I won't even the score between my kind? The last time I truly used it, a male was killed. And it was all my fault!"

Wilder blinked.

He opened his mouth and then shut it. If she weren't afraid of what she had admitted, it would be comical seeing him gape like a fish.

"How?"

Tears of rage stung her eyes. "I don't know. I was a child myself. I just remember he wouldn't get off me—he wouldn't listen—and then darkness. When I came to, he was dead, and my father was dragging me to that sea witch. I never touched it again. No matter how bad it got. I couldn't be trusted."

"So you'd rather let the males unleash horrors … and not even try to stop it? I hadn't pegged you as a coward, Legs."

Lyra swallowed and turned away from him. "I'm not a coward. I just refuse to be a murderer," she muttered.

Peering out the window, the rolling hills gave way to the thicket, and a shadow blanketed their journey. A cloud overhead descended. Rain was on its way.

She could feel his eyes on her, prodding and questioning, but she didn't have it in her to speak any longer. He wouldn't understand.

No one would ever understand the burden she carried and the endless responsibility that was imminent the moment she began using her magic.

The rocking sway of the carriage, coupled with the darkening sky, had Lyra sinking further into the plush cushion of the seat and leaning her head back.

She didn't even try to keep her eyes open as sleep tugged her under and her breath slipped out in a slow and steady rhythm.

61
STRANGE SILENCE

She believed her magic was murder. That's why she had never touched it.

Sure, there was always a fear, but to have the power to change the world for the better and not even try to learn how to? That was something he couldn't fathom.

He watched as she slipped into a fitful slumber and whistled to halt the carriage.

The magic responded, and the carriage slowed. Maelys, Otto, and Ridge halted and looked back at him. Cyrus, Dust, and Oak approached the carriage and then stopped by the door.

"She's asleep. Cyrus, take your *ordered* position. I want my horse back."

Cyrus' nostrils flared, and Wilder primed for a fight. This was what he had been hoping for.

There was a storm brewing inside of him, and without the ability to take it out on Lyra, the ill-tempered guard was the next best thing.

But in a move that ripped the wind from Wilder's sails, the guard nodded and slipped off the horse.

They switched places, and as Wilder swung up onto the black stallion, Maelys watched.

"Are you sure that's a good idea?"

"He was ordered by the king to be on carriage duty. And I can't take one more moment stuck in there with her." Wilder shook his head and rode up beside Maelys. "I just don't understand her sometimes."

Maelys cocked her head to the side. "Why are you even trying to?"

"Because it helps me understand her decisions better. Why did she agree to the bargain with my father? What's the play here?"

They nudged their horses forward, and the carriage wheels creaked. Wilder threw a glance behind them to see Oak and Dust stay beside the carriage for a moment before dropping back.

She would be safe with all of them guarding her, even if he wasn't inside the carriage. But something about not being there irked him. He shook it off and turned forward again.

"I think there's a lot about her you won't be able to understand," Maelys replied with a shrug.

"Like what?" he snapped. Otto and Ridge shared a look before dropping back.

"For starters, she's not the monster our kind has been led to believe. She was never given the ability to grow and learn on her own. She's been caged and stifled. This is her first taste of being on her own, and she's still technically under someone else's thumb. Can you imagine what that must be like?"

A weight settled on his chest. He could and had experienced it for himself. But his capture had not been as peaceful as Lyra's had been. Not even close. The scars on his back were evidence of that.

"I do," he whispered with quiet rage.

"I know you do," Maelys replied. "But when you were returned, things had changed. You were allowed freedom, and your father attempted to understand you better."

That was also true. But by the looks of things now, it hadn't lasted as long as he had hoped.

"If she returns, if she's not killed immediately, her life will be even more miserable than it was before she left. She has no friends, or at least no one that you or I would consider a friend. The entirety of her choices, from the books she reads to the food she would prefer, will be stripped away. It's a cage, Wilder. And it will kill her."

Wilder sighed and shook his head to clear it from the thoughts that sliced at him.

"So, it makes sense that her motives or actions are not logical to you. They're probably the impulse of the moment for her."

The journey passed quietly after that. Wilder thought through what Maelys had explained, and the idea of it made sense. He hadn't realized how similar their paths had been.

Wilder stood firm in his decision not to take on his father's mantle. It was his choice, like it was Lyra's choice not to take on the weight of what her power would dictate. She was exercising the only bit of control she had in what she thought was the safest way possible.

Late in the evening, rain fell. Big, fat droplets hindered his ability to hear anything outside of their perimeter. But with the moisture in the air, it increased his ability to scent their surroundings.

He raised a fist in the air, halting them. A mangy scent filled his nose, and the hair on the back of his neck rose. Wulvers.

They weren't close, but they were there.

"I smell them," Maelys whispered.

Ridge and Otto pressed forward, and Wilder glanced at Otto.

"I can't see what they plan or if they know we are here. But I will keep checking."

"Let's find shelter for the night and set up camp," Wilder ordered.

He was surprised Lyra had not been sticking her head out of the carriage window every hour to complain about being stuck in there with Cyrus, or that she needed to relieve herself, or eat. She hadn't spoken at all.

Dread sliced like ice through his veins, and he hopped off his horse and stalked towards the carriage. Wilder ripped the door open to find a sleeping Lyra and a glaring Cyrus.

"Has she been sleeping the whole time?" Wilder asked, his gaze bouncing from Cyrus to Lyra.

"No," Cyrus replied, a devilish smirk tugging at his lips.

"Did she not need anything?" Wilder asked.

Maelys approached from behind him, and he could feel the irritation radiating off of her.

"Not that she told me." Cyrus shrugged.

Something didn't feel right, but without Lyra awake to corroborate the story, there wasn't much he could do about it right now.

Wilder's eyes raked over her one more time. Her lashes fluttered against her ivory skin. There was a line on her cheek, from pressing her face against the seat cushion, as she was slumped in the most strange position.

"We're setting up the camp. Get out and help," Wilder ordered.

Irritation glowed in Cyrus' eyes, but he got out of the carriage and shoved past Maelys. She gave him a wide berth, but her shoulders stiffened and she whipped her head back to Lyra.

"Is she alright?" Maelys whispered.

"She's asleep," Wilder replied.

He turned around to see Cyrus, hands in his pockets, walking towards Dust and Oak, who were pitching their tents.

Something didn't feel right.

"Wake her up," Wilder said to Maelys. "I don't believe his story."

Maelys nodded and slipped into the carriage across from Lyra. Worry etched into the lines on her face as she gently stroked Lyra's knee to wake her.

It was nice to see, Wilder thought. That care and concern Maelys had for Lyra. He was glad someone did.

62
FIND YOUR
MARK

L yra felt disconnected from her limbs. She didn't know if
she preferred that over the usual ache her legs gave her,
but when she tried to move her arms and couldn't, fear over-
took her.

She fought with everything she had, thrashing about in her
mind, to get them to move a fraction. The numbness gave way,
and then she really was thrashing around in the close confines
of the carriage.

"Lyra!" Maelys yelled, gripping her as firmly as she could
without injuring her. "It's alright!"

Lyra stilled, but her chest still heaved with each breath.

Maelys slid from the bench across from Lyra to the vacant
seat beside her and wrapped an arm around her shoulder. She
shushed her with a tenderness that made Lyra's chest ache.

The slow, gentle pats on her arm had her leaning into
Maelys' embrace.

"Was it a nightmare?" Maelys asked.

Lyra shook her head, and tears trailed down her cheeks before plopping onto her lap.

"I don't know what happened. I just couldn't move," Lyra whispered.

She glanced up then to see the blackness of night outside the carriage window. She had been sleeping all day?

"Do you remember anything before you fell asleep?"

Lyra shook her head. She remembered speaking to Wilder and then dozing off, and then a flash of something, and then nothing. Nothing at all.

"Do you remember Wilder being in the carriage?"

Lyra nodded and sank deeper into Maelys' embrace.

"What about Cyrus?"

Lyra flinched at those words and out of Maelys' arms. There was a flash of dark hair and a sneer, but nothing else.

"Not really," Lyra whispered.

Maelys' eyes narrowed in a way that promised violence.

"I need you to tell me everything you remember. A smell, a sound, anything at all."

Lyra closed her eyes and then wanted to vomit. There had been an unusual smell …

"There was a sharp smell—" Lyra began.

Maelys tore out of the carriage, and the door slammed against the side.

Lyra blinked, staring outside into the night. From the glow of the fire, she could see Maelys hurtling towards Cyrus.

"You son of a—" she screamed at him, pulling a dagger from the holster at her thigh.

In a single heartbeat, Maelys had kicked him off the stump he was sitting on and had her boot pressed against his throat.

"Maelys!" Wilder yelled. "What are you doing?"

Ridge was already at Maelys' side, his hands raised in a placating gesture.

Otto sat still and blinked.

"Wilder ..." he breathed. "Don't."

Wilder whipped his head back and forth.

"Someone explain. Now."

"He. Drugged. Her." Maelys pointed at Cyrus' chest.

Lyra gripped the side of the carriage and pulled herself out. Her legs wobbled, and she locked her knees to remain upright.

"What?" she whispered, clutching her chest with her other hand.

She watched as Maelys removed her boot and Ridge pulled Cyrus to his feet.

Wilder approached like a shadow over the moon. He was terrifying. Wrath twisted his features into a nightmare come to life.

"Is this true?" he snarled in Cyrus' face.

"She shouldn't still be here!" Cyrus yelled, pulling against the wall that was Ridge.

Otto stood, dropping the bowl of food onto the ground.

"Wilder," he called. "They're coming."

Cyrus smiled, and it was more vicious than anything she had ever seen before. "He wants her back."

And there it was.

The traitor in the Wilds Kingdom—Cyrus.

"*Who* wants her back?" Wilder asked, pointing at Lyra.

Cyrus continued to grin a maniacal grin. Maelys stepped closer, pointing her blade at his throat.

Ridge pulled Cyrus by the hair, baring his throat to Maelys' blade.

"Who. Wants. Her. Back." Maelys growled each word like she was conjuring a spell.

Cyrus closed his eyes and smiled broadly.

The howls grew closer, springing up around them in a circular pattern. Lyra's legs wobbled, and her throat dried out.

There must be at least ten of them, which meant they were outnumbered, and with her still recovering from being drugged, she would be more of a hindrance than a help.

Maelys nicked Cyrus' throat with her blade. A drop of darkened blood welled up and dribbled down the strong column of his throat.

His eyes flashed open, and he opened his mouth.

"She's his, and he will take her. He will—"

Goosebumps erupted on Lyra's exposed skin, and the hair on the back of her neck stood on end. But Cyrus never got the chance to finish.

Maelys split his throat from ear to ear at the same time Wilder lunged forward, piercing his heart.

They had both killed him—for her.

Wilder turned and looked at her. There was something unreadable on his face.

But when Maelys looked at her, there was only pure rage, not at Lyra, but at what had been done to her.

"I am sorry," Wilder began, stepping closer to her. "I should have realized." His voice cracked.

Otto, Maelys, and Ridge stared wide-eyed at him.

Tears welled in Lyra's eyes when he reached a hand out towards her face. He froze, not daring to touch her without her permission first. When she nodded, he sighed, and his fingertips grazed her cheek.

"I need you to get in the carriage and stay there until I call for you. Do you understand?" His voice was low, an order to be obeyed.

"I can—can try to …" Lyra began.

"No. You will stay in that carriage. I will not ask you to meddle with powers you have no control over. We can handle this without you."

The howls grew closer now, and Lyra could see Wilder's pupils narrow in the dim light.

Dust and Oak shifted in her peripheral view, their armor glinting in the moonlight.

"Get in the carriage. Stay there," Wilder commanded.

Maelys gripped Lyra under her elbow.

"Here, I'll help you in."

Lyra acquiesced and let Maelys tug her back to safety. She wobbled on her feet but did not fall.

The carriage door creaked open as Maelys held it for Lyra to slip inside.

"Take this," Maelys said, holding out the dagger she had killed Cyrus with. "If someone other than us breaches those doors, I implore you to use it if you won't use your power."

Lyra took it, and her bottom lip quivered. It was more dangerous than she thought if Maelys was arming her.

"I know you know how to use it. Aim for the soft bits and the major arteries. Neck, thighs, and even the wrists if they reach for you, okay?"

Lyra nodded, still staring at the dagger in her grip.

"If it comes down to it—you need to save yourself first, Lyra. Do you understand?"

With those words, Lyra's head whipped up. A question bubbled up, but popped with the slamming of the door.

She couldn't hear anything outside the carriage. It had fallen inexplicably silent.

There was not a clang of metal, a crack of a twig, or even the whistle of wind. It's as if the entire world had fallen away outside.

All she could hear was the roaring in her ears and the heaving of her breath.

Lyra thought through all the worst-case scenarios. What would happen to her if they all died? That thought made her hands shake. She couldn't lose all of them. That damage would be irreparable.

Her pounding heart and burning lungs were nothing

compared to the fear that sliced through every part of her. And that's when it hit her.

Maelys was standing out there, Ridge, Otto, Dust, and Oak. They were all out there protecting her.

Wilder was out there, facing his worst fears—for her.

He was standing between her and creatures who had held him hostage and tortured him for a decade. Fury burned through her, staining her vision crimson.

Lyra stared down at the dagger gripped in her hand.

The nothingness that was coming from outside set her teeth on edge.

Slow and steady, she squared her shoulders, preparing herself for what she would face on the other side of the carriage door.

The thread of magic flared within her, and she brushed against it.

"Find your mark," she commanded the dagger, and then threw the door open.

63
SHE KILLS

Wilder kept his back to the carriage door. They had surrounded the carriage under his order, which was to protect Lyra at all costs. She was the key to restoring balance, and he felt that if he had more time with her, then he could get her to control that power that flowed through her.

Otto stood on his right, a large ax held out in front of him.

"There are twelve," he murmured. "They'll surround us and go for her."

Ridge stiffened on the other side of Wilder.

"Clan?"

"Igneous."

Wilder's chest tightened. It had been years since he had faced his captor's clan. But there was a debt to settle, and he would gladly exact his revenge.

"Casualties?" Ridge asked, his eyes bouncing from Wilder to Otto. Ridge knew there was only so much he could ask without Wilder stopping him.

"One. Not ours," Otto replied.

Ridge nodded, lifting his broadsword higher.

Wilder focused on listening. He could hear Lyra's heart fluttering like a hummingbird's wing, and the panting of her breath slipping through her lips from inside the carriage behind him. He could hear the twelve wulvers approaching each from a different direction.

Their breathing was steady, except for one. A low, gravelly breathing that signified him as an elder.

Tilting his head to the sky, he inhaled, channeling the wind to swirl around them, stirring up their scents and bringing them to him.

It was the Igneous Clan, and Igneous himself had come to this fight.

They breached the clearing and stood around the perimeter. Smudges of darkness in the shadows of the trees.

The wulver who had captured him stepped one foot closer than the rest. Wilder's fury stirred, and he bit down on his tongue to keep from yelling at the beast. He gripped his blade tighter but lowered it a fraction.

It was a show of disrespect to the elder wulver, and it was intentional.

"You have something that belongs to the sea," Igneous spoke.

He was fifty yards away but still spoke as if Wilder had been standing right beside him.

Maelys' breath caught in the back of her throat, and Wilder could feel her shifting on her feet. She knew that voice and the beast it belonged to.

"I think Lyra would disagree about belonging to anyone," Wilder replied.

Igneous stepped into a beam of moonlight. His black fur gleamed, and a splattering of silver hairs shone on his elongated snout. But it was the protracted claws on long fingers that had

Wilder squaring up. The scars from those claws still marred the skin on his back.

"You will give her to me, and we will leave here without spilling blood," Igneous responded.

"That's not going to happen," Ridge whispered.

But Igneous and his wulvers heard the words, anyway.

"You seek to spill blood, *child*?" The reddened wulver on Igneous' right answered.

"If you think you're coming any closer—absolutely." Ridge widened his stance, backing up his threat.

Killing Igneous would spark a war with all the wulvers, not just this clan. But he was under strict orders to protect Lyra at all costs. His father could handle a war with those beasts. And it would satisfy Wilder's need for revenge.

But first, he needed answers.

"Who did you make a deal with? Besides, your dead informant over there." Wilder jutted his chin towards the cooling body of Cyrus.

Igneous didn't even spare the male a glance.

"You're stalling."

He wouldn't tell Wilder, not even with a blade through his chest.

Dust and Oak slid into defensive stances at the tone of Igneous' voice. Strange Otto had said there had been only one casualty, and it wasn't on their side. And if anyone was going to kill a wulver and spark a war—it would have to be Wilder.

This is why he hated knowing his future. Now the decision didn't feel like his own, but another thread in the great tapestry of fate.

Igneous took another step, and Wilder relaxed his grip on the sword.

He already knew he would kill the wulver, and now he could savor the ending.

"You're willing to die for a mermaid, Igneous?"

There were snarls from the wulvers surrounding them.

"It is you who will die, Prince," the red wulver dared to speak again.

Wilder looked between the empty tract of land that separated the wulver from him. "Someday, sure. But not today. And between us right now is *nothing and nobody.*"

The threat rang like a struck bell, and the wulver had the intelligence to back up a step.

Igneous slid his black eyes towards Otto. Word of his powers had no doubt spread to all the creatures of the realm. But even if Otto had spoken the truth to Wilder, that didn't mean the wulvers would believe it as such. It all could be a ruse.

"Enough of this," Igneous snarled. "Give us the mermaid so we can return her to the waves."

Wilder cocked his head.

"Does the *water* miss her?" Wilder chuckled.

Igneous opened his mouth for a quick retort before snapping it shut.

"You will not goad the answers out of me, boy."

The glittering malice in Igneous' eyes reminded Wilder of all those years of torture. He could do it, could kill the beast that was the root of so much anguish and torment in his mind.

Igneous stepped closer. "How about I make her scream as I did you, Prince?"

An exhale slipped through Wilder's parted lips. Another step from Igneous and Wilder would charge the beast and slit him from neck to navel.

"How about you let the lady speak for herself?" Igneous' words halted Wilder's swelling fury.

The creak of the carriage door had his chest seizing up. Without turning around, he knew she was there.

The scent of her wrapped around him in a gentle embrace,

but where he expected the tang of fear, he found the sharpness of fury.

"Lyra—get back inside. *Now.*"

"They've come for me. I will speak to them," she retorted as haughtily as she had spoken to him that first day.

"It's as it should be," Otto whispered, settling Wilder's nerves.

"*Speak,*" she ordered the clan leader of the largest wulver clan.

She asserted as much dominance in her voice as one would use to a wayward pup.

If he hadn't been so unnerved by her presence, he would have cracked a smile at her tone.

"You are to return to the sea and I am to escort you," Igneous replied.

His patience was slipping, and Wilder could tell by the way Igneous cracked his jaw.

Lyra's shoulders stiffened. They were offering her a way home—would she take it?

She had made a bargain with his father, but that wouldn't keep her here—would it?

"And who requests my return? The same male who bargained for my kidnapping?" Her voice did not waver, and the scent of her fury swelled.

Igneous shrugged his shoulders. "I do not know any information outside of my bargain."

"The name," she spat.

The wulvers on either side of Igneous bristled at her tone.

Lyra gripped the handle of the dagger and stepped beside Wilder. She hadn't completed enough training to think she could fight her way out of this. Protecting her would be a liability, and now, with her standing this close to him, she was a distraction.

"I will not stand here and be questioned by a girl or by a *coward* who had to be rescued by his father. You will come—"

Igneous didn't get to finish his demand.

The pommel of Lyra's dagger quivered from between his eyes. He hadn't seen her move, hadn't felt her arm raise before she had launched the dagger between them.

The clearing froze.

No one dared to move or breathe; even the wind ceased. It was as if time had stopped altogether.

Igneous dropped to his knees and then fell to his stomach. The blade on the dagger was pure silver and had belonged to Maelys.

Wilder prepared for retaliation, for the rest of the clan to charge them now that their leader was killed. But the wulver on the right, the beta, looked at the corpse of the alpha and stepped back.

Lyra's chest heaved, and she stepped in front of Wilder, raising her hands in challenge.

She looked like a goddess summoning her power.

The wind swirled through the clearing, bringing Wilder the scent of death. The remaining wulvers peeled off and out of the clearing, disappearing into the thick of the forest.

This would not be the end.

When the clearing was empty except for the seven of them, Wilder whirled on her.

"What the fuck were you thinking?"

"He was going to take me."

"And I was here to prevent that from happening!" He beat a fist to his chest.

Otto snickered beside him, and he whipped his head towards him.

"It's as it should be." Otto patted his shoulder and walked past him. "They won't be back tonight. Rest easy."

Wilder jutted his chin down and then turned back to Lyra. "Why?" His voice went hoarse.

"Because he deserved it. He caused nothing but pain and suffering."

Wilder's brow rose as he stared down. "Even if it was mine?"

Lyra looked at her hands, dropping her chin. "Especially yours."

64
FEMININE RAGE

Lyra squeezed her hands together and twisted her fingers until her knuckles whitened. She had killed that wulver. She had brushed against her magic and now its euphoria surged through her.

It was the same pleasure Wilder had brought her in the carriage. She was relieved no one had realized what she had done.

As Maelys retrieved her blade and stomped across the clearing, she smiled at Lyra.

"Looks like you learned something after all."

Lyra cracked a smile in return and shrugged, trying to hide the trembling of her hands.

"You never displayed that level of skill in training," Maelys said, stopping beside her.

Lyra's stomach clenched. If Maelys figured out she was capable of using her magic, then she would be forced to use it time and time again.

"I never had someone in front of me that I *wanted* to kill," Lyra replied.

Maelys chuckled. "I should have you aim for Wilder at the next training."

Ridge appeared beside Maelys. "I don't think that would work anymore."

His voice wasn't louder than a whisper, but it still felt as if he had shouted it.

"That's not true," Lyra argued.

She tasted the lie as soon as she spoke it.

Ridge crossed his massive arms over his chest and leveled Lyra with a look.

"Don't play dumb with us. Even I can sense what's brewing between you two."

Lyra slid her eyes over to Wilder, who was directing Dust and Oak on where to set up their tents. His black hair gleamed as if it were kissed by the night sky. He was beautiful, she had always thought that, but seeing him stand so rigidly in front of Igneous highlighted the pain he had hidden below his curated surface.

"I have no idea what you're talking about." Her eyes never left Wilder, and as if he sensed her stare, he turned and looked at her.

"Sure ya don't," Maelys whispered in her ear as she passed with a still chuckling Ridge.

"Lyra! We're setting you up right here," Otto called, waving a pillow above his head to get her attention.

A canopy tent had been pitched beside the carriage in front of a thicket of brush that Oak was collecting for a fire.

"Is that safe?" Lyra asked.

She stood in front of her tent with her hands on her hips. They hadn't started a fire once on their journey from Terra to the Wilds. Now it seemed counterintuitive.

"They already know where we are," Oak replied with a shrug. "Might as well be warm."

Otto pressed the pillow into Lyra's stomach, and she wrapped her arms around it.

"You did well. Found that fire in your veins after all," Otto murmured.

Lyra squeezed the pillow to her chest and tucked her chin into it. She hadn't known where it had come from, that rage. Maybe it had to do with being used as a pawn again. Maybe it was because she thought they had all been in danger.

But maybe more than any of that, it had to do with protecting him.

"You'll do wonderful things … now that you finally found your voice, too."

Lyra's eyes flashed, but she huffed and pushed through the flapping fabric that made up her tent door. Leaving a bewildered Otto staring after her.

The tent was small. No bigger than the cot that took up most of the floor space. Her trunk had been unloaded from the carriage and was placed beside a stack of quilts.

Lyra closed her eyes and tilted her head back. Sighing through her nose, she thought back to her room at the castle. She missed Daisy, she missed the bathing chamber, and she missed her big, fluffy bed.

The thread of gold around her heart was muted, dulled in a way that told her she was empty right now. She had used all of her power in one go to kill that wulver. But she wasn't afraid. She knew it would come back.

When she blinked her eyes open again, she noted the netting that made up the tent roof. The night sky was ablaze with millions of twinkling lights. Lyra curled up onto her cot, kicking off her boots, and she lay back looking up at the blanket of stars in the sky.

Constellations that told stories over a millennium. Heroes

and villains, ordinary people making decisions that would cast them into the oblivion of legends.

She hadn't felt the guilt she had the last time she used her power. Although she was a child then, she could still vividly remember the anguish she had felt when she had learned the fate of that boy.

But now—she felt still.

Her eyes slipped closed, and she thought of her decisions. Where would these choices lead her ...

65
CHOICE

Wilder sat on the ground, out of reach of the swaying flaps of Lyra's tent. She had been asleep for a while now. Her rhythmic breathing had placed him in a trance as he listened.

She was prone to nightmares, and he listened for them now.

"I see no ambush this night," Otto murmured from his left. He poked at the burning branch with a long twig.

"So you've said," Wilder replied.

"Ridge couldn't scent out Cyrus because he was never a traitor. He stayed true to his cause—the wulvers."

Wilder nodded, having puzzled that much out already. Cyrus wasn't technically a bad seed in the general sense of the word.

"But that's not why you are still awake, is it?" Otto asked.

Wilder rolled his eyes, but did not reply. Oak and Dust twitched in their sleep on their bedrolls beside the fire. The tent that Ridge and Maelys had pitched for themselves had eventually fallen silent. Wilder envied them. Envied their freedom in each other and finding their releases.

"I know you do not like to know—" Otto began, his brow scrunched and worry dimming his eyes.

"Then do not tell me," Wilder snapped.

"It does not end well," Otto whispered, ignoring Wilder's order.

Otto never disregarded an order like that. Wilder stared long and hard at the man he'd known his entire life. From the tightening white skin around his eyes to the gray irises themselves.

"Who is fate to tell me how to live my life?" Wilder huffed. "It is my choices that dictate its very weaving."

Otto shook his head, his white hair sliding over his shoulder as he did. "We are but threads in Her world, moving as she instructs."

Wilder spat into the fire and glared.

There were some things he chose to believe about life and the meaning of it all, and there were some things he chose to ignore. This was one of those things. That nothing was by choice, that everything was predetermined to happen a certain way, no matter what you chose or believed.

It was disheartening to know you had no free will over your own life.

Otto's eyes turned glassy again, and Wilder froze.

"There is a way ..."

"*No*," Wilder ordered. "We will not speak of it."

Otto closed his eyes and then scrubbed a hand down his face. The beads in his hair glimmered in the light as he shook his head. It must be exhausting seeing things as they are decided and played out. A constant barrage of images and pathways.

Maelys slipped out of the tent and plopped down on the other side of Otto. Her eyes were bright, and a small smile graced her face.

"What're we talking about?"

"Nothing," Wilder snapped, as Otto opened his mouth.

Maelys pressed her lips together to hide her budding smile. "Ahh, Fate's plan?"

Otto shook his head and mimed locking up his lips.

Maelys sighed and looked over at the corpse of Cyrus. It grew quiet—cold, even.

"How did she do it?" Maelys whispered, looking out of the clearing where they had faced off with the wulvers.

"I'm still trying to figure that out," Wilder replied.

"Anger," Otto replied after a moment. "She finally wielded that anger. It was a kindling to the fire already growing within her."

"She hadn't shown an ounce of that during training," Maelys murmured.

Otto chuckled. "Sure, she had. When Wilder was pissing her off."

The realization clicked for Maelys, and she nodded. "Anger can be a powerful tool. So can protecting those you care about."

Otto smiled, big and broad. His eyes sparkled like the stars overhead. "Just you wait ..."

"I don't like the sound of that," Ridge chimed in.

Maelys grinned, and it was predatory. "A woman scorned is as savage as the sea in a hurricane."

Wilder nodded. He had seen a glimpse of that monster beneath her skin. It lay in wait for the catalyst that would launch her into a bloodthirsty frenzy. He would weather that storm, though. He had no doubt in his mind that whatever she threw at him, he could take. But that was the point of her not touching her powers, wasn't it? She didn't want to slip into the unrestrained.

That explained her thirst for knowledge.

If you know a thing, you cannot be afraid of a thing. He should do that with her magic, too.

Maybe if she learned about it, she would no longer fear it.

66
UNICORN

Morning light shone through the tiny holes in the canvas tent as Lyra stretched awake. A shadow darkened the bottom half of her door, and she lurched upright. Judging by the height and shape, it was a male, but which one of her companions she wasn't sure. She threw her legs off the side of her long cot and set to putting her boots back on.

The shadow moved then and cleared its throat.

"Yes?" Lyra asked.

But there was no reply.

An unusual noise had her sitting up taller. It was a squelching sound, like when your boot gets stuck in mud.

Then there was a groan. A groan deep enough that her cheeks heated.

Surely not, she thought as she tiptoed to the tent door and peered out.

It absolutely was.

Ridge sat very rigidly as Maelys lay between his spread

thighs. The shaft of what looked to be an enormous cock slid in and out of her mouth.

Lyra's eyes bulged as Maelys worked Ridge into a pulsing, thrusting mass of male.

Sunlight shone on Maelys' golden brown hair as she bobbed her head up and down, at the same time she twisted her fist around him.

Lyra knew it was possible because Wilder had done that very thing to her, but she couldn't understand why he hadn't asked her to do that in return. It was obviously enjoyable if Ridge's bucking hips were any indication.

When Ridge increased his thrusting from his seated position, Maelys popped off and stood.

"Hurry and fuck me before they return," she whispered as she grabbed Ridge's hand and scurried off into the trees.

Lyra stood frozen as a statue. The intimacy of that moment was not hers to partake in, but she had enjoyed it. The freedom that Maelys exhibited, the power she held over Ridge at that moment, was astonishing.

Lyra hadn't realized something like that was truly possible. Or that you could take pleasure in it.

With slow, deep breaths, she worked to calm her pounding heart.

After what felt like an hour, she had mastered herself enough to step out of the tent and into the dappled light.

The campsite was empty.

Maelys and Ridge were probably not too far away from finding their completion. But where had the others gone?

Instead of doing something stupid like searching for any member of their guard, Lyra plopped down beside the ash remains of their fire.

The sky was turning a powdery blue, and the birds chirped in the trees. They had to be getting close to the Mannereds. The land felt different here. More orderly than what they had come from.

A shimmer caught her eye, and she turned to see a creature appear from between two large ash trees. Lyra's breath caught, and she scrubbed her eyes with her fists. There was no way. With a stuttering breath, she smiled at the unicorn.

Its white mane glittered iridescently, like that of the pearls from the ocean. Its twisting horn dripped with blood and gore.

It took a step closer to her, and Lyra stood. She had read so many stories as a child about them, but she never fathomed they were anything but a fairy tale.

Once more, she blinked to see the creature taking another step towards her. It was magic. Pure undiluted magic. The unicorn was majestic, but with the gore dripping from its horn, it was also monstrous.

Lyra considered the juxtaposition of it all. The creatures associated with rainbows and sunshine were the same creatures that mutilated or murdered others. Like her.

Outstretching her hand, she took another step closer, at the same time the unicorn did until she brushed her hand up its snout. It felt like velvet before she got to the long mane. Up close, the hair was white, but also every shade of color.

It smelled like the fluffy purple petals that had been in the Wilds. Closing her eyes again, she savored this moment. The feel of the life next to her, the softness of its warmth, and the lightness of its scent.

The wind sang through the trees, and with it, the unicorn's ears flicked. It stood up taller and backed away before it disappeared into the thicket again.

"Farewell," Lyra whispered.

Her life felt complete now that she had pet a unicorn.

"Who are you talking to?" Maelys asked, tightening her scabbard back around her waist.

"A unicorn."

Maelys started laughing so hard she bent over at the waist. Ridge appeared out of the tree line and stalked towards them.

"What's so funny?" He had the expression of a man who had hoped that laughter wasn't about him.

"Lyra," Maelys breathed in between laughing. "Said she was talking to a unicorn."

Ridge chuckled then, but Lyra crossed her arms over her chest and leaned to the side, jutting her hip out.

"What is so funny? I did!"

Maelys straightened and wiped the tears from her eyes. Silently, Wilder and the others appeared, looking dirty but happy.

"Why is Maelys crying?" Dust asked.

"She was laughing at Lyra because she saw a unicorn," Otto confirmed.

Maelys froze. "She really did?"

"We were out there for hours," Wilder growled, turning to Otto.

"You don't like to know."

Lyra looked from person to person. "What is happening?"

Dust cracked a grin and shook his head. "We were out looking for a unicorn all morning. They're practically impossible to find, and Wilder has been looking every time we've come here for the last, I don't know how many years."

"One hundred. One hundred years." Wilder continued glaring but shook his head. "Let's pack up and head out before the wulvers decide to follow us."

Lyra smirked at Wilder as he passed, and he returned it with one of his own.

"You didn't tell me," Lyra said, stepping behind him and following back to the center of camp.

"Tell you what?"

"That the unicorns existed. I told you about all those books I read," Lyra replied.

Wilder halted, and she stopped with him. "I didn't know if they truly were real and didn't want to get your hopes up."

He jostled the pack on his back, and the flap covering the contents shifted enough that she could see the twine of a rope.

"Were you planning on catching it?"

Wilder's eyes never left her face, and they even seemed to soften. "Maybe."

"Why?"

"So that you could see it too."

67

TREE

The rest of the journey to the Mannereds passed uneventfully—it came as a surprise and a relief to Wilder. Lyra rode alone in the carriage, but as expected, she did not stay quiet.

From flowers, birds, or rock formations, she pointed everything out with childish wonder. Dust and Oak found it endearing, Ridge and Maelys were used to it, and Otto gestured to everything he thought she would admire but had missed.

Wilder stayed quiet, enjoying the companionship of those around him while staying trapped in his thoughts. His feelings towards Lyra had shifted—that much was obvious. She was unexpected. Had leapt into his life as gracefully as a wildfire, consuming everything in her path.

He had wanted to do things for her, the unicorn for starters, but more. He had wanted to be there when she had woken, with the unicorn in hand, to see the happiness in her eyes. To know that he was the cause of such joy.

The forest around them became ordered with fewer brambles underneath the large canopies and more intentionally placed shrubbery. They were still far from the castle, but Queen Titania's grip over her realm was already evident.

A pathway lined with tulips and foxglove opened up before them, leading them up and over a hill that overlooked the large plateau in the distance where the castle emerged. It was still a day's ride away.

Something rustled in the distance, outside his periphery. A shadow, lying in wait. It wasn't the Queen's guards that monitored their perimeter; it was something else.

A creature of which he had only heard whispers. Wilder whistled low under his breath, a tone that only Maelys would hear. She urged her horse forward and beside him, leaving Ridge to fall back in line with the carriage.

"Yes?"

"We're being followed," he said, no louder than the breeze. "Animal?"

Maelys' grip on her reins tightened as she felt for the animals around them.

"No."

Wilder nodded, and she fell back in line.

"Otto?"

"I see nothing," he replied.

Wilder squared his shoulder and reached for the sword strapped to his side. The creature melded with the shadows but kept pace with them. It wasn't threatening, per se. It wasn't welcoming either.

"What is it?" Lyra called from the window of her carriage.

Half of her body was leaning out of the opening, and she gripped the bottom of the window to keep herself from tipping out.

"Nothing," Wilder replied.

"It doesn't look like nothing. Your shoulders are stiff."

Wilder did his best to let the tension melt away. It was futile. He caught a better glimpse of what was trailing them and gleaned it wasn't a threat, but a surprise to be sure.

It was a tree—one of the sentient trees that stood between their two courts.

Wilder halted their pace and dismounted.

"Of the King," the tree spoke. Its voice was as soft as the wind in its branches.

Wilder bowed and touched his brow. "Of the Wilds."

"You've traveled some way, my prince."

"And we have a way yet to go." Wilder looked up into the gnarled face of the tree. Lined with centuries of life and weather. It was like looking at the beginning of the world and seeing what it had become.

"You travel with a creature not of land." Its words were not unkind, but there was an edge to them.

"I do. We travel with a princess of the sea."

"I have not looked upon the water in some time. I will see her."

No other creature could have demanded such a thing of the Prince. But as a royal of the Wilds, his stewardship prioritized nature.

"Lyra," Wilder called.

He heard the clatter of the carriage door opening before the crunch of her light footsteps against the forest floor. Turning as she approached, he had to stifle a laugh at the wonder and astonishment widening her eyes and dropping her jaw.

"Is that—" she whispered.

"A lady of the sea," the tree remarked.

Lyra halted, her gaze sweeping from the tree to Wilder. He held out his hand, and with equal astonishment, she took it.

"I am, er, sir?"

The tree laughed, and the leaves rustled. "I am not a male or female. I simply am."

"My apologies," she lamented, and shame colored her face.

"Do not fret. How could you have known?"

Lyra sighed and took a step closer. "May I?"

Wilder watched in wonder as the tree nodded as she approached, resting her brow upon its bark. For someone who had little knowledge of their customs, she certainly behaved in a way that was similar.

"Why have you come?"

Lyra tipped her head back to meet the wise eyes of the sentient wood.

"I was taken and agreed to a bargain."

"And yet you are afraid."

Lyra shifted, and Wilder could tell the words stung.

"I am unsure of how to uphold my bargain," she uttered.

"You fear the desires in your heart."

She didn't have an answer for that, and Wilder felt he had become an unwanted outsider.

"Stay, Prince."

Wilder nodded. Lyra sighed and worried her bottom lip.

"What if I am the monster they always said I was?"

"You will bear the burden. There is no other."

Wilder watched as all the sun-kissed color drained from her face. Her freckles now stood out starkly.

"What is magic if not the bindings of our fragile realm? Elvethamian would cease to exist without magic. The gods will see to it."

Elvethamian.

Only the wisest and oldest knew its true name.

Lyra closed her silver-lined eyes. A single tear dripped down her cheek.

"What if I fail?"

"See to it that you do not. Or in violent waves we all perish."

He could see the anger flash across her face, a tinge of red to her cheeks, and then the clenching of her fists.

The tree's branches swayed and jostled as it turned; long roots rose and fell as it walked away.

"It was a pleasure, Lyra of Atlantis."

Lyra stood frozen as the tree ambled away with slow, crunching strides.

"Was that a dream?" she spoke at last when the sun speared through the thinner canopy of the hawthorns.

"It was not."

Wilder watched as her face turned from anger to wonder, and, lastly, to horror.

"I think—I think I'm going to be sick."

She bent over at the waist and proceeded to catch her breath. He rubbed lazy strokes over her back, and she didn't pull away.

"It's going to be okay."

"How? How is it going to be okay?"

"The library at the Mannereds is second to none. And if I know anything about you, it is that you have a thirst for knowledge. You're afraid of your magic because you know nothing about it. You fear the unknown and the lies that were spewed. We simply need to increase your knowledge to decrease your fear." He said it with as much authority as his title held.

"And you think that will help?"

"I know it will."

She shifted on her feet and squeezed her fingers together in a way that was most out of character for her.

"I killed someone. What if it happens again?" Her voice was quiet and timid.

All at once, it hit him—she needed a vote of confidence, someone to believe in her when she couldn't believe in herself.

"I believe you are capable of anything you put your mind to. You have lived through so much in your short life—I see that now. You were only a child, and it was an accident. It was not your fault. I see the scars you hide, the tremble in your voice when you can't contain your anger, I see the fire in your eyes when you've been wronged, and the way you try to stifle it. I want you to wield that anger, Lyra. Wield it as a blade against everyone who has ever wronged you."

She stared and stared into his eyes.

"Even against me, if you must."

Her eyes slipped closed as she nodded.

"Give me a moment, please?" she asked, her voice shaking again.

"Anything you wish," he murmured.

And he left her standing in the grove of hawthorn trees as he trudged back to the carriage.

68
Mind the Manners

The air was thick, and her limbs were numb. Lyra stood alone—breathing. That's all she could do.

Everything pressed down upon her. To stand and fight for the world felt like learning to run before you could walk.

And she knew exactly what that felt like.

A song wove through her veins; something was calling to her. But it wasn't the land—it was the sea. It called to her; it needed her.

Something was happening in Atlantis, and she could feel it like an oppressive cloud ruining an otherwise sunny day.

Birds sang and leaves rustled, pulling her back to the present. The scent of earth and moss and sunshine seeped into her bones, and she sighed.

"Lyra," Maelys called. "Are you alright?"

"Just a moment!"

Lyra traced her finger down the trunk of the nearest tree.

The roots of this tree reached the roots of the next and the next, an underground network that sprawled across the entire realm.

"I need your help," she whispered to the tree. "If you're listening and grant wishes, I need all the luck a girl could get." Lyra closed her eyes and pressed her brow against the bark. Tiny white petals floated down from its branches and gathered on her hair and eyelashes. She fluttered her eyelashes and wrapped her arms as wide as she could around the tree. "Give me strength. I do not want to fail."

Lyra stepped away from the tree and headed back to the carriage, throwing one last look over her shoulder. She could have sworn she saw the tree lean towards the one beside it.

"Is everything well?" Maelys asked, walking towards Lyra and pulling her horse behind her. It whinnied and stomped when Maelys stopped.

"As well as it could be," Lyra muttered.

Maelys reached out, gripping Lyra's fingers. "We're all here for you."

"Thank you."

Lyra clambered into the back of the carriage. The enchantment pulled it along behind Wilder. Maelys and Ridge flanked either side, and Dust, Oak, and Otto brought up the rear. Lyra watched as the orderly groves turned into orderly bushes resembling a large hedgerow on either side.

The bushes gave way to circular patches of flowers. Circles are not natural in nature. And perfect ones were a strange sight to behold.

Hanging out of the side of the carriage, Lyra watched as Wilder unstrapped his sword from his waist and attached it to the saddlebag before digging around in it and pulling out a cape of emerald green. Throwing it over his shoulders, she watched as the sun refracted off the fabric, casting rainbows all around him.

He was a visiting royal, and now he looked the part. As if he could feel her watching, he turned to look at her.

His gaze lingered, and she felt the heat bloom high on her cheekbones.

"I'm not allowed weapons. It's part of the treaty," he murmured.

She didn't listen to his words; it felt intimate—that stare, like he could see every part of her as clearly as if he had crawled between her legs again.

Free from his gaze, she took a deep breath and stared out at the castle that loomed on the horizon. It was like something out of an ancient fable. Towering battlements, gothic windows, and clumps of dangling purple flowers.

Wisteria—that was the vine that wound up the watch towers.

She could smell the floral fragrance from here. It was lovely as it floated towards them on a gentle breeze. Wilder raised a single hand in front of him, and only then did she realize he was controlling the wind.

"That's my favorite part," Maelys said beside her. "The fragrance. It's inviting, isn't it?"

"Mhm," Lyra replied.

"Keep your wits about you here. The elves of the Mannereds are a different sort."

"How so?"

The clomping of hooves reached her ears, and she saw a group of five horses with glittering riders heading towards them.

"You're about to find out."

The troop of riders reached them, and Wilder halted their procession. Lyra couldn't help but stare.

Stunning. Every single rider looked as if they were hewn from granite. Strong, chiseled, and extremely attractive. There weren't any flaws to behold among the five of them.

Three had hair the color of spun gold, one the richest chestnut, and the last had hair that shimmered like a blackbird's wings. Each of their eyes gleamed with keen intelligence, but more than that, they resembled jewels. Sapphire, emerald, and amber.

It was unnatural, that beauty. Bows of ash wood were strapped to their backs, and silver pommels of swords rested on their sides. Their uniforms were white as the puffy clouds overhead. The insignia of a thistle was embroidered on their chests.

These weren't just any guards, but the Queen's guards.

The black-haired elf slid off his mount and into a quick bow as he noticed Wilder's briar crown. His skin rivaled the night sky, and Lyra was enraptured by his beauty.

"We're here to escort you, Your Highness." The rich timbre of his voice rumbled as the clopping of the hooves had.

"Word traveled quickly, I see," Wilder responded.

"A missive arrived early this morning from the High King. Queen Titania is pleased to welcome Princess Lyra."

His eyes shifted to Lyra, and she didn't squirm under his gaze like she did under Wilder's. For all the beauty this male possessed—it was empty.

Wilder nodded, and the guard hopped back in the saddle.

"Was there trouble on the way? We expected you sooner."

Again, Wilder nodded. "Wulvers."

The guard brightened with the news. "I'm sure that would be no trouble for a Prince of your skill. How did you kill them?"

"It was Lyra who killed the alpha."

The guard turned to gape at her. "How?"

Lyra gave him a bored look. "He made me angry."

Maelys and Ridge chuckled at the horrified expressions from several of the guards. But not Wilder. He gazed at her with something akin to pride.

They traveled silently to the castle. It differed greatly from the Wilds. There was no sprawling city to travel through before you reached the entrance.

From Lyra's vantage point, she had no idea where the elves of the Mannereds made their homes, but what she couldn't see was the city behind the castle and the cottage-style homes along the cliffs. Cliffs that stood like stewards against the sea. She had read about it long ago, but never dreamed she would one day see it.

It was a jagged line that marked the land from the sea. An ancient game of tug-of-war that would know no victor in the end. Lyra thought she heard the faint crashing of waves against the stone, like the ocean was knocking for entry.

"The queen waits in her throne room."

Wilder nodded as they crossed through the pearly gates. This close to the sea, Lyra noticed that the details of the castle reflected its relation to the water.

With a deep inhale, she relished the salty air. So close—she was so close to the water, and her blood hummed.

"Can you taste the salt in the air?" Otto asked.

"I can," she whispered. "It tastes like home."

Trumpets sounded their arrival, and Lyra raised her chin. The clatter of hooves and the creaking of the wheels against the smooth stone ground fell away. It was polished to a near-mirror shine. Everything was pristine, perfect, almost. It was over-whelming.

Large oak doors carved with filigree and wisteria blooms opened, and a short stairway rose ahead as light speared through the doorway like a shot arrow.

The carriage halted, and as the others dismounted, the guards led their horses away. Wilder opened the carriage door and offered her a hand.

A vice tightened around her chest.

"Legs?" Wilder asked, his brow furrowing.

She placed her hand in his, and he gave her a gentle squeeze.

"Nervous?"

"No," she snapped, raising her chin to look down her nose at him.

"Are you cold then?"

"What's with all the questions?"

He leaned closer so that only she could hear. "Your hand is trembling."

Lyra gripped him tighter.

"Is not."

69

SURPRISE

The castle of Queen Titania was that of legend. Wilder tried to see this place as Lyra might. This is where the fables came from. Glittering white stone walls showcased art that spanned millennia.

Their reflections shone on the polished floor, and their footsteps echoed before they stepped onto the crimson runner that led down the main hall.

Lyra moved slowly, gazing from painting to painting. A sculpture of a winged woman stood in the center of the wide hallway. The carved wings were so thin you could see through the granite. It was the epitome of feminine grace.

Their procession down the hallway halted as Lyra spied the statue. She stopped, and her hand trembled as she reached out to graze a fingertip down the stone of the cascading gown.

Silver lined her eyes as she stared, enraptured. He had felt like that once, too. A well of emotions was bubbling up to swallow him whole. Wilder recalled the first moment he saw the sculpture. It had almost brought him to his knees.

"It's breathtaking," Lyra whispered.

Wilder studied each minute reaction that played across Lyra's face. "It is."

Her eyes flashed to his, and a slow, genuine smile tugged up the corner of her lips.

He was done for.

His reaction to the sculpture hadn't been as visceral as his body's reaction to her smile. The world stopped spinning, and he balled his hands into fists to keep them at his sides instead of where he wanted them—on her.

Footsteps resonated down the hall, pulling her attention from him. Wilder felt the absence immediately, like a cool breeze against bare skin.

"Son of Oberon," a masculine voice boomed. It was loud, like the crack of a whip.

"Consort of Titania," Wilder replied.

Lyra froze; even her chest stopped moving with her breathing as she took in the elf standing before them.

Baelwyn wore a robe of silver, like moonlight had spilled from the sky. Dark thread embroidered the sleeves with a forest scene of grazing stags alongside unicorns. He looked to be everything you'd expect from an elvish king consort, from the top of his long white hair wrapped in a wreath of ivy to the long ash staff he walked with.

"Ah, and this must be the Princess Lyra." Baelwyn shifted his green eyes to Lyra.

There wasn't malice in his gaze, but Wilder shifted closer to shield her from it. Baelwyn was a kind male and had never given Wilder an inkling of ill will, but those ancient eyes saw things most did not.

Lyra bobbed her head with respect before holding her head up high. "I am."

"Such violent waves we've seen since your arrival."

His words echoed around the silent hall, and Lyra shifted towards Wilder.

"Violent waves?" she asked, a shade quieter than he thought possible.

"Great violence, indeed. They batter the cliffs like fists on a door."

Lyra swallowed audibly and looked at Wilder.

"He will come for me …" she whispered.

"Your father?"

Her head nodded of its own volition, and she trapped her bottom lip between her teeth.

Wilder searched her eyes. She had wanted to return to the sea. Had bargained for a deal to return to the water. So why did she seem so reluctant to be found?

"The queen awaits," Baelwyn murmured, interrupting Wilder's scrutiny.

Otto cleared his throat, and Lyra flinched.

Baelwyn turned on a heel, and they followed behind him. When Lyra slipped her hand into Wilder's, he did not hesitate to grip hers. She was afraid.

"Queen Titania is kind," Wilder whispered, knowing damn well everyone in the hall could hear his words.

Lyra shook her head once, and Wilder's brow furrowed.

"Later," she mouthed.

Stone doors opened on silent hinges. The metal ivy filigree flanking each door unwound itself to allow entry, and they stepped through the threshold.

Wilder heard Lyra's breath catch in her throat.

Evening light poured through rainbow-tinted windows in the ceiling. Archways made of the white, glittering stone led to the tall dais on which the crescent-moon-shaped throne sat.

Queen Titania sat regally in a high-collar navy gown embroidered with silver thread. The light danced upon the thread, casting tiny rainbows around her like bobbing butterflies.

Wilder walked with steady legs to the queen, who would have been his mother-in-law.

"Wilder," she breathed, her voice as soft and lovely as a spring breeze.

He dropped to one knee and bowed. Lyra dropped alongside him, and the queen tutted.

"Such formalities," she giggled. "Up, up, my child!"

Wilder didn't know who she spoke to until Baelwyn stepped alongside Lyra and offered her a hand to lead her up the steps.

Lyra walked with such grace that he stared with astonishment. She had never been that steady on her feet before.

Titania stood and clasped Lyra's hands in hers. A rustle of her gown was all that could be heard as she moved Lyra into a beam of light.

"Pray, child, who is your mother?"

Lyra opened her mouth and then shrugged. Wilder continued to stare, his ears pricking as he listened to their conversation from down the stairs.

"My father had her dragged to shore."

"Your father? King Auris?"

Lyra bobbed a nod, and Titania reached out, plucking a loose strand of auburn between her fingertips.

"Only one other female in the world had hair of this color …" she breathed.

Otto cleared his throat, and Wilder's eyes flashed to his friend.

Baelwyn gasped, and Titania looked down from her throne to Otto.

"Am I correct?"

Lyra looked from person to person, not quite understanding what was happening. Which made two of them.

"Blessed three," Maelys blurted out.

Ridge clapped a hand over her mouth and grimaced with an apology.

Dust and Oak shared a look and then shrugged.

Wilder turned back to Otto, who bowed low to the queen.

Tears filled Titania's eyes. "You are my granddaughter, the daughter of Odette."

Wilder could hear Lyra's breath come out in a whoosh, like someone had punched her in the stomach.

Baelwyn stepped closer, resting a hand on her shoulder. Wilder moved towards the stairs as if he would support her.

But as a cry escaped Lyra, she threw her arms around the queen.

Titania wrapped her in an embrace, and Baelwyn circled both of them with his powerful arms.

"You're my family," Lyra said between sobs.

"We had heard whispers of you, but never in our wildest dreams did we think they were true," Titania whispered, stroking Lyra's hair.

Wilder's head spun. She was the daughter of the princess he was supposed to marry.

"What happened to her?" Lyra asked.

Titania looked at Baelwyn, and he nodded. "She is here … but she is unwell."

"What do you mean?" Lyra pulled out of her arms.

The queen's face pinched in worry, and Wilder held his breath.

"We don't really know. The witches believed her heart had been broken so badly that her mind had fragmented. We had her put under a spell until we could figure out what to do. By the time we did—she wouldn't wake."

Lyra's eyes flashed, and Wilder's foot smashed against the bottom stair.

"Heartbroken?"

Titania nodded. "A mother's love." She cupped Lyra's cheek. "Would you like to see her?"

Lyra nodded, and Titania gathered the train of her gown in her hand.

"Come with me."

Titania sauntered down the stairs, with Lyra and Baelwyn following her. As the queen passed, she patted Wilder's cheek.

"You should probably come too."

Her eyes slid to his group of friends and back to him.

"Stay," he ordered Otto and the others as he took up a position beside Baelwyn.

"We'll be right here," Maelys murmured to Lyra.

There had been no murmurs that Odette had returned, not even the wind spoke of her arrival. It had been a very well-guarded secret.

Titania turned down a shadowed hallway and then another. The air grew colder, but not stale. It was crisp, like freshly fallen snow.

A nondescript wooden door appeared at the end of the hidden hallway. A blue flame glowed in an iron torch beside it. The door creaked as Titania turned the handle, and Wilder held his breath as they stepped into the room.

It was a circular room that belonged to one of the towers that flanked the south wall of the castle. The windows overlooked the seaside cliffs, and gulls cried loudly as they flew in the lavender-colored sky.

A lavish bed sat in the middle of the room with a clear view of the sea in the distance. Odette lay still and peaceful in her slumber.

A cornflower gown of silk clad her frail body. Locks of auburn framed her pale face, the color identical to Lyra's but muted somehow, as if the life had vanished from her. If Wilder hadn't spied the slight imperceptible rise and fall of her chest, he would have thought she was deceased.

Lyra stood beside the bed but made no move to reach for her mother.

"I thought she had died," she whispered, gazing at the face that was a mirror of hers.

"She wanted to," Titania replied. "Your mother was a wanderer and had longed to live beneath the waves."

Lyra looked at the queen. "But she's an elf?"

Baelwyn draped an arm around his mate and tugged her close to him. "She bargained for a witch's spell."

"Such a thing is possible?" Lyra's gaze swept to Wilder, and he nodded.

"How else did you think we planned to send you home?"

Baelwyn and Titania looked at Lyra with such sorrow. "You wish to return to the depths?"

Lyra gripped the white down comforter and looked back at her mother. "I belong to the sea."

Wilder couldn't stop the words that flew from his mouth. "You belong to no one but yourself."

Her head whipped back to his.

"You decide what you want, not what you think you should do."

"I made a bargain," she whispered.

"To balance magic, not return to the sea."

"It will require me to return to Atlantis to break it."

Wilder shook his head and could feel the weight of his crown pressing into his flesh. "You don't know that."

"What bargain are you breaking?" the queen asked.

"The Tidal Tithe."

Titania hummed her agreement. "Then Lyra is correct."

Wilder's jaw clenched, and Lyra sucked in a breath.

"If she is to break the Tidal Tithe, it will require her to undo each knot. One in the sea and one in Badenvaria."

His eyes widen with her words. "No creature has ever set foot in the mortal's palace."

"A bargain was struck there. At least one creature must have entered," Baelwyn replied.

It was a death sentence, then. The humans would never let a mermaid leave their palace walls.

"We'll have to find another way," he declared.

He watched as a range of emotions flitted across her face. Sorrow, fear, and then anger.

"You are the reason I am stuck in this position."

Lyra's eyes narrowed on him, and the light outside seemed to vanish entirely. Flames erupted in sconces around the room, and the timing was so startling he almost retreated a step.

"I did not know," he whispered with a plea.

A plea for her to listen, for her to forgive.

Titania spoke, "What do you mean?"

Lyra turned to face them. "I did not come here of my own accord. Wilder kidnapped me under orders from the High King."

Titania gasped, and Baelwyn glowered.

"Tell me that isn't true?" Titania shifted scornful eyes to Wilder.

He couldn't meet them, but he nodded.

"If there was ever a time for you not to follow an order, that would have been it," Baelwyn grumbled.

Wilder's eyes slid shut. "It was my duty."

Lyra watched the exchange with a snarled expression and squeezed her arms across her chest.

"How many atrocities have you committed under the guise of 'duty'?"

Wilder flinched at her question, and her arms lowered to her sides.

"Lyra," Titania whispered. "There is much more to his story than that."

"I know his story. It's similar to mine."

Wilder had opened his mouth to reply, but Odette opened her eyes.

She must have squeezed Lyra's fingers because she jumped away from the bed before returning.

"Mother?"

Titania was weeping, tears running in rivulets down her cheeks as she stared at her waking daughter. Baelwyn had a strong arm wrapped around his wife, not for moral support, but to keep her on her feet.

"Alyra …" a voice croaked with a dry and disused throat.

Lyra clung to her mother, but her other hand clutched the charm that hung from the silver necklace she never took off.

That name, Alyra. He never knew that her name had been shortened.

And apparently, she hadn't known that either.

"That was my name," Lyra whispered.

It broke something in Wilder to see her reduced to such anguish, and he had nothing to offer her—or nothing that she would allow him to give.

With that thought, he slipped out of the room, giving Lyra and her family privacy.

70
REVELATIONS

L yra lay beside Odette, speaking into the early hours of the morning. The sun was rising outside when she had fallen silent. She had told her mother everything.

Every miserable second of her existence had led to this moment. And her mother listened, not once shying away from the darker parts of Lyra's life.

From her killing that boy to poisoning the maid who turned over her books. Sneaking away from the castle for weeks until King Auris dragged her back in nets made of acid kelp that would melt away her flesh when she struggled too much.

The time he thought he could cut the power from her and had her strapped to a table as he cut perfect lines between her ribs that protected her heart. She stabbed Marina with her sharp nails after she had touched her shell necklace to change the dressings after her torture. All the cruel tendencies she was partial to after the treatment she had suffered under the king.

Odette had remained quiet or asked, "What else?" to keep Lyra talking.

She stroked her daughter's auburn hair and pressed kisses into the crown of her head. It had probably felt like waking from a nightmare to set eyes on her infant daughter, who was now well into womanhood.

When Lyra had told her about her engagement to Drystan, Odette had stiffened. Lyra turned to look up into her mother's eyes and saw the words written in them. Drystan's father had been one of the mermen who had dragged Odette to the surface and left her there.

The very fate that Odette had begged not to include Lyra in was already in motion, and her mother had been trapped here, helpless.

"Father ordered me to kill him after we consummated our vows," Lyra whispered.

"So that you would become the heir and no other mermen would rise and try to claim his title. It's a smart move politically —but cruel. Rulers are meant to be challenged so that they may prove they are still worthy."

Her mother spoke with such wisdom and humility that she could feel her heart aching. How different would her life have been if they hadn't taken her away? Would she have become as kind as her?

"Why did you go to Atlantis in the first place?"

Odette seemed to slip back in time. A small smile graced her tired face.

"I craved an adventure."

Lyra smiled. She had once felt the same.

"King Auris wasn't as he is now. He was … charming and romantic."

Bile burned the back of Lyra's throat to hear her monstrous father spoken about in such a way.

"His wife had perished, and I was such a lost girl. We fit, in a strange way. Completed each other. He secured the throne and was at a loss for how to keep it. A single father of six daughters. It was such an enormous burden. And having been raised here, in an elvish court, I was no stranger to court politics and machinations. But he took my advice and twisted it. I thought we were building something stronger—better—together. When he held you in his arms, felt the power inside you—I lost everything that day."

Guilt washed over Lyra like a rogue wave, pulling her down into its inescapable depths.

It had been her fault.

She had come into the world and ruined their lives.

Odette felt Lyra shift beside her and pulled her close.

"No, my daughter," she breathed. "This was not of your doing. Not now—not ever. I failed you."

Lyra shook her head, tears overflowing down her cheeks. "Why would you think that? He is the monster."

Odette's jaw clenched. "I should have seen the signs of his madness and left long before then. I thought his holding of something so innocent and pure would heal him and put an end to the sanctions he was implementing against mermaids."

"You had no idea I would be born with such power," Lyra argued.

"Even if you hadn't been born with power, I still would have been bringing you into a realm ruled by a monster. I should have protected you first instead of believing my love for him would be enough. Will you forgive me?"

Lyra gripped her mother back, her head nestled against her neck.

"There's nothing to forgive."

Odette sighed, and Lyra could feel her mother's strength waning.

"Get some rest. I will be here when you wake."

Odette nodded, her eyes fluttered closed, and Lyra slid off

the bed and onto her feet. She stumbled to the door, throwing one last look at her mother.

When she pulled the door open, she came face-to-face with Wilder. He sat against the opposite wall with one knee up, and his head rested back against the stone wall.

A comfortable, relaxed position by all outward appearances, but it was the look on his face—the devastation. He had heard her. Heard every word.

Lyra pulled the door closed behind her and then crossed her arms over her chest and leveled a look at him.

"No one likes an eavesdropper."

"I'm sorry." His voice cracked, and Lyra's arms dropped to her sides as she stepped closer to him. He stood in one swift motion and wrapped her in his arms.

"I am so sorry. The pain I must have caused. The nightmares that I inflicted. I am sorry."

Her arms were trapped to her sides, so even if she had wanted to, she couldn't have held him back, and she had wanted to.

He let go a fraction and looked down at her. And that's when she saw it.

The haunting horrors that weighed on him even now. He felt the same things she had.

"Walk with me," Lyra breathed.

Wilder tilted his head and then looked out the window to the end of the hall.

"Don't you need sleep?"

Lyra shook her head.

"I actually think I want to be close to the sea."

Wilder nodded and grabbed her hand in his. Interlacing their fingers together felt natural, normal even. He led her down and out of the castle, which sat precariously on a cliff that overlooked the vast sea.

There were stairs carved down the cliff face. They took the

steps one at a time. Mists from the tide had slicked the shale steps and made the descent treacherous.

Wilder didn't let go of her for a second. When they reached the sandy bottom, Lyra inhaled, savoring the brine in the air.

The line between the sea and the land felt like the words of a sentence separated from one page of a book to the next; still the same sentence, but a great leap of space.

She walked closer to the shore, following the path that the water took to crawl closer. It was as if it were reaching for her. One wild thing recognizing another.

After a few hundred feet, she finally stopped and sat on the sand. The sky was the kind of clear blue she had always hoped it would be—the same shade as Wilder's eyes. He sat beside her, and she leaned into his side.

They lounged together all morning while the sun rose. He didn't prompt her to speak. He sat with her, making sure she had all the time and space she needed. The freckles on her nose had darkened, and a flush sat high on her cheeks.

Wilder looked darker, too. A deep olive tone was now apparent on his skin, and if she looked closely, she could see that his hair wasn't purely dark. It was like a raven's wing with a gleaming blue tone that highlighted his eyes. As beautiful as the sky.

He interlaced their fingers together again, and she sighed.

"I see you," he said against her head. "I see all of you, and I am not disgusted by the parts you try to hide."

Lyra gazed into his eyes.

"I see you too."

He kissed her then, slow and thoroughly. It was a claiming, tying them together irrevocably. He tasted of freedom and the deepest, clearest waters. He felt like hers.

Wilder's lips were soft and gentle as he wrapped a hand in her hair and tugged her to him. They broke apart and grinned at each other. He understood her, saw her, and accepted her. She had never felt like this before.

"I think I love you," she whispered.

A breath slipped through his lips before he said, "I know I love you."

The waves stopped crashing against the shore.

She slowly turned from Wilder's gaze and stared at the ocean. Something wasn't right. A prickle itched her palms, and a weight dropped in her stomach.

Wilder must have felt the change, too, because he rose to his feet.

A light started glowing past the incoming waves that had flattened and stilled.

"What is that?" Lyra asked, clambering to her feet beside him.

Wilder took a step closer to the water, but Lyra gripped his hand, halting him.

"Stop."

He looked from her to the water and then back again.

"What is it?"

"They're coming—for me."

71
IN VIOLENT WAVES

A bubble rose from the water on a giant wave that carried a dozen mermen to shore.

Drystan was at the center. A golden helm couldn't hide his familiar sneer from her. Lyra felt her stomach sink, and a weight settled on her chest.

"Go back to the castle," Wilder ordered. He patted his side for the sword that was usually there, but came up empty.

They were unarmed and outnumbered.

And it was already too late.

A dozen guards, tails splitting into powerful thighs and calves, were marching through the surf and towards them.

"Lyra—go." When she did not move, he said again, "I command you to go." Wilder's voice thundered with the authoritative quality that only a crowned prince of the Wilds could instill.

"You do not command me," Lyra hissed, her eyes scouring his face for any hint of the elf she had come to love.

Wilder stared back at her and lowered his chin only once.

The mermen circled them, and Wilder pulled Lyra close to his side.

Drystan stood in front of them. Bedecked in royal armor of glittering gold scales, carrying the trident that belonged to her father. Lyra hesitated at what that could mean.

"Well, well. If it isn't my blushing bride," Drystan addressed Lyra before turning his nastiness to Wilder. "You dare touch what is mine?"

"I belong to no one," Lyra seethed and stepped in front of Wilder.

"Our engagement says otherwise."

The guards flanking them shifted. Several weapons were pointed directly at Lyra and Wilder. Golden spears and broadswords were all held in their fists, ready and waiting for the order to kill them.

She didn't recognize a single guard, and the emblem on their chests was not her father's. An eel wrapped around a barracuda. It was the Ithicais house crest.

"Why are you here?"

Drystan looked from her to Wilder.

"Are you the crowned prince of the Wilds?"

Wilder ground his teeth, and Lyra could feel him stiffen behind her.

"The princess asked you a question," was his only reply.

Drystan smirked. "A crown of briars on raven-black hair. You must be Wilder Vale."

Wilder nodded only once, and Drystan smirked.

"I made a bargain with your father." Lyra could feel her heart stop. "A bargain he did not uphold."

"What bargain?" Lyra asked and took a step forward. Wilder wrapped his fingers around her wrist to keep her from taking another step away from him.

"He was to hold you captive until I could complete my plans.

And then return you to the sea. But it seems Oberon had other plans in mind and kept you. I've come to claim what is mine."

"I am not yours!" Lyra's chest heaved with her scream. "And I refuse to return to the sea."

Wilder tightened his grip, and she took a step back, bumping against his chest, and her breathing slowed.

"What did my father get out of this bargain?"

The superiority on Drystan's face made Lyra's chest hurt. "Lyra would have been a common enemy. He assumed her presence would remind you of your duty. You've been a bit wayward again, and the wulvers were beneficial last time. That, and of course, he would want to be in my good graces."

A breath slipped through her lips. It appeared he had no idea about the bargain she had struck with Oberon.

Drystan threw the trident from one hand to another, keeping his eyes on them.

"But aren't you curious as to why I have this?"

She was. Despite herself, she was curious about how he had acquired her father's trident. Was it given willingly? Or stolen?

"No."

Drystan tutted, pointing it at her. "Such an accomplished liar."

Lyra's spine stiffened, and Wilder leaned forward. "Easy," he whispered.

"I am the ruler of the seven seas."

The ocean waves ceased, and the constant blowing of the wind halted.

"What did you do?"

"That's why I needed you out of the way, my bride. It'd be hard to conquer a kingdom with you standing in the way with that power of yours."

"I have no power," she hissed.

Drystan snorted and shook his head. "Did you forget who I am? Where I am from? The sea witch told me as soon as she glimpsed the power within you. Why do you think I agreed to the wedding arrangements in the first place?"

Lyra ground her teeth together. "The sea witch lied. I have no magic."

"I have ways of making you cooperate, Lyra. Don't push me." Drystan now pointed the trident at Wilder.

"Whatever happens," he whispered. "You save yourself, Legs."

"No," she ground out, clinging to his hand in hers.

"You will come with me now, Lyra. Or I will kill everything you have come to love. And I know you have enjoyed your time here on land." Drystan's eyes slid from her to Wilder.

"When I say run," Wilder whispered so that only she could hear. "You run, and you do not look back."

"No," she whimpered. "I can't leave you."

"I don't think she will be going with you," Wilder said to Drystan.

Drystan's jaw flexed, and he aimed the trident at Wilder's chest. The trident held no magic, but the threat was clear.

Lyra felt the magic within her flare once more. He was threatening what was hers. And she would not have it.

"Don't," Wilder ground out to her. As if he could feel her magic coiling to strike.

"You will come with me now."

Lyra shook her head, and Drystan nodded to the guards, who crept towards them.

Closer and closer, they closed in.

When the points of their weapons were in striking range, Wilder's hand slipped from her wrist and gripped her shoulder.

"One," he breathed. "Two." The points of their weapons gleamed in the sunlight. "Run!"

Wilder shoved her towards the castle and let loose his magic.

A wall of wind surged from around them, throwing the guards to the sand and clearing a path for Lyra to race to the castle.

Sand kicked up behind her as she darted out of reach of several guards.

She had to get to Maelys, Ridge, and Otto. She had to get help.

Guards clambered to their feet, half splitting to catch her and the other half circling Wilder.

They wouldn't make it.

Wilder fought them off with his bare hands and well-placed kicks. Surges of his wind pushed them backwards, but there were too many for him to hold off alone.

Grunts of pain and shouts of anger rang out behind her.

He would die before she could make it back with help.

Lyra threw herself to a stop and felt several bodies collide against her.

Manacles were shackled to her wrists as she was hauled to her feet and carried back to Drystan.

He stood leaning against his trident, looking on as Wilder was forced to his knees by a guard with a broadsword.

"Well, that was quick," he sighed. "I expected more from the great Wilder Vale."

"Give me a sword and even the odds, then."

Drystan snorted and rolled his eyes. "I'm not stupid."

"Could have fooled me," Lyra sang as she was dragged to his feet.

"Lyra," Wilder shushed her.

But his eyes were pleading. He had failed her, and she could see it plain as day in his eyes. She winked at him, and he frowned.

"I will go with you," Lyra said to Drystan. "On one condition."

Drystan arched a brow.

"Let him go."

Drystan shook his head. "He touched you. His life is penance."

Lyra smirked. "I touched him—and liked it."

Drystan's face turned a ruddy shade of red as his fury grew.

"Lyra," Wilder snapped.

A sword pressed against his throat, silencing him.

All her swagger evaporated. She couldn't imagine a world without him in it.

"Let him go!" Lyra shrieked. "Let him go, and I will go willingly. But harm him, and I will fight. Every day of my life, I will do nothing but make your life miserable. And you know I will succeed."

Drystan shook his head as if clearing the images of her touching Wilder from his head.

"Let him go, please," Lyra begged.

If anything happened to him, she couldn't bear the thought of it. Of everything she had come to love, taken away from her.

"You will do as I bid?" Drystan asked.

Her magic. He was after her magic. But it was her life or Wilder's now.

Lyra nodded.

"No!" Wilder barked out before the sword pressed against his skin.

Lyra looked back at him with pleading eyes and trembling hands. "Stop," she mouthed. And prayed that he would listen.

"Fine," Drystan agreed. He grabbed hold of her chains and tugged her to him. But he turned around to face Wilder.

"I see how much he means to you," Drystan whispered in her ear. And the nearness made her stomach roil. But it was the edge in his voice that had her heart racing. Drystan nodded to the guard, and he removed his sword. "And because of that. He cannot live."

Lyra sucked in a sharp inhale, and her eyes widened. The guard reared back with his sword in an arc meant to decapitate Wilder.

"Stop," Lyra commanded, plucking on that thread of her

magic. Her voice rang out with the dominance of the entire universe.

Everything stopped.

The sea, the wind, and the birds flying in the sky.

Everything froze.

"You will not harm him."

The sword thunked as it landed in the sand.

She couldn't imagine one more scar upon Wilder's body, much less the end of his life.

Wilder stared, enthralled. And it broke her heart into a million pieces.

The thread within her went out, the magic all used up.

She had never practiced how to wield it to last and had burned through it already. There was nothing left for her to save herself.

All at once, the world started spinning again. The waves crashed against the shore, the birds flew by, and the wind blew her hair in her face.

The guard picked up his sword and stepped past Wilder as if he weren't there. The guard holding Wilder let go and stepped towards the sea. Drystan whirled her around to face him.

"I knew it," he spat. Tugging her close to him, he dragged her through the surf.

It was as if Wilder didn't even exist.

A slow breath slipped through her lips. The magic held—they could not harm him.

Wilder clambered to his feet and raced towards her.

But it was too late.

Drystan shoved a vial down her throat.

"For your legs." He glared down at them.

The jelly-textured liquid slid down her throat, and she choked on it as they dragged her further into the sea.

"Lyra," Wilder screamed. Trudging through the waves to get to her.

Her heart splintered at the sound of the anguish in his voice. She looked over her shoulder as her legs dropped beneath her and dragged her body.

They were going to take her now, and there was nothing she could do about it but let it happen.

Tears ran in rivulets down her cheeks. She didn't want to go—didn't want him to see her being taken.

"I will come for you!" Wilder promised, still trying to swim through the waves.

His head bobbed above the water before a wave crashed down on him.

Her legs fused, and the skin stitched itself back together. Her toes elongated, and it felt like bones piercing through her flesh as her fins grew back.

The familiarity of her form was a balm to the anguish she felt suffocating her.

"I will find you!" Wilder roared, coming up for air again.

It was the last words she heard as they swam beneath the surface and back towards her home.

But it wasn't Lyra's home any longer, and she wasn't returning as the mermaid who had left.

She was returning as the monster they made.

THE END

ACKNOWLEDGMENTS

Firstly, my sweet, amazingly kind husband, Justin. You're the best partner a girl could ever ask for, and I am eternally grateful for all your support and love. None of this would ever have been possible without you. Thank you for putting up with my manic writing episodes and my crippling self-doubt. You're the best.

Jordan, my sister, I love you so much. I am so grateful to have you in my life. From pushing me to write, to pushing me to run, to just pushing me. I love you forever. Thank you so much for loving and accepting me. When I grow up, I hope to be half the woman that you are.

Kira, you're an angel! From being my very first beta reader to a voice I rely on for every single thing I write. You're so kind and have been an integral part of this journey.

Aurora, I'm keeping you forever. You're so uplifting and supportive, and your insight has been a necessity in making this book come to life. Thank you so much!

Sammy and Charity, you two are stuck with me now! Thank you so much for reading all my crappy first drafts and saying only kind things. I hope you love this final draft just as much as the first and hope you appreciate the very specific suggestions I made sure to add just for you guys.

Laura, oh my, I don't even know where to start. The absolute best editor, graphic maker, and late-night brainstorming genius. I am wholly and utterly grateful for your wisdom and insight. You are also mine forever now.

About the Author

J. A. Townsend was born and raised outside the city of Dallas, in the large state of Texas. Townsend considers her five children and wonderful husband to be the adventure of her life. But when she's not spending time with them, she's lost in a project or buried in a book.